SCIENCE & HISTORY

Preventing Youth Violence
in a Multicultural Society

Preventing Youth Violence in a Multicultural Society

Edited by
Nancy G. Guerra and
Emilie Phillips Smith

American Psychological Association
Washington, DC

Published by
American Psychological Association
750 First Street, NE
Washington, DC 20002
www.apa.org

To order
APA Order Department
P.O. Box 92984
Washington, DC 20090-2984
Tel: (800) 374-2721
Direct: (202) 336-5510
Fax: (202) 336-5502
TDD/TTY: (202) 336-6123
Online: www.apa.org/books/
E-mail: order@apa.org

In the U.K., Europe, Africa, and the Middle
East, copies may be ordered from
American Psychological Association
3 Henrietta Street
Covent Garden, London
WC2E 8LU England

Typeset in Goudy by World Composition Services, Inc., Sterling, VA

Printer: Sheridan Books, Ann Arbor, MI
Cover Designer: Aqueous Design, Bethesda, MD
Project Manager: Debbie Hardin, Carlsbad, CA

The opinions and statements published are the responsibility of the authors, and such opinions and statements do not necessarily represent the policies of the American Psychological Association.

Library of Congress Cataloging-in-Publication Data

Preventing youth violence in a multicultural society / edited by Nancy G. Guerra and
    Emilie Phillips Smith.—1st ed.
        p. cm.
    Includes bibliographical references and index.
    ISBN 1-59147-327-6
    1. Youth and violence—United States—Prevention. 2. Violence—United States—
Prevention. 3. Pluralism (Social sciences)—United States. I. Guerra, Nancy.
II. Smith, Emilie Phillips.

HQ799.2.V56P746   2005
303.6'0835—dc22   2005016567

British Library Cataloguing-in-Publication Data
A CIP record is available from the British Library.

Printed in the United States of America
First Edition

For Stephen G., Andrew E., and so many youth and families
affected by youth violence.

CONTENTS

CONTRIBUTORS

Ioakim Boutakidis, University of California, Riverside

Sabine E. French, University of California, Riverside

Nancy G. Guerra, University of California, Riverside

La Mar Hasbrouck, Centers for Disease Control and Prevention, Atlanta, GA

Cynthia Hudley, University of California, Santa Barbara

Samantha Hurst, University of California, San Diego

Tia E. Kim, University of California, Riverside

Jack Laird, Indian Health Council, Pauma Valley, CA

Gregory Yee Mark, Sacramento State University, Sacramento, CA

David T. Mayeda, University of Hawaii, Honolulu

Brenda Mirabal-Colón, University of Puerto Rico School of Medicine, San Juan

Robert Nash Parker, University of California, Riverside

Olivia Pillado, University of California, Riverside

Linda A. Revilla, University of Hawaii, Honolulu

Emilie Phillips Smith, Pennsylvania State University, University Park

Fernando Soriano, California State University, San Marcos

April Taylor, California State University, Northridge

Louis Tuthill, University of California, Riverside

Thomas Tsutsumoto, University of Hawaii, Honolulu

Carmen Noemí Vélez, University of Puerto Rico, San Juan

Kirk R. Williams, University of California, Riverside

Joan C. Wright, University of Michigan, Ann Arbor

Marc A. Zimmerman, University of Michigan, Ann Arbor

ACKNOWLEDGMENTS

We are thankful to a number of people who have been helpful in the preparation of this volume. First, numerous youth, families, community members, and policy makers have participated in the research projects described. Their insights and experiences have contributed to our perspectives on youth violence prevention in diverse communities. Second, several of the authors of this book are affiliated with the National Centers for Academic Excellence in Youth Violence Prevention. These investigators would like to acknowledge the funding support provided by the National Center on Injury Control and Prevention at the Centers for Disease Control and Prevention to the University of California, Riverside (Grant no. 918589), the University of Michigan (Grant no. 518605), the University of Puerto Rico (Grant no. 218618), and the University of Hawaii–Manoa (Grant no. 918619). We are also grateful to the staff at the Centers for Disease Control, Joan Hoffman, Marci Feldman, Michele Hoover, Candice Jackson, Joanne Klevens, and Monica Swahn, who have been helpful in fostering collaborative endeavors among this group. Third, we are indebted to our own families and communities, who are our sources of support and inspiration.

Preventing Youth Violence
in a Multicultural Society

INTRODUCTION

EMILIE PHILLIPS SMITH AND NANCY G. GUERRA

Youth violence is a pressing social problem that compromises the health and well-being of countless young people and their victims. Although official rates of serious violence typically rise and fall across different historical periods and, in fact, seem to be on a downward trajectory in the United States in recent years, violence still represents one of the most significant health risks for children and youth. Homicide is the second leading cause of death among young people, resulting in higher rates of mortality than for all diseases combined—in 1999, nearly 5,000 youth between the ages of 15 to 24 were murdered and another 467,000 were injured because of nonfatal violence (Centers for Disease Control and Prevention, 2001). For every child who dies because of violence, more than a thousand more are treated in emergency rooms or hospitalized. Violence results in substantial costs to society and years of youthful lives lost. It also results in emotional costs to the families, siblings, and peers who are left to cope with serious emotional and physical injures or mourn the untimely deaths of so many young people.

The surgeon general's recent *Report on Youth Violence* (U.S. Department of Health and Human Services, 2001) echoes this concern. For example, this report indicates that arrest rates for violent crimes committed by youth of ages 10 to 17 continue to be 15% higher than in 1983, the year that saw the beginning of a significant surge in arrests for violent crimes. Similarly, rates for aggravated assaults are still 70% higher than in 1983. Perhaps the most disturbing findings have come from self-reported prevalence studies that generally have failed to show declines in rates of youth violence (Elliott, 1994).

Although the youth violence problem cuts across all ethnic groups and social classes, there continues to be an ongoing overrepresentation of ethnic minority youth from disadvantaged ecological niches among both perpetrators and victims of violence. The size of the gap depends, in part, on the source of information. In some cases this information is limited simply because these breakdowns have not been systematically included in epidemiological studies of youth violence. When ethnic categories are included they are often limited to comparisons between a few general groups, for instance, African American versus White versus "other" youth.

Most data available for ethnic minority youth are for African Americans; these data point to the disproportionately severe consequences for this group. Indeed, homicide is the leading cause of death for African American youth. Official arrest data also indicate that African American youth are disproportionately arrested for violent crimes, although the discrepancy between African Americans and other ethnic groups varies by type of crime. In terms of calculation of lifetime health risks, homicide is one of the three major factors (along with heart disease and cancer) that contribute to the 6 years of reduced life expectancy of African Americans (Centers for Disease Control and Prevention, 2001). Less information is available about violence rates among other ethnic groups. For instance, although Latinos account for approximately 12.5% of the U.S. population, similar to representation of African Americans, a number of important reports and studies of youth violence do not examine violence or victimization among Latinos. Available data do seem to indicate elevated risk for perpetration and victimization (Anderson, 2002).

In addition, youth violence is becoming a problem with some groups that are typically invisible to the field, often falling in the "other" category. For example, limited data suggest that youth violence is becoming an increasingly significant problem among other minority youth such as Asian and Pacific Islander and American Indian youth. This concern about disproportionately high rates of youth violence among ethnic minority youth is even more urgent in light of the increasing number of citizens from these groups in the United States, which is increasingly becoming a multicultural society. Currently, ethnic minority and multiethnic citizens make up approximately one third of the U.S. population, and predictions suggest these numbers will increase significantly in the coming years.

The United States is becoming a society where the number of ethnic minorities are increasing and may soon make up the majority in several regions and across the country. Since youth violence is a continuing threat to public health, it becomes more important to look carefully at the role of ethnicity and culture in understanding and preventing youth violence in a multicultural society. This requires a focused dialogue about key themes including (a) development of a common language and terminology relevant to culture and ethnicity that represents the overlap and interplay between these terms as well as captures intra-group variation; (b) specification of the shared and unique mechanisms of risk and resilience that influence violence among various ethnic groups; (c) description of how these shared and unique risk and resilience factors operate specifically in different ethnic groups with elevated or increasing rates of youth violence; (d) attention to the interaction between ethnicity and culture and the social ecologies of youth in reducing and increasing risk for youth violence; and (e) careful elaboration of how best to incorporate ethnic and cultural characteristics, experiences, norms, values, behavioral patterns, beliefs, and other ecological forces into the development, implementation, and evaluation of youth violence prevention and intervention programs.

This book provides direction for youth violence prevention and intervention efforts with youth from diverse backgrounds in a multicultural society by addressing these themes. To begin with, the authors acknowledge the general lack of precision in terminology when discussing ethnicity, culture, and related constructs. We define terms as used in this book in the glossary; however, we acknowledge that choice of terminology is often determined by a host of generational, political, and conventional factors.

This issue is even more complex when we address variation within ethnic groups. For instance, the terms "Hispanic" and "Latino" frequently are used interchangeably to refer to a broadly defined population that includes peoples from different ethnic groups, distinct cultures, and a shared language (Spanish). *Hispanic* has been used to connote linkages to Spain, and *Latino* has been used to connote heritage from Latin America, although in practice these distinctions are blurred. For example, although Brazilians are not Spanish-speaking they may or may not be included conceptually in the term Hispanic/Latino. Further refinements in terminology hinge on country of origin and immigration status, such as Mexican versus Mexican American versus Chicano. Similarly, the term "Asian and Pacific Islander" (API) refers to Asian peoples of the Far East, Southeast Asia, or the Indian subcontinent as well as Pacific Islanders originally from Hawaii, Guam, Samoa, or other Pacific Islands. Because of the complexity of these categories, chapters that discuss violence etiology and prevention within specific ethnic groups provide a detailed discussion of terminology and criterion for inclusion.

The chapters in this volume draw on a multidimensional, ecological framework for understanding and preventing youth violence. This framework emphasizes the learning of aggression over time and across contexts, and how ethnicity and culture can influence both development and behavior. Rather than treat ethnicity as a nuisance variable, as is frequently done in psychological research, we view it as a central contextual variable that can help explain behavior. So often when the term *ethnicity* is used for a group of people in the research literature, we are unaware of the unexplained processes for which the term is considered as a proxy.

We focus specifically on how ethnicity and culture can increase or decrease risk for youth violence. We emphasize three specific mechanisms that highlight risk factors that are shared and risk factors that are unique to either minority groups or specific ethnic groups as follows: (a) risk and resilience factors that are common across minority and majority ethnic and cultural groups but that may be more or less likely to emerge in relation to the specific developmental ecologies of ethnic minority youth; (b) risk and resilience factors related to the minority experience and associated adjustment processes that may be shared across minority groups depending on their past and current status vis-à-vis oppression, racism, and other aspects of the minority experience in the United States (but would not be shared by mainstream society); and (c) risk and resilience factors that are unique to the historical conditions and cultural practices of different ethnic or cultural groups that may have meaning only within that context. We emphasize the interaction of individual risk factors with environmental conditions associated with ethnicity and culture.

SHARED RISK FACTORS

In many cases, factors that influence risk and resilience for youth violence are common across majority and minority ethnic and cultural groups. Individual-level factors such as impulsivity, low self-control, low empathy, and aggressive behavior are all likely to increase violence risk across ethnic and cultural groups. One of the most robust findings in the literature on aggression and violence that holds across cultures and settings is that early aggression predicts future aggression and antisocial behavior during childhood, adolescence, and adulthood (Huesmann, Eron, & Dubow, 2002). Still, child-rearing styles that vary by ethnicity or culture may contribute in different ways to the emergence and development of these individual-level factors. Cultural practices that encourage self-control and empathy for others are more likely to facilitate development of these competencies beyond individual proclivities. In a similar vein, the limited opportunities that exist for members of some ethnic groups may interfere with the development of protective factors such as school achievement that promote resilience and reduce risk for violence (Gerard & Buehler, 2004). From this perspective, risk factors that do not vary in magnitude of influence across different groups may still vary in the likelihood they will unfold in these groups because of nonshared ecological contexts.

RISK LINKED TO THE MINORITY EXPERIENCE

In contrast, some risk factors may be linked directly to the particular experiences of ethnic minority youth. Indeed, it is also the case that the "minority experience" provides an additional developmental context that can increase risk for violence. History has been different for individuals from many ethnic and cultural groups in the United States. Many ethnic minorities have historically been subject to racism, discrimination, and limited economic opportunities, all of which may significantly influence their attitudes and behavior. The history of youth gangs in the United States is linked, in part, to a history of oppression and exclusion. For example, the origins of Latino street gangs can be traced back to the anti-Mexican sentiment of the Alamo, the Treaty of Guadalupe Hidalgo in 1848 (where the United States paid Mexico $18 million for large portions of the Southwest), and the rapid growth of Los Angeles during the early 1900s. Feelings of displacement and resentment fueled the fires of solidarity that bound Latino youth together against the establishment. The first prison gang in California, La Eme (the "Mexican mafia") was formed in the 1950s as a response to this exclusion and discrimination. As Latino immigration patterns have shifted, new gangs have emerged representing regional subgroups within Latino culture, such as the relatively new Mara Salvatrucha gangs (Valdez, 1999).

Many of the ethnic groups we highlight vis-à-vis youth violence have a similar shared history of oppression and discrimination that represents a common experience based on minority status. However, even within the larger constellation of ethnic minority youth, not all minority youth necessarily share the same minority experience nor do they share the same historical circumstances behind this experience (for instance, African American youth must deal with a legacy of slavery that is not experienced by most other ethnic minority youth). Similarly, even within a particular ethnic minority group there are intergroup differences in strategies, coping, and ethnic group identification. To the extent that youth experience a shared history of oppression within their ethnic group as defined by minority status, themes related to ethnicity and its links to development may also be more salient. For example, ethnic minority youth are more likely than majority youth to struggle with the meaning of their ethnicity, particularly during the adolescent years when issues of identity are most salient (Phinney & Alipuria, 1990). Programs that foster positive ethnic identity development for minority youth may be particularly important to counteract perceptions of discrimination or alienation and to promote positive identity development.

UNIQUE RISK FOR EACH ETHNIC GROUP

Another perspective on preventing youth violence in a multicultural society emphasizes the unique conditions experienced by members of a particular ethnic group growing up under a set of circumstances that influence the meaning of risk for members of that group. This perspective speaks to the importance of examining specific risk factors within specific ethnic groups. For example, a large literature has documented the importance of "authoritative" parenting styles for healthy development and prevention of problems. Although these studies demonstrate the links between this type of parenting style and healthy outcomes for children, much of this research has been conducted with White middle-class families. More recent studies have shown that under some circumstances, for instance, for African American children, more parent-directed decision making may be warranted and adaptive (Brody & Flor, 1998; Lamborn, Dornbusch, & Steinberg, 1996). This suggests that some risk factors play out differently in each ethnic group and must be examined as potentially unique risk factors within each ethnic group.

OVERVIEW OF CHAPTERS

In Section I, "Understanding Youth Violence and Prevention in Context: The Role of Ethnicity and Culture," we elaborate on our multidimensional ecological model by examining the specific developmental ecologies of ethnic minority children in the United States, and how the experience of being a minority youth and being a member of a specific minority group can influence development and behavior, including violence. In chapter 1, Guerra and Williams examine the mechanisms by which elevated rates of violence by ethnic minority youth in the United States reflect their disproportionate exposure to problematic ecologies of development. They emphasize structural changes in communities where ethnic minority children are more likely to grow up and how these changes influence violence via their impact on resource scarcity, concentrated disadvantage, and danger.

In chapter 2, French, Kim, and Pillado consider the role of ethnic identity in youth violence and implications for prevention. As the authors discuss, the importance of ethnic identity is not the same for majority and minority youth, nor is it necessarily the same across youth from different ethnic minority groups. They discuss two distinct models of ethnic identity development, the "mainstream path" that emphasizes the importance of ethnic identity as one of many social identities that would impact ethnic minorities in a similar fashion, versus the "underground path" that emphasizes the unique and nonshared features that impact youth because of their particular ethnic background. To address the lack of consistent research findings on ethnic identity and youth violence, they examine this relation further using data from the Adolescent Pathways Project (Seidman, 1991). In chapter 3, Boutakidis, Guerra, and Soriano focus on the unique circumstances experienced by ethnic minority groups who are recent immigrants to the United States As they point out, immigration, per se, is not likely to affect youth violence. However, the process of acculturation and adaptation can unfold in a problematic fashion that may increase risk via the specific stress experience as well as shifting cultural and normative frameworks.

In Section II, "Youth Violence and Prevention in Specific Ethnic Groups," we review current knowledge regarding prevalence, etiology, and prevention of youth violence among five distinct ethnic groups: Latinos, Asian and Pacific Islanders, African Americans, American Indians, and White youth. Although we are clearly interested in examining youth violence among individuals from historically disadvantaged ethnic minority groups in the United States, we realize that a discussion of the role of ethnicity and culture in youth violence requires a broader conceptualization that goes beyond minority status. For this reason, we also include a chapter on violence among White youth that focuses on the concept of "whiteness" as related to youth violence. We also address the need to consider intragroup variability within ethnic groups, including factors such as national origin, socioeconomic status, and regional variation.

In each chapter in this section, the authors begin by describing the demographic characteristics of the ethnic group and terminology used for membership. Next they review data on youth violence trends, incorporating findings from both official reports and self-report surveys. Following this, they review what is known about shared risk and resilience factors (e.g., across ethnic groups), with particular attention to cultural factors or ecological circumstances that may increase the emergence of these risk and resilience factors. Emphasis also is placed on distinguishing individual, family, peer, and community risk factors related to unique practices of each ethnic group and subgroup, as well as the significance of minority or majority status within a given setting. Implications for designing and delivering prevention and intervention programs are discussed, particularly as they address ecological influences on violence risk and the need for tailoring programs for specific ethnic minority groups.

In chapter 4, Mirabal-Colón and Vélez discuss the rapid growth among Latino youth and families as well as the more difficult social and economic circumstances they live in. As they point out, consistent with a main theme of this book, Latinos are exposed to more difficult living conditions marked by scarce resources, low-wage work, and other roadblocks to success and adjustment. Similarly, although they indicate that accurate information on youth violence rates for Latinos in particular is sketchy, findings from multiple sources suggest that rates of youth violence and gang activity are relatively high and are increasing. The authors point to studies suggesting that many risk factors for youth violence are, indeed, shared across ethnic groups, although disadvantaged circumstances make these more likely to occur for Latinos. Further, they discuss unique characteristics of Latino culture that can serve as risk or protective factors for violence, as well as the history and circumstances surrounding the emergence of Latino gangs in the United States that contribute to youth violence.

Shifting the focus to American Asian Pacific Islander (API) youth, Mark, Revilla, Tsutsumoto, and Mayeda in chapter 5 highlight the invisibility and paucity of information on youth violence prevalence, etiology, and prevention among this group. This is, in part, because of the general habit of including API in the "other" category in most risk and prevalence studies. As the authors point out, many risk factors and recommendations for prevention for API youth are shared across ethnic minority groups, including the experience of racism, minority status, and disadvantaged child-rearing environments. However, there is also a great deal of diversity within API groups, and in some cases (for instance, among Hmong populations) historical circumstances including refugee status create unique risk profiles and must be addressed via focused interventions.

In chapter 6, Hurst and Laird report startling statistics about prevalence of youth violence and associated problems (such as depression, substance use, child abuse, and fetal alcohol syndrome) that affect American Indian youth living in cities and on reservations. Not only are American Indian youth and families exposed to structural disadvantage and difficult living conditions, but they have experienced historical trauma in the form of organized oppression and isolation from mainstream "White" society that contributes to their unique experience as ethnic minorities in the United States. This historical trauma includes government policies since the 1800s that have attempted to extinguish Indian identity through programs such as forced removal of entire communities, relocation to urban areas, and adoption by non-Indian families. Issues of identity and connectedness to mainstream society loom large. For this reason, violence prevention and youth development programs must integrate and build on the strengths of native culture. As an example, Hurst and Laird discuss the Tribal Youth Program that is designed to empower American Indian communities to determine the resolution of their social problems, using both the spiritual and cultural aspect of their specific Native traditions.

As Smith and Hasbrouck discuss in chapter 7, much of the concern about disproportionate minority representation in youth violence statistics has focused on the high rates for African Americans, particularly adolescent and young adult males. They review risk and protective factors that are shared across ethnic groups (such as hyperactivity and parenting approaches) but discuss how developmental ecologies for African Americans may affect the likelihood of emergence of these factors. In addition, they highlight unique risk factors for African Americans that may be shared with other ethnic groups based on the minority experience, as well as uniquely experienced by African Americans based on their particular historical circumstances (such as segregated schooling). They review preventive interventions that have involved large numbers of African Americans, although not tailored to African Americans, as well as culture-specific programs that are more sensitive to ethnic history and/or practices.

In chapter 8, Parker and Tuthill examine the fact that although ethnic minority youth may be disproportionately represented in youth violence statistics, the majority of youth violence is perpetrated by White youth. In addition to understanding similarities and differences in the ecological circumstances of White and ethnic minority youth vis-à-vis youth violence, they also point to the troublesome phenomenon of White ethnic violence linked to antiminority bias and a belief system focused on the superiority of the White race. They discuss different manifestations of White ethnic violence including White supremacists, White survivalists, skinheads, hate crimes, White youth gangs, and school shooters.

In Section III, "Developing Culturally Competent Youth Violence Prevention Programs and Strategies," we turn to broader issues of cultural competence and the development, implementation, and evaluation of culturally competent interventions. The authors review different approaches to enhancing cultural competence, including increasing awareness of cultural practices of the population to be served; providing interventions focused specifically on issues of ethnicity, culture, and diversity; developing focused interventions for specific ethnic groups; and engaging professionals in violence prevention with participants from a range of economic, ethnic, and cultural backgrounds.

In chapter 9, Wright and Zimmerman emphasize the concepts of deep structure and surface structure as related to cultural sensitivity in preventive interventions. As they point out and illustrate through various examples of youth violence prevention programs, deep structure reflects how cultural, social, psychological, environmental, and historical factors influence behavior differently across ethnic groups, including an awareness of how individuals in a particular subgroup perceive the problem and its solutions. In contrast, surface structure emphasizes the external characteristics of culture that enhance "fit" or receptivity to the implementation of interventions, including use of appropriate food, language, and music familiar to and preferred by the selected population.

The role of cultural competence in violence prevention is discussed by Hudley and Taylor in chapter 10. The authors emphasize the importance of looking at culture in a broad and general sense, including the multiple ways it can be infused into prevention programming and practice. They also provide examples of best practices in violence prevention that address important elements of cultural competence. Finally, they suggest general principles that emphasize building positive competencies across multiple settings to guide to the development of culturally competent violence prevention programming.

Finally, we conclude in chapter 11 (Guerra and Smith) by reviewing the major themes of this volume and their relevance to future research and practice. These include (a) ethnicity as a marker for culture, (b) ethnicity and disadvantage, (c) ethnicity and gangs, (d) levels of culture, (e) prevention in a multicultural setting, and (f) strengths-based cultural competence. We highlight the challenges of developing and implementing youth violence prevention programs in a multicultural society, and suggest directions for future research and practice.

REFERENCES

Anderson, R. (2002). Deaths: Leading causes for 2000. *National Vital Statistics Report, 50*, 16.

Brody, G. H., & Flor, D. L. (1998). Maternal resources, parenting practices, and child competence in rural, single-parent African American families. *Child Development, 69*, 803–816.

Centers for Disease Control and Prevention. (2001). Influence of homicide on racial disparity in life expectancy, U.S., 1998. *Morbidity and Mortality Weekly Report, 50*, 780–783.

Elliott, D. S. (1994). Serious violent offenders: Onset, developmental course, and termination. The American Society of Criminology 1993 presidential address. *Criminology, 32*, 1–21.

Gerard, J. M., & Buehler, C. (2004). Cumulative environmental risk and youth maladjustment: The role of youth attributes. *Child Development, 75*, 1832–1849.

Huesmann, L. R., Eron, L. D., & Dubow, E. F. (2002). Childhood predictors of adult criminality: Are all risk factors reflected in childhood aggressiveness? *Criminal Behavior and Mental Health, 12*, 185–208.

Lamborn, S. D., Dornbusch, S. M., & Steinberg, L. (1996). Ethnicity and community context as moderators of the relations between family decision making and adolescent adjustment. *Child Development, 67*, 283–301.

Phinney, J. S., & Alipuria, L. (1990). Ethnic identity in older adolescents from four ethnic groups. *Journal of Adolescence, 13,* 271–281.

Seidman, E. (1991). Growing up the hard way: Pathways of urban adolescents. *American Journal of Community Psychology, 19,* 173–205.

U.S. Department of Health and Human Services. (2001). *Youth violence: A report of the surgeon general.* Rockville, MD: U.S. Government Printing Office.

Valdez, A. (1999). *A history of California's Hispanic gangs.* National Alliance of Gang Investigators Associations. Retrieved November 15, 2004, from http://www.nagia.org

I

UNDERSTANDING YOUTH VIOLENCE AND PREVENTION IN CONTEXT: THE ROLE OF ETHNICITY AND CULTURE

1

ETHNICITY, YOUTH VIOLENCE, AND THE ECOLOGY OF DEVELOPMENT

NANCY G. GUERRA AND KIRK R. WILLIAMS

Understanding the relationship between ethnicity and youth violence requires an analysis of specific developmental contexts that can vary by ethnicity. One of the most important developmental contexts for children is the community where they grow up. In the United States and elsewhere, children from certain ethnic groups have disproportionately grown up in neighborhoods characterized by high levels of segregation and disadvantage, as indicated by poverty and inequality (Evans, 2004; Hernandez, 2004; Massey & Denton, 1996; Wilson, 1996). Several aspects of these disadvantaged contexts can interfere with successful adaptations to prosocial behavioral expectations and facilitate the learning, use, and escalation of aggressive, violent, and delinquent behavior during childhood and into adulthood (Sampson & Laub, 2004).

Ethnic minority youth often grow up in ecological contexts that have fewer resources to foster the development of protective factors that reduce risk for violence compared with their nonminority peers. Otherwise stated, a child's ethnicity can increase the likelihood that he or she will be raised in a particular "ecological niche" that will hinder rather than promote successful development. An ecological niche refers to the sociospatial location where specific groups of people reside. It forms a child's developmental environment by providing a stage where social interactions occur, offering a normative or regulatory structure that includes costs and benefits of distinct courses of action, and providing opportunities for learning, development, and social interaction. This ecological niche can influence both individual propensities for aggression as well as the circumstances under which aggression is learned over time (Guerra & Huesmann, 2004). The niche provides a broad context for development that includes proximal sources of social influence (such as family and peers) nested within it, and yet it is situated within a larger, more distal historical, political, national, and global context.

This chapter examines the intersection of ethnicity and the ecology of development in the genesis of violence among minority youth in the United States. First, we review studies that show how elevated rates of violence by ethnic minority youth reflect their disproportionate exposure to problematic ecologies of development. We discuss research that links these elevated violence rates not only to economic disadvantage but also to the myriad of accompanying social transformations that have changed the quality of life in many communities. As Sampson and Wilson (1995) argued, it is these structural differences among communities rather than ethnicity that produce heightened rates of violence and other problems. We emphasize the role of *resource scarcity*, *concentrated disadvantage*, and *danger*, and how they are disproportionately more likely to occur in poor, urban neighborhoods where many ethnic minority children live.

These structural differences clearly affect the course of individual development for children growing up in these contexts. We also discuss the processes and mechanisms by which these structural differences can increase the likelihood that an individual child will engage in aggressive and violent behavior. We review individual biological and psychosocial predictors of violence and examine how neighborhood effects can influence risk across different developmental periods. We emphasize the socialization, learning, and developmental processes involved in violence that occur over time from before birth through adolescence. This discussion highlights the linkages between both social structural and individual explanations of violence. Rather than asking what it is about the nature of communities that influences violence or what it is about the nature of individuals that influences violence, we examine how individual development unfolds within a specific ecological niche, and how this unfolding affects behaviors such as violence. This approach highlights the different contexts within which ethnic minority children are raised and how these developmental ecologies contribute to violence.

SOCIAL TRANSFORMATIONS AND THE DISADVANTAGED
ECOLOGICAL NICHE

Many researchers have documented the massive transformations that have reshaped the landscape of urban America during the past few decades (Berry & Kasarda, 1977; Hagan, 2004; Hernandez, 2004; Kasarda, 1989; Massey & Eggers, 1990; Massey, Gross, & Shibuya, 1994; Wilson, 1987, 1996). Although these researchers differ in both their methodologies and theoretical arguments (for a review, see Massey & Fischer, 2000), they largely agree that the transformations have created ecological niches for ethnic minorities that are scarred by multiple forms of disadvantage. The decades since the 1970s have witnessed a significant deindustrialization of the U.S. economy, resulting in an exodus of manufacturing jobs out of the country or into the suburbs. The decline of such work has been associated with greater unemployment, prolonged joblessness, and detachment from conventional work and related values and skills within urban settings. Other transformations have included the movement of middle-class families into the suburbs, retention of low-income families in the inner city because of declining housing values and rents, and increasing segregation (Wilson, 1987, 1996). Massey and Fischer (2000) summarized these structural changes.

> The structural transformations of the U.S. economy from goods production to service provision generate a strong demand for workers with high and low levels of schooling, but offered few opportunities for those with modest education and training. Central cities lost hundreds of thousands of high-paying, unionized manufacturing jobs and these were replaced by non-union service positions that paid high salaries to an expanding class of managers and professionals, but low wages to displaced factory workers and new job seekers who lacked educational credentials. In the post-industrial economy that emerged after 1973, labor unions withered, the middle class bifurcated, income inequality grew and poverty deepened. This new stratification in the socioeconomic sphere was accompanied by a growing spatial separation between classes in the spatial sphere. As inequality rose so did the degree of class segregation, as affluent and poor families increasingly came to inhabit different social spaces. These trends undermined the socioeconomic well-being of all racial and ethnic groups in the United States. (p. 670)

Massey and Fischer (2000) further asserted that income stagnated, inequality increased, and geographic separation intensified for all ethnic minorities, but especially for African Americans living in large cities.

In short, these social transformations have resulted in the de facto segregation of ethnic minority populations in ecological niches of urban disadvantage. To illustrate, Kasarda (1993) found that as of 1990, 83% of poor, inner-city African Americans in the United States lived in neighbor-hoods that were at least 20% poor. A more striking illustration is that Sampson and Wilson (1995) analyzed census data for the 171 largest cities in the United States "to get some idea of the concentrated dislocations by race" (p. 129) in terms of poverty and families with children headed by a single parent. Here is how they summarize their findings.

> In not one city over 100,000 in the United States do blacks live in ecological equality with Whites when it comes to these basic features of economic and family organization. Accordingly, racial differences in poverty and family disruption are so strong that the "worst" urban contexts in which Whites reside are considerably better than the average context of black communities. (Sampson & Wilson, 1995, p. 129)

The social transformations and accompanying forms of concentrated disadvantage described have placed a heavy burden on ethnic minorities in the United States. Much of the early work on community disadvantage by Wilson and colleagues (Sampson & Wilson, 1995; Wilson, 1987) focused particularly on social isolation and its impact for African Americans. How-ever, social transformations and disadvantage are experienced across many ethnic minority groups. For instance, recent work examining the effects of burgeoning immigrant populations has identified a somewhat distinct set of factors that increase disadvantage and isolation of ethnic minority immigrant groups, including overcrowded housing, linguistic barriers, low-wage work without benefits, lack of familiarity with the educational system, and citizen-ship status (e.g., Hernandez, 2004; Portes & Rumbaut, 2001).

Still, two issues must be addressed before proceeding with this discus-sion. First, it is important to clarify the meaning of the term "disadvantage." Second, it is important to elaborate further on the implications that disad-vantage has for the relation between ethnicity and youth violence. Consider the first issue. Claiming neighborhoods, social spaces, or ecological niches are disadvantaged can have pejorative connotations, suggesting a blanket attribution of deficits to an entire area or social location. Such a claim could be viewed as a form of environmental labeling, insensitive to the diverse features of life in those settings. It is a conceptual gloss that can blind observers to the positive features of an ecological niche that may support people in making successful adaptations to their life circumstances. Hence, the term *disadvantage* is used here to refer to the variable properties of social spaces or ecological niches that reduce the life chances of people in those settings; that is, these niches interfere with the healthy adaptations that facilitate constructive developmental pathways. Ecological niches can be more or less disadvantaged along multiple dimensions, which we discuss below, having behavioral consequences that may be moderated by other features of the setting or individuals within those settings possessing strengths or assets.

Second, interpretations with pejorative connotations too often accompany reported findings that ethnic minorities, particularly African Americans, have higher rates of serious violence compared with non-Hispanic Whites. A case in point is the subculture of violence thesis, alleging that ethnic minorities are carriers of a violent culture, which accounts for their higher involvement in violent behavior (Wolfgang & Ferracuti, 1982). Besides bordering on a blatant tautology, such an explanation amounts to a cultural indictment that minimizes the structural location and circumstances of ethnic minorities and how their ecological niche can influence cultural beliefs and practices, adaptive to the circumstances of living. Causal priority is thus given to the massive transformations structuring disadvantage in the ecological niches in which ethnic minorities have become increasingly situated. To the extent that cultural beliefs and practices incorporate violence, they are a function of the structural dynamics confronted by ethnic minorities. These beliefs and practices are adaptive phenomena, not internalized norms that assume a life and character of their own and thus persist independent of their structural roots (for a recent study of the intersection of structural and cultural explanations of violence, see Kubrin & Weitzer, 2003).

Disadvantage can be manifested in multiple forms across ecological niches. Although poverty is clearly a marker for disadvantage, it does not adequately capture the dimensions of disadvantage. Furthermore, the effects of poverty on youth violence are more evident when considering the mechanisms by which poverty and associated features can affect violence. Indeed, this recognition is one of the advances in violence research that has often associated disadvantage merely with poverty (Elliott et al., 1996; Kovandzic, Vieraitis, & Yeisley, 1998; Krivo, Peterson, Rizzo, & Reynolds, 1998; Peterson & Krivo, 1999). We highlight three dimensions of disadvantage that are central to the relation between ethnicity and youth violence: resource scarcity, concentrated disadvantage, and danger.

Resource Scarcity

Broadly defined, resources refer to assets of an ecological niche that can be mobilized to promote human development. They can be physical or material resources, human resources, or social resources. This is compatible with the distinction between physical, human, and social capital (Coleman, 1988; Field, 2003; Portes, 1998; Putnam, 2000; Warren, Thompson, & Saegert, 2001; Woolcock, 1998). Physical capital includes obvious assets such as income and quality of the environment (e.g., housing stock, parks, and recreation centers). Human capital includes acquired personal competencies that enhance the chances of achievement, making healthy adaptations, and meeting the performance requirements of social settings, such as family, school, and work. Education and training as well as the development of a positive identity, self-regulation skills, social problem-solving and social relationship skills, prosocial goal orientation, and a system of prosocial beliefs would be examples of human capital. Social capital consists of the interconnections among people within an ecological niche and between them and resources in the larger community that provide the foundation for reciprocal interaction, the development of mutual trust, and action to promote personal well-being and the common good.

Resource scarcity among poor ethnic minority families living in the inner city has been well-documented, particularly in terms of physical capital. In terms of developmental implications, health risk conditions and access to health care are particularly critical. Several studies have shown that health risk conditions are higher for inner-city children and families. One of the most frequently discussed health risks for children is lead poisoning, with children in poverty, particularly African American children, at elevated risk for lead exposure (Sherman, 1994). Additional research has shown that economic, linguistic, and cultural barriers also significantly affect the use of health care services among minority families (Guendelman & Schwalbe, 1986; Lessard & Ku, 2003) and that the health status of minority children is often compromised (Garcia Coll, 1990; Takanishi, 2004).

Once physical resources are compromised, the development of human and social resources becomes problematic. Human resources would include the prevalence of people in the ecological niche with the skills and knowledge necessary to achieve or to help others achieve, either through their direct supportive involvement or indirectly by serving as role models. Social resources refer to the availability of social networks, "making possible the achievement of certain ends that in [their] absence would not be possible" (Coleman, 1990, p. 300). These social resources are closely linked to child health, as well as to child neglect and abuse—prevalence estimates of child neglect and abuse reveal elevated rates among the poor, urban minorities, with African American children five times more likely than White children to die from neglect and abuse (National Research Council, 1993).

This conception suggests that social resources include the social organizational characteristics of an ecological niche that can also be mobilized to support families and their children. This notion has been extended in the conceptualization of "collective efficacy," which embraces the resource potential of organizational networks but infuses it with action-oriented expectations relating to mutual trust and a willingness to intervene for the common good, particularly in the active support and social control of children (Sampson, 2004; Sampson, Morenoff, & Gannon-Rowley, 2002; Sampson, Raudenbush, & Earls, 1997). Social resources, therefore, provide the safety net and supportive mechanisms inherent in strong organizational ties within an ecological niche. Unfortunately, such ties never develop or are ravaged by the disorganizing influences of the massive transformations discussed earlier and their consequences for diminishing the physical resources of ecological niches. Resource scarcity, particularly as reflected in types of neighborhoods and stress on family structure, threatens the life chances of ethnic minority youth and thus increases their risk of violence (Sampson, Morenoff, & Raudenbush, 2005).

Concentrated Disadvantage

Research on the structural transformations during the past three decades has shown that disadvantage has deepened, fallen heavily on ethnic minorities, and has become increasingly concentrated (Hernandez, 2004). *Concentration* has a dual meaning. On the one hand, it denotes the density or dispersion of an ethnic population in geographic space. On the other hand, it denotes the extent to which that population is separated from and perhaps even devalued by the broader society. This second meaning is similar to the notion of "social isolation," referring to "the lack of contact or of sustained interaction with individuals and institutions that represent mainstream society" (Sampson & Wilson, 1995, p. 135). These scholars consider social isolation as a consequence of concentrated poverty.

However, the degree of concentration can also be viewed as a variable characteristic of ecological niches that is clearly correlated with the nature and extent of resource scarcity yet analytically distinct. For example, some inner-city African American communities are characterized by circumscribed spaces with intense resource scarcity, whereas others are more disperse yet with equally scarce resources, as in the rural south. Many Latino communities in the Southwest also suffer scarce resources but are not as geographically concentrated (U.S. Census Bureau, 2000). More important, the degree of concentration is a key feature in understanding the development of adaptive strategies to disadvantage, particularly the rise of alternative means to surviving in an austere and potentially hostile environment. Thus, it is the combination of resource scarcity with intense concentration that must be considered in understanding patterns of violence (Anderson, 1990, 1999; Canada, 1995; McCord, 1997).

Concentration and poverty too often exacerbate the perception among ethnic minorities that they are marginalized from the broader society. Density, residential segregation, and social exclusion accentuate the devaluation of these groups. Residents may feel that their voices are not heard and their needs are ignored. Proximity can create a collective identity of the disenfranchised. When one looks closely at the human costs of concentrated disadvantage for ethnic minorities, one often finds a sense of separateness, lack of self-esteem, and a low level of personal self-efficacy to change things or make them better (McMahon & Watts, 2002).

Although ethnic minority youth are more likely than nonminority youth to live in disadvantaged communities, studies that have compared violence rates in neighborhoods with a relatively high prevalence of both minority and nonminority disadvantage have largely found that disadvantage has the same pattern of effects in both communities. Furthermore, violence rates are lower in minority neighborhoods with low disadvantage when compared with either minority or nonminority neighborhoods with extreme disadvantage (Krivo & Peterson, 1996). In other words, when structural conditions are controlled, violence rates are more comparable across ethnic groups. However, ethnic minority youth in the United States are more likely to live under conditions of extreme and concentrated disadvantage associated with higher rates of violence.

Danger

Danger is often overlooked as an important dimension of disadvantage. This is a serious oversight because it plays a significant role in shaping the day-to-day cultural beliefs and practices within an ecological niche. Participation in dangerous life situations heightens the risk of violent posturing and violent behavior. Such settings also increase levels of fear and create a need for responses that help youth manage this fear (Vigil, 1988). Dangerous settings are particularly common in urban, ecological niches suffering from resource scarcity and concentrated poverty (Krivo et al., 1998; Sampson & Wilson, 1995).

For example, in their research in inner-city neighborhoods in New York City, Fagan and Wilkinson (1998a) reported that adolescent males regularly discussed the lack of personal safety in their communities and a strong sense of danger that permeates the public landscape. As respondents noted, expectations of violence are high, and behavior on the streets is guided by the knowledge that violence can erupt at any moment. This creates an *ecology of danger* "where social interactions are perceived as threatening or lethal, and where individuals are seen as harboring hostile intent and the willingness to inflict harm" (p. 130).

As a result, possessing a firearm plays an important role in personal safety as both a preemptive and defensive strategy. Participants in the Fagan and Wilkinson (1998a) study reported that most young males can and did have guns, and that guns are available to just about anyone who has the means to buy, borrow, or steal them. A number of surveys and interview studies support these findings. For example, in a large study of gun access among inner-city juveniles in high schools and correctional facilities, Sheley and Wright (1995) found that 84% of inmates (before incarceration) and 22% of students said that they possessed guns; 74% of inmates and 41% of students said they could acquire a gun on the street or from a family member with no trouble at all. For those who purchased guns, average cost was less than $100, and guns could be acquired even more cheaply through informal networks. Access to guns is highest among ethnic minority, urban adolescent, and young adult males.

Although adolescents frequently mention self-protection as a primary reason for gun carrying, the presence of guns on the street also increases (rather than decreases) the likelihood of violence (Blumstein, 2002). Guns raise the stakes in conflict—individuals who show guns must also be willing to use guns, limiting the number of choices for resolving conflicts. Furthermore, carrying guns fosters a cognitive and behavioral readiness to aggress that can lead to proactive as well as reactive forms of violence. As Shapiro, Dorman, Burkey, Welker, and Clough (1997) reported, adolescents who carry guns tend to believe that guns are exciting and provide power and safety. Carrying guns is also related to overall levels of comfort with physical aggression and the belief among youth that any sign of "disrespect" must be counteracted with aggressive retaliation. In summary, guns are functional in dangerous settings but simultaneously contribute to the perpetuation of danger and likelihood of violence in these settings.

In terms of the developmental and learning implications of danger, there is also an increased likelihood that children will be exposed to and witness neighborhood violence in these settings from a young age (Bell & Jenkins, 1991; Osofsky, Wewers, Hann, & Fick, 1993). During the past few decades, studies have consistently demonstrated that children in inner-city neighborhoods are exposed to extremely high rates of violence. Many of these studies examine rates of exposure within specific groups of children and adolescents (e.g., inner-city youth) and demonstrate high levels of violence exposure, particularly for males and particularly for inner-city youth (Farrell & Bruce, 1997). Short-term longitudinal research also has revealed a link between witnessing community violence and subsequent aggressive behavior. For example, Gorman-Smith and Tolan (1998) found that exposure to community violence predicted subsequent aggression among inner-city elementary and middle school boys. Furthermore, recent studies have found that community violence exposure also contributes to the development of beliefs supporting aggression that, in turn, increase the likelihood of aggressive and violent behavior (Guerra, Huesmann, & Spindler, 2004). Thus, violence exposure is a correlate of living under conditions of danger with implications for future beliefs and behavior. We now turn to a discussion of how these dimensions of disadvantage are linked to the development and learning of aggression among ethnic minority youth.

AN ECOLOGICAL APPROACH TO UNDERSTANDING PREDICTORS OF YOUTH VIOLENCE FOR ETHNIC MINORITY YOUTH

Structural characteristics of neighborhoods and communities typically have been linked with differences in rates of violence between communities that vary on these characteristics. Additional variation within communities (e.g., not all parents lack social networks) has also been put forth as an explanation for different levels of violence within a community, particularly because most youth are not involved in violent acts even within the most distressed communities. A somewhat different research perspective involves the identification of predictors of risk that vary between individuals such as attention difficulties (Moffitt, 1990), hormonal levels (Olweus, Mattsson, Schalling, & Low, 1988), peer difficulties (Coie & Dodge, 1997), and poor parenting (Eron, Huesmann, & Zelli, 1991), to name a few. Although there are clearly multiple risk factors for violence, no one causal factor by itself explains more than a small portion of individual differences. Furthermore, lists or matrices or risk factors do not illuminate the linkages between individual and contextual risk factors and the mechanisms of influence on aggression and violence over time.

How can one better understand the interconnectedness between these individual and contextual factors and how they are affected by ethnicity? One strategy is to examine how individual development unfolds within a specific ecological niche, including how environments facilitate or inhibit development and risk. Although developmental researchers have become increasingly aware of the transactional nature of individual–environmental interactions (Sameroff & Fiese, 1990), the specific ecological niches occupied by many ethnic minority children have not been systematically assessed in terms of their impact on development. As Garcia Coll and colleagues (1996) noted, "most of the prevalent conceptual frameworks do not emphasize the social stratification system, or the social positions that comprise the scaffolding or structure of the system (i.e., social class, ethnicity, and race) and the processes and consequences that these relative positions engender for a child's development" (p. 1892). Indeed, traditional paradigms may offer little insight into the developmental adaptations of ethnic minority children (Spencer, 1990). As French, Kim, and Pillado (chap. 2, this volume) note, the minority experience in the United States presents a unique and additional context, reflecting historical and political conditions that influence development and behavior for all ethnic minority groups and for members of ethnic minority groups who have experienced a unique history of racism and oppression.

Similarly, although a large literature is available on the effects of poverty and concentrated disadvantage on community indicators of youth and adult violence, little research has focused directly on the effects of these structural characteristics on children's development. Sociological investigations that have examined potential mediators of neighborhood structural characteristics on developmental outcomes (including violence) generally have focused on a single proposed mechanism or set of social mechanisms that affect the lives of children. For example, as discussed previously, Sampson and colleagues (Sampson, 1997; Sampson, Morenoff, & Earls, 1999; Sampson, Morenoff, & Raudenbush, 2005) have examined the importance of spatial dynamics in generating collective efficacy for childrearing. Collective efficacy operates as a type of informal social control, demonstrated in such acts as monitoring play groups or confronting people who are threatening public space in some way. Thus, collective efficacy represents one mediating mechanism by which community context can influence children's development.

In the present chapter, we look more broadly at some of the primary processes by which ecological contexts influence children's development and behavior as well as specific mediating mechanisms that occur in different proximal environments (e.g., peers, families, schools) during different developmental periods. Although the general processes involved in the learning of aggression should not vary significantly by setting, what is learned and opportunities for learning can vary greatly across different contexts. In particular, we emphasize the role of resource scarcity, concentrated disadvantage, and danger on children's socialization over time, and how these dimensions of disadvantage relate to the learning of aggression and violence. We emphasize two distinct but related processes linked to the disadvantaged ecological niches of many ethnic minority children.

First, these contexts increase the chance that development will be compromised from before birth through adolescence. Although disadvantage theoretically can affect all children regardless of their ethnicity, in the United States at this time, ethnic minority children are more likely to experience such disadvantage. In turn, this creates conditions that do not facilitate and are likely to inhibit the healthy development of children. This can occur through a variety of mediating mechanisms such as lack of adequate prenatal care, lack of access to care, lead exposure in substandard housing, family structure, lack of role models, consequences of stress, and low levels of parental monitoring and supervision. Not only is optimal development problematic, but any type of "downward slide" is likely to continue without adequate remediation. This is quite important in the etiology of violence because many of the prominent risk factors represent inadequate developmental adaptations at different stages (e.g., lack of secure attachment relationship with primary caregiver during infancy; Sampson & Laub, 2004). Although the relation between risk factors and violence should not vary by ethnicity, the likelihood of these risk factors emerging and/or spinning a web of cumulative risk is much higher for ethnic minority children growing up under conditions of disadvantage.

Second, there is an increased likelihood that violence will emerge as a normalized type of social currency to navigate these difficult contexts (Ng-Mak, Salzinger, Feldman, & Stueve, 2002). As recent evolutionary theorizing suggests, a defining characteristic of humans is our ability to adjust our behavior quickly to the demands of the situation and to choose between multiple possible courses of action. Indeed, much emphasis has been placed on the importance of "calibration" of response systems (such as aggression) to match the needs and demands of the environment (Malamuth & Heilmann, 1998). However, contexts can also vary greatly in terms of the adaptive value of aggression. As Buss and Schackelford (1997) pointed out, "In principle, the mechanisms producing aggression could remain dormant for the entire life of an individual, if the relevant contexts are not encountered" (p. 612). In this fashion, resource scarcity, concentrated disadvantage, and danger can lead to the emergence of a cultural structure where aggression and violence are more likely to be adaptive under certain conditions.

The specific mechanisms of influence of dimensions of disadvantage are also likely to vary in salience during infancy, childhood, and adolescence. However, given that early aggression and related behaviors during childhood are among the strongest predictors of later violent and delinquent behavior (Huesmann, Eron, Lefkowitz, & Walder, 1984; Moffitt, 1993, 2004), it is critically important to examine these predictors across development, and determine how they unfold in certain contexts. Let us now turn to a more detailed description of the influence of structural characteristics on the development and learning of aggression and violence.

Infancy and the Preschool Years

Environmental factors associated with disadvantaged ecological niches can compromise development and affect both innate and acquired propensities for aggression from the very earliest stages of development—prenatal care can be inadequate, low birth weight is more prevalent, nutrition is often poor, and the incidence of fetal exposure to toxins is greater. These factors can contribute to an array of nervous system problems including hyperactivity, poor attention, verbal skill deficits, problems with self control, low IQ, and poor school performance (Evans, 2004). For example, malnourished infants appear to have greater attention difficulties, are more easily distracted, and are less socially skilled. Even if nutrition improves during the preschool years, these characteristics tend to endure, and the damage done by malnutrition is significantly higher in disadvantaged urban contexts (Barrett & Frank, 1987). In turn, nervous system problems have been linked with aggressive and delinquent behavior in childhood and adolescence through a variety of mechanisms (Moffitt & Henry, 1991). For example, problems with hyperactivity and inattention, particularly when reaching clinical levels as seen in children with attention-deficit/hyperactivity disorder (ADHD), have been shown to set the stage for a chain of events beginning with early aggression and culminating in more serious forms of juvenile violence (Loeber, Green, Keenan, & Lahey, 1995; Moffitt, 2004).

To a certain extent, neuropsychological problems can contribute directly to aggression. Clearly, characteristics such as low self-control will increase the likelihood of aggression under conditions of provocation or anger. Similarly, low verbal skills can compromise a child's ability to negotiate solutions to problems with others and increase the likelihood of aggression. In addition, these (and other) negative child characteristics may also elicit problematic social interactions from caregivers, especially under conditions of economic disadvantage and high levels of stress (Tarter, Hegedus, Winsten, & Alterman, 1984). In other words, the challenges of dealing with a difficult child also can set in motion a sequence of problematic adult–child interactions that continue to compromise development during childhood and beyond. This can occur in the classroom, as teachers struggle to cope with children who talk out of turn or act out, and culminate in poor school performance. It can also occur in the home environment, particularly among parents with limited skills and resources, who themselves are coping with the daily challenges of disadvantage. Along the way, the mastery of many important developmental tasks can be compromised, further increasing the likelihood of behaviors such as aggression (Shaw, Gilliom, Ingoldsby, & Nagin, 2003).

Consider the importance of the infant–caregiver attachment relationship. In this context, attachment refers to a cumulative process of reciprocal interchanges between a child and a caregiver during infancy and beyond. An important outcome of this interchange is the development of a close and trusting relationship. This positive emotional exchange has been linked to the development of empathy and emotional sensitivity in relationships. It has also been found to correlate with specific neurochemical and structural processes involved in early brain development (Schore, 1994). When the attachment process goes awry, emotional development can be severely affected. If these early relationships provide a working model for later interactions, as Bowlby (1988) has proposed, then children with insecure attachments will be forced to navigate the social world without a template for successful relationships. Studies examining the relation between early attachment problems and children's aggression have supported this conclusion, with avoidant attachment measured in infancy significantly predicting school-age aggressive behavior in poor, urban settings (Renken, Egeland, Marvinney, Mangelsdorf, & Sroufe, 1989).

The ability to develop positive emotional relationships and healthy social interactions is perhaps most significantly compromised for children who are victims of severe abuse and neglect. As mentioned previously, rates of abuse and neglect are highest among inner-city ethnic minority children. Child abuse is the fourth leading cause of death for children ages 1 to 4 and the second leading cause of death for African American children in that age group (National Clearinghouse on Child Abuse and Neglect Information, 2004). Although there are multiple causes of abuse and neglect, it is quite easy to understand how conditions of disadvantage can contribute to this behavior. Clearly, resource scarcity increases levels of stress, and this is exacerbated for parents who are both young and single. Social support may be harder to access, and role models for effective parenting may be absent. This is even more problematic for young parents who were themselves raised under harsh conditions, with high levels of physical punishment or abuse. As Widom (1989, 1998) detailed in her "violence begets violence" studies, parents tend to raise their children as they have been raised—being the victim of abuse predicts later abusive behavior toward one's children.

Furthermore, such victimization predicts aggression and violence during childhood, adolescence, and adulthood. Studies have documented this relation as early as the preschool years. For instance, Howes and Eldredge (1985) found that abused and neglected children attending a day care center were more likely than their nonabused counterparts to respond to peer aggression with retaliation. Other studies extending into elementary school have found that abused and neglected children are more likely to respond to aggression with aggression, while failing to respond to friendly social interactions (Dodge, Bates, & Pettit, 1990; Jacobson & Straker, 1982). The relation between early abuse and later violent criminal behavior is also strong, especially when serious violence is considered. In a longitudinal study examining predictors of youth violence and delinquency, Smith and Thornberry (1995) reported that abuse during childhood (from official records) significantly predicted serious violence and delinquency during middle school and high school.

High levels of neighborhood violence can compromise early development in several ways. To begin with, even if resources (e.g., health care, counseling) are available, parents may be afraid to venture out on a regular basis. Danger also limits opportunities for positive engagement with one's children and with other parents, such as meeting at the park or playground. Instead, parents are more likely to stay at home and keep their children inside with them. When children do venture outside, witnessing violence, particularly from an early age, can quickly overload the brain's alarm system, creating children who are hypervigilant to stress and who overreact to environmental cues (Pynoos, Steinberg, & Ornitz, 1977). Recent studies of early brain development have shown that the blueprint for responding to danger and stress is written early in development, and early overstimulation of the alarm system through violence exposure can set the stage for later aggression (Perry, 1997).

For example, early stress and violence exposure may lead to the development of what has been labeled *persistent fear response* (Perry, 1999). Because fear is necessary for human survival, the brain is uniquely designed to process and store information related to potential threats, and to organize responding accordingly. However, chronic stress or repeated exposure to violence can alter the biological system. Chronic activation of the fear response system can actually interfere with development of other parts of the brain involved in cognition and memory. Early trauma can also interfere with brain development and result in extreme anxiety, depression, and difficulty forming attachments (Schore, 1994). Chronic activation of the neural pathways involved in the fear response can also remain permanently etched on the brain in a manner that shapes future perceptions and responses. In this way, early brain development under hostile conditions can shape the brain's architecture in a way that may be difficult to alter, even if environmental conditions change (Shore, 1997).

Childhood

Many of the factors related to risk during infancy and the preschool years carry forward into childhood. Lack of access to health and other resources, poor parenting because of high stress levels and lack of role models, abuse and neglect, and exposure to neighborhood violence continue to affect children's development in a similar fashion. Neural connections are being formed and pruned during the elementary school years, and characteristic patterns of thought and behavior begin to emerge. Once established, these patterns contribute to a high level of stability in aggression from childhood through adolescence and adulthood (Huesmann et al., 1984).

Children are learning cognitive scripts for behavior that guide information processing and responding. As they develop characteristic styles of thinking across a restricted range of increasingly familiar contexts, these scripted responses become highly automatic. More aggressive children learn more aggressive scripts and rely on them more regularly (Guerra & Huesmann, 2004). In particular, aggressive scripts can be seen as an adaptive response to social interactions marred by potential danger. Given the heightened likelihood of victimization in disadvantaged settings, it may be wise to "be prepared" in terms of readiness to fight or defend oneself.

Childhood also marks the child's formal entry into the school system. The school experience adds a new dimension to risk for aggression in terms of academic progress, peer relations, and the sense of connectedness or "bonding" the child develops to school as a conventional social institution

(O'Donnell, Hawkins, & Abbott, 1995). Clearly, children from disadvantaged settings who begin school with emotional, behavioral, or neuropsychological problems are less likely to succeed from the start. The snowball of cumulative disadvantage starts earlier and rolls faster in this context (Lee & Burkham, 2002).

Resource scarcity may severely limit the ability of schools to offer any type of special help or remediation. Teacher expectations for poor, ethnic minority children may also be low. In a subtle fashion, children may actually be learning that they cannot succeed (Woolfolk, 1995). Parents are also less able to help their children. Inadequate social capital can make it harder for parents to work together to access needed services. In the case of immigrant ethnic minority families, language and cultural issues may hinder the child's development as well as the parent's ability to provide effective guidance. Parents with little formal education may also feel unprepared and anxious when dealing with school issues (Takanashi, 2004).

The lack of opportunities and resources clearly limits the achievement of ethnic minority children growing up in disadvantaged settings. These differential achievement patterns have been documented in a number of studies and reports. Although this achievement gap appears to be narrowing, ethnic minority youth still complete fewer years of school and score lower on most standardized achievement tests than White youth (Ogbu, 1992). This difference is most striking for African American students (Bruschi & Anderson, 1994). However, it is important to note that neighborhood effects loom large in these differences, particularly poverty and the prevalence of single-parent families (Steinberg & Darling, 1994).

Underachievement and aggression are also likely to co-occur. The causal sequence appears to be reciprocal over time during the school years (Hinshaw, 1992; Huesmann, Eron, & Yarmel, 1987). On one hand, aggression may be a reaction to early learning problems. That is, children may become frustrated with not being able to learn the material presented to them and act out aggressively. On the other hand, academic achievement can be impeded by aggression. Aggressive children may have fewer learning opportunities if classmates and teachers avoid them because of their behavior. Aggressive children may also have greater difficulty with self-control and engage in more inappropriate behavior that interferes with learning.

This problem is compounded for ethnic minority youth. Aggression not only leads to academic underachievement but increases the likelihood of school dropout. One study of urban, African American children reported that first grade aggressive behavior predicted higher rates of high school drop out (Ensminger & Slusarcick, 1992). It has been argued that early aggression may propel a cycle of problems that inhibits a child's ability to learn. This behavior, if unchecked, may lead to confrontations with teachers and authority figures, and set in motion a cycle of failure. Over time, this failure can alienate a child from school, particularly for disadvantaged ethnic minority children growing up in a context of alienation and isolation.

As a consequence, some ethnic minority students may become part of a *resistance culture*. Students reject the behaviors that would make them successful in school—things such as studying, cooperating with teachers, and coming to class. Such a stance allows them to show others they are not "selling out" and helps to maintain status within the peer groups. In some African American peer networks, achieving in school is frowned on because it signals that students are "acting White" (Rodkin, Farmer, Pearl, & Van Acker, 2000). Other studies have found that ethnic minority youth, particularly boys, often value students who are low achievers rather than high achievers (Taylor, Graham, & Hudley, 1997; Woolfolk, 1995). Peer group networks often encourage skipping classes or dropping out, even when students and their parents value academic success (Horowitz, 1983). Thus, a type of resistance peer network forms that is held together by opposition to school and what it represents for conventional status. This may be particularly problematic as children enter adolescence, when they begin to think more about who they are and where they are going.

Adolescence

Although adolescent violence often represents another step in a continuing sequence of misbehavior from the early years, it is during this developmental period that such behavior becomes more frequent and more extreme. As epidemiological data indicate, serious violence begins to escalate during the early adolescent years and peaks during midadolescence and early adulthood, particularly for ethnic minority youth. Furthermore, juveniles are most likely to be implicated in serious crimes such as homicide, including those that involve multiple perpetrators, are gang-related, and involve felonies (Bureau of Justice Statistics, 2003).

What is it about adolescence that contributes to this surge in violence and other problem behaviors? What is it about adolescence for poor, ethnic minority youth that further increases the likelihood of violence? What are the particular developmental tasks of adolescence that contribute to youth violence? Stated differently, what is it about adolescence as a stage of development that facilitates involvement in violence? How does this play out differently for ethnic minority youth? Furthermore, how do these developmental process interact with contextual influences, including families, peers, and neighborhoods? Finally, what are the unique experiences of ethnic minority youth growing up in disadvantaged ecological niches that can adversely impact their development and contribute to violence in this age group?

First, adolescence is a time of rapid biological and social changes. Biological changes during puberty are marked and often dramatic, including a rapid acceleration in growth, development of primary and secondary sex characteristics, changes in body shape and composition, and an increase in physical strength and fitness. Among boys, testosterone concentration can increase as much as twentyfold during adolescence (Faiman & Winter, 1974). These biological changes are part of a complex process that physically transforms the child into an adult. Increases in physical growth, strength, and testosterone can also transform the child into a more physically capable aggressor, as well as affect others' perceptions, particularly if this maturation occurs relatively early. Early maturation and accompanying physical change is also more common within some ethnic minority groups, suggesting that this may represent a unique characteristic of minority versus nonminority youth that can contribute to higher levels of aggression. For example, in a study of African American children, Spencer, Dobbs, and Swanson (1988) found that boys tended to be taller, heavier, and often mature earlier than their White peers. They suggest that both early maturation and increased size might interfere with age-appropriate social interactions and create the impression that these youth are a threat to others, increasing the likelihood of problematic social exchanges and aggressive behavior.

Adolescence also has been described as an "emotional rollercoaster" of despair about self and identity (Larson & Richards, 1994). In a now classic work, Erikson (1968) described adolescence as a period of time that focuses on autonomy and the search for identity. This involves the search for a stable sense of self that provides adolescents with a direction guided by knowledge of who and what they are and where they are going—giving both meaning and purpose to their lives as they enter adulthood (Brinthaupt & Lipka, 2002; Harter, 2003). As French, Kim, and Pillado (chap. 2, this volume) discuss, identity development for ethnic minority adolescents also involves understanding the meaning of membership in their ethnic group, such that ethnicity becomes part of the identity search. As they point out, perceptions of being stigmatized or undervalued because of one's ethnicity may interfere with the development of a healthy identity.

The search for identity evolves in a context that includes both the past and the present. Youth can easily become ensnared in the consequences of earlier problems that effectively narrow (or even close) the gates of opportunity. A history of academic and social problems can limit a teenager's ability to cope with the changing demands of adolescence—a type of cumulative disadvantage that might increase the likelihood that children with early behavior problems or "early starters" continue and escalate this behavior during adolescence (Moffitt, 2004). Furthermore, an ongoing lack of resources can severely curtail the current and future options available for youth. Consider the lack of meaningful employment in many inner city communities. There is little incentive for school success when future opportunities consist largely of unstable, low-paying jobs or no jobs at all. In contrast, gainful employment seems to protect ethnic minority youth from a delinquent career. For instance, Elliott (1994) found that although twice as many African Americans as Whites continue their violent careers into early adulthood, this difference disappears for those who are employed.

In addition to lack of resources linked to past, present, or future disadvantage, marginalization can influence identity development and violence by compromising the ability of parents and other adults to serve as role models, mentors, and monitors for youth during this process. Indeed, related studies have shown that the proportion of affluent neighbors has a positive impact on adolescent development (Brooks-Gunn, Duncan, Kato, & Sealand, 1993). Additional evidence for the importance of adults as role models and mentors and the significance of youth–adult relationships is found in an intriguing study by Schwartz (1987). He focused on the nature of the relationships between adolescents and adults in authority in neighborhoods that varied on multiple dimensions. In comparing an affluent, White suburban area, an inner-city Mexican community, and a lower-class Italian neighborhood in the same city, he reported striking differences in the ability of adults to exercise authority. Adults who lacked status and power within the larger society and were not perceived as valuable role models were afforded less authority. This was particularly evident in the Mexican community—the perceived marginalization of Mexican adults within the larger society decreased their ability to serve as role models and mentors, leaving youth more vulnerable to peer pressure. As Schwartz (1987) noted, "What is missing . . . is the kind of intergenerational alliance between nonfamilial authority figures that would support a redefinition of a youth's identity that could override the assessment of his peers" (p. 223).

Just as parents and adults may be less able to serve as positive role models for youth, certain neighborhood conditions appear to compromise their ability to monitor both their children and the children in the neighborhood. One of the most robust findings in the delinquency literature is that low parental monitoring is associated with higher levels of delinquent behavior (Dishion & Kavanagh, 2003; Loeber & Stouthamer-Loeber, 1986). At the neighborhood level, this monitoring may also be important and vary as a function of concentrated disadvantage. For instance, Sampson and colleagues found that certain components of concentrated disadvantage, namely concentrated affluence, low population density, and residential stability, indirectly affected youth crime through their effects on collective efficacy. Collective efficacy includes both mentoring and monitoring, as seen in "shared expectations and mutual engagement by adults in the active support and social control of children" (Sampson, Morenoff, & Earls, 1999, p. 635).

Marginalization can also lead to a sense of hopelessness and rage as youth recognize the limited opportunities available to poor, ethnic minorities. Coupled with an increasing awareness of danger on the streets, the lure of violence can increase. Exposed to the potential danger within an ecological niche, youth may perceive violence as instrumental for self-protection, deterring others through threatened or actual preemptive violence, protecting turf, or retaliating against those who have violated one's self, setting, or others within it (Fagan & Wilkinson, 1998a, 1998b). Furthermore, adolescents who perceive the setting as "aversive" with no avenue of escape or legal means of eliminating or neutralizing "noxious stimuli" may engage in anger-based violence and delinquency (Agnew, 2001).

Previous research on youth violence has documented how it can instill a sense of power in those otherwise feeling powerless, achieving and verifying personal and public images of status based on respect as perceived by self or others. Such images are typically created and sustained through resources such as conventional opportunities for achievement (e.g., prosocial peers and activities, successful engagement in school, a nurturing and supportive family, etc.). Building status through conventional activities allows youth to have feelings of accomplishment and a strong grounding in their positive self-images. However, when conventional opportunities are unavailable, violence often becomes an alternative means of building and protecting those images (Fagan & Wilkinson, 1998a, 1998b). Threats of violence, the occurrence of violence, and pervasive hostility foment the development of toughness as a posture toward the ecology of danger. Whether through blocked conventional opportunities for personal attainment or blocked methods of escaping or modifying an aversive condition, youth may substitute violence as an alternative method of navigating daily life. Violence may come to be seen as an acceptable currency for social interactions that is tolerated and even respected as a sign of toughness and resilience (Ng-Mak et al., 2002). In many cases, this respect for violence may be instilled in youth from an early age by parents who realize the need for street smarts. For example, recounting his mother's admonition to his 6-year-old brother after his jacket had been stolen by another boy, Canada (1995) recalled her words: "You go out there and get your brother's jacket or when you get back I'm going to give you a beating that will be ten times as bad as that little thief could do to you . . . both of you better bring that jacket back here" (p. 5).

A number of writers have described how displays of toughness become necessary for self-preservation and positioning one's self in a dominance hierarchy (Anderson, 1990, 1999; Canada, 1995; Guerra, 1997). Those displays demonstrate a predisposition to violence in affirming one's self and involve a variety of symbolic forms of "impression management," ranging from physical posturing and facial expressions to verbal expression and other methods of conveying toughness, including carrying and "flashing" handguns. As Fagan and Wilkinson (1998b) pointed out, although such patterns are commonplace in inner-city settings, "toughness has always been highly regarded and a source of considerable status among male adolescents in a wide range of adolescent subcultures, from street-corner groups to gangs" (p. 65). Toughness can also form the core of a youth's developing identity that must then be preserved at all costs. This involves not only defensive aggression when attacked but often escalates into an ongoing spiral of revenge or "pay back" (Anderson, 1999).

When opportunities and avenues for exploration of personal identity are limited, groups may provide a particularly salient basis for identity formation (Hogg, 2003). In an ecological niche with few opportunities for belonging to conventional groups, gangs can provide a group-based identity, often solidified through conflict (Sanchez-Jankowski, 1991). Such conflict tends to reinforce group cohesion and push the gang identity on the group. This identity is further established through rigid rites of passage, informal and formal rules, and the use of graffiti as a symbolic form of gang conflict.

Ethnic segregation also facilitates the development of a coherent identity as part of both an ethnic group and a gang. Although some exceptions have been noted, in general, gangs are individuals with similar ethnic and racial backgrounds. This ethnic categorization is further refined by geographic affiliation, either regional (e.g., northern versus southern California), by neighborhood, or even by the block where one lives. For the most part, gang violence on the streets is usually within ethnic groups but between subgroups based on territory. In dangerous and disadvantaged neighborhoods, violence becomes a currency for social exchange and forms the basis for group identity that can be "represented" through a variety of mechanisms (and must usually be defended at all costs). Although gangs vary in activities (e.g., degree of criminal orientation, involvement in drug markets, connection with gang "nations"), overall they are responsible for a high percentage of urban youth violence (Miller, 2001).

CONCLUSION

Although we have described various mechanisms by which individual and contextual factors operate to increase risk for violence within the ecological niche of ethnic minority youth, it is also true that most youth in disadvantaged settings do not engage in serious forms of violence. By all accounts, it is still a relatively low base rate behavior. Things "go right" for youth even though they may face significant individual or contextual challenges in their lives (Katz, 1997; Lackey & Williams, 1995). Given multiple adversities and their cumulative effects, it is striking that violence is still the exception rather than the rule in most neighborhoods.

Several reasons for the apparent resilience of many children to adverse settings have been proposed, ranging from individual characteristics to variations among disadvantaged communities themselves in structural and cultural conditions (Sampson, 1997, 2004). Clearly, not all children begin life with the same biological birth certificate. Similarly, just as poverty, disadvantage, and social climate vary within and across neighborhoods, the capacity of families, adults, and social institutions to foster children's development in those settings also varies greatly. As we have argued, being poor and part of an ethnic minority in the United States often carries with it a larger package of adversities that influences children's development from infancy through adolescence. These adversities, rather than just poverty or ethnicity, increase the likelihood of aggressive responses as children calibrate their behavior to the contextual demands they face. Thus, the link between ethnicity and youth violence is a link between the ecological niches of many ethnic minority youth and the adaptive function of violence in those niches. Attempts to prevent or intervene to prevent youth violence in a multicultural society must respond to this ecology of development and provide supports and opportunities that minimize adversity and foster developmental competencies from birth onward.

REFERENCES

Agnew, R. S. (2001). An overview of general strain theory. In R. Paternoster & R. Bachman (Eds.), *Explaining criminals and crime* (pp. 161–174). Los Angeles: Roxbury.

Anderson, E. (1990). *Streetwise: Race, class, and change in an urban community.* Chicago: University of Chicago Press.

Anderson, E. (1999). *Code of the streets: Decency, violence, and the moral life of the inner city.* New York: Norton.

Barrett, D., & Frank, D. (1987). *The effects of undernutrition on children's behavior.* New York: Gordon & Breach Science.

Bell, C. C., & Jenkins, E. J. (1991). Traumatic stress and children. *Journal of Health Care for the Poor and Underserved, 2,* 175–185.

Berry, B. J., & Kasarda, J. D. (1977). *Contemporary urban ecology.* New York: Macmillan.

Blumstein, A. (2002). Youth, guns, and violent crime. In *The future of children* (Vol. 12, pp. 39–53). Princeton, NJ: David & Lucile Packard Foundation.

Bowlby, J. (1988). *A secure base: Parent–child attachment and healthy human development.* New York: Basic.

Brinthaupt, T. M., & Lipka, R. P. (2002). Understanding early adolescent self and identity: An introduction. In T. M. Brinthauupt & R. P. Lipka (Eds.), *Understanding early adolescent self and identity: Applications and interventions* (pp. 1–21). Albany: State University of New York Press.

Brooks-Gunn, J., Duncan, G., Kato, P., & Sealand, N. (1993). Do neighborhoods influence child and adolescent behavior? *American Journal of Sociology, 99*, 353–395.

Bruschi, B. A., & Anderson, B. T. (1994, February). *Gender and ethnic differences in science achievement of nine-, thirteen-, and seventeen-year-old students.* Paper presented at the annual meeting of the Eastern Educational Research Association, Sarasota, FL.

Bureau of Justice Statistics. (2003). *Homicide trends in the U.S.* Washington, DC: U.S. Government Printing Office.

Buss, D. M., & Schackelford, T. K. (1997). Human aggression in an evolutionary psychological perspective. *Clinical Psychology Review, 17*, 605–619.

Canada, G. (1995). *Fist, stick, knife, gun.* Boston: Beacon.

Coie, J. D., & Dodge, K. A. (1997). Aggression and antisocial behavior. In N. Eisenberg (Ed.), *Handbook of child psychology* (Vol. 3, pp. 779–862). New York: Wiley.

Coleman, J. S. (1988). Social capital in the creation of human capital. *American Journal of Sociology, 94*(Suppl.), S95–S120.

Coleman, J. S. (1990). *Foundations of social theory.* Cambridge, MA: Harvard University Press.

Dishion, T. J., & Kavanagh, K. (2003). *Intervening in adolescent problem behavior: A family-centered approach.* New York: Guilford Press.

Dodge, K. A., Bates, J. E., & Pettit, G. S. (1990). Mechanisms in the cycle of violence. *Science, 250*, 1678–1683.

Elliott, D. S. (1994). Serious violent offenders: Onset, developmental course, and termination. *Criminology, 32*, 1–21.

Elliott, D. S., Wilson, W. J., Huizinga, D., Sampson, R. J., Elliott, A., & Rankin, B. (1996). The effects of neighborhood disadvantage on adolescent development. *Journal of Research in Crime and Delinquency, 33*, 389–426.

Ensminger, M. E., & Slusarcick, A. L. (1992). Paths to high school graduation or dropout: A longitudinal study of first-grade cohort. *Sociology of Education, 65*, 95–113.

Erikson, E. H. (1968). *Identity: Youth and crisis.* New York: Norton.

Eron, L. D., Huesmann, L. R., & Zelli, A. (1991). The role of parental variables in the learning of aggression. In D. Pepler & K. Rubin (Eds.), *The development and treatment of childhood aggression* (pp. 169–188). Hillsdale, NJ: Erlbaum.

Evans, G. W. (2004). The environment of childhood poverty. *American Psychologist, 59*, 77–92.

Fagan, J., & Wilkinson, P. (1998a). Guns, youth violence, and social identity in inner cities. In M. Tonry & M. H. Moore (Eds.), *Crime and justice, Vol. 24: Youth violence* (pp. 373–456). Chicago: University of Chicago Press.

Fagan, J., & Wilkinson, P. (1998b). Social contexts and functions of adolescent violence. In D. S. Elliott, B. Hamburg, & K. Williams (Eds.), *Violence in American schools* (pp. 55–93). New York: Cambridge University Press.

Faiman, C., & Winter, J. S. D. (1974). Gonadotropins and sex hormone patterns in puberty: Clinical data. In M. M. Grumbach, G. D. Grave, & F. E. Mayer (Eds.), *Control of the onset of puberty* (pp. 32–61). New York: Wiley.

Farrell, A. D., & Bruce, S. E. (1997). Impact of exposure to community violence on violent behavior and emotional distress among urban adolescents. *Journal of Clinical Child Psychology, 26,* 2–14.

Field, J. (2003). *Social capital: Key ideas.* London: Routledge.

Garcia Coll, C. (1990). Developmental outcome of minority infants: A process-oriented look into our beginnings. *Child Development, 61,* 270–289.

Garcia Coll, C., Lamberty, G., Jenkins, R., McAdoo, H. P., Crnic, K., Wasik, B. H., et al. (1996). An integrative model for the study of developmental competencies in minority children. *Child Development, 67,* 1891–1914.

Gorman-Smith, D., & Tolan, P. H. (1998). The role of exposure to community violence and developmental problems among inner-city youth. *Developmental Psychopathology, 10,* 101–116.

Guendelman, S., & Schwalbe, J. (1986). Medical utilization by Hispanic children. *Medical Care, 26,* 925–940.

Guerra, N. G. (1997). Intervening to prevent childhood aggression in the inner city. In J. McCord (Ed.), *Violence and childhood in the inner city* (pp. 256–312). New York: Cambridge University Press.

Guerra, N. G., & Huesmann, L. R. (2004). A cognitive–ecological model of aggression. *Revue Internationale de Psychologie Sociale, 17,* 177–203.

Guerra, N. G., Huesmann, L. R., & Spindler, A. (2004). Community violence exposure, social cognition, and aggression among urban elementary school children. *Child Development, 74,* 1507–1522.

Hagan, J. (2004). Crime and capitalization: Toward a developmental theory of street crime in America. In T. P. Thornberry (Ed.), *Developmental theories of crime and delinquency* (pp. 287–308). New Brunswick, NJ: Transaction.

Harter, S. (2003). The development of self-representations during childhood and adolescence. In M. R. Leary & J. P. Tangney (Eds.), *Handbook of self and identity* (pp. 610–642). New York: Guilford Press.

Hernandez, D. J. (2004). Demographic change and the life circumstances of immigrant families. *Children of immigrant families.* Retrieved March 30, 2005, from http://www.futureofchildren.org

Hinshaw, S. P. (1992). Externalizing behavior problems and academic underachievement in childhood and adolescence: Causal relationships and underlying mechanisms. *Psychological Bulletin, 111,* 127–155.

Hogg, M. A. (2003). Social identity. In M. R. Leary & J. P. Tangney (Eds.), *Handbook of self and identity* (pp. 462–479). New York: Guilford Press.

Horowitz, R. (1983). *Honor and the American dream.* New Brunswick, NJ: Rutgers University Press.

Howes, C., & Eldredge, R. (1985). Responses of abused, neglected, and non-maltreated children to the behaviors of their peers. *Journal of Applied Developmental Psychology, 6,* 261–270.

Huesmann, L. R., Eron, L. D., Lefkowitz, M. M., & Walter, L. O. (1984). Stability of aggression over time and generations. *Developmental Psychology, 20,* 1120–1134.

Huesmann, L. R., Eron, L. D., & Yarmel, P. W. (1987). Intellectual functioning and aggression. *Journal of Personality and Social Psychology, 52,* 232–240.

Jacobson, R. S., & Straker, G. (1982). Peer group interaction of physically abused children. *Child Abuse and Neglect, 6,* 79–88.

Kasarda, J. D. (1989). Urban industrial transition and the underclass. *Annals of the American Academy of Political and Social Sciences, 501,* 26–47.

Kasarda, J. D. (1993). Inner city concentrated poverty and neighborhood distress: 1970–1990. *Housing Policy Debate, 4,* 253–302.

Katz, M. L. (1997). *On playing a poor hand well: Insights from the lives of those who have overcome childhood risks and adversities.* New York: Norton.

Kovandzic, T. V., Vieraitis, L. M., & Yeisley, M. R. (1998). The structural covariates of urban homicide: Reassessing the impact of income inequality and poverty in the post-Reagan era. *Criminology, 36,* 569–600.

Krivo, L. J., & Peterson, R. D. (1996). Extremely disadvantaged neighborhoods and urban crime. *Social Forces, 75,* 619–650.

Krivo, L. J., Peterson, R. D., Rizzo, H., & Reynolds, J. R. (1998). Race, segregation, and the concentration of disadvantage: 1980–1990. *Social Problems, 45,* 61–80.

Kubrin, C. E., & Weitzer, R. (2003). Retaliatory homicide: Concentrated disadvantage and neighborhood culture. *Social Problems, 50,* 157–180.

Lackey, C., & Williams, K. R. (1995). Social bonding and the cessation of partner violence across generations. *Journal of Marriage and the Family, 57,* 295–305.

Larson, R., & Richards, M. H. (1994). *Divergent realities: The emotional lives of mothers, fathers, and adolescents.* New York: Basic.

Lee, V. L., & Burkham, D. T. (2002). *Inequality at the starting gate: Social background differences in achievement as children begin school.* Washington, DC: Economic Policy Institute.

Lessard G., & Ku, L. (2003, Spring). Gaps in coverage for children in immigrant families. *Future of Children: Health Insurance for Children, 13,* 101–116.

Loeber, R., Green, M. S., Keenan, K., & Lahey, B. (1995). Which boys will fare worse? Early predictors of the onset of conduct disorder in a six-year longitudinal study. *Journal of American Academy of Child and Adolescent Psychiatry, 34,* 499–509.

Loeber, R., & Stouthamer-Loeber, M. (1986). Family factors as correlates and predictors of juvenile conduct problems and delinquency. In M. Tonry &

N. Morris (Eds.), *Crime and justice* (Vol. 7, pp. 29–149). Chicago: University of Chicago Press.

Malamuth, N. M., & Heilmann, M. F. (1998). Evolutionary psychology and sexual aggression. In C. H. Crawford & D. L. Krebs (Eds.), *Handbook of evolutionary psychology* (pp. 515–542). Hillsdale, NJ: Erlbaum.

Massey, D. S., & Denton, N. A. (1996). *American apartheid: Segregation and the making of the underclass.* Cambridge, MA: Harvard University Press.

Massey, D., & Eggers, M. L. (1990). The ecology of inequality: Minorities and the concentration of poverty. *American Journal of Sociology, 95,* 1153–1188.

Massey, D., & Fischer, M. J. (2000). How segregation concentrates poverty. *Ethnic and Racial Studies, 23,* 670–691.

Massey, D., Gross, A. B., & Shibuya, K. (1994). Migration, segregation and the concentration of poverty. *American Sociological Review, 59,* 425–445.

McCord, J. (Ed.). (1997). *Violence and childhood in the inner city.* New York: Cambridge University Press.

McMahon, S. D., & Watts, R. J. (2002). Ethnic identity in urban African American youth: Exploring links with self-worth, aggression, and other psychosocial variables. *Journal of Community Psychology, 30,* 411–432.

Miller, W. B. (2001). *The growth of youth gang problems in the United States: 1970–1998.* Washington, DC: Office of Juvenile Justice and Delinquency Prevention.

Moffitt, T. E. (1990). Juvenile delinquency and attention-deficit disorder: Developmental trajectories from age 3 to 15. *Child Development, 61,* 893–910.

Moffitt, T. E. (1993). "Life-course persistent" and "adolescence-limited" antisocial behavior: A developmental taxonomy. *Psychological Review, 100,* 674–701.

Moffitt, T. E. (2004). Adolescence-limited and life-course-persistent offending: A complementary pair of developmental theories. In T. Thornberry (Ed.), *Developmental theories of crime and delinquency* (pp. 55–100). New Brunswick, NJ: Transaction.

Moffitt, T. E., & Henry, B. (1991). Neuropsychological assessment of executive functions in self-reported delinquents. *Development and Psychopathology, 1,* 105–118.

National Clearinghouse on Child Abuse and Neglect Information. (2004). *Child maltreatment 2002: Summary of key findings.* Washington, DC: Department of Health and Human Services, Administration for Children and Families.

National Research Council. (1993). *Understanding child abuse and neglect.* Washington, DC: National Academy Press.

Ng-Mak, D. S., Salzinger, S., Feldman, R., & Stueve, A. (2002). Normalization of violence among inner-city youth: A formulation for research. *American Journal of Orthopsychiatry, 72,* 92–101.

O'Donnell, J., Hawkins, J. D., & Abbott, R. D. (1995). Predicting serious delinquency and substance use among aggressive boys. *Journal of Consulting and Clinical Psychology, 63,* 529–537.

Ogbu, J. U. (1992). Adaptation to minority status and impact on school success. *Theory Into Practice, 16*, 287–295.

Olweus, D., Mattsson, A., Schalling, D., & Low, H. (1988). Circulating testosterone levels and aggression in adolescent males: A causal analysis. *Psychosomatic Medicine, 50*, 261–272.

Osofsky, J. D., Wewers, S., Hann, D. M., & Fick, A. C. (1993). Chronic community violence: What is happening to our children? *Psychiatry, 56*, 36–45.

Perry, B. D. (1997). Incubated in terror: Neurodevelopmental factors in the cycle of violence. In J. D. Osofsky (Ed.), *Children in a violent society* (pp. 124–149). New York: Guilford Press.

Perry, B. D. (1999). *Memories of fear: How the brain stores and retrieves physiologic states, feelings, behaviors and thoughts from traumatic events.* Retrieved August 4, 2005, from http://www.childtrauma.org/ctamaterials/memories.asp

Peterson, R. D., & Krivo, L. J. (1999). Racial segregation, the concentration of disadvantage, and Black and White homicide victimization. *Sociological Forum, 14*, 465–493.

Portes, A. (1998). Social capital: Its origins and applications in modern sociology. *Annual Review of Sociology, 24*, 1–24.

Portes, A., & Rumbaut, R. G. (2001). *Legacies: The story of immigrant second generation.* Berkeley: University of California Press.

Putnam, R. D. (2000). *Bowling alone: The collapse and revival of American community.* New York: Simon & Schuster.

Pynoos, R., Steinberg, A. M., & Ornitz, E. M. (1977). Issues in the developmental neurobiology of traumatic stress. *Annals of the New York Academy of Sciences, 821*, 176–193.

Renken, B., Egeland, B., Marvinney, D., Mangelsdorf, S., & Sroufe, L. A. (1989). Early childhood antecedents of aggression and passive withdrawal in early elementary school. *Journal of Personality, 57*, 257–281.

Rodkin, P. C., Farmer, T. W., Pearl, R., & Van Acker, R. (2000). Heterogeneity of popular boys: Antisocial and prosocial configurations. *Developmental Psychology, 36*, 14–24.

Sameroff, A. J., & Fiese, B. H. (1990). Transactional regulation and early intervention. In S. J. Meisels & J. P. Shonkoff (Eds.), *Handbook of early child intervention* (pp. 119–191). New York: Cambridge University Press.

Sampson, R. J. (1997). The embeddedness of child and adolescent development: A community level perspective on urban violence. In J. McCord (Ed.), *Violence and childhood in the inner city* (pp. 31–77). New York: Cambridge University Press.

Sampson, R. J. (2004). Networks and neighborhoods: The implications of connectivity for thinking about crime in the modern city. In H. McCarthy, P. Miller, & P. Skidmore (Eds.), *Network logic: Who governs in an interconnected world* (pp. 157–166). London: Demos.

Sampson, R. J., & Laub, J. H. (2004). A life-course theory of cumulative disadvantage and the stability of delinquency. In T. P. Thornberry (Ed.), *Developmental theories of crime and delinquency* (pp. 133–162). New Brunswick, NJ: Transaction.

Sampson, R. J., Morenoff, J. D., & Earls, F. (1999). Beyond social capital: Spatial dynamics of collective efficacy for children. *American Sociological Review, 64,* 633–660.

Sampson, R. J., Morenoff, J. D., & Gannon-Rowley, T. (2002). Assessing neighborhood effects: Social processes and new directions in research. *Annual Review of Sociology, 28,* 443–478.

Sampson, R. J., Morenoff, J. D., & Raudenbush, S. (2005). Social anatomy of racial and ethnic disparities in violence. *American Journal of Public Health, 95,* 224–232.

Sampson, R. J., Raudenbush, S., & Earls, F. (1997). Neighborhoods and violent crime: A multilevel study of collective efficacy. *Science, 277,* 918–924.

Sampson, R. J., & Wilson, W. J. (1995). Toward a theory of race, crime, and urban inequality. In J. Hagan & R. D. Peterson (Eds.), *Crime and inequality* (pp. 37–54). Stanford, CA: Stanford University Press.

Sanchez-Jankowski, M. (1991). *Islands in the street.* Berkeley: University of California Press.

Schore, A. N. (1994). *Affect regulation and the origin of self: The neurobiology of emotional development.* Hillsdale, NJ: Erlbaum.

Schwartz, G. (1987). *Beyond conformity or rebellion: Youth and authority in America.* Chicago: University of Chicago Press.

Shapiro, J. P., Dorman, R. L., Burkey, W. M., Welter, C. J., & Clough, J. B. (1997). Development and factor analysis of a measure of youth attitudes towards guns and violence. *Journal of Clinical Child Psychology, 26,* 11–32.

Shaw, D. S., Gilliom, M., Ingoldsby, E. M., & Nagin, D. (2003). Trajectories leading to school-age conduct problems. *Developmental Psychology, 39,* 189–200.

Sheley, J., & Wright, J. (1995). *In the line of fire: Youth, guns and violence in urban America.* New York: Aldine de Gruyter.

Sherman, A. (1994). *Wasting America's future: The Children's Defense Fund report on the costs of child poverty.* Boston: Beacon.

Shore, R. (1997). *Rethinking the brain.* New York: Families & Work Institute.

Short, J. F. (1997). *Poverty, ethnicity, and violent crime.* Boulder, CO: Westview Press.

Smith, C., & Thornberry, T. P. (1995). The relationship between childhood maltreatment and adolescent involvement in delinquency. *Criminology, 33,* 451–477.

Spencer, M. B. (1990). Development of minority children: An introduction. *Child Development, 61,* 267–269.

Spencer, M. B., Dobbs, B., & Swanson, D. P. (1988). Afro-American adolescents: Adaptational processes and socioeconomic diversity in behavioral outcomes. *Journal of Adolescence, 11*, 117–137.

Steinberg, L., & Darling, N. (1994). The broader context of social influence in adolescence. In R. Silbereisen & E. Todt (Eds.), *Adolescence in context* (pp. 25–45). New York: Springer.

Takanishi, R. (2004). *Leveling the playing field: Supporting immigrant children from birth to eight.* Retrieved March 30, 2005, from http://www.futureofchildren.org

Tarter, R. E., Hegedus, A. M., Winsten, N. E., & Alterman, A. I. (1984). Neuropsychological, personality, and familial characteristics of physically abused delinquents. *Journal of the American Academy of Child Psychiatry, 23*, 668–674.

Taylor, A. Z., Graham, S., & Hudley, C. (1997, April). *Falling stars: The valuing of academic achievement among African American, Latino, and White adolescents.* Paper presented at the biennial meeting of the Society for Research in Child Development, Washington, DC.

U.S. Census Bureau. (2000). *Census 2000. Public Use Microdata Sample (PUMS).* Washington, DC: U.S. Department of Commerce Economics and Statistics Administration.

Vigil, D. (1988). *Barrio gangs.* Austin: University of Texas Press.

Warren, M. R., Thompson, J. P., & Saegert, S. (2001). The role of social capital in combating poverty. In S. Saegert, J. P. Thompson, & M. R. Warren (Eds.), *Social capital and poor communities* (pp. 60–88). New York: Russell Sage Foundation.

Widom, C. S. (1989). Does violence beget violence? *Psychological Bulletin, 104*, 3–28.

Widom, C. S. (1998). Child victims: Searching for opportunities to break the cycle of violence. *Journal of Applied and Preventive Psychology, 7*, 225–234.

Wilson, W. J. (1987). *The truly disadvantaged: The inner city, the underclass, and public policy.* Chicago: University of Chicago Press.

Wilson, W. J. (1996). *When work disappears: The world of the new urban poor.* New York: Knopf.

Wolfgang, M. E., & Ferracuti, F. (1982). *The subculture of violence.* Thousand Oaks, CA: Sage.

Woolcock, M. (1998). Social capital and economic development: Toward a theoretical synthesis and policy framework. *Theory and Society, 27*, 151–208.

Woolfolk, A. E. (1995). *Educational psychology* (6th ed). Needham Heights, MA: Allyn & Bacon.

2

ETHNIC IDENTITY, SOCIAL GROUP MEMBERSHIP, AND YOUTH VIOLENCE

SABINE E. FRENCH, TIA E. KIM, AND OLIVIA PILLADO

Research in the area of youth violence has identified multiple causes and pathways of development that lead to aggression, violence, and other problem behaviors (Patterson, DeBaryshe, & Ramsey, 1989; Tolan, Guerra, & Kendall, 1995). An array of risk and protective factors has been delineated emphasizing individual, peer, family, and community predictors. Given the disproportionate rates of youth violence among ethnic minority youth, it is particularly important to examine the salience of these risk factors for children from distinct ethnic groups as well as to examine risk factors directly linked to an individual's ethnic background.

In general, this area of inquiry has been somewhat neglected. In particular, there is a paucity of research that focuses on the psychological processes related to ethnicity that increase or decrease the risk of youth violence. For the most part, the link between ethnicity and violence has been attributed

Data collection for the work reported in this chapter was supported by grants from the National Institute of Mental Health (MH43084) and the Carnegie Corporation (B4850) awarded to Edward Seidman, J. Lawrence Aber, LaRue Allen, and Christina Mitchell. We would like to express appreciation to the adolescents and schools whose cooperation made this study possible.

to the socioeconomic and neighborhood disadvantage experienced by ethnic youth and their families, as described by Guerra and Williams (chap. 1, this volume). However, an individual's ethnicity and the meaning derived from this label also may have a strong impact on psychological well-being that in turn affects development and behavior.

Ethnic identity is one aspect of ethnicity that may be particularly important for youth. Indeed, as Wright and Zimmerman (chap. 9, this volume) discuss, a number of youth development and prevention programs are currently being implemented to strengthen ethnic identity and promote well-being. The relation between ethnic identity, as a component of ethnicity and culture, and youth violence is less obvious and more complex. In order to examine the nature of this relation in youth, it is first important to understand ethnic identity as part of a larger process of identity formation during adolescence.

This chapter examines potential mechanisms linking ethnic identity and youth violence. We begin by delineating the process of identity development in adolescence, with particular attention to the work of Erikson (1968) and Marcia (1966, 1980). Next, the important role of ethnicity in the development of an identity is discussed. We review several models including Phinney's (1989, 1992) ethnic identity model, Cross's (1971, 1991) racial identity model, and Helms's (1990) White racial identity model. Differences in ethnic identity across ethnic groups are noted as well as the positive effects of high ethnic identity on overall well-being for adolescents. We then examine the relation of ethnic identity and delinquency with data from the Adolescent Pathways Project (Seidman, 1991). Although these data do not include specific items on violence, violence and delinquency are highly correlated and many types of serious violence are classified as delinquent offenses (e.g., seriously injuring someone in a fight). Finally, we discuss how interventions can enhance ethnic identity to prevent youth violence.

IDENTITY DEVELOPMENT

The major developmental task of adolescence is the establishment of an identity. Adolescents try on a variety of roles and lifestyles to determine the best fit for themselves (Markstrom-Adams & Spencer, 1994). In searching for an identity, adolescents are trying to discover a sense of who they are and what their place is among various environmental contexts, including family, peer groups, school, work, culture, and religion (Berzonsky & Adams, 1999). Furthermore, identity develops within the context of role relationships (Stets & Burke, 2003; Swanson, Spencer, & Petersen, 1998). These role relationships typically occur within the community of people and their values that surround an adolescent. In some cases, there can be confusion about which community is the most appropriate reference group, particularly for ethnic minority youth. For example, children of immigrant families have the difficult task of negotiating multiple identities in their identity formation because they belong to numerous communities. These adolescents face cultural dissonance because they not only have to adapt to a new culture but one that is different from the culture of their parents (Suarez-Orozco, 2000).

Erikson's (1968) seminal work, *Identity: Youth and Crisis*, identified the search for and development of identity as the critical "crisis" of adolescence. Having a healthy, developed identity through the process of search and commitment was proposed as essential to the mental health of an individual. Erikson's (1968) discussion of identity development centered on the individual's need to have a sense of self and meaning in his or her life. The identity crisis of adolescence is defined by reconciling the identities imposed on oneself by one's family and society with one's need to assert control and seek out an identity that brings satisfaction, feelings of industry, and competence. Through this search for one's own identity, an individual develops his or her own ideology regarding political, religious, and societal matters. Only on completion of a satisfactory period of exploration, discovery, and acceptance of one's identity can the individual truly engage in critical functions of life, such as developing intimate relationships and being a productive member of society.

Marcia (1966, 1980) conceptualized identity development as a four-stage process. A person's identity crisis or exploration (the search for one's identity) and commitment (accepting one's identity) define the four stages as follows: (a) *foreclosure*—when individuals have committed to an identity based solely on family values and goals without going through an identity crisis period; (b) *moratorium*—when individuals are in an identity crisis period; (c) *identity diffusion*—when individuals may or may not have gone through an identity crisis but have not committed to an identity; and (d) *identity achievement*—when individuals have experienced an identity crisis and have resolved it by committing to an identity. This stage model is based on the notion that having an achieved identity is the ideal end point to identity development. Failure to achieve a satisfying identity can have negative psychological consequences for adolescents. For instance, being low in ego identity has been related to low self-esteem (Phinney, Lochner, & Murphy, 1990). Similarly, Rotheram-Borus (1989) found that those adolescents who were in the moratorium stage had significantly more behavior problems, lower social competence, and lower self-esteem than those in the other three stages.

THE ROLE OF ETHNICITY IN IDENTITY DEVELOPMENT

Before examining the role of ethnicity in identity development, we first must define what we mean by ethnicity and how it is the same or different from the concept of race. As discussed by Smith and Guerra (introduction, this volume), ethnicity is defined as group membership based on a perceived shared heritage typically derived from a sense of ancestry or geography. Individuals can choose whether to subscribe to that perceived heritage. Race is defined as social construction based on a collection of perceived shared phenotypical (and possibly genotypical) features. Race is often used to refer to group membership and collective identity that may carry a specific social meaning based on the individual's perception or the perception of others.

However, as these definitions illustrate, there are many different nuances and interpretations that accompany discussions of ethnicity and race. In some cases, choice of the term "ethnic" or "racial" to signal a type of identity development is a matter of preference for one term or the other; for instance, ethnic identity based on perceived racial grouping would be called racial identity. In other cases, the concept of racial identity has been differentiated from ethnic identity in that it is presumed to incorporate a political awareness of the existence of racism and its implications for development. In the present chapter, we emphasize ethnic identity development and its relation to youth violence; however, we incorporate previous models on both ethnic identity development and racial identity development and label these accordingly.

Because establishing an identity is a major task of adolescence, ethnicity may be a particularly important factor during this developmental period. Rotheram-Borus and Wyche (1994) contend that ethnicity shapes the adolescent's exploration and commitments to occupational, religious, political, and gender roles. One of the unique aspects of ethnic group membership (which in some cases may overlap racial group membership) is that unlike occupational, political, or religious group memberships, ethnicity is relatively impermeable, that is, individuals cannot choose or change ethnic groups (similarly, they cannot choose or change racial groups). Living in the United States where there are many different ethnic groups makes ethnicity particularly salient. Each ethnic group has a culture, history, and features that differentiate it from other ethnic groups, although they may share the minority experience.

In considering who they are and who they want to be, adolescents must also adopt a stance toward their ethnic group (Markstrom-Adams & Spencer, 1994). This task is clearly more salient for ethnic minority adolescents. The question for them is not only "Who am I" but also "What does my ethnic group membership mean to me and what does minority group membership mean to me." Thus, a minority adolescent's ethnicity and minority status becomes a focus of the identity search. More specifically, it appears that this may provide barriers to developing a healthy identity. For instance, the stigma associated with belonging to a particular minority group could make the successful completion of a healthy identity difficult (Aries & Moorehead, 1989; Garrett, 1995; Rotheram-Borus & Wyche, 1994). These adolescents are part of a social context that often does not support or value them because of their minority status, and they are faced with issues such as racism, poor education, and a lack of employment that can thwart their development.

Models of ethnic and racial identity development have taken two paths in the literature (Gaines & Reed, 1994, 1995). The first path is the "mainstream path" that primarily focuses on one's ethnic or racial group membership as one of many social identities and seeks to find the universal cognitive and affective processes associated with one's social identity. Much of the work on ethnic identity has built on this path. The second path, the "underground path," has focused on examining each ethnic or racial group separately, including their history, culture, and position in society, with an emphasis on what it means to be a member of that group. The underground path is so named because of the reluctance of mainstream psychology to examine ethnic or racial identity within the context of a specific group's history. The underground path model typically has focused on only one ethnic or racial group and on the awakening of political awareness and action in regard to being a member of a devalued group in the context of a racist society. Most frequently, this approach has formed the basis of models specifically labeled as racial identity.

For our purposes, it is important to consider ethnic identity as both a process of integration of beliefs about one's ethnicity and a set of circumstances related to being a member of a specific (and often) devalued group vis-à-vis youth violence. This is consistent with mechanisms of influence set forth by Smith and Guerra (introduction, this volume) whereby ethnicity may influence youth violence by its association with factors (a) that are unique to the conditions experienced by different ethnic groups (e.g., the salience and role of ethnic identity may only be important in communities where ethnic group members are the minority); and (b) by the minority experience that may be shared across ethnic groups (who are devalued within the context of a racist society).

MODELS OF ETHNIC (AND RACIAL) IDENTITY

Ethnicity shapes the acquisition of values, attitudes, and patterns of behavior from childhood through adulthood (Rotheram-Borus & Wyche,

1994). The dominant culture influences ethnic minority adolescents through constant contact. Therefore, minority youths establish an idea of their ethnicity within the context of the dominant culture. This process results in the formation of ethnic identity, which is one component of personal identity and refers to one's sense of belonging to an ethnic group, as well as to the part of one's thinking, feelings, perceptions, and behavior that is attributable to ethnic group membership. Ethnic identity is also formed by incorporating one's group membership into self-perception (Yancey, Aneshensel, & Driscoll, 2001). Ethnic identity develops over time through interactions with members of one's ethnic group and with groups other than one's own. It is a multidimensional concept that includes not only self-identification as a group member, but a sense of belonging and attachment, positive attitudes or feelings about one's group, and participation in social activities and cultural traditions.

Phinney has written extensively on the ethnic identity development of African Americans, Asian Americans, European Americans, and Latinos in the United States. Similar to Erikson, Phinney (1989) has proposed that the initiation of ethnic identity development takes place during adolescence, although it does not necessarily have to conclude during adolescence. Over the years, researchers have conceptualized ethnic identity in many different ways; however, Phinney (1992) focused on four dimensions of ethnic identity: (a) *self-identification*—this is how one labels oneself ethnically; (b) *ethnic behaviors and practices*—this involves engagement in social activities with members of one's ethnic group and participation in cultural traditions; (c) *affirmation and belonging*—this has been defined as positive feelings and attachment toward one's group and feelings of pride and group esteem; and (d) *ethnic identity achievement*—this is primarily a sense of clarity of what it means to be a member of one's ethnic group.

Basing her model of ethnic identity development on Marcia's (1980) conceptualization of Erikson's (1968) theory of identity development, Phinney (1989) proposed a model of ethnic identity development for members of all racial or ethnic groups where individuals progress through three stages—*unexamined ethnic identity, ethnic identity search*, and *achieved ethnic identity*. In the unexamined stage, individuals endorse either a positive, indifferent, or negative ethnic identity based solely on the values taught to them (or not taught to them in the case of those who are indifferent) by their parents and family. Individuals have not thought about or engaged in a personal search for the meaning of being a member of their ethnic group. During an ethnic identity search, individuals wrestle with what it means to be a member of their ethnic group. Individuals are likely to seek out members of their ethnic group, engage in discussions about their ethnic group, and examine the meaning of cultural practices. It is important to note that Phinney does not suggest any reason, contextual or psychological, for the initiation of an ethnic identity search—merely that it is likely to happen during adolescence. In the final stage, achieved ethnic identity, individuals have accepted their ethnic group membership and are clear about what it means to them. Again, this is only possible after going through a period of ethnic search. Although positive group esteem is not part of the definition of this stage, having a positive sense of ethnic group membership is often expected of individuals who have an achieved ethnic identity and is highly correlated with ethnic identity achievement (Phinney, 1992).

Ethnic identity has not been found to have similar salience for all ethnic groups. In particular, studies have found that European Americans do not possess high levels of ethnic identity compared with other ethnic groups (Branch, Tayal, & Triplett, 2000; Yancey et al., 2001). There are several possible explanations for this finding. For instance, ethnic identity may be a difficult concept for European Americans to comprehend, especially because many of them are generations removed from their ethnic roots and they are part of the dominant mainstream group, which makes ethnicity less salient. They may be unaware of their ethnicity apart from being American (Phinney, 1989). Although African Americans are also generations removed from their African roots, as members of a minority group in the United States, their ethnicity is made to be more salient.

Members of the dominant group often say they have no heritage. Martinez and Dukes (1997) suggested that this means that their ethnic identity is so secure that they take it for granted and are not aware of it. On the other hand, being a minority in a dominant culture pushes ethnic minority adolescents to become more familiar with their ethnic heritage and affirm it. Thus, having a strong sense of ethnic identity may serve as a protective mechanism for ethnic minorities. Indeed, Martinez and Dukes found that Native Americans had low ethnic identity, but unlike the European American counterparts who possessed low ethnic identity, Native Americans scored low on well-being. However, African Americans, Latinos, and Asian Americans in the same study possessed a generally high level of ethnic identity, and this seemed to mitigate the negative effects of discrimination on well-being.

Most adolescents of European descent are inclined to identify themselves as White (a racial label) rather than associating with a place of origin. Pro-White sentiments may be seen as being anti-other and, thus, European Americans may be more reluctant to show strong same-group ties. Yancey et al. (2001) suggested that European Americans may express socially desirable answers when responding to ethnic identity questions. In other words, ethnic identity among European Americans may be of similar intensity as among other groups but be artificially suppressed by social desirability. However, more recent European immigrant adolescents living in ethnic enclaves are more likely to self-label themselves with an ethnic term (e.g., Italian,

Russian, etc.) and more likely to endorse high levels of group esteem (French, Seidman, Allen, & Aber, 2005). Immersion in this type of culture may result in an awareness of one's heritage and allow one to have a high sense of ethnic identity, especially because social contexts give greater or lesser salience to ethnic identity issues.

Turning to models emphasizing racial identity fostered via the experience of racism and oppression for specific groups, the most well-known model is Cross's (1971) Nigrescence model, a five-stage model for African Americans that emphasizes moving from self-hatred to self-love. The stages include *pre-encounter, encounter, immersion–emersion, internalization,* and *internalization–commitment* (Cross, 1971, 1991). Originally, Cross (1971) viewed individuals in the pre-encounter stage to be anti-Black and pro-White. In a reassessment of his model, however, he suggested that individuals could also believe that race did not matter (Cross, 1991). The encounter is a critical facet of the model. This was originally conceptualized as the occurrence of a traumatic, racially prejudiced event that shakes individuals from their original view. However, Cross (1991, 1995) later suggested that many small and negative eye-opening incidents that build up over time could initiate an encounter, and he even allowed room for positive experiences with African Americans to initiate an encounter.

During the encounter stage, the old identity begins to seem inappropriate, and individuals feel ashamed of their previous views and/or lack of awareness. Individuals now decide to be "Black" and fully immerses themselves into everything that is "Black" in the immersion–emersion stage. In this stage, individuals are filled with anger toward Whites and toward oppression. After emerging from the immersion–emersion stage, individuals enter the internalization stage where they are confident and proud of their identity as a Black person and are no longer filled with hatred for White people. Individuals in the internalization–commitment stage take their confidence in and commitment to their race one step further and work toward elevating the status of African Americans and eliminating racism in our society. Cross (1995) also noted that there are some African Americans who have been socialized from childhood to have a positive Black identity and racial awareness and are not in need of Nigrescence.

A racial identity model similar to Cross's has been proposed for Mexican Americans (Arce, 1981). Although Latinos are an ethnic group and not a racial group, Arce's model is included as a racial identity model because it involves an awakening of a political awareness of the existence of racism. He did not formally specify the process of Mexican American or Chicano identity development into a set of stages. However, the process he discusses can be conceptualized into five stages. At first, individuals have an identity that is forced on them, either by members of their in-group, such as their family, or members of the out-group, such as their teachers, which they accepted blindly and without thought. Then individuals go through an internal search—a cognitive and emotional process—examining their cultural roots and question the legitimacy of the majority group telling them who to be and what they are. Next, individuals shift the locus of the responsibility for their group's oppressed status from members of their group to the discriminatory practices of the majority group. Here, they also reclaim negative terms and stereotypes associated with their group and make them positive, such as "Brown Power." Finally, individuals develop an internalized identity that allows them to have a deep sense of belonging to their group and a desire to work collectively for the betterment of the group.

Models of White racial identity development are quite different from models of African American or Mexican American racial identity development. Due to the privilege of Whiteness, European Americans do not have to face the realities of the oppression of their group or reconcile negative images and stereotypes of themselves in the media. Helms (1990) developed a stage model of racial identity for European Americans that involves the realization of Whiteness, the recognition of the oppression that the White American majority imposes on people of color, and movement away from being blind to racism.

Helms (1990) described White racial identity development as a process through six statuses: *contact, disintegration, reintegration, pseudo-independence, immersion–emersion,* and *autonomy.* There is a lack of racial awareness in the contact status. Individuals in this status purport to be blind to race while judging people of color by White standards of behavior. After an awareness of racial issues, one moves to disintegration. Here, one realizes that the "colorblind" perspective does not work, and that racial inequalities exist and feels guilty about it. But one also becomes aware of the rules of race relations and the price that White individuals will pay if they do not maintain those rules.

The frustration that may develop from this stage may lead to reintegration. Here one believes that the privileges that Whites enjoy are earned and deserved and that people of color are truly socially, morally, and intellectually inferior. It takes a significant event to move one from the reintegration status. One must choose to abandon racism and to examine one's long-held beliefs about race to move forward to pseudo-independence. In general, this involves looking to people of color for the solutions to fight racism, without understanding that the solution can only come from the group that maintains the institution of racism, White Americans. These individuals still avoid self-examination and the role they have played in maintaining the status quo. Immersion–emersion is the next status where individuals have come to understand that they must challenge racism. They also seek accurate information about people of color.

In the last status of autonomy, one has freed oneself from the denial of the existence of racism. An individual no longer holds on to individual, institution, or cultural racism, so he or she is better able to appreciate exchanges and experiences with people of color without judging them as deficient relative to European Americans. An individual in this status is secure in her or his Whiteness without a reliance on Whiteness meaning superiority. This theory of racial identity monitors the process of developing racial consciousness (Leach, Behrens, & LaFleur, 2002). Although, the racial identity theory for European Americans describes different levels of sensitivity to other racial/ethnic groups, it does little to adequately describe White identity. One could argue that those involved in White supremacist hate groups exhibit an extremely high level of racial identity in which the appreciation and love for their culture is taken to extremes (see Parker & Tuthill, chap. 8, this volume). However, this type of White racial identity is not incorporated into Helms's White Racial Identity model.

Overall, these models of ethnic and racial identity have a great deal in common. They all suggest that individuals begin in a state of unawareness or disinterest in what it means to be a member of their racial or ethnic group. From this initial state, individuals move through a process of exploration into their race or ethnicity and perhaps experience a racial or ethnic awakening. Ideally, after this process, individuals are able to come to terms and are satisfied with their sense of self as a member of their racial or ethnic group. The primary difference lies in the expectation of the ethnic identity models that all racial and ethnic groups will follow the same path regardless of historical precedents. These models do not take into account the experience or the impact of racism. In contrast, the racial identity models examine each racial group independently and incorporate the legacy of racism in the United States in how one perceives racial group membership.

ETHNIC IDENTITY, RISK, AND RESILIENCY

Ethnic identity can contribute to the understanding of risk and resilience. Yancey et al. (2001) suggested that attitudes toward one's ethnicity are central to the overall health and psychological functioning of youth, especially for those who live in societies where their group is poorly represented and where they are discriminated against. Furthermore, when youth are struggling with the consequences of low socioeconomic status, the impact of ethnicity on identity achievement is particularly important. Having a strong ethnic identity may allow minority youth to overcome the effects of a hostile environment and may be linked to resilience and successful adaptation.

In general, an increase in ethnic identity should portend a correspond-ing increase in psychological well-being. Adolescents who have the opportu-nity to think about their ethnic group membership may come to understand the issues of ethnicity more clearly. Identification with the heritage and culture of their ancestors can help them find a secure sense of self. As a result, they may accept themselves more fully and be able to function more effectively. In general, research has substantiated the directionality of this relation.

For instance, in a sample of 12,386 adolescents, Martinez and Dukes (1997) found that greater ethnic identity was related to higher self-esteem, purpose in life, and self-confidence. Moreover, the authors suggested that achieved ethnic identity may blunt the negative effects of social denigration and stereotyping. Howard (2000) also asserted that a strong ethnic identity is related to high self-esteem. Furthermore, ethnic identity appears to be a malleable characteristic and may be a potential mechanism through which deleterious behaviors may be modified. For example, Belgrave, Chase-Vaughn, Gray, Addison, and Cherry (2000) were able to increase the ethnic identity of African American preadolescent females in an intervention program. Findings from this study elucidate the potential to enhance ethnic identity in adolescents via interventions.

Belgrave and colleagues' (2000) findings are important in light of findings linking lower levels of ethnic identity with adverse psychological outcomes and higher levels of identity with psychological well-being. Brook, Balka, Brook, Win, and Gursen (1998) suggested a paradigm whereby ethnic identity can enhance the beneficial effects of protective factors related to decreased drug use in African American adolescents. Some dimensions of ethnic identity appear to enhance the effects of other protective factors while buffering against the effect of some risk factors. More specifically, in a study of drug use among African American adolescents, Brook et al. (1998) found that the attachment to one's ethnic group as well as ethnic awareness, two components of ethnic identity, moderated the effects of drug-related personal risks, family drug tolerance, peer deviant attitudes, and availability on drug use.

IDENTITY AND YOUTH VIOLENCE

Much of the work on ethnic identity and adolescent development has examined the link with healthy adjustment. In general, a positive sense of ethnic identity appears to predict greater adjustment. For instance, Smith, Walker, Fields, Brookins, and Seay (1999) examined the relation of ethnic identity to self-esteem, perceived self-efficacy, and prosocial attitudes in a sample of 100 early adolescents. They found that both self-esteem and ethnic identity emerged as influences on the adolescents' perception of their ability to achieve academically and professionally and ultimately on prosocial values of goal attainment. Self-esteem and ethnic identity most influenced prosocial attitudes by affecting the youths' perception of their academic and career possibilities. The results of this study suggest that ethnic identity may be an important component in developing positive and prosocial cognitive and behavioral orientations.

Clearly, positive outcomes such as self-esteem, prosocial attitudes, and academic self-efficacy should also reduce risk for violence. Less is known about the direct relation between ethnic identity and youth violence. The few studies that have been conducted mirror the findings with adjustment. That is, they suggest that a positive sense of ethnic identity leads to less violent tendencies. In one study of African American and Latino adolescents, Arbona, Jackson, McCoy, and Blakely (1999) examined whether ethnic identity would predict attitudes toward fighting in the presence of parental involvement and negative peer influences. They found that feelings of pride and commitment to one's ethnicity were related to self-reported attitudes and skills in resolving conflicts with peers in nonviolent ways for African Americans. For Latinos, ethnic identity did not account for additional variance beyond that accounted for by parental involvement and negative peer influences in predicting attitudes toward fighting, suggesting that ethnic identity may operate in a different fashion for youth from different ethnic backgrounds.

In another related study with African American adolescents, McMahon and Watts (2002) found that higher levels of ethnic identity were associated with lower rates of aggressive behavior and fewer beliefs supporting aggression. Similarly, Whaley (1992) found that strong identification among African American males with their ethnicity was negatively associated with Black-on-Black crimes. In examining Hawaiians, Austin (2004) found that individuals that reported greater pride in being Hawaiian reported less violent behavior than those who reported little pride in their Hawaiian heritage. On the other hand, Caldwell, Kohn-Wood, Schmeelk-Cone, Chavous, and Zimmerman (2004) did not find a direct link between racial identity of African Americans and violent behavior. However, they did find that young adults who believed that other groups hold more positive attitudes toward African Americans and who experience more racial discrimination engaged in more violence than those who believed that other groups hold more negative attitudes toward Blacks.

However, other evidence suggests that a strong ethnic identity may actually increase one's likelihood of violence or aggression. Minority youth who live in poorer neighborhoods may have a difficult time figuring out who they are, and gangs can provide an outlet to discover their identity, even if it is negative. As illustrated by Mark, Revilla, Tsutsumoto, and

Mayeda, (chap. 5, this volume), recent Chinese immigrants banded together to form gangs to protect themselves from American-born Chinese youth who rejected their Chinese heritage. In this case, those with the strong ethnic identity banded together into violent groups to maintain their ethnic identity and protect themselves. Garrett (1995) also provided support for this idea, stating that African American adolescents often join gangs because they provide a clearly delineated sense of identity and enhanced self-esteem. People strive for a social identity based on group membership (Gaskell & Smith, 1986). The identity that many minority members adopt is that of the social group around them. Unfortunately, in disadvantaged communities with low resources and limited access to services, "conventional" identities may be largely unavailable to many youth. However, violent, "gang-banger" identities may be more available and, indeed, seen as viable strategies to secure desirable outcomes including economic rewards, protection, and status.

In this manner, violent behavior and membership in violent groups can become part of an adolescent's identity. Not only do some adolescents define their world in relation to violence, but they are proud of their toughness and willingness to fight (Bracher, 2000; Rothstein, 1999). As Mayeda, Chesney-Lind, and Koo (2001) illustrated through their qualitative research on at-risk ethnic minority youth in Hawaii, some adolescents derive their self-concept and self-worth from engaging in delinquent or violent behavior. In turn, if adolescents derive their identity from violent acts, they must also continually seek out opportunities to practice and display this behavior. In some sense, gangs provide this function, with much routine violence occurring within gangs.

OUR STUDY

To further test the association between ethnic identity and violence, we examined data from the Adolescent Pathways Project (APP), a longitudinal study of ethnically diverse, urban, early and middle adolescents attending eastern urban public schools with high concentrations of poor children (Seidman, 1991). Because this study was not designed to test directly the relation between ethnic identity and youth violence, we rely on comparable measures of outcomes, for instance, delinquency versus violence.

Sample Description

The sample for this study consisted of African American, Latino, and European American students on whom at least two consecutive waves out of three waves of data were available. In all, 621 adolescents are included in the analyses. The sample is composed of 456 early adolescents (152 African Americans, 79 European Americans, and 225 Latinos; 256 girls and 200 boys) and 165 middle adolescents (51 African Americans, 37 European Americans, and 77 Latinos; 119 girls and 46 boys). At wave 1, the mean age was 11.33 (SD = 0.90) for early adolescents and 14.22 (SD = 1.08) for middle adolescents.

Retention/Attrition

Three waves of data were collected from two cohorts of adolescents. Wave 1 data were collected between March and early June of the last year of elementary or junior high school. Approximately 1 year later, after the transition to junior high school or senior high school, respectively, a second wave of data was gathered. Approximately 1 year after the second wave of data collection, a third wave of data was collected. In wave 1, ethnic identity was the final measure in a lengthy protocol, and unfortunately when time fully elapsed this measure was not completed. Analyses were conducted to examine differences between youth who did not complete the ethnic identity measure in wave 1 and those who had completed it in both waves 1 and 2, with regard to all the dependent and demographic variables at wave 1 employed in this study. There were no significant differences between the two groups.

Data Collection

Data were collected in group settings at schools by APP staff of different ethnic backgrounds. Instructions and questions were read aloud to the group. Staff members circulated to answer students' questions and spot-check measures where directions were more complicated.

Measures

The measures used in the study are discussed in the sections that follow.

Ethnic Identity

The ethnic identity measure was adapted from J. S. Phinney and L. L. Alipuria (personal communication, December 31, 1987). This measure consisted of seven items, answered on a 4-point scale, from *very true* to *not at all true*. (For a more detailed explanation of this measure, see French et al., in press.) Two subscales, group esteem and exploration, were employed in this study. Group esteem was based on 3 items, α = .71 ("I feel good about being in my ethnic group") and exploration was based on 4 items, α = .76 ("I talk with my friends about our ethnic group and how it affects our lives").

Delinquency

This measure consisted of five items for the early adolescents in wave 1 and 10 items for the middle adolescents at all times and waves 2 and 3 for the early adolescents. Students were asked whether they had committed a list of violent and criminal acts (e.g., "stolen something worth less than five dollars" and "bodily harm against a student"). Each item was weighted by its severity; more severe violent or delinquent acts were weighted more heavily. The weighted scores were summed to create a total delinquency score. Test–retest reliability over a 2-year time period was $r = .36$ for the early adolescents and was $r = .46$ for the middle adolescents (Adolescent Pathways Project, 1995).

Results

To examine the relation between ethnic identity and delinquency both cross-sectionally and longitudinally, we examined Pearson correlations and hierarchical linear regressions. We first list all the means and standard deviations within cohort, race/ethnicity, and gender, as shown in Tables 2.1 and 2.2. We then examine correlations both within time and across time within cohort and race/ethnicity, as shown in Table 2.3. Next, two sets of hierarchical regressions were conducted. The first set had wave 2 delinquency as the dependent variable, gender, and time one delinquency as control variables in the first step, wave 1 group esteem and exploration as predictors in the second step. The second set had wave 3 delinquency as the dependent variable, gender, and wave 2 delinquency as control variables in the first step, wave 2 group esteem and exploration as predictors in the second step, as shown in Table 2.4.

Examining the correlations, we see that among the early adolescents, there is essentially little relation between delinquency and either measure of ethnic identity. Within one time point (see correlations in bold), although the correlations are not significant, in general the small correlations are negative correlations; the only significant correlation is between exploration and delinquency in wave 3. Surprisingly, this correlation is positive, such that as exploration rises, delinquency rises as well. We see two across time correlations that are marginally significant for the African American early adolescents: wave 1 group esteem and wave 2 delinquency (positively correlated), wave 3 exploration and wave 2 delinquency (negatively correlated). Examining the correlations for the middle adolescents, we see a somewhat

TABLE 2.1
Means and Standard Deviations on Delinquency and Ethnic Identity for Early Adolescents

Cohort	Race/ethnicity	Gender	Delinquency T1	Delinquency T2	Delinquency T3	Group esteem T1	Group esteem T2	Group esteem T3	Exploration T1	Exploration T2	Exploration T3
Early adolescents			1.32 (1.42)	2.33 (3.10)	2.12 (2.98)	2.97 (.87)	3.40 (.75)	3.42 (.71)	2.46 (.82)	2.53 (.91)	2.63 (.90)
	African American		1.43 (1.47)	2.54 (3.22)	2.14 (3.06)	2.80 (.94)	3.40 (.82)	3.48 (.77)	2.37 (.84)	2.56 (.94)	2.68 (.91)
		Girls	1.03 (1.0)	2.23 (3.03)	1.59 (2.02)	2.89 (.91)	3.46 (.80)	3.51 (.71)	2.48 (.81)	2.60 (.95)	2.77 (.88)
		Boys	2.02 (1.83)	3.02 (3.45)	3.00 (4.07)	2.67 (.98)	3.32 (.86)	3.42 (.87)	2.21 (.87)	2.50 (.94)	2.55 (.94)
	European American		1.18 (1.41)	2.23 (2.34)	2.07 (2.61)	3.27 (.71)	3.49 (.59)	3.40 (.70)	2.52 (.80)	2.58 (.82)	2.60 (.88)
		Girls	.87 (1.04)	1.98 (1.97)	1.51 (1.98)	3.28 (.55)	3.35 (.65)	3.46 (.58)	2.58 (.73)	2.56 (.86)	2.74 (.85)
		Boys	1.49 (1.65)	2.49 (2.67)	2.74 (3.11)	3.25 (.84)	3.62 (.48)	3.32 (.82)	2.47 (.87)	2.60 (.80)	2.42 (.89)
	Latino		1.30 (1.38)	2.22 (3.25)	2.11 (3.04)	2.92 (.85)	3.38 (.76)	3.38 (.68)	2.53 (.81)	2.49 (.93)	2.61 (.91)
		Girls	.97 (1.09)	2.23 (3.05)	1.23 (1.87)	2.89 (.91)	3.41 (.70)	3.32 (.71)	2.41 (.82)	2.43 (.89)	2.47 (.91)
		Boys	1.69 (1.59)	2.22 (3.49)	3.26 (3.79)	2.96 (.78)	3.34 (.82)	3.46 (.63)	2.69 (.77)	2.55 (.96)	2.78 (.89)

Note. T = time.

TABLE 2.2
Means and Standard Deviations on Delinquency and Ethnic Identity for Middle Adolescents

Cohort	Race/ethnicity	Gender	Delinquency			Group esteem			Exploration		
			T1	T2	T3	T1	T2	T3	T1	T2	T3
Middle adolescents			1.68	1.87	1.85	3.08	3.48	3.51	2.56	2.62	2.78
			(2.71)	(2.90)	(2.85)	(.81)	(.62)	(.59)	(.78)	(.86)	(.87)
	African American		1.30	2.22	2.11	2.70	3.38	3.38	2.53	2.49	2.61
			(1.38)	(3.25)	(3.04)	(.90)	(.76)	(.68)	(.81)	(.93)	(.91)
		Girls	.83	1.95	1.39	2.72	3.34	3.61	2.39	2.66	2.89
			(1.23)	(3.31)	(1.69)	(.93)	(.69)	(.55)	(.80)	(.78)	(.81)
		Boys	2.25	1.33	3.00	2.65	3.67	3.83	2.22	2.43	3.16
			(1.98)	(2.24)	(2.78)	(.78)	(.55)	(.31)	(.81)	(.86)	(.67)
	European American		1.91	1.76	1.76	3.27	3.56	3.43	2.64	2.48	2.52
			(2.18)	(2.48)	(2.51)	(.69)	(.50)	(.61)	(.76)	(.84)	(.92)
		Girls	1.22	1.57	1.28	3.39	3.57	3.48	2.82	1.44	2.50
			(1.93)	(1.69)	(2.67)	(.49)	(.44)	(.55)	(.70)	(.75)	(.97)
		Boys	2.79	2.00	2.33	3.11	3.54	3.38	2.42	2.53	2.53
			(2.22)	(3.29)	(2.26)	(.88)	(.58)	(.69)	(.81)	(.97)	(.97)
	Latino		1.13	1.94	2.01	3.39	3.49	3.45	2.75	2.67	2.81
			(1.43)	(2.97)	(3.42)	(.61)	(.64)	(.62)	(.73)	(.91)	(.89)
		Girls	.88	1.68	1.63	3.48	3.51	3.49	2.69	2.68	2.83
			(1.20)	(2.48)	(3.30)	(.59)	(.59)	(.61)	(.74)	(.91)	(.90)
		Boys	1.86	2.62	3.05	3.07	3.43	3.35	2.94	2.69	2.74
			(1.79)	(3.99)	(3.59)	(.57)	(.77)	(.63)	(.73)	(.93)	(.87)

Note. T = time.

TABLE 2.3
Correlations of Delinquency With Group Esteem and Exploration by Cohort and Race/Ethnicity

African American early adolescents		Delinquency		
		T1	T2	T3
Group esteem	T1	-.12	.17[a]	.10
	T2	-.01	.07	.07
	T3	.03	-.08	.04
Exploration	T1	-.10	.08	.00
	T2	-.04	.05	.08
	T3	-.04	-.18[b]	.02

European American early adolescents		Delinquency		
		T1	T2	T3
Group esteem	T1	-.06	.07	.04
	T2	-.10	.03	-.06
	T3	.00	.15	-.12
Exploration	T1	-.09	-.03	-.18
	T2	-.06	-.04	-.10
	T3	-.08	.16	-.10

Latino early adolescents		Delinquency		
		T1	T2	T3
Group esteem	T1	-.03	.12	.11
	T2	-.01	-.01	-.09
	T3	-.03	-.09	-.08
Exploration	T1	.00	.07	-.10
	T2	.11	-.04	.07
	T3	.01	-.05	.15[b]

African American middle adolescents		Delinquency		
		T1	T2	T3
Group esteem	T1	-.10	-.47[c]	-.12
	T2	.15	-.29[b]	.18
	T3	.23	-.33[b]	.14
Exploration	T1	-.02	-.38[b]	-.02
	T2	-.06	-.31[b]	.09
	T3	.17	-.29[a]	.04

European American middle adolescents		Delinquency		
		T1	T2	T3
Group esteem	T1	-.13	.26	-.08
	T2	.13	-.06	.29
	T3	-.30	.04	-.10
Exploration	T1	-.42[a]	.21	-.49[a]
	T2	.06	.07	-.13
	T3	-.26	.06	-.07

Latino middle adolescents		Delinquency		
		T1	T2	T3
Group esteem	T1	-.28[a]	.07	.09
	T2	.08	-.02	.01
	T3	.10	-.35[c]	-.01
Exploration	T1	.20	.13	.27
	T2	.07	-.15	-.02
	T3	.33*	-.07	.07

Note. T = time.
[a]p < .10; [b]p < .05; [c]p < .01.

TABLE 2.4
Hierarchical Regression Analyses: Delinquency Predicted From Ethnic Identity by Cohort and Race/Ethnicity

African American

	Early adolescent						Middle adolescent					
	T2			T3[a]			T2[b]			T3		
	B	SE	β	B	SE	β	B	SE	β	B	SE	β
Step 1: ΔR^2	.01			.05[b]			.01			.10		
Delinquency T1 (T2)	.26	.24	.10	.01	.08	.02	-.09	.24	-.06	.00	.10	.00
Gender	-.17	.75	-.02	1.40[b]	.53	.22	-.70	1.42	-.08	1.40+	.82	.27
Step 2: ΔR^2	.02			.01			.24[c]					
Group esteem T1 (T2)	.48	.48	.11	.18	.36	.05	-1.5[b]	.70	-.41	.30	.54	.10
Exploration T1 (T2)	.28	.52	.06	.24	.31	.07	-.47	.79	-.11	.00	.42	.00

European American

	Early adolescent						Middle adolescent					
	T2			T3			T2			T3[b]		
	B	SE	β	B	SE	β	B	SE	β	B	SE	β
Step 1: ΔR^2	.00			.07			.10			.15[a]		
Delinquency T1 (T2)	-.06	.21	-.03	-.11	.14	-.10	.23	.16	.38	.37[b]	.15	.38
Gender	.59	.55	.13	1.31	.66	.25	-.37	.67	-.13	1.1	.76	.22
Step 2: ΔR^2	.01			.01			.10			.20[b]		
Group esteem T1 (T2)	.34	.42	1.0	.06	.57	.01	.26	.61	.12	2.24[b]	.82	.45
Exploration T1 (T2)	-.18	.36	-.06	-.38	.39	-.12	.49	.61	.26	-.99[a]	.49	-.34

Latino

	Early adolescent						Middle adolescent					
	T2			T3[d]			T2			T3		
	B	SE	β	B	SE	β	B	SE	β	B	SE	β
Step 1: ΔR^2	.00			.11[d]			.02			.06[a]		
Delinquency T1 (T2)	-.12	.17	-.08	-.05	.06	-.05	.03	.24	.02	.20	.14	.17
Gender	.45	.54	.09	2.0[d]	.40	.32	1.38	1.3	.21	1.31	.90	.17
Step 2: ΔR^2	.01			.01			.04			.00		
Group esteem T1 (T2)	.38	.37	.13	-.29	.30	-.07	1.05	1.07	.23	.15	.73	.03
Exploration T1 (T2)	-.19	.37	-.07	-.25	.24	.08	-.82	.87	-.21	-.01	.50	-.00

Note. T = time; B = unstandardized regression coefficient; SE = standard error; β = standardized regression.
[a] $p < .10$; [b] $p < .05$; [c] $p < .01$; [d] $p < .001$.

stronger relation between ethnic identity and delinquency. Within each time point we see significant and marginally significant negative correlations. Across time points we also see more and larger negative correlations.

The goal of the hierarchical regressions was to determine whether ethnic identity at one time point predicts delinquency 1 year later. Again, we examine the results for the early adolescents first. Group esteem and exploration do not significantly predict later delinquency for any of the three ethnic groups. However, examining the middle adolescents we see a different picture. Ethnic identity as a step significantly predicts delinquency for African Americans (ΔR^2 = .24, p < .01). Examining the coefficients, we see that wave 1 group esteem significantly predicts wave 2 delinquency, such that as group esteem rises, delinquency is lower. For European Americans, ethnic identity at wave 2 is a significant predictor of delinquency 1 year later (ΔR^2 = .20, p < .05). Group esteem is positively associated with delinquency, such that as group esteem rises, delinquency rises.

Discussion

These results suggest both unique developmental and ethnic group difference patterns between ethnic identity and delinquent behavior. First, the lack of association between delinquency and ethnic identity for the early adolescents may be because of ethnic identity not being fully developed or salient during this age period. It is possible that the lack of cognitive maturity weakens the link between how one feels about one's ethnic group and how one behaves. Previous research found no relation between ethnic identity and self-esteem over time for early adolescents, while finding such a relation with middle adolescents (French, 2005). This supports the idea that ethnic identity is not sufficiently established in this early adolescent time period to critically affect future behavior.

In contrast, although it is not consistent at every time point or for every group, we do see that there is a greater association between ethnic identity and delinquency for the middle adolescents, suggesting that ethnic identity may be more established and critical at this developmental level. Middle adolescents have had a greater period of time to think about what it means to be a member of their group and have the cognitive ability to recognize the repercussions of such group membership. More important, it seems that the majority of associations between ethnic identity and delinquency indicate that a positive sense of ethnic identity is protective, in that it is associated with less delinquency. The pride that these students take in their group membership seems to make them less likely to fulfill the negative stereotype that adolescents of color are violent and dangerous.

Not surprisingly we see different patterns of the association between ethnic identity and delinquency for the different ethnic groups. For African

Americans, group esteem negatively predicted subsequent delinquency—students with higher levels of group esteem reported lower levels of delinquency 1 year later. Although the longitudinal association between group esteem and delinquency also was significant for the European American middle adolescents, it was in the opposite direction when compared with African American students. European American students with greater levels of group esteem reported more delinquency 1 year later. However, European American students with higher levels of exploration reported lower levels of delinquency 1 year later.

Clearly group esteem means different things to African Americans and European Americans. It may be that African Americans' sense of group esteem is within the context of being the devalued group in society, and the positive sense of group esteem is despite this devaluation. European Americans are in the dominant position in society and hence have a sense of invulnerability; thus group esteem for them can carry a different meaning. The fact that those with higher levels of group esteem report more delinquent acts may reflect a certain confidence in one's Whiteness as untouchable and invulnerable—even to acts of delinquency and violence. Interestingly, the European Americans with higher levels of exploration were less likely to report delinquent acts. Again, the role of group esteem and exploration may serve different purposes for the European Americans. It may be that European Americans who take the time to actually explore what it means to be White or a member of their White ethnic group (e.g., Italian, Greek) may be more sensitive to issues of race, their position in society, and the link to their behavior. Surprisingly, there was no association between ethnic identity and delinquency in the regression equations for the Latinos. The correlations between the two constructs were also weak.

These results also support the notion of the uniqueness versus universality of ethnic identity. Two competing perspectives have been discussed wherein it has been suggested that (a) all ethnic groups will experience their ethnic identity in a similar manner (typically called ethnic identity models), or (b) each group's history and collective experience will play a role in defining how one perceives one's group membership and the impact that it will have on other factors (typically called racial identity models). Given that the three ethnic groups had different relations between their group esteem, exploration, and delinquency, this suggests that the way one identifies with one's group is not universal and may be specific to a particular group history. Furthermore, differences between African Americans and Latinos, both members of ethnic minority groups in the United States, suggests that differences are because of more than a shared or nonshared minority experience.

Overall, this study lends support to the notion that there is a link between ethnic identity and delinquency. In general, it is protective for

African Americans, such that a more positive sense of ethnic identity leads to more positive behaviors, specifically in terms of avoiding violence and delinquency—suggesting that prevention-oriented researchers are right to include ethnic pride in violence prevention programs. Given the lack of relations for the Latino students, we need to continue to study ethnic identity and delinquency and determine why the relation is not there— whether it is unimportant or it was not properly assessed for this group in this study. In terms of European American students, it is clear that too great a level of group esteem may be detrimental—as members of the dominant group, a great sense of pride in one's group may be harmful to those around them. Looking back through the past century, we have seen many acts of violence against people of color in the name of "White pride." We need to better understand the protective role of exploration for European Americans. With more knowledge in this realm, we may be able to prevent hate crimes committed by European Americans against people of color.

PROGRAMS TO ENHANCE ETHNIC IDENTITY

In light of findings (such as those from the APP described earlier) that support a link between ethnic identity and violence and delinquency, efforts have been made to address barriers to positive ethnic identity formation encountered by minority youth. Results from various programs that have incorporated an ethnic identity component suggest that it may be a malleable characteristic that can also be useful as part of a more comprehensive program to promote adjustment and to prevent adolescent problem behaviors such as youth violence. Enhancing ethnic identity appears to have positive effects for minority adolescents, ranging from academic motivation to health promotion to decreasing attrition in interventions (Bass & Coleman, 1997; Greene, Smith, & Peters, 1995; Weeks, Schensul, Williams, Singer, & Grier, 1995).

In chapter 9 of this volume, Wright and Zimmerman review a number of health promotion and prevention programs that incorporate efforts to instill a positive ethnic identity in youth as part of a health promotion and prevention strategy often linked to violence prevention. As they point out, many of these programs are designed for African American youth and draw on a rites-of-passage approach. Indeed, during the past two decades, rites-of-passage models have been integrated into a broad range of prevention and intervention efforts including family therapy interventions (Quinn, Newfield, & Protinsky, 1985), independent living programs to help adolescents in foster care (Gavazzi, Alford, & McKenry, 1996), and adolescent health promotion programs (Harvey & Rauch, 1997).

We turn briefly to consideration of the mechanisms by which these efforts are believed to promote ethnic identity and to protect adolescents from problem behaviors such as youth violence. First, these programs help define what a culture expects for individuals within this culture. To the extent that ethnic minority adolescents are unclear about the appropriate reference group for anchoring their identity search, such programming should provide conceptual clarity for youth based on clearly delineated norms, beliefs, and values of the culture.

Second, such programs may help ethnic minority youth, particularly those who have been disenfranchised by the minority experience, to see their ethnic heritage as a positive rather than a negative influence, linked more to pride than to anger or resentment. In this manner, rites-of-passage programs can help adolescents develop self-protective competencies that aid in the psychological prowess to resist and constructively counter the negative images, attitudes, and behaviors perpetuated by the social environment (Brookins, 1996). Thus, rites-of-passage programs may help adolescents by serving as a cultural and social inoculation process that facilitates healthy development and protects them against the detriments of a racist, capitalist, oppressive society (Bass & Coleman, 1997).

Third, such programs can serve as rituals or events that function as markers of change in the individual's status within that culture. As such, they can serve an important role in the transition from childhood to adulthood that may be particularly salient for ethnic minority youth, but is salient to some degree for all youth (i.e., understanding one's heritage and its meaning). This transition may be particularly problematic for African American youth. According to Brookins (1996), rites-of-passage interventions ultimately help prepare African American adolescents for coping with the many challenges they may encounter as they enter adulthood by providing a structured and formalized process through which youth develop the basis for a strong positive identity and orientation toward the future.

CONCLUSION

An important developmental task of adolescence is establishment of a positive identity to organize self-knowledge and provide direction and guidance for the future. Identity provides a sense of self as well as one's place among family, peers, school, work, culture, and religion. Part of one's identity reflects beliefs and values related to ethnic heritage and its salience— one's ethnic identity. In particular, the importance of ethnic identity may be even greater for minority youth who are more likely to have grown up with a set of unique (and perhaps negative) experiences related to their minority status.

As we have discussed, ethnic identity can serve as a protective factor to promote healthy adjustment, helping minority youth overcome effects of a hostile environment. Furthermore, a healthy ethnic identity may be accompanied by the belief that one's ethnic group is viewed positively by others, which may be reflected in more positive attitudes toward other groups as well. Still, it is clear from the relatively few studies examining relations between ethnic identity and youth violence over time and in diverse ethnic groups that caution must be exercised when infusing ethnic identity enhancement into preventive interventions.

Otherwise stated, when designing and implementing programs to enhance or promote ethnic identity, researchers must take into account various factors. It is important to consider developmental trends and recognize that the association between ethnic identity and problem behavior may not be static but may instead depend on the adolescents' level in development. As illustrated in the APP data previously discussed, the link between ethnic identity and delinquent behavior may be strongest for middle adolescents. Therefore, providing interventions to enhance ethnic identity may be more beneficial during middle adolescence. Finally, researchers must consider the notion that the strength of the association between ethnic identity and delinquent behavior may differ by ethnic group. Although higher ethnic identity in African American adolescents appears to be greatly associated with lower levels of delinquency in the current APP study, the association between ethnic identity and delinquency is not as clear for Latino adolescents and seems to reverse for European Americans. Clearly, rather than making blanket statements about the needs of ethnic minority youth vis-à-vis identity development and implications for violence prevention, we must consider carefully the role that ethnic identity plays for all youth, the role it plays for ethnic minority youth, and the role is plays for youth from different ethnic groups.

REFERENCES

Adolescent Pathways Project. (1995). *Delinquency index: Psychometric development summary.* New York: New York University.

Arbona, C., Jackson, R. H., McCoy, A., & Blakely, C. (1999). Ethnic identity as a predictor of attitudes of adolescents toward fighting. *Journal of Early Adolescence, 19,* 323–340.

Arce, C. H. (1981). Reconsideration of Chicano culture and identity. *Daedalus, 110,* 177–191.

Aries, E., & Moorehead, K. (1989). The importance of ethnicity in the development of identity of Black adolescents. *Psychological Reports, 65,* 75–82.

Austin, A. A. (2004). Alcohol, tobacco, other drug use, and violent behavior among native Hawaiians: Ethnic pride and resilience. *Substance Use and Misuse*, 39, 721–746.

Bass, C. K., & Coleman, H. L. K. (1997). Enhancing the cultural identity of early adolescent male African Americans. *Professional School Counseling, 1*, 48–51.

Belgrave, F. Z., Chase-Vaughn, G., Gray, F., Addison, J. D., & Cherry, V. R. (2000). The effectiveness of a culture- and gender-specific intervention for increasing resiliency among African American preadolescent females. *Journal of Black Psychology, 26*, 133–147.

Berzonsky, M. D., & Adams, G. R. (1999). Reevaluating the identity status paradigm: Still useful after 35 years. *Developmental Review, 19*, 557–590.

Bracher, M. (2000). Adolescent violence and identity vulnerability. *Journal for the Psychoanalysis of Culture and Society, 5*, 189–211.

Branch, C. W., Tayal, P., & Triplett, C. (2000). The relationship of ethnic identity and ego identity status among adolescents and young adults. *International Journal of Intercultural Relations, 24*, 777–790.

Brook, J. S., Balka, E. B., Brook, D. W., Win, P. T., & Gursen, M. D. (1998). Drug use among African Americans: Ethnic identity as a protective factor. *Psychological Reports, 83*, 1427–1446.

Brookins, C. C. (1996). Promoting ethnic identity development in African American youth: The role of rites of passage. *Journal of Black Psychology, 22*, 388–417.

Caldwell, C. H., Kohn-Wood, L. P., Schmeelk-Cone, K. H, Chavous, T. M., & Zimmerman, M. A. (2004). *American Journal of Community Psychology*, 33, 91–105.

Cross, W..E. (1971). Negro to Black conversion experience. *Black World, 20*, 13–27.

Cross, W. E., Jr. (1991). *Shades of black: Diversity in African American identity.* Philadelphia: Temple University Press.

Cross, W. E., Jr. (1995). The psychology of nigrescence: Revising the Cross model. In J. G. Ponterotto, J. M. Casas, L. A. Suzuki, & C. M. Alexander (Eds.), *Handbook of multicultural counseling* (pp. 93–122). Thousand Oaks, CA: Sage.

Erikson, E. H. (1968). *Identity: Youth and crisis.* New York: Norton.

French, S. E. (2005). *The development of ethnic identity and its relationship to self-esteem among urban adolescents.* Manuscript submitted for publication.

French, S. E., Seidman, E., Allen, L., & Aber, J. L. (in press). The development of racial and ethnic identity during adolescence. *Developmental Psychology*.

Gaines, S. O., & Reed, E. S. (1994). Two social psychologies of prejudice: Gordon W. Allport, W. E. B. DuBois and the legacy of Booker T. Washington. *Journal of Black Psychology, 20*, 8–28.

Gaines, S. O., & Reed, E. S. (1995). Prejudice: From Allport to DuBois. *American Psychologist, 50*, 96–103.

Garrett, D. (1995). Violent behaviors among African American adolescents. *Adolescence, 30*, 209–217.

Gaskell, G., & Smith, P. (1986). Group membership and social attitudes of youth: An investigation of some implications of social identity theory. *Social Behaviour, 1*, 67–77.

Gavazzi, S. M., Alford, K. A., & McKenry, P. C. (1996). Culturally specific programs for foster care youth: The sample case of an African American rites of passage program. *Family Relations, 45*, 166–174.

Greene, L. W., Smith, S. M., & Peters, S. R. (1995). "I have a future" comprehensive adolescent health promotion: Cultural considerations in program implementation and design. *Journal of Health Care for the Poor and Underserved, 6*, 267–281.

Harvey, A. R., & Rauch, J. B. (1997). A comprehensive Afrocentric rites of passage program for Black male adolescents. *Health and Social Work, 22*, 30–38.

Helms, J. E. (Ed.). (1990). *Black and White racial identity: Theory, research and practice.* Westport, CT: Greenwood Press.

Howard, J. A. (2000). Social psychology of identities. *Annual Review of Sociology, 26*, 67–93.

Leach, M. M., Behrens, J. T., & LaFleur, N. K. (2002). White racial identity and White racial consciousness: Similarities, differences, and recommendations. *Journal of Multicultural Counseling and Development, 30*, 66–80.

Marcia, J. E. (1966). Development and validation of ego-identity status. *Journal of Personality and Social Psychology, 3*, 551–558.

Marcia, J. E. (1980). Identity in adolescence. In J. Adelson (Ed.), *Handbook of adolescent psychology* (pp. 159–187). New York: Wiley.

Markstrom-Adams, C., & Spencer, M. B. (1994). A model for identity intervention with minority adolescents. In S. L. Archer (Ed.), *Interventions for adolescent identity development* (pp. 84–102). Thousand Oaks, CA: Sage.

Martinez, R. O., & Dukes, R. L. (1997). The effects of ethnic identity, ethnicity, and gender in adolescent well-being. *Journal of Youth and Adolescence, 26*, 503–516.

Mayeda, D. T., Chesney-Lind, M., & Koo, J. (2001). Talking story with Hawaii's youth: Confronting violent and sexualized perceptions of ethnicity and gender. *Youth and Society, 33*, 99–128.

McMahon, S. D., & Watts, R. J. (2002). Ethnic identity in urban African American youth: Exploring links with self-worth, aggression, and other psychosocial variables. *Journal of Community Psychology, 30*, 411–432.

Patterson, G. R., DeBaryshe, B. D., & Ramsey, E. (1989). A developmental perspective on antisocial behavior. *American Psychologist, 44*, 329–335.

Phinney, J. S. (1989). Stages of ethnic identity development in minority group adolescents. *Journal of Early Adolescence, 9*, 34–49.

Phinney, J. S. (1992). The multigroup ethnic identity measure: A new scale for use with diverse groups. *Journal of Adolescent Research, 7*, 156–176.

Phinney, J. S., Lochner, B. T., & Murphy, R. (1990). Ethnic identity development and psychological adjustment in adolescence. In A. R. Stiffman & L. E. Davis (Eds.), *Ethnic issues in adolescent mental health* (pp. 53–72). Newbury Park, CA: Sage.

Quinn, W. H., Newfield, N. A., & Protinsky, H. O. (1985). Rites of passage in families with adolescents. *Family Process, 24*, 101–111.

Rotheram-Borus, M. J. (1989). Ethnic differences in adolescents' identity status and associated behavior problems. *Journal of Adolescence, 12*, 361–374.

Rotheram-Borus, M. J., & Wyche, K. F. (1994). Ethnic differences in identity development in the United States. In S. L. Archer (Ed.), *Interventions for adolescent identity development* (pp. 62–83). Thousand Oaks, CA: Sage.

Rothstein, D. A. (1999). Lethal identity: Violence and identity formation. In M. Sugar (Ed.), *Trauma and adolescence* (pp. 225–250). Madison, CT: International University Press.

Seidman, E. (1991). Growing up the hard way: Pathways of urban adolescents. *American Journal of Community Psychology, 19*, 173–205.

Smith, E. P., Walker, K., Fields, L., Brookins, C. C., & Seay, R. C. (1999). Ethnic identity and its relationship to self-esteem, perceived efficacy, and prosocial attitudes in early adolescence. *Journal of Adolescence, 22*, 867–880.

Stets, J., & Burke, P. (2003). A sociological approach to self and identity. In M. R. Leary & J. P. Tangney (Eds.), *Handbook of self and identity* (pp. 128–152). New York: Guilford Press.

Suarez-Orozco, C. (2000). Identities under siege: Immigration stress and social mirroring among the children of immigrants. In A. C. Robben & M. M. Suarez-Orozco (Eds.), *Cultures under siege: Collective violence and trauma* (pp. 194–226). New York: Cambridge University Press.

Swanson, D. P., Spencer, M. B., & Petersen, A. (1998). Identity formation in adolescence. In K. Borman & B. Schneider (Eds.), *The adolescent years: Social influences and educational challenges* (pp. 18–41). Chicago: National Society for the Study of Education.

Tolan, P. H., Guerra, N. G., & Kendall, P. C. (1995). A developmental–ecological perspective on antisocial behavior in children and adolescents: Toward a unified risk and intervention framework. *Journal of Consulting and Clinical Psychology, 63*, 579–584.

Weeks, M. R., Schensul, J. J., Williams, S. S., Singer, M., & Grier, M. (1995). AIDS prevention for African American and Latina women: Building culturally and gender-appropriate intervention. *AIDS Education and Prevention, 7*, 251–263.

Whaley, A. L. (1992). A culturally sensitive approach to the prevention of interpersonal violence among urban Black youth. *Journal of the National Medical Association, 84*, 585–588.

Yancey, A. K., Aneshensel, C. S., & Driscoll, A. K. (2001). The assessment of ethnic identity in diverse urban youth populations. *Journal of Black Psychology, 27*, 190–208.

3

YOUTH VIOLENCE, IMMIGRATION, AND ACCULTURATION

IOAKIM BOUTAKIDIS, NANCY G. GUERRA,
AND FERNANDO SORIANO

Despite recent downward trends, youth violence continues to be a significant concern in the United States, as evidenced by recent calls for action (Office of the Surgeon General, 2001). Furthermore, rates of youth violence in this country are still among the highest in the industrial world (Cunningham, 2000). As discussed by Smith and Guerra (introduction, this volume) and throughout this book, epidemiological studies generally show that ethnic minority youth are disproportionately and adversely affected by violence, both as perpetrators and victims.

Much of the work examining the plight of ethnic minority groups in light of the changing urban landscape and the impact on violence has emphasized conditions and consequences for African Americans (as discussed by Guerra and Williams, chap. 1, this volume). However, attempts to increase one's understanding of the relation between ethnicity and youth violence in the United States also must consider the influence of immigration and acculturation on development and behavior. Indeed, since the passage of the Immigration Act of 1965, there has been a sharp increase in the number of immigrants to the United States. Clearly, certain children and adolescents from specific ethnic groups that make up this immigration surge are the primary focus of attention. For example, recent estimates indicate that approximately 40% of the Latino population and 60% of the Asian Pacific Islander population are foreign-born (U.S. Census Bureau, 1997, 2004). Since 1990, the number of children in immigrant families has expanded almost seven times faster than for native-born families (Hernandez, 2004). As a result, many ethnic minority youth have at least one foreign-born parent. It is difficult to provide an accurate portrait of these youth without taking into account the impact of being raised by parents who were themselves raised in a different culture.

Being the child of immigrants can exert a profound impact on development and behavior. Clearly, this impact is greatest for children who were born in a different country but came to the United States during childhood and for children who are first-generation residents (i.e., they were born in the United States to parents who were born outside of the United States). In this chapter, we examine a subset of mechanisms related to immigrant families that are likely to be of greatest relevance for youth violence etiology and prevention. First, we describe the immigrant population in terms of relevant background characteristics, including socioeconomic status, areas of settlement, access to resources, language ability, and school achievement. These factors can either increase risk for violence or buffer children from adverse circumstances. Next, we review the literature on acculturation and adaptation, with a particular focus on the mechanisms through which this process can contribute to aggression and violence. In particular, we highlight the importance of cultural frameworks and cultural norms related to violence of both the native and host culture and the impact of stressors associated with acculturation. Of most relevance to youth violence, we emphasize those stressors that place additional burdens on the family system. We then turn to a discussion of biculturalism and its influence on adjustment. We conclude with a discussion of implications of immigration and acculturation for youth violence prevention research and practice.

IMMIGRANT YOUTH: RECENT TRENDS

Before the 1950s, most immigrants to the United States were from northern and western European countries; however, the latter part of the 20th century saw a marked shift in immigration patterns. Whereas European immigration fell to about 10% of total immigrants, there was a large increase in immigration from other countries. Indeed, approximately 85% of immigrants were from Asia and Latin America, followed by immigrants from Caribbean countries (Martin & Midgley, 1994). Although on average, immigrants who entered the United States in the 1980s or later are more economically disadvantaged than native-born Americans or those who entered pre-1980, there is still a great deal of socioeconomic diversity among immigrants. These differences tend to follow national origin, although there are additional variations within regions.

Immigrants from Latin America and the Caribbean tend to be less educated and less occupationally skilled than immigrants from Asia (Hernandez, 2004). This difference can be traced to the admission criteria specified in the Immigration Act of 1965. Country origin was eliminated as a qualification for obtaining an immigrant visa (which had given preference to European relatives), and a preference system was established that gave priority to individuals with special skills needed in the U.S. labor market or with family members already in the country. Because of earlier exclusionary policies, few individuals from Asia were already living in the United States by midcentury; therefore, the majority of Asian immigrants during this time were admitted by virtue of their occupational and professional skills.

There are also regional differences within Asian immigrants that stem from historical and political circumstances. For instance, a large number of immigrants from Laos and Cambodia were admitted to the United States under special humanitarian provisions, many of whom are members of rural groups, such as the Hmong and Lao, with little formal education and high levels of poverty. Although there are also distinctions among Latino immigrants, in many cases, they entered the United States as agricultural workers or manual laborers, with relatively little formal schooling. Many of these workers were granted residency in the 1980s based on an amnesty policy. Still, there are a disproportionate number of undocumented Latin American immigrants, and this contributes to their disadvantaged socioeconomic status and associated problems (Fix & Passel, 1994; Nightingale & Fix, 2004).

Throughout history, entry into the United States was often a ticket to improved economic status. In recent years, times have been more difficult for immigrants. Globalization and deindustrialization have placed constraints on the economy with fewer opportunities for upward mobility. Immigrants of color also face roadblocks not experienced by their White, European counterparts (Nightingale & Fix, 2004). As McLoyd (1998) noted, "European immigrants confronted dilemmas born of conflicting cultures, but they had the advantage of being uniformly White" (p. 7). Furthermore, most recent immigrants have settled in large, urban metropolitan areas such as Los Angeles, New York, and Chicago. To the extent that these immigrants are poor and unskilled, they are also more likely to reside in some of the most disadvantaged neighborhoods of these urban centers.

In these settings, immigrant families are more likely to be exposed to harsh conditions, including exposure to violence, scarce resources, and difficulty accessing services. These difficulties are likely to be compounded additionally for nonlegal residents who are often uninformed about available services or reluctant to access those services. Limited language proficiency and lack of knowledge about local school systems can compromise parents' abilities to serve as brokers for their children's education and development. In overburdened and troubled urban school systems, a lack of parental involvement can compound any difficulties children might already face (Fix & Passel, 2003; Takanashi, 2004). Because children of immigrant parents often are more proficient in English than their parents, they frequently serve as translators. In this role, the parent–child status hierarchy is inverted, and children can easily filter information parents receive about their progress (e.g., reports from school, grades, etc.). In addition, although educational research suggests that some teachers encourage the aspirations of ethnic minority and immigrant students, there are also studies that point to low teacher expectations for students from immigrant families and the resulting detrimental effects on academic progress (McDonnell & Hill, 1993).

Still, there is not a clear-cut relation between immigrant status and educational achievement. There appears to be great variation within ethnic subgroups as well as across generations. In general, earlier generations tend to perform better than later generations, particularly among Asian families (Fuligni, 1997). Children from certain Asian countries, such as Japan, Korea, and Vietnam tend to outperform children from Latin American countries (Kao & Tienda, 1995), but they also tend to outperform children from other Asian groups such as the Lao and Hmong (Rumbaut, 1994). Researchers have suggested that this declining emphasis on education by subsequent generations also may portend an increase in problem behaviors across generations (Steinberg, 1996).

The differential outcomes for immigrant children most likely depend on a host of factors related to the adaptation process. These outcomes (e.g., low school achievement, parental discord), in turn, can increase risk for violence. As discussed by Smith and Guerra (introduction, this volume), many risk factors are shared across all majority and minority ethnic groups (e.g., low school achievement) but are more likely to be experienced by some ethnic minority groups because of the conditions of development they face. For this reason, a better understanding of the adjustment process and how it affects development and behavior can also increase one's understanding of risk for violence among children from immigrant families. A salient component of this adjustment process involves the manner by which these families acculturate to the standards, norms, rules, and demands of the host society. Furthermore, this adjustment often involves adjustment to multiple cultural realms. As Boykin and colleagues have discussed (Boykin, 1986; Boykin & Toms, 1985), immigrant families who are members of disadvantaged ethnic minority groups in the United States have to negotiate three cultural realms: (a) the indigenous ethnic culture and associated values from their native country; (b) the new mainstream culture of the host country;

and (c) the component of the new host country culture that embodies the elements of minority ethnic status.

ACCULTURATION AND ADAPTATION

To date, most research examining cultural issues has focused primarily on acculturation. Acculturation involves an ongoing adjustment to the social and cultural differences between one's country of origin and the new country of residence. Several definitions that highlight different aspects of acculturation have been offered. For instance, Moyerman and Forman (1992) defined acculturation as the "process whereby the attitudes and/or behaviors of persons from one culture are modified as a result of contact with a different culture" (p. 78). Berry (1995) defined acculturation as the steadily increasing influence of cultural forces that exist outside of one's native, first, or heritage culture. Acculturation, therefore, must be distinguished from *enculturation* or socialization where the influencing forces come from within one's culture (Segall, Dasen, Berry, & Poortinga, 1999). In this volume, the authors use acculturation to refer to "differences and changes in values and behaviors that individuals make as they gradually adopt the cultural values of the dominant society" (Smith & Guerra, introduction, this volume).

Early research considered acculturation as a unilinear, unidimensional construct that followed a continuum from fully unacculturated to fully acculturated (to the new culture). More recently, these two-dimensional frameworks have been questioned. Rather than characterizing individuals as more or less traditional or American on certain salient dimensions, different frameworks for understanding the acculturation process have been offered. For instance, Berry (1994) has delineated four acculturation outcomes in relation to adolescent adjustment. Adolescents who reject their native culture in the process of fully adopting the host culture are considered to be *assimilated*. An adolescent that manages to remain strongly connected and affiliated to both the native and host culture is said to be *bicultural*. Adolescents that reject the majority culture in favor of maintaining their native culture have been labeled *separatist*, while adolescents who cannot seem to establish and maintain affiliations to either culture are known as *marginal*.

These broad categorizations are somewhat simplified for the purposes of easy classification. In reality, the individual process of acculturation may be fluid and change quite often across time. There are also many different subcultures in the United States that children and youth are exposed to. Rather than determining overall "high" and "low" scores on broad levels of cultural adjustment, it may be useful to explore the specific aspects of the old and the new culture (or subculture) that are accepted or rejected. In this manner, the important question is not whether or not children acculturate to the United States, but to which aspects of American culture they will acculturate. This is particularly important in relation to youth problem behaviors and violence, as the "acceptability" of these behaviors within the normative youth culture in the United States is generally rather high.

Furthermore, the desires of an individual to assimilate may be met by resistance from members of the majority culture. An immigrant's desires or plans for how the process of acculturation should proceed must be met by an accommodating society. On the other hand, attempts at biculturalism may be met by members of one's ethnic community with resistance, such as accusations of "selling out." Overall, research has shown that members of different immigrant ethnic groups experience unique sociostructural circumstances that may limit avenues of acculturation. This process has been detailed in Zhou's recent work on *segmented assimilation* (Bankston & Zhou, 1997; Zhou, 2003). Other researchers are also wary of closed statements regarding acculturation and assimilation, preferring to view them as dynamic, intergenerational processes (Suarez-Orozco & Suarez-Orozco, 1995).

Acculturation, Adjustment, and Youth Violence

Acculturation is a multifaceted process with a complex influence on adjustment. One prominent line of research has focused on the relation between acculturation and a range of adjustment difficulties. For instance, acculturation has been associated with a number of negative outcomes including child abuse (Mitchell, 1980), delinquency (Berlin, 1987; Buriel, Caizada, & Vasquez, 1982), gang membership (Soriano, 1995), and substance abuse (Caetano, 1987; Hartung, 1987; Neff, Hoppe, & Perez, 1987). Acculturation has also been linked to mental health difficulties including personality adjustment problems (Hoffmann, Dana, & Bolton, 1985; Padilla, Wagatsuma, & Lindholm, 1985), self-disclosure (Franco, Malloy, & Gonzales, 1984; Pomales, 1987), expressions of pathology in psychiatric patients (Price & Cuellar, 1981), stress (Martinez, 1983; Mena, Padilla, & Maldonado, 1987), and a variety of other mental disorders (Burnham, Hough, Karno, Escobar, & Telles, 1987).

The link between acculturation and violence is even more complex. Indeed, some studies have found a link between low levels of acculturation and violence, while other studies have shown that higher levels of acculturation are associated with violence. For example, with regard to domestic violence among Latino populations, some studies have found that acculturation is significantly correlated with male partner violence, with higher levels of acculturation linked to higher levels of female partner assaults (Sorenson

& Telles, 1991). In contrast, other research suggests the opposite pattern (Champion, 1996). Still other studies indicate that average-to-high levels of acculturation are most detrimental. In one recent study of Latino couples, Caetano and Schafer (2000) found that medium-acculturated couples showed the highest levels of male-to-female and female-to-male violence followed by those scoring highest on acculturation.

Although few studies have looked at the direct link between acculturation and youth violence, they tend to suggest the negative impact of acculturation. For example, Sommers, Fagan, and Baskin (1993) found higher levels of adolescent acculturation were also associated with higher levels of interpersonal violence. The literature on acculturation and risk factors associated with youth violence also seems to point to the negative consequences of acculturation. Indeed, a recent study by Soriano, Rivera, Williams, Daley, and Reznik (2004) found that although ethnic identity and bicultural self-efficacy were protective factors, acculturation was a potential risk factor for youth violence. Similar patterns have been found when looking at other types of adolescent problem behavior. For example, studies have shown more highly acculturated youth to be at greater risk for substance use (Caetano, 1987; Marin & Flores, 1994; Markides, Krause, & Mendes-DeLeon, 1988) and delinquency (Rodriguez, 1996; Wong, 1997).

Clearly these discrepant findings suggest that the influence of acculturation on outcomes including violence is not necessarily straightforward. Otherwise stated, different facets of the acculturation process may contribute to adjustment, albeit in a somewhat different fashion. As mentioned previously, we propose that acculturation impacts violence via two primary mechanisms: (a) the cultural frameworks and cultural norms related to violence of both the native and host culture; and (b) the impact of stressors associated with acculturation, particularly those stressors that compromise the family system.

Cultural Frameworks and Cultural Norms

There is a long history of research in the social sciences examining the influence of culture on cognition and behavior (Goodnow, 1997; Markus & Kitayama, 1998; Triandis, 1994, 1995). Some of this research has focused on broad frameworks that highlight distinct dimensions of culture. Other studies have examined specific norms and values that influence behavior. Connecting this to the acculturation process, it may be that acculturation from a less violent culture (based on dimensions and norms) to a more violent culture predicts increases in violence, while acculturation from a more violent to a less violent culture predicts decreases in violence. In this manner, whether acculturation, per se, relates to an increase in violence depends, in part, on the norms of the host and new cultures and the extent of the individual's acculturation. These cultural influences on violence may stem from broad dimensions of a culture or specific norms, as described below.

Triandis (1996) developed a cultural classification system to distinguish cultures on key dimensions. These dimensions include individualism–collectivism, cultural complexity, and tight versus loose cultures. Individualistic cultures stress individual goals, achievements, and rights as well as personal autonomy and independence. Collectivistic cultures emphasize group goals, group harmony, and group needs, often subordinating individual needs. Cultural complexity is a wide-ranging dimension, covering everything from the number of languages spoken in a community and occupational opportunities, to the number of recognized religions. Tightness versus looseness refers to tolerance of deviations from cultural norms. Typically, the more heterogeneous a society, the more loose the system. These dimensions can and do interact to produce unique systems. For example, complex cultures tend also to be loose because of the degree of heterogeneity present, which provides members a variety of groups to join or leave, making enforcement of norms more difficult. Nevertheless, classification along any one dimension does not necessarily predict the classification in the remaining ones. For example, the United States is considered an individualistic, complex, and loose culture, whereas Thailand is considered collectivistic, complex, and loose (Pelto, 1968).

Dimensions such as individualism versus collectivism are useful tools for characterizing cultures and societies and may be particularly relevant to one's understanding of violence. However, within this framework, these tools do not apply to individuals. Rather, individuals may be classified as having tendencies toward *idiocentrisim* (inwardly and achievement-oriented) or *allocentrism* (outwardly and socially oriented; Triandis, Leung, Villareal, & Clack, 1985). Therefore, one may have idiocentrics within collectivistic cultures and allocentrics within individualistic ones. This classification system can provide valuable information at the broad country and culture level, as well as the individual level, allowing for both a nomothetic and idiographic understanding of the role of culture in human behavior.

The framework of individualism and collectivism was originally meant to classify large groups, often based on nationality (Singelis, 1994). The United States, for example, is considered an individualistic nation. In contrast, Japan is considered a highly collectivistic culture. As such, interpersonal harmony and the avoidance of conflict is not only highly valued, it is among the most important cultural principles and goes hand in hand with being Japanese (Markus & Kitayama, 1998). Given this cultural priority, the Japanese have created social institutions and customs in the service of avoiding interpersonal conflict (Ohbuchi, Fukushima, & Tedeschi, 1999). It should come as no surprise, then, that Japan has among the lowest rates of interpersonal violence in the industrialized world, with one seventh the per-capita homicide rate of the United States (*White Paper on Crime*, 1998).

Other studies point to the tendency for individuals in collectivistic cultures to prefer nonconfrontational methods of conflict resolution. In contrast, more confrontational and adversarial methods tend to be more prevalent within individualistic cultures, increasing the likelihood of violent outcomes (Gire & Carment, 1997). For example, Chinese individuals are more likely to use obliging and compromising tactics when faced with interpersonal conflict, as compared with European Americans (Ting-Toomey, 1985). Likewise, native Latino populations regularly endorse the culturally salient value of *simpatia* that calls for individuals to avoid interpersonal conflict in favor of harmony and to defer to elders (Padilla, 1995), as well as emphasizing a sense of obligation to the family that can serve to motivate youth (Cooper, 2003). Both Chinese and native Latino cultures have been classified as collectivistic.

Individualism and collectivism also have been linked with associated risk factors for violence. For example, one outcome of living in a collectivistic culture is a much lower risk of family disruption and divorce. Collectivistic cultures report much lower rates of divorce and single-parent families than more individualistic cultures, such as in the United States (Triandis, 1994). In the case of lower divorce rates, collectivistic cultures may be tied to the emphasis on familial obligation and cohesion as well as the subordination of individual desires (Dion & Dion, 1993). In turn, a more stable family system may foster a greater degree of adolescent adjustment, while a less stable family system (e.g., absentee fathers, single-parent households) may increase risk for violent and delinquent behavior (Lykken, 2000; Triandis, 1994).

Although collectivism appears to be predictive of lower overall violence rates, this relation is also complex. What it may do is create circumstances and social expectations that reduce the likelihood of certain kinds of violence. For example, although the average rates of interpersonal violence are lower in collectivistic cultures, group-on-group violence is often higher (Triandis, 2000). Furthermore, within any given country or society, there are many subgroups defined along lines such as ethnicity, socioeconomic status, and geographic location. These subgroups have their unique cultural frameworks and associated subcultural values that emerge at the regional and local levels (Sanchez-Burks, Nisbett, & Ybarra, 2000).

For instance, elaborate norms around youth violence often develop within specific neighborhoods. These norms often emerge in response to the difficult circumstances experienced by many youth, particularly those growing up in disadvantaged inner-city settings. A compelling example of the influence of local belief systems related to violence has been illustrated by Anderson (1994, 1999). He described the "codes of the street" that have emerged in many African American inner-city communities in response to harsh circumstances, lack of resources, and recurring danger. These circumstances led to the creation of an oppositional, street subculture in which violent and criminal behavior became a viable alternative to more mainstream values. In part, this street culture emerged because of the lack of a responsive, conventional structure that could provide economic and social opportunities for advancement and security. In this sense, the cultural values, or "street codes" are functionally no different than that of any cultural group that must adapt to specific conditions.

Both cultural frameworks and cultural norms provide rules for social interaction that can decrease or increase the likelihood of violence within any group or setting. As discussed earlier, the United States is considered an individualistic culture that relies more on confrontation and adversarial exchanges than cooperation and harmony. In many disadvantaged areas, street codes have emerged that also sanction violence. Although the majority of individuals do not engage in violent and disruptive behaviors, rates of violence are still extremely high. As Hudley and Taylor note (chap. 10, this volume), efforts to understand the influence of culture on violence in the United States must consider the long history of violence in America. Not only is the United States among the most violent countries in the industrialized world, but violence in this country is often directed toward historically disadvantaged and disenfranchised groups. Furthermore, popular youth culture frequently glorifies violence as seen in media portrayals, video games, Internet sites, and sports. Given the "normative" status of violence, particularly among adolescents and young adults, adopting these mainstream values and norms may actually interfere with the positive development of youth from immigrant families and increase their risk for violence.

Against this normative backdrop, immigrant groups may also develop more violent subcultural norms in response to their particular life circumstances. Much as the code of the streets (Anderson, 1994, 1999) emerged in response to limited economic opportunities and high levels of fear and danger in African American communities, many immigrant youth develop their own codes to navigate their status and circumstances. As highlighted by French, Kim, and Pillado (chap. 2, this volume), youth from disadvantaged minority groups often have direct experiences with discrimination and lack of economic resources. In areas where these youth are concentrated, they may band together around a common belief system that articulates a set of reasons and causes for their plight.

In many cases, American society is viewed as denying access to conventional opportunities to ethnic minorities, particularly immigrants. White society may be seen as ultimately at fault, but youth from different ethnic groups or different regions within their ethnic group are seen as competitors

(Sanchez-Jankowski, 1991). Thus, a specific subculture emerges based on in-group/out-group differences that relies on violence to settle these differences, although the in-group/out-group differences are actually recreated within an ethnic group. For example, the southeastern part of the United States has seen a recent surge in Latino gang violence from gangs such as the Mara Salvatrucha 13 (MS–13) who were formed in Los Angeles in the early 1980s by guerrillas and refugees fleeing the war in El Salvador but who have expanded over time across the country. Although they may profess anger against White society, much of their violence is intra-Latino, often between Central American and Mexican gangs (and including children of the earlier immigrants; Campo-Flores, 2003).

Acculturative Stress and Family Systems

The dilemma faced by ethnic youth in general, albeit more powerfully for *immigrant* ethnic youth, is striving to find a balance between the formative powers of their native or heritage culture and those of the majority culture. Efforts to establish a balance are often met with obstacles, whether they be driven by a desire to internalize fully and accept the values of one culture over another or a need to sift through and select certain aspects of each culture to follow. These obstacles can come from the adolescent's family and friends or from social institutions such as school and work. Whatever their source, these obstacles can produce stress in the adolescent. This stress, in turn, may increase an adolescent's vulnerability to a wide array of adjustment problems and other maladaptive outcomes. This process has been labeled *acculturative stress*. Berry (1994) has characterized acculturative stress as acculturation that is marked by difficulties in adjusting to the majority culture as well as an ambivalence between wanting to maintain ethnic values that create in-group cohesion and wanting to fit into the larger, dominant society and its culture.

Acculturative stress has been associated with negative outcomes for adults including psychological distress and reduced quality of life (Thoman & Suris, 2004). Similarly, it has been shown to portend negative adolescent outcomes, including increased drug and alcohol use, mental health problems, intrafamilial conflict, and even increased risk of physical illness (Masi, 1989; Nwadiora & McAdoo, 1996; Vega & Gil, in press). Indeed, research indicates that acculturative stress hits adolescents particularly hard. One affected domain is the parent–adolescent relationship. Immigrant parents may fear that their children will gain undesirable traits and values from the new culture, while at the same time wanting them to gain the skills necessary to succeed in school and future occupational settings (Xenocostas, 1991). This dual demand may place added stress on the adolescent and be a source of conflict between parent and child that taxes the family system.

Immigrant families to the United States have always faced the prospect of having children who are torn between the traditional, ethnic values of their parental generation and the new and dynamic American cultural values. Rumbaut and Portes (2002) have conceptualized this as acculturative *dissonance*, defined as parent–child conflicts that arise when different cultural orientations clash. This is typically manifested when parents continue to adopt the cultural orientation of their native national or ethnic group while their children adopt values and goals connected more to the youth culture in the United States. In this fashion, high acculturation in adolescent youth may be linked to problems in parental control. For instance, in a recent study, Rumbaut and Portes (2002) found a high degree of dissonant acculturation and related lack of parental control in a Mexican immigrant sample. Similarly, Filmore (1991) found that immigrant parents reported difficulties in monitoring their children's behavior when children did not speak their parent's native language.

If high acculturative dissonance among children of immigrant families does, indeed, weaken parents' abilities to monitor their children's behavior, it is also likely to portend increased problem behavior, given the well-known link between family functioning and adolescent maladjustment. In general, studies have shown that family problems including lack of emotional closeness, lack of involvement, and low levels of parental monitoring predict violence, delinquency, and future criminal behavior (Dishion & Kavanaugh, 2003; Gorman-Smith, Tolan, & Henry, 2000; Hawkins, Laub, & Lauritsen, 1998; Lipsey & Derzon, 1998). Furthermore, there is some evidence that family factors may be especially important for ethnic minorities. For example, Smith and Krohn (1995) found that family variables accounted for about twice as much of the variance in delinquent outcomes for Latino adolescents as compared with their non-Hispanic White and African American counterparts.

In addition to the impact of acculturation on family functioning, it may also create a sense of injustice, particularly for children who did not experience the conditions of their parents' native country. Immigrant parents may have come to the United States short on money and skills but long on hopes for a better future. Rather than poverty and lack of opportunity, they see a wealth of options tied to their willingness to work hard and sacrifice. However, their children, who may have been born in the United States or immigrated at a young age, see oppression rather than opportunity as their parents struggle to make ends meet, particularly when their parents are members of a disadvantaged ethnic minority group. They see "White" society as taking advantage of their parents and consequently may feel further disenfranchised from conventional society. This disenfranchisement can lead to anger, frustration, and a search for like-minded youth to provide a collective refuge. In this fashion, the acculturative process can fuel the development of antisocial peer groups and youth gangs, both of which greatly increase risk for involvement in violence (Sanchez-Jankowski, 1991; Short, 1997).

Another issue related to acculturative stress involves the particular developmental demands that arise in adolescence. Concurrent with their attempts at acculturating successfully, adolescents are also faced with issues of separation, individuation, and identity that arise at this developmental stage (Baptiste, 1993). As discussed by French, Kim, and Pillado (chap. 2, this volume), adolescence marks a critical age in establishing a unique and autonomous self-identity. For an adolescent to successfully navigate this stage, he or she must integrate various identities and roles, for example, as a son or daughter, as a friend, as a student, and so on, despite the fact that these roles may seem to be incompatible. Successful integration leads to a cohesive sense of self versus a prolonged state of identity crisis and role confusion (Erikson, 1968).

This developmental task is equally relevant for immigrant adolescents, but it is somewhat more complicated. In addition to the various roles a native adolescent must integrate, immigrant and first-generation adolescents (and to a meaningful, but lesser extent, second-generation ethnic youth) must also cope with the often incompatible cultural roles they face. For example, adolescent youths immigrating from rural Mexico to Los Angeles, face the challenge of combining a traditional, collectivistic Mexican cultural outlook with the more individualistic, industrialized, rapid-paced cultural outlook of a metropolitan American city. Not only must they deal with forming a cohesive sense of self, but this must be done while dealing with the added complications of differing cultural senses of self and the acculturative stress this may entail.

BICULTURALISM AND ADJUSTMENT

As discussed earlier, the process of blending the native culture of one's family with the host culture of a new country can create difficulties on several levels. Regardless of the particular models of acculturation or mechanisms for characterizing this process, it is clear that adaptations must be made as "integration" into the new culture unfolds. Different models have also been offered to describe the resolution of this process. For example, LaFromboise, Coleman, and Gerton (1993) discussed five distinct models of biculturalism that have been used to describe this integration: *assimilation*, *acculturation*, *alternation*, *multicultural*, and *fusion* models.

Of greatest relevance to youth development and violence prevention, the alternation model highlights the importance of bicultural competence and its relation to adjustment. According to this model, an individual is able to gain competence within two cultures without having to choose between them. In this fashion, an individual can incorporate aspects of both their native and the majority culture, and choose the degree of affiliation with either culture. Bicultural youth are able to navigate through twin cultural *processes* (that of the native as well as that of the host culture) and to adopt and integrate cultural *values* from two cultural groups. In so doing, they are able to navigate and function within both their ethnic community milieu as well as that of the host culture, altering their behavior to fit the specific demands of a particular social context. The alternation model assumes that youth can have a sense of belonging linked to both cultures without compromising their own cultural identity.

This type of biculturalism implies that the ability to effectively switch between cultures will lessen an individual's anxiety and increase cognitive, behavioral, and psychological functioning (Rogler, Cortes, & Malgady, 1991). As LaFromboise et al. (1993) commented, "Research suggests that individuals living in two cultures may find the experience to be more beneficial than living a monocultural life-style. The key to psychological well-being may well be the ability to develop and maintain competence in both cultures" (p. 402). For adolescents, bicultural competence can increase their ability to negotiate a number of important contexts and relationships, serving as a buffer against problem behavior and violence. In particular, bicultural competence has been associated with academic success, lower acculturative dissonance, close family relationships, positive self-identity, and access to supportive social capital. Bicultural competence, therefore, may be termed *positive acculturation*.

For example, Bankston and Zhou (1995) found strong positive associations between factors that mark biculturalism, for example, the ability of a child to speak his or her parents' native language fluently and strong ethnic identification, and measures of academic success and motivation for adolescents of Asian ethnicity. Similarly, Bankston and Zhou (1997) have shown that Chinese and Indian American children are more likely to succeed academically and avoid delinquent outcomes when they can cultivate both an "American" identity around values and goals alongside of a deliberate cultivation of their own ethnic heritage. This effect is robust and remains even after other factors are controlled for, including socioeconomic status, length of U.S. residence, and hours spent on homework.

Studies have also linked biculturalism to improvements in parent–adolescent relationships. This effect may be associated, in part, with the different rates of acculturation between immigrant parents and their adolescent children. Studies have shown that immigrant children born elsewhere acculturate to the host, majority culture quite rapidly when compared with their immigrant parents (Buriel, Perez, De Ment, Chavez, & Moran, 1998). First-generation adolescents who have immigrant parents, but were themselves born in the United States, also exhibit more typically Western traits, attitudes, and characteristics. For example, first-generation Asian Americans tend to endorse more Western individualistic goals and aspirations than their immigrant parents. This has been reflected in measures that have found increasing "de-ethnicization" (i.e., drops in ethnic identity measures) across generations, which corresponds to increasing acculturation to the American society (Zhou & Gatewood, 2000).

Bicultural youth, by definition, may avoid much of this dissonance because of their dual frames of reference, allowing them to understand and appreciate both their parents' native culture as well as that of the majority culture. Although relatively few studies have investigated this possibility, evidence does appear to be supportive. For example, Hao and Bonstead-Burns (1998) proposed that a greater degree of acculturative consonance (the degree to which parents and adolescents can share their cultural values) predicts positive youth outcomes such as academic success. The authors posit that immigrant groups such as Asians and Cubans, who both actively learn English and adopt some aspects of American culture, but at the same time maintain their own language and customs, appear to exhibit more generational consonance versus Mexican immigrants who do not.

Thus, bicultural youth are more likely to agree with their parents' expectations and values, relative to highly acculturated youth. Otherwise stated, it is reasonable to believe that parents and adolescents who agree on a greater percentage of expressed expectations and goals will enjoy greater relationship harmony compared with those with lower agreement. Studies have supported this hypothesis. For instance, Hao and Bonstead-Burns (1998) found that Chinese and Korean immigrant adolescents agree with a greater percentage of parental expectations and goals, in comparison to Mexican immigrant adolescents. Chung (1998) found that differential rates of acculturation among Asian American families often leads to a clash of values, usually involving issues of adolescent autonomy and independence and marked by challenges to parental authority. Other studies have shown that both adolescents from immigrant families who are fluent in English but also manage to maintain fluency in their parents native language (a key marker of biculturalism) report better relationships with their parents, including greater relationship satisfaction, cohesion, parent–adolescent respect, and decreased intrafamilial conflict (Jackson, Bijstra, Oostra, & Bosma, 1998; Tseng & Fuligni, 2000; Yao, 1985). Bicultural youth also have access to the social capital of two cultural communities—that of the native culture as well as that of the majority culture. Social capital refers to social networks and relations that youth have access to outside of the immediate family. Social capital can involve something as simple as having a support group of friends, or it may involve institutional structures, such as community support groups, church and other religious groups, charity organizations, and after-school and job placement programs. In explaining the concept of *segmented assimilation*—the different prospects of acculturation paths faced by different ethnic groups—Bankston and Zhou (1997) noted how important social capital is for successful acculturation and economic adaptation, especially for new immigrants. For example, as they pointed out, Chinese ethnic enclaves are notably filled with such social support centers and provide recent immigrants with a convenient and effective means of overcoming the initial obstacles of living in a foreign country. Bicultural youth are able to access both ethnically centered social capital institutions, staffed by people who are from the same or similar native cultural background, as well as more widely available programs and services provided for all youth and families.

IMPLICATIONS FOR YOUTH VIOLENCE PREVENTION RESEARCH AND PRACTICE

To a certain extent, all ethnic youth must navigate distinct cultural realms derived from their native culture, mainstream culture, and minority culture. For immigrant youth, these distinctions are likely to be more obvious and salient. Still, they are important to consider when developing any type of youth prevention strategy that considers ethnicity and culture. Up to this point, we have reviewed the various mechanisms by which immigrant and minority status can contribute to either adjustment or problem behaviors in youth. We now turn to a discussion of possible intervention points that address factors most critical in violence risk and prevention.

We propose that the adjustment of youth from immigrant families (and the prevention of problem behaviors such as violence) can be facilitated by addressing three key factors. These are (a) fostering bicultural competence and bicultural efficacy; (b) building on cultural dimensions and beliefs that promote harmony and nonviolence; and (c) promoting intergroup understanding and positive attitudes toward other ethnic/cultural groups.

Bicultural Competence and Bicultural Efficacy

As we have discussed, bicultural competence implies an understanding of both one's native and host cultures, the ability to adopt and integrate values from both cultures, and the ability to effectively switch between cultures in response to specific contextual demands. Bicultural youth appear to do better on a number of personal and social adjustment indices when compared with youth who are monocultural, assimilated, or acculturated. Bicultural competence can also provide individuals with a broad knowledge of diverse cultures as well as the skills needed to select an optimal course of action. As youth become aware of the expectations within each culture, they learn about a wider range of acceptable behaviors and how best to navigate these multiple demands. Bicultural competence can also help shape a positive sense of identity as a member of a valued ethnic culture and also as a member of the mainstream culture. Negative messages from "White" culture can be counterbalanced by an appreciation and a celebration of the unique contributions of members of one's ethnic group and/or individuals from one's native country.

An important cognitive component of bicultural competence is bicultural efficacy. LaFromboise et al. (1993) defined bicultural efficacy as the "belief, or confidence, that one can live effectively, and in a satisfying manner, within two groups without compromising one's sense of cultural identity" (p. 404). In this fashion, bicultural efficacy should enhance an individuals' confidence that they can learn and sustain a bicultural orientation, develop effective support networks in both the ethnic and the majority culture, and persist in efforts to resolve competing demands as they unfold.

How can one encourage the development of bicultural competence and bicultural efficacy among ethnic and immigrant youth? One strategy is to actively encourage learning, opportunities, and experiences that cultivate knowledge and appreciation of ethnic culture in general, the specific ethnic culture(s) of participants, and skills in navigating ethnic and mainstream cultures. This conscious socialization process has been labeled *proactive socialization* (Hill, Soriano, Chen, & LaFromboise, 1994; Spencer, 1985). Studies have shown that families who practice proactive socialization, where children are taught directly about the richness of their ethnic heritage as well as the consequences of their ethnicity in mainstream society, have children who are more competent and well-adjusted (Bowman & Howard, 1985). Social institutions such as schools, clinics, neighborhood organizations, and volunteer groups can facilitate bicultural development by engaging in deliberate and active efforts to strengthen bicultural competence. This may be done as part of a general approach that highlights the contributions and strengths of one or more ethnic cultures. It also may be developed via specific training. For example, Szapocznik and colleagues provided bicultural effectiveness training to Cuban American families in conflict (Szapocznik, Santisteban, Kurtines, Perez-Vidal, & Hervis, 1984). They found that families who were able to develop a repertoire of bicultural social skills were less likely to report conflicts, and children were less likely to engage in problem behaviors such as drug use.

In addition to proactive socialization and direct intervention, bicultural competence is facilitated by the development of stable external support networks in both cultures. Individuals and families who can call on the resources of both their ethnic culture as well as the mainstream culture should be better able to manage the stress of acculturation. This cultural social capital can be enhanced by programs and policies that link immigrants and ethnic groups together (e.g., housing practices, cultural centers) as well as programs that increase access to mainstream services for immigrant families.

Cultural Support for Harmony and Nonviolence

Cultures vary on general dimensions (e.g., individualism vs. collectivism) as well as specific beliefs, values, and norms. In some cases, these variations fluctuate by factors such as region, neighborhood, income, generational status, subculture, or ethnic identification. Still, these cultural influences can work to encourage or discourage violence. For example, collectivist cultures place greater emphasis on group needs and group harmony as compared with individual needs. This emphasis has been associated with lower rates of interpersonal violence, and is likely to promote harmony rather than conflict. In contrast, the United States has been classified as an individualistic culture, with relatively high rates of interpersonal violence.

As such, strategies that build on the collectivistic values of ethnic and immigrant cultures should be helpful in preventing youth violence. In many of these cultures different core values can be identified that best reflect these dimensions. For Latinos, *simpatia* emphasizes the importance of avoiding interpersonal conflict in favor of harmony and deference to elders. Asian cultural codes emphasize connection to the sociocultural order that is sustained through harmonious social relations. Native American culture, although varied across tribal entities, frequently emphasizes harmony, respect, generosity, and community responsibility for individual problems. Traditional African American culture also emphasizes collective values such as harmony, interrelatedness, communalism, mutuality, and spirituality.

In some cases, these collectivistic values and associated norms can promote violence when they are tied to specific subcultures or groups of ethnic individuals bonded together against other groups. This bonding together within a smaller ethnic enclave, although perhaps adaptive in terms of access to resources and social capital, can also result in an extreme case of collective identity that is strengthened by competition with nonmembers. Consider the history of ethnic gangs in the United States—immigrant and ethnic youth often bound by ethnic and neighborhood identification and frequently engaged in intraethnic conflict based on distinctions such as country of origin, regions within an area, or even specific streets in a neighborhood (Sanchez-Jankowski, 1991). For this reason, it is important to simultaneously promote cultural beliefs and values within a group and to promote understanding of the cultural beliefs and values of other groups (Wessler, 2003).

Promoting Intergroup Understanding and Positive Attitudes

One of the risks of promoting awareness of an individual's ethnic culture is that the differences rather than the similarities across cultures may become more salient. Pride in one's ethnic group may generate disdain for other groups, particularly if those groups are perceived as somehow related to one's disadvantaged status. Arguably, ethnic minority and immigrant youth in the United States may hold negative attitudes toward the dominant White society resulting in anger, frustration, and lack of engagement in conventional (i.e., "White") opportunities. However, this in-group/out-group bias may also occur within any ethnic group where others are perceived as being responsible for their plight (e.g., see Parker & Tuthill's discussion of White violence in chap. 8, this volume). The history of war is often a history of ethnic, religious, or national conflict based on intergroup differences.

In this regard, bicultural (or multicultural) competence should be seen as a reciprocal process whereby individuals simultaneously learn about their own ethnic heritage and learn to appreciate the diverse ethnic heritage of others. This can be facilitated by educational interventions that teach youth about different cultures. It can also be facilitated via opportunities for contact with youth and adults from other cultures. Indeed, the length and time of contact individuals have with members of other cultural groups has a strong impact on their attitudes toward both their own and other cultures (Berry, 1984).

CONCLUSION

Attempts to understand ethnicity, culture, and youth violence and to develop appropriate prevention strategies and programs must consider the effect of immigration to the United States on large groups of minority youth and families. In addition to ethnic minority status, immigrant children often face additional roadblocks not encountered by their more acculturated or native peers. Prevention strategies that enhance bicultural competence, build on norms and beliefs promoting nonviolence, and promote intergroup acceptance are particularly important for immigrant youth. These strategies should be evaluated carefully in future research on youth violence prevention with ethnic and immigrant youth.

REFERENCES

Anderson, E. (1994). The code of the streets. *Atlantic Monthly*, 5, 81–94.

Anderson, E. (1999). *Streetwise: Race, class, and change in an urban community*. Chicago: University of Chicago Press.

Bankston, C. L., III, & Zhou, M. (1995). Effects of minority-language literacy on the academic achievement of Vietnamese youths in New Orleans. *Sociology of Education*, 68, 1–17.

Bankston, C. L., III, & Zhou, M. (1997). The social adjustment of Vietnamese–American adolescents: Evidence for a segmented-assimilation approach. *Social Science Quarterly*, 78, 508–523.

Baptiste, D. A. (1993). Immigrant families, adolescents and acculturation: Insights for therapists. *Marriage and Family Review*, 19, 341–363.

Berlin, A. R. (1987). An examination of the relationship among acculturation, school achievement, and family level of income with Hispanic students labeled behavior disordered. *Dissertation Abstracts International*, 47, 1539A.

Berry, J. W. (1984). Cultural relations in plural societies: Alternatives to segregation and their socio-psychological implications. In M. Brewer & N. Miller (Eds.), *Groups in contact* (pp. 11–27). New York: Academic Press.

Berry, J. W. (1994). Acculturative stress. In W. J. Lonner & R. S. Malpass (Eds.), *Psychology and culture* (pp. 211–215). Needham Heights, MA: Allyn & Bacon.

Berry, J. W. (1995). Psychology of acculturation. In N. Goldenberg & J. B. Veroff (Eds.), *The culture and psychology reader* (pp. 457–488). New York: New York University Press.

Bowman, P. J., & Howard, C. (1985). Race-related socialization, motivation, and academic achievement: A study of Black youths in three-generation families. *Journal of the American Academy of Child Psychiatry*, 24, 134–141.

Boykin, A. W. (1986). The triple quandary and the schooling of Afro American children. In U. Neisser (Ed.), *The school achievement of minority children* (pp. 57–92). Hillsdale, NJ: Erlbaum.

Boykin, A. W., & Toms, F. (1985). Black child socialization: A conceptual framework. In H. McAdoo & J. McAdoo (Eds.), *Black children* (pp. 33–51). Beverly Hills, CA: Sage.

Buriel, R., Calzada, S., & Vasquez, R. (1982). The relationship of the traditional Mexican American culture to adjustment and delinquency among three generations of Mexican American male adolescents. *Hispanic Journal of Behavioral Sciences*, 4, 41–55.

Buriel, R., Perez, W., De Ment, T. L., Chavez, D. V., & Moran, V. R. (1998). The relationship of language brokering to academic performance, biculturalism, and self-efficacy among Latino adolescents. *Hispanic Journal of Behavioral Sciences*, 20, 283–297.

Burnham, M. A., Hough, R. L., Karno, M., Escobar, J. I., & Telles, C. A. (1987). Acculturation and lifetime prevalence of psychiatric disorders among Mexican Americans in Los Angeles. *Journal of Health and Social Behavior, 28,* 89–102.

Caetano, R. (1987). Acculturation and drinking patterns among U.S. Hispanics. *British Journal of Addiction, 82,* 789–799.

Caetano, R., & Schafer, J. (2000). Intimate partner violence, acculturation and alcohol consumption among Hispanics couples in the U.S. *Journal of Interpersonal Violence, 15,* 30–46.

Campo-Flores, A. (2003, December 8). Gangland's new face. *Newsweek,* 41.

Champion, J. D. (1996). Woman abuse, assimilation, and self-concept in a rural Mexican American community. *Hispanic Journal of Behavioral Sciences, 18,* 508–521.

Chung, R. (1998, August). *Measuring intergenerational conflict in Asian American families: A report of the Intergenerational Conflict Inventory.* Paper presented at the 106th annual meeting of the American Psychological Association, San Francisco.

Cooper, C. R. (2003). Bridging multiple worlds: Immigrant youth identity and pathways to college. *International Society for the Study of Behavioural Development, 2,* 1–3.

Cunningham, N. (2000). A comprehensive approach to school–community violence prevention. *Professional School Counseling, 4,* 126–134.

Dion, K. K., & Dion, K. L. (1993). Individualistic and collectivistic perspectives on gender and cultural context of love and intimacy. *Journal of Social Issues, 49,* 53–69.

Dishion, T. J., & Kavanaugh, K. (2003). *Intervening in adolescent problem behavior: A family-centered approach.* New York: Guilford Press.

Erikson, E. (1968). *Identity, youth, and crisis.* New York: Norton.

Filmore, L. W. (1991). When learning a second language means losing the first. *Early Childhood Research Quarterly, 6,* 323–346.

Fix, M., & Passel, J. S. (1994). *Immigration and immigrants: Setting the record straight.* Washington, DC: Urban Institute.

Fix, M., & Passel, J. S. (2003). *U.S. immigration, trends and implications for schools.* Washington, DC: Urban Institute.

Franco, J. N., Malloy, T., & Gonzales, R. (1984). Ethnic and acculturation differences in self-disclosure. *Journal of Social Psychology, 122,* 21–32.

Fuligni, A. J. (1997). The academic achievement of adolescents from immigrant families: The role of family background, attitudes, and behavior. *Child Development, 68,* 261–273.

Gire, J. T., & Carment, D. W. (1992). Dealing with disputes: The influence of individualism–collectivism. *Journal of Social Psychology, 133,* 81–95.

Goodnow, J. J. (1997). Parenting and the "transmission" and "internalization" of values: From social–cultural perspectives to within-family analyses. In J. E.

Grusec & L. Kuczynski (Eds.), *Handbook of parenting and the transmission of values* (pp. 333–361). New York: Wiley.

Gorman-Smith, D., Tolan, P. H., & Henry, D. B. (2000). A developmental–ecological model of the relation of family functioning to patterns of delinquency. *Journal of Quantitative Criminology, 16,* 169–198.

Hao, L., & Bonstead-Burns, M. (1998). Parent–child difference in educational expectations and academic achievement of immigrant and native students. *Sociology of Education, 71,* 175–198.

Hartung, B. D. (1987). Acculturation and family variables in substance abuse: An investigation with Mexican American high school males. *Dissertation Abstracts International, 48,* 264–268.

Hawkins, D. F., Laub, J. H., & Lauritsen, J. L. (1998). Race, ethnicity and serious juvenile offending. In R. Loeber & D. P. Farrington (Eds.), *Serious and violent juvenile offenders: Risk factors and successful interventions* (pp. 30–46). Thousand Oaks, CA: Sage.

Hernandez, D. J. (2004). Demographic change and the life circumstances of immigrant families. *Children of immigrant families.* Retrieved March 30, 2005, from www.futureofchildren.org

Hill, H. M., Soriano, F. I., Chen, S. A., & LaFromboise, T. D. (1994). Sociocultural factors in the etiology and prevention of violence among ethnic minority youth. In L. Eron, J. Gentry, & R. Schlegel (Eds.), *Reason to hope: A psychological perspective on violence and youth* (pp. 59–97). Washington, DC: American Psychological Association.

Hoffmann, T., Dana, R. H., & Bolton, E. (1985). Measured acculturation and MMPI–168 performance of Native American adults. *Journal of Cross-Cultural Psychology 16,* 243–256.

Jackson, S., Bijstra, J., Oostra, L., & Bosma, H. (1998). Adolescents' perceptions of communication with parents relative to specific aspects of relationships with parents and personal development. *Journal of Adolescence, 3,* 305–322.

Kao, G., & Tienda, M. (1995). Optimism and achievement: The educational performance of immigrant youth. *Social Science Quarterly,* 1–19.

LaFromboise, T., Coleman, H. L. K., & Gerton, J. (1993). Psychological impact of biculturalism: Evidence and theory. *Psychological Bulletin, 114,* 395–412.

Lipsey, M. W., & Derzon, J. H. (1998). Predictors of violent and serious delinquency in adolescence and early adulthood: A synthesis of longitudinal research. In R. Loeber & D. Farrington (Eds.), *Serious and violent juvenile offenders: Risk factors and successful interventions* (pp. 86–105). Thousand Oaks, CA: Sage.

Lykken, D. T. (2000). Psychology and the criminal justice system: A reply to Hanney and Zimbardo. *General Psychologist, 35,* 11–15.

Marin, B. V., & Flores, E. (1994). Acculturation, sexual behavior, and alcohol use among Latinas. *International Journal of the Addictions, 29,* 1101–1114.

Markides, K., Krause, N., & Mendes-DeLeon, C. F. (1988). Acculturation and alcohol comsumption among Mexican Americans: A three-generation study. *American Journal of Public Health, 78,* 1178–1181.

Markus, H. R., & Kitayama, S. (1998). The cultural psychology of personality. *Journal of Cross-Cultural Psychology, 29,* 32–61.

Martin, P., & Midgley, E. (1994). Immigration to the U.S.: Journey to an uncertain destination. *Population Bulletin, 49,* 2–45.

Martinez, A. (1983). Acculturation, self-concept, anxiety, imagery and stress as related to disease in Mexican-Americans. *American Doctoral Dissertations, 159,* 1981–1982.

Masi, R. (1989). Multiculturalism, medicine, and health. Part IV: Individual considerations. *Canadian Family Physician, 35,* 69–73.

McDonnell, L. M., & Hill, P. T. (1993). *Newcomers in American schools: Meeting the educational needs of immigrant youth.* Santa Monica, CA: Rand.

McLoyd, V. C. (1998). Changing demographics in the American population: Implications for research on minority children and adolescents. In V. C. McLoyd & L. Steinberg (Eds.), *Studying minority adolescents* (pp. 3–28). Mahway, NJ: Erlbaum.

Mena, F. J., Padilla, A. M., & Maldonado, M. (1987). Acculturative stress and specific coping strategies among immigrants and later generation college students. *Hispanic Journal of Behavioral Sciences, 9,* 207–225.

Mitchell, M. C. (1980). *An application of attachment theory to a socio–cultural perspective of physical child abuse in the Mexican–American community.* Unpublished doctoral dissertation, University of California, Santa Barbara.

Moyerman, D. R., & Forman, B. D. (1992). Acculturation and adjustment: A meta-analytic study. *Hispanic Journal of Behavioral Sciences, 14,* 163–200.

Neff, J. A., Hoppe, S. K., & Perez, P. (1987). Acculturation and alcohol use: Drinking patterns and problems among Anglo and Mexican American male drinkers. *Hispanic Journal of Behavioral Sciences, 9,* 183–206.

Nightingale, D. S., & Fix, M. (2004). *Economic and labor market trends.* Retrieved March 30, 2005, from http://www.futureofchildren.org

Nwadiora, E., & McAdoo, H. (1996). Acculturative stress among Amerasian refugees: Gender and racial differences. *Adolescence, 31,* 477–487.

Office of the Surgeon General. (2001). *Report of the Surgeon General on youth violence.* Washington, DC: U.S. Department of Health and Human Services.

Ohbuchi, K., Fukushima, O., & Tedeschi, J. T. (1999). Cultural values in conflict management: Goal orientation, goal attainment, and tactical decision. *Journal of Cross-Cultural Psychology, 30,* 51–71.

Padilla, A. M. (1995). *Hispanic psychology: Critical issues in theory and research.* Thousand Oaks, CA: Sage.

Padilla, A. M., Wagatsuma, Y., & Lindholm, K. J. (1985). Acculturation and personality as predictors of stress in Japanese and Japanese–Americans. *Journal of Social Psychology, 125,* 295–305.

Pelto, P. J. (1968) The differences between "tight" and "loose" societies. *Transaction, 5,* 37–40.

Pomales, J. (1987). The effects of level of acculturation on Hispanic students' perceptions of counselor, willingness to self-disclose, and preference for counseling style. *Dissertation Abstracts International, 47,* 2461-A.

Price, C. S., & Cuellar, I. (1981). Effects of language and related variables on the expression of pathology in Mexican American psychiatric patients. *Hispanic Journal of Behavioral Sciences, 3,* 145–160.

Rodriguez, L. J. (1996). *East side stories: Gang life in East LA.* New York: Power House.

Rogler, L. H., Cortes, D. E., & Malgady, R. G. (1991). Acculturation and mental health status among Hispanics. *American Psychologist, 46,* 585–597.

Rumbaut, R. G. (1994). The crucible within: Ethnic identity, self-esteem, and segmented assimilation among children of immigrants. *International Migration Review, 28,* 748–794.

Rumbaut, R. G., & Portes, A. (2002). *Ethnicities: Coming of age in immigrant America.* Berkeley: University of California Press.

Sanchez-Burks, J., Nisbett, R. E., & Ybarra, O. (2000). Cultural styles, relationship schemas, and prejudice against outgroups. *Journal of Personality and Social Psychology, 79,* 174–189.

Sanchez-Jankowski, M. S. (1991). *Islands in the street: Gangs and American urban society.* Berkeley: University of California Press.

Segall, M. H., Dasen, P. R., Berry, J. W., & Poortinga, Y. H. (1999). *Human behavior in global perspective.* Boston: Allyn & Bacon.

Short, J. F. (1997). *Poverty, ethnicity, and violent crime.* Boulder, CO: Westview Press.

Singelis, T. M. (1994). The measurement of independent and interdependent self-construals. *Personality and Social Psychology Bulletin, 20,* 580–591.

Smith, C., & Krohn, M. D. (1995). Delinquency and family life among male adolescents: The role of ethnicity. *Journal of Youth and Adolescence, 24,* 69–93.

Sommers, I., Fagan, J., & Baskin, D. (1993). Sociocultural influences on the explanation of delinquency for Puerto Rican youths. *Hispanic Journal of Behavioral Sciences, 15,* 36–62.

Sorenson, S. B., & Telles, C. A. (1991). Self reports of spousal violence in a Mexican American and non-Hispanic White population. *Violence and Victims, 6,* 3–15.

Soriano, F. I. (1995). *Conducting needs assessments: A multidisciplinary approach.* Newbury Park, CA: Sage.

Soriano, F. I., Rivera, L. M., Williams, K. J., Daley, S. P., & Reznik, V. M. (2004). Navigating between cultures: The role of culture in youth violence. *Journal of Adolescent Health, 34,* 169–176.

Spencer, M. B. (1985). Black children's race awareness, racial attitudes, and self-concept: A reinterpretation. *Annual Progress in Child Psychiatry and Child Development,* 616–630.

Steinberg, L. (1996). *Beyond the classroom.* New York: Simon & Schuster.

Suarez-Orozco, C., & Suarez-Orozco, M. (1995). *Transformations: Migration, family life, and achievement motivation among Latino adolescents*. Stanford, CA: Stanford University Press.

Szapocznik, J., Santisteban, D., Kurtines, W., Perez-Vidal, A., & Hervis, O. (1984). Bicultural effectiveness training: A treatment intervention for enhancing intercultural adjustment in Cuban–American families. *Hispanic Journal of Behavioral Sciences, 6*, 317–344.

Takanashi, R. (2004). *Leveling the playing field: Supporting immigrant children from birth to eight*. Retrieved March 30, 2005, from http://www.futureofchildren.org

Thoman, L. V., & Suris, A. (2004). Acculturation and acculturative stress as predictors of psychological distress and quality-of-life functioning in Hispanic psychiatric patients. *Hispanic Journal of Behavioral Sciences, 26*, 293–311.

Ting-Toomey, S. (1985). Toward a theory of conflict and culture. In W. Gudykunst & L. S. Ting-Toomey (Eds.), *Communication, culture and organizational processes* (pp. 71–86). Beverly Hills, CA: Sage.

Triandis, H. C. (1994). *Culture and social behavior*. New York: McGraw-Hill.

Triandis, H. C. (1995). *Individualism and collectivism*. Boulder, CO: Westview Press.

Triandis, H. C. (1996). The psychological measurement of cultural syndromes. *American Psychologist, 51*, 407–415.

Triandis, H. C. (2000). Culture and conflict. *International Journal of Psychology, 55*, 145–152.

Triandis, H. C., Leung, K., Villareal, M. J., & Clack, F. L. (1985). Allocentric versus idiocentric tendencies: Convergent and discriminant validation. *Journal of Research in Personality, 19*, 395–415.

Tseng, V., & Fuligni, A. J. (2000). Parent–adolescent language use and relationships among immigrant families with East Asian, Filipino and Latin American backgrounds. *Journal of Marriage and the Family, 62*, 465–476.

U.S. Census Bureau. (1997). *Current population reports: The foreign-born population: 1996*. Washington, DC: U.S. Government Printing Office.

U.S. Census Bureau. (2004). *Statistical abstract of the United States: 2003*. Washington, DC: U.S. Government Printing Office.

Vega, W. A., & Gill, A. G. (in press). Acculturative stress and drug use behavior among immigrant and U.S.-born Latino adolescents: Toward an integrated model. In M. R. De La Rosa & R. Lopez (Eds.), *Conducting drug abuse research with minority populations*.

Wessler, S. (2003). *The respectful school: How educators and students can conquer hate and harassment*. Baltimore: Association for Supervision and Curriculum Development.

White Paper on Crime. (1998). Tokyo: National Police Agency, Ministry of Justice.

Wong, S. (1997). Delinquency of Chinese Canadian youth. *Youth and Society, 29*, 112–133.

Xenocostas, S. (1991). Familial obligation: Ideal models of behaviour for second generation Greek youth in Montreal. In S. P. Sharma, A. M. Ervin, &

D. Meintel (Eds.), *Immigrants and refugees in Canada* (pp. 294–315). Saskatoon, Canada: University of Saskatchewan.

Yao, E. L. (1985). Adjustment needs of Asian immigrant children in the schools. *Elementary School Guidance and Counseling, 19,* 222–227.

Zhou, M. (2003). Urban education: Challenges in educating culturally diverse children. *Teachers College Record, 105,* 208–255.

Zhou, M., & Gatewood, J. V. (2000). Mapping the terrain: Asian American diversity and the challenges of the twenty-first century. *Asian American Policy Review, 9,* 2–29.

II

YOUTH VIOLENCE AND PREVENTION IN SPECIFIC ETHNIC GROUPS

4

YOUTH VIOLENCE PREVENTION AMONG LATINO YOUTH

BRENDA MIRABAL-COLÓN AND CARMEN NOEMÍ VÉLEZ

Youth violence is a significant public health problem that affects all ethnic groups in the United States and worldwide. Indeed, the World Health Organization has estimated that more than 40 million children and youth are victims of violence in the world (Concha-Eastman & Villaveces, 2001). In the United States, youth violence tends to be more prevalent among families that experience greater levels of economic disadvantage, fewer opportunities, scarce resources, and a host of related stressors. As discussed in other chapters in this volume, these conditions and associated higher rates of youth violence disproportionately affect members of traditionally underrepresented and underserved ethnic minority groups, including Latinos, Asian Pacific Islanders, American Indians, and African Americans.

According to the U.S. Census Bureau, the percentages of these traditionally underrepresented minority group members have changed radically (U.S. Census Bureau, 2000b). Indeed, minorities represent the fastest growing segment of the population. For instance, it is estimated that by the year 2020, 40% of all children in the United States will be African American or Latino. Projected increases are greatest for Latinos; as McLoyd (1999) noted, between 2000 and 2010 the Latino population is expected to increase by 42%. This is driven, in part, by higher immigration and higher fertility rates, compared with native-born Americans (Martin & Midgley, 1994). Given this rapid increase in population, it is imperative to focus attention on the types of problems these youth and their families are likely to confront, as well as the types of solutions that are most likely to succeed.

This chapter will focus on the problem of violence among Latino youth in the United States. To understand violence in this population it is important to have an understanding of the various groups encompassed by the term *Latino* as well as the sociodemographics of this group in the United States. For this reason, we begin by clarifying the meaning of the term, followed by a description of relevant demographic information. Next, we present youth homicide rates, intentional injuries, official crime statistics, and national youth surveys to illustrate the magnitude of the problem among Latino youth. Finally, we provide a brief review of risk and protective factors and their relevance to Latino youth and discuss effective youth violence prevention strategies and initiatives.

SOCIODEMOGRAPHICS

In this chapter (and in the introduction, this volume) we use the terms *Latino* and *Hispanic* interchangeably to refer to a broadly defined population that includes different ethnic groups who share a common language, Spanish, but represent distinct cultures. This usage is consistent with the U.S. Census Bureau category of *Hispanic/Latino* (U.S. Census Bureau, 2000b). It reflects terms that are generally used across a wide range of settings. (For example, we report survey data using the specific nomenclature of the survey, i.e., Hispanic or Latino.) However, it is important to note that an individual's choice of designation can depend on many factors, including where a person is from, generation, identity, and political beliefs. These and other terms do have precise meanings.

For instance, *Hispanic* is most frequently used collectively to refer to all Spanish speakers. It connotes a lineage or cultural heritage related to Spain. Yet, millions of Spanish-speakers are not of true Spanish descent, or do not live in Latin America, or do not claim Spanish heritage. The term *Latino* is used to refer to people from or claiming heritage from Latin America. This is actually a superset of nationalities. The term "Latin" comes into use because individuals from Latin America speak one of the Romance languages (and so Brazilians technically could be included). Even more broadly, the term *Spanish people* is frequently used in the United States to refer to anyone who speaks Spanish. It is really a proper name for people of Spain, and is somewhat imprecise to denote a shared heritage.

Additional refinements based on country of origin and ethnic identity are also commonly used. This is most obvious among Mexican immigrants.

For instance, *Mexican* refers only to individuals who claim nationality as inhabitants of Mexico. This is an appropriate term for Mexican citizens who visit or work in the United States, but it is not appropriate for those who were born in the United States or are naturalized citizens who are of Mexican ancestry. *Mexican American* is commonly used to refer to U.S. citizens who are descendants of Mexicans. However, this term is often not acceptable for those who identify with a Spanish rather than a Mexican heritage or for those who do not view themselves as Americans by choice. Furthermore, many individuals of Mexican extraction view themselves as temporarily displaced from Mexico by economic circumstances, maintain strong family ties in Mexico, and plan to return as soon as they can become economically secure. Finally, a relatively recent term that has been used to refer to individuals of Mexican descent is *Chicano*. This term became popular during the 1960s and 1970s in the U.S. Southwest and represented a type of social and political activism. It has now become quite common, particularly among those who are searching for a new ethnic and cultural identity that embraces social empowerment and ethnic pride.

These distinctions are also important because they speak to the diversity within the larger group of individuals classified as Hispanic or Latino. Looking at this combined group, we see that they are, indeed, the largest ethnic minority group in the United States, with about 37 million people (Miller, 2003). Recent data show that approximately 39% of the Latino population is foreign-born. For this reason, as discussed by Boutakidis, Guerra, and Soriano (chap. 3, this volume), considerations of immigration and its effects on development and behavior of youth are particularly important for Latinos. Latinos are also a diverse group in terms of countries represented. Mexicans are by far the largest group of Latinos (58%), followed by Puerto Ricans (9%) and Cubans (3.5%). The other Hispanic/Latino category (28%) measured in the 2000 census included Dominicans (2%), Central Americans (5%), and South Americans (4%; Therrien & Ramirez, 2000). *Latino* is also an ethnic designation based on heritage and not race. This has created some confusion because Latinos can be of any race, although they are predominantly Caucasian/White. Indeed, a large number of Latinos do not consider themselves either White or Black when asked to designate their race (Grieco & Cassidy, 2001).[1]

Different Latino groups also reside in different geographic areas of the continental United States Mexicans are located mainly in the West and

---

[1] In this chapter, we use the term *White* to refer to anyone who is not an individual of color rather than as a racial designation. This would include non-Hispanic Whites and European Americans. We also use the terms *African American* and *Black* interchangeably as an ethnic category to refer to individuals bound by perceived physiology as well as by shared experiences, beliefs, and values.

Southwest, Cubans mainly reside in the Southeast (Florida), and Puerto Ricans are located mostly in the East Coast. An additional 3.8 million Puerto Ricans reside in Puerto Rico. Latinos are also a relatively young population, with approximately one third of the population under the age of 18. However, the age distribution of the Latino population also varies by country of heritage. For instance, Mexicans have the youngest population of all the Latino groups, with 42% being 19 years or younger. Cubans tend to be somewhat older; only 20% are less than 19 years old (U.S. Census Bureau, 2000b).

As mentioned previously, Latino youth confront significant roadblocks in the United States related to economic and educational opportunities. Approximately 25% of Latinos live below the poverty line, compared with only 8% of Whites. This is even more acute in Puerto Rico, where more than 45% of the families live below the poverty level. The per capita income on the island was $8,185 in 1999; the median household income was $14,412 and the median family income was $16,543, only one third of the United States median income (U.S. Census Bureau, 2000a). Data on income earned from full-time employment in the United States shows that income levels are significantly lower among Latinos; 44% of Latinos report incomes of less than $20,000 compared with 19% of Whites. Education data also reveal lower rates of high school completion; almost half of Latinos (43%) have not completed high school compared with 12% of Whites (U.S. Census Bureau, 2000b).

CRIME AND VIOLENCE AMONG LATINOS

We consider data on crime and violence from two main sources in the general population—official statistics and sample surveys. Each source has its limitations. Official statistics only reflect crimes that result in arrests. These can be biased for several reasons: (a) different ethnic groups may vary in their police reporting behavior; (b) types of crimes committed by different groups may have a different likelihood of resulting in arrest; and (c) the arrest rates may vary by the ethnicity of the offender (Hawkins, Laub, Lauritsen, & Cothern, 2000). Furthermore, the rates generated by official statistics are incident-based as opposed to person-based. As noted in the recent report by the surgeon general, this means that official statistics cannot identify how many individuals commit crimes or how many crimes are committed (Office of the Surgeon General, 2001). On the other hand, surveys are often not able to capture meaningful ethnic differences. They are often limited to a specific region of the country, or when they are national, fail to capture regional, generational, and other intra-ethnic distinctions among Latino groups.

The problem with official criminal statistics is compounded for Latinos. Important databases and reports simply do not include the Latino or Hispanic category; they only identify Black and White and sometimes the category "other." This is evident in some sections of the U.S. Department of Justice (DOJ) *Sourcebook*, a publication that includes important data sets for the analysis of crime and criminal justice statistics. For instance, two important chapters in this book, "Nature and Distribution of Known Offenses" and "Characteristics and Distribution of Persons Arrested" do not present data for Latinos. Another report, the 1999 *National Report Series (Juvenile Justice Bulletin)* that focused on minority youth also included few tables with Latinos as a category for analysis (DOJ, 1999).

Official Crime Statistics: Homicide

Homicide is a common indicator of fatal injuries caused by interpersonal violence. The World Health Organization (WHO) estimates there were 520,000 global deaths because of homicides in the year 2000—a total homicide rate of 8.8 per 100,000 (World Health Organization [WHO], 2002). Gender is a major risk factor for homicide victims. In 2000, 77% of homicide victims in the world were males. Furthermore, males 15 to 29 years of age had the highest homicide rate, reaching 19.4 per 100,000.

Every day, 565 youth (10- to 29-years-old) are victims of homicide worldwide. In 2000 the rate of homicides was twice as high in the low/middle income countries (32.1 per 100,000) as in high-income ones (14.4 per 100,000; WHO, 2002). Among the countries that report to the World Health Organization, the highest rates are in Latin America (Colombia and El Salvador), the Caribbean (Puerto Rico), the Russian Federation, and some countries in southeast Europe. In Latin America and the Caribbean, high levels of poverty and inequality are among the most intractable problems that contribute to social and domestic violence (Buvinic, Morrison, & Shifter, 1999). The western European countries and Asia have the lowest homicide rates (WHO, 2002).

The United States has the highest homicide rate of all developed countries, even in light of recent decreases (Concha-Eastman & Villaveces, 2001). In 2002, there were 17,638 homicide deaths in the United States, an age-adjusted death rate of 6.1 per 100,000. Moreover, approximately one third of murder victims and almost half the offenders are under the age of 25 (U.S. DOJ, 2005b). Overall, homicides constitute the second cause of death in youth 15 to 24 years of age in the United States and the third cause of death from 25 to 34 years (Centers for Disease Control and

Prevention [CDC], 2005). Male youth have three times the risk of females of being victims of homicide (U.S. DOJ, 2005b).

However, homicide rates vary greatly according to ethnicity. In the 15-to-24 age group, homicide is the leading cause of death for African Americans and the second leading cause of death for Latinos (Anderson & Smith, 2003). These minorities are also at highest risk of victimization; they have 10 and 4 times, respectively, the risk of being murdered than their White peers (U.S. DOJ, 2005b). The homicide rate is highest in the 18- to 24-year-old age group, at 17.2 per 100,000 (U.S. DOJ, 2005a, 2005b). In 2002, 5,435 people from 10 to 24 years of age were murdered—51 less than in 2001 (CDC, 2005). In the United States, firearms are an important factor in youth homicides. More than 80% of youth homicides in the 15- to 19-year-old group have been related to firearms since 1989 (Dahlberg & Potter, 2001). In 2002, 82% of homicide victims ages 10 to 24 were killed with firearms, an increase from 79% in 2001 (CDC, 2005).

A total of 790 murders were reported in Puerto Rico during 2004, approximately two murders per day (Rosa, 2005). There were more murders in Puerto Rico that year than in New York City (571), Los Angeles (511), and Chicago (445; Rosa, 2005). Puerto Rico has a rate of 20.1 murders (homicides and nonnegligent manslaughter) per 100,000 residents. When it is grouped with all 50 states and the District of Columbia, Puerto Rico ranks second in most murders per capita (Federal Bureau of Investigation, 2004). The District is ranked number one, but its rates may be slightly elevated because of the urban density of the geographical area measured. Of the 774 homicides that occurred in Puerto Rico in 2002, 87% were a result of death by firearm. More than 60% of the homicides in Puerto Rico are related to illegal drug trafficking (Rosa, 2005).

Homicides are currently the leading cause of death for Puerto Rican youth 15 to 24 years of age, with a rate of 47.2 per 100,000 in 2002 (Puerto Rico Health Department, 2004). During the same year, the homicide rate for males 20 to 24 years old, in Puerto Rico reached 130 per 100,000, four times the rate of their Latino peers, and comparable to their African American cohort in the mainland (Puerto Rico Health Department, 2004).

Fatal and Nonfatal Injuries

Another important indicator of violence is the report of violence-related deaths and injuries. A recent report on fatal and nonfatal firearm-related injuries (1993–1998) includes the category of Hispanics in most of its tables (Gotsch, Annest, Mercy, & Ryan, 2001). The nonfatal injuries data in the report comes from the National Electronic Injury Surveillance System and the data on deaths comes from the Center for Disease Control National Vital Statistics System. The estimates for nonfatal injuries are based on patients in a national and representative sample of emergency departments in hospitals. In the analysis of this data set White Hispanics were classified as Hispanics and Black Hispanics were classified as Black. For the fatal injuries analysis, Black Hispanics were also classified as Blacks. This represented 0.2% (n = 462) of all deaths studied and 3.7% of all Hispanic deaths in the sample.

In the 6-year period studied (1993–1998), an estimated average of 115,000 firearm injuries occurred, including 79,000 nonfatal and 35,000 fatal injuries. This data set, however, does not include Puerto Rico. The analysis showed the rates per 100,000 firearm-related injuries (fatal and nonfatal) were highest among the young and among Black males (53.6%). In general, rates for Hispanics (25.6%) were lower than among Blacks (53.6%) but higher than for Whites (18.4%). The latter is particularly interesting in view of the fact that according to the *National Survey on Private Ownership and Use of Firearms*, Hispanics are less likely (11%) than Whites (27%) and Blacks (16%) to own guns (Cook & Ludwig, 1997). Because the study used telephone interviews in a probability sample of adults (18 or older) fluent in English or Spanish, it is conceivable that its estimates are somewhat biased because minorities, especially Latinos, may be less likely to have telephones (Aquilino, 1992; Federal Communications Commission, 2000; McAuliffe, Labrie, Woodworth, & Zhang, 2002).

The National Trauma Data Bank (NTDB) also collects information concerning injuries attributable to violence. The American College of Surgeons established the database as a repository of trauma data—coded using the International Classification of Diseases—to be used by hospitals, health planners, and government agencies. The 2004 *National Trauma Data Bank Report* includes data from 405 trauma programs in the United States. A total of 633,435 patients were reported to the NTDB from 1993 to 2003; 164,353 (26%) were 10 to 24 years of age. In this report, 12% of the total hospital days were because of intentional injuries (gunshot wounds, stab wounds, and fights). Firearm injuries, which peak at 19 years of age, are the second cause of death and are associated with 16.5% of deaths (American College of Surgeons, 2004). The data bank collects valuable descriptive information about intentional and unintentional injuries. The report, however, does not include ethnicity as a variable, limiting its interpretation and use.

The Puerto Rico Trauma Center is the only trauma center on the island; it provides services to victims of moderate to severe intentional and unintentional injuries. The Puerto Rico Trauma Center Registry, opened in April 2000, collects data on all trauma admissions and reports to the National Trauma Data Bank. In 2004, 106 youth from 10 to 24 years of age were registered with intentional injuries. Of these, 79% were caused by firearms and 21% were stab wounds. All intentional firearm injury victims and 96% of those with stab wounds were males (Puerto Rico Trauma Registry, 2005).

Latinos and the Criminal Justice System

Another important issue is the treatment of Latino youth in the criminal justice system. Latino youth are six times more likely than White youth to be found unfit for juvenile court and transferred to adult court in Los Angeles County, according to a study published in 2000 by Building Blocks for Youth, a multiyear initiative funded by Office of Juvenile Justice Delinquency Prevention (OJJDP) to promote effective juvenile justice policies (Males & Macallair, 2000). The study found that racial disparities accumulate as the youth moves into the adult system. Compared to their proportion of the population and of juvenile offenders, minority youth are overrepresented at all stages of the juvenile justice system. Compared with White youth, minority youth are approximately three times as likely to be arrested for a violent crime, six times as likely to wind up in adult court, and seven times as likely to be sent to prison by adult courts (Males & Macallair, 2000). When White and minority youth were charged with the same offenses, minority youth with no previous admissions were six times more likely to be incarcerated in public facilities than White youth. Meanwhile, Latino youth were three times more likely than White youth to be incarcerated (Poe-Yamagata & Jones, 2000).

In 2000, Latinos represented 13% of the U.S. population but accounted for 31% of those incarcerated in the federal criminal justice system, according to *Lost Opportunities*, a report coauthored by the National Council of La Raza, the Center for Youth Policy Research, and Michigan State University's Office of University Outreach & Engagement (Senger, 2004). The study found that Latinos are more likely to be incarcerated than Whites charged with the same offenses. It also reported that Latinos were disproportionately charged with nonviolent, low-level drug offenses, were arrested by the Drug Enforcement Agency in 2001 at a rate almost three times their proportion in the general population, and accounted for nearly half (43%) of the individuals convicted of drug offenses in 2000.

Survey Data

There are a few surveys collecting data on violence among youth that also include the category of Latino or Hispanic in their data collection instruments; these include the CDC's Youth Risk Behavior Surveillance System (YRBSS; CDC, 2002); Substance Abuse and Mental Health Services Administration's (SAMSHA) National Household Drug Use Survey (NHDS; Office of Applied Studies, 1998, 1999, 2000, 2001); the DOJ's

National Crime Victimization and its the School Crime Supplement Survey (SCSS; Rennison, 2002); and the National Longitudinal Study of Adolescent Health (NLSAH; Carolina Population Center, 2002). Another important ongoing survey, Monitoring the Future, does not identify Hispanics in the survey (Johnston, Bachman, O'Malley, & Schulenberg, 2004).

The YRBSS is a national school-based survey conducted by the CDC. It monitors several health-risk behaviors among youth including behaviors that contribute to unintentional injuries and violence. The YRBSS collects national, state, territorial, and local school-based data on students in grades 9 to 12. A self-administered questionnaire is completed by students ages 12 to 18 years during a regular class period (CDC, 2002). Data are presented for Hispanics, Blacks, and Whites in the continental United States and for Puerto Rican youth surveyed on the island. In the United States overall, physical fighting has declined significantly in all ethnic groups, from 42.5% in 1991 to 33.0% in 2003. Physical fighting has also declined significantly among all subgroups except 11th-grade students, where it has remained level since 1999 to 2003. Physical fighting on school property also declined significantly, from 16.2% in 1993 to 12.8% in 2003 (Brener, Lowry, & Barrios, 2004). Even though 17.1% of students reported they had carried a weapon during the month preceding the 2003 survey, carrying a weapon on school property has also declined significantly, from 11.8% in 1993 to 6.1% in 2003, including Hispanics. No significant changes were detected, however, in the prevalence of being threatened or injured with a weapon on school property during 1993–2003 (CDC, 2004b).

Carrying a handgun is an infrequent behavior among all ethnic groups studied. Vélez (2003) has documented a similar pattern among Puerto Rican students surveyed on the island. Nationwide, 6.1% of students had carried a gun during the month preceding the 2003 YRBSS survey (CDC, 2004b). Not going to school because of safety concerns increased significantly, from 4.4% in 1993 to 5.4% in 2003. No significant changes were detected during 1993 to 2003 among male, Black, Hispanic, 9th-, 10th-, and 12th-grade students (CDC, 2004b).

In Puerto Rico, the Center for Hispanic Youth Violence Prevention, which was established in 2000 as 1 of 10 Academic Centers of Excellence funded by the CDC (Mirabal-Colón, 2003), conducted a self-administered middle school survey in 2002 to determine violence prevalence and identify risk and protective factors. A total of 260 students participated. The survey revealed a relatively low prevalence of fighting on school property (5%). However, 9% of students reported carrying a razor to school (the weapon most commonly reported), and 7% reported carrying a gun on school property. Safety concerns were significant. Almost one of every four students (23%) reported feeling unsafe at school or on the way to and from school compared with 5.4% of students in the United States (CDC, 2004b).

In contrast to the YRBSS, the NHDS is a household survey whose target is the civilian, noninstitutionalized population aged 12 or older. It is designed to produce drug and alcohol use incidence and prevalence estimates and reports the consequences and patterns of use and abuse. In addition, since 1998 it included various items about violent behavior in its questionnaire. Looking at prevalence of serious fighting for Blacks, Whites, and Latino youth between the ages of 12 and 17 from 1998 to 2001, between one-fourth and one-fifth of the students in each ethnic group reported engaging at least once in this behavior during the year before the survey. Attacking someone with the intent to seriously hurt him or her was a less frequent behavior. Between 6% and 12% of the students in each ethnic group reported this behavior in each survey.

Data from the NHDS looking at neighborhood violence and related perceptions also demonstrate marked ethnic differences. For example, between 1998 and 2000, approximately 25% of Latino youth reported that there was a lot of crime in their neighborhood. This is considerably higher than reports of White youth (about 15%) but lower than reports of Black students (about 37%). Finally, the National Longitudinal Study of Adolescent Health, wave 1, of the Carolina Population Center at the University of North Carolina at Chapel Hill, also revealed important information regarding safety issues in adolescents from 11 to 21 years of age. In this survey, 33% of all adolescents who reported they were almost certain to be killed by age 21 were Hispanic, even though only 12.2% of the total respondents were Hispanic (Carolina Population Center, 2002).

CRIMINAL VICTIMIZATION

The National Crime Victimization Survey is one of the largest continuous household surveys conducted by the federal government. In the survey, people who identify themselves as from any Spanish Origin are defined as Hispanic (Bureau of Justice [BOJ], 2002). In 2002, the BOJ reported that for the period 1993–2000, the most likely victims of violent crimes were males, juveniles between 12 and 17 years of age, those of lower income (under $7,500), and those who had never married. The most prevalent form of crime reported was simple assault (59%), followed by robbery (20%) and aggravated assault (19%). In all ethnic groups surveyed, the youngest respondents reported the highest rates of victimization. For all ethnic groups surveyed, the rates of victimization decreased with age.

For all ages, the victimization rates for Latinos were lower than that of Blacks and Whites. It should be mentioned, however, that for the period between 1993 and 1999, the rate of homicides per 100,000 for Latinos (12.6) was higher than the national rate (8.9%; Rennison, 2002). Latinos were more likely to be victimized by a stranger (52%) than were all other ethnic groups (except Asian). The study also found that, in general, Latinos are as likely as other ethnic groups to report violence to police. In addition, the age distribution of victims that report violence to the police showed that youth ages 12 to 17 are less likely (29%) to report crimes than any other age group.

The National Crime Victimization Survey collects data on middle and high school students as well. Between 1994 and 1999, the *DOJ Sourcebook of Criminal Justice* reported the data on nonfatal violent crimes against young adolescents (students ages 12 to 18) occurring either at school or going or coming from school. The data show a significant reduction across the 5-year period. In 1994, the majority of Latino students surveyed (64%) reported a violent crime against them, and in 1999 only about one fifth of the Latino students reported this event. A similar reduction in violent crime against the students was observed in all ethnic groups studied (Pastore & Maguire, 2002).

The most frequently reported hate-related behavior toward school children (ages 12 to 18) is hate-related graffiti. Slightly more than one third of the students (Latinos, Whites, and Blacks) report seeing it at school. In addition, between 12% and 16% of the groups studied reported being the target of hate-related words. More Latino students reported street gangs present at school (28%) than Blacks (25%) and Whites (13%). According to the survey, the estimated annual rates (per 1,000) of violent victimization among the different ethnic groups of students (12 to 17 years) surveyed between 1993 and 2000 were similar—Black (99.9), White (98), and Hispanic (90.1). These rates are the largest of any other age group surveyed. In 1999, more Black and Hispanic students reported fear of being attacked at school (9% and 8.1% respectively) than did White students (3.9%). These proportions are lower for all three ethnic groups than those reported in 1995 (13.5%, 15.5%, and 6.3% respectively).

Taken together, the results from these multiple sources suggest that youth violence is a significant problem among Latino youth, although in recent years it has decreased in some areas and for some behaviors. Although it does not appear to be as prevalent as among African American youth, rates typically are consistently higher than for White youth. Furthermore, the problem seems to be more acute among males. Still, lack of consistent data for Latinos and lack of attention to intraethnic variations limits our ability to link these data to differential patterns of risk. Indeed, as we discuss in the next section, much of what we know about risk and protective factors for youth violence has been extrapolated from the general literature and has not been specifically focused on Latino populations. However, there have also been recent efforts to examine specifically aspects of Latino culture that may increase or decrease risk as well as portend viable targets for prevention and intervention.

RISK AND PROTECTIVE FACTORS

As discussed in chapters 1 through 3 of this volume, many risk and protective factors for violence affect all youth (e.g., biological, psychological, behavioral, and developmental and community social factors). However, the likelihood of these risk factors being present or developing is greater for ethnic minority youth, including Latino youth, because of the multiplicity of socioeconomic, educational, and environmental disparities they face.

Overall, studies that have included a significant number of Latino youth or focused specifically on Latino youth have reported similar findings on specific risk and protective factors. For example, Reyes (2003) analyzed the results of "Consulta Juvenil," a questionnaire survey of a representative sample of public and private elementary, middle, and high school students in Puerto Rico, conducted to determine the prevalence of drug use, violence, and risk and protective factors. He studied the sample of middle and high school students surveyed during the second semester of 2000–2001 to determine the prevalence of violence and identify risk and protective factors. He identified several individual risk factors, including male gender, early antisocial behavior, and illicit drug use such as Ecstasy/MDMA. Antisocial behavior/attitudes of the parents were a significant risk factor, as well as association with antisocial peers. The only protective factor identified in this survey was active participation in family activities (Reyes, 2003).

Other studies that have examined Latino youth outside of the United States have also demonstrated a similar pattern of findings. For example, resilience in Colombian youth has been associated with strong family support and structure, less exposure to serious life stress, and greater control and coherence in their lives (Klevens & Roca, 1999). Literature on resiliency and academic success (that protects against violence) has identified five key protective factors of families, schools, and communities (Chavkin & González, 2000):

- supportive relationships, particularly with school personnel and other adults;
- individual characteristics, such as self-esteem, motivation, and acceptance of responsibility;
- family factors, such as parental support/concern and school involvement;
- community factors, such as community youth programs (sports, clubs, hobbies); and
- school factors, such as academic success and prosocial skills training.

Many of these resiliency factors can be seen as integral components of cultural practices that emphasize group welfare, social capital, and community development. Indeed, Rodríguez and Morrobel (2002) emphasize that collective endeavors build on many core values within Latino communities, and they underscore the importance of building connections of Latino youth within and across their communities. Overall, these core values highlight the importance of the group versus the individual. Let us now turn to a discussion of specific aspects of Latino culture vis-à-vis risk and protective factors for youth violence.

Culture as a Risk and Protective Mechanism

Culture also contributes to the individual's psychosocial development, interpersonal relationships, and interaction with his or her environment. Cultural factors and their relationship to youth violence have not been well studied as specific risk or protective factors. However, core cultural values can play an important role in understanding both etiology and prevention of violence within distinct ethnic/cultural groups. Although there is clearly a good deal of intra-ethnic variation, certain core cultural values within the Latino community have been identified that merit discussion (Marin & Marin, 1991; Maternal and Child Health Bureau, 1999; National Alliance for Hispanic Health, 2001). These include *colectivismo* (collectivism), *familismo* (family-centered), *respeto* (respect), *simpatia* (pacifism), *personalismo* (person as a whole), and *religiosidad* (religiosity).

Colectivismo is a cultural value that differentiates the Latino culture from the individualistic, competitive, and achievement-oriented U.S. society. It involves mutual empathy, where personal desires are subordinated to the interests of the group. There is a preference to belong to and work in groups, as a tightly knit community that provides a sense of belonging. On the surface, this value appears antithetical to violence, given the focus on group versus personal interests. However, in many cases, youth violence is part of a group or collective response, particularly when gangs are involved. Therefore, the cultural value of *colectivismo* can serve to draw youth to gangs as alternative groups, particularly when participation in conventional group activities is limited or unavailable.

Familismo describes a cultural value that places the family at the center of an individual's life. The needs of the family come first, while family members are expected to provide support to individual members in need. It creates a support system of nuclear and extended family members that provides strong emotional and material support. It includes a deep sense of obligation to the family, as well as a belief that relatives serve as both guides and supporters of one's actions. Again, similar to the notion of *colectivismo*, the emphasis on the family can be a protective factor, particularly when family support is positive and geared toward productive engagement. However, bonding to a gang-involved family (as in the case of multigenerational gangs) or a less engaged family, can serve to draw youth to gangs and increase their function as surrogate families.

Respeto literally means "respect" and represents a value placing great social worth and decision-making power on authority figures. There are clear distinctions based on one's status and expertise. This can be seen in attitudes and behaviors involving deference to (and often uncritical support for) decisions of elders, parents, teachers, physicians, law enforcement personnel, politicians, and others in higher status positions. It is reflected in careful use of the informal (*t*) and formal (*Usted*) designation for addressing others in Spanish, whereby it is considered quite disrespectful to address someone in authority by the informal term. Again, the significance of this value as a risk or protective factor hinges on the nature of the group authority structure that generates deference (e.g., conventional authority such as law enforcement versus unconventional authority such as gangs). Otherwise put, without support for conventional authority figures, unconventional and delinquent authority figures may gain support.

Simpatia is a cultural value that discourages interpersonal conflict and encourages individuals to behave in ways that keep the peace. It discourages conflict, aggression, and even assertiveness. This core value seems most antithetical to violence, particularly at the interpersonal level. *Personalismo* refers to the importance of interpersonal relationships and the need to be treated by professionals that show genuine interest in the person as a whole. This can be either a risk or protective factor, depending on whether the relationships are positive or negative influences.

Finally, *religiosidad* is often a central tenet of Latino culture, and is primarily defined by Roman Catholicism and its extensions. For example, Mexican American interpretation of religious symbols and the sacred is often referred to as *religiosidad popular* (popular religion). It is an integration of Roman Catholicism with native beliefs. God's will, the spirit world, miracles, and folk healing are powerful influences on the individual's view of the world. Hardship, suffering, and death are accepted as inevitable and integral parts of life. Sacrifices and suffering are perceived as a means for redemption or transformation. Again, this belief system can serve as a protective factor against youth violence but also as a risk factor, particularly to the extent that suffering and death are seen as inevitable.

Latino Gangs and Youth Violence Risk

Although gangs are a factor in youth violence across ethnic groups in the United States, they are more common among ethnic minority youth. Furthermore, within distinct ethnic groups (e.g., African American versus Latino), the history and dynamics of gangs varies significantly. In examining youth violence among Latinos, it is important to understand how the history and significance of gangs has been shaped specifically for Latinos, and how it is similar and/or different from the history and significance of gangs within other ethnic groups.

The OJJDP published a report titled *The National Youth Gang Survey Trends from 1996 to 2000*, which highlighted findings from the five national youth gang surveys conducted annually since 1996 by the National Youth Gang Center, funded by OJJDP (National Youth Gang Center, 2002). The national representative sample of 3,018 law enforcement agencies included (a) all police and sheriff's departments of cities and suburban counties with a population greater than 25,000 and (b) a randomly selected sample of police and sheriff's departments in rural counties and cities with populations between 2,500 and 25,000. Youth gangs were defined as "a group of youths or young adults in your jurisdiction that you or other responsible persons in your agency or community are willing to identify or classify as a gang." Motorcycle gangs, hate or ideological groups, prison gangs, and adult gangs were excluded from the survey. In spite of an overall decline of gangs and gang members during this period, persistent gang activity was observed in all large cities with populations greater than 250,000 and in 86% of cities with populations between 100,000 and 250,000. The prevalence of youth homicides was highest in large cities with populations more than 100,000.

The National Youth Gang Center estimates that more than 24,500 gangs were active in the United States in 2000—a decrease of 5% from 1999. However, cities with populations greater than 25,000 experienced a 1% increase. The estimated number of gang members in the United States was greater than 750,000 for each year of the 5-year period. In 1999, 37% of gang members were younger than 18 years of age. That year, the ethnic distribution of gang members was reported as 47% Latino, 31% African American, 13% Caucasian, 7% Asian, and 2% "other." In 2000, 94% of gang members were males; however, 39% of all youth gangs had female members (National Youth Gang Center, 2002)

As can be seen, Latinos constitute the majority of all gang members. They are also the fastest growing type of gang in the United States and include the relatively new Mara Salvatrucha gang linked to Central America (Valdez, 2000). Still, it should be noted Latino gangs are mostly distributed in the state of California and the southwestern region of the United States Latino gangs also have a reasonably long history in the United States, particularly in the Southwest. Indeed, the origins of Latino street gangs can be traced back to the anti-Mexican sentiment of the Alamo, the Treaty of Guadalupe Hidalgo in 1848 (where the United States paid Mexico $18 million for large portions of the Southwest), and the rapid growth of Los Angeles during the early 1900s. The first prison gang in California, La Eme (the "Mexican Mafia") was formed in the 1950s and exerts influence over street activity to this day (Valdez, 1999).

Although new Latino gangs have emerged in recent years, it is still the case that many of the Chicano gangs in areas such as Los Angeles are multigenerational. It is typically the case that youth involved in these gangs have parents and grandparents who were also members of the same gang, so that family and gang ties are intertwined. For example, in several interviews with Chicano gang members, Sánchez-Jankowski (1991) found that 11% of those interviewed reported that four generations of men in their family had been in the same gang, for example, the grandfather, father, and son will all have belonged to the same gang while they were younger. In this manner, gangs often become infused in the community, providing supports and resources that partially counteract the frustration and resentment of immigrant and poor ethnic groups living with scarce resources. On the other hand, for some youth, gangs become surrogate families that satisfy the unmet psychological and emotional needs of youth, particularly when families are unable to provide adequate attention, supervision, and monitoring (Adler, Hocevar, & Ovando, 1984; Belitz &Valdez, 1994).

Buriel (1984) suggested that because of the constant assimilation attempts by the dominant society in the United States, many Latinos may be left stranded between traditional Latino culture and the dominant culture, resulting in a sociocultural disconnection or deculturation. Vigil (1988) proposed that difficulties in development of self-identity in some Latinos was related to ethnic group generational conflicts. These Latino youth satisfied their desire for self-identity through roles within the subculture of the street gang. The influences of the gang member ideals contributed to the development of an alternative or delinquent achievement orientation. Meanwhile, Suarez-Orozco (1989) discussed the "culture of terror" and the internalization of fear, imposed via violence on certain Latinos. Later, Suarez-Orozco and Suarez-Orozco (1995) used a cross-cultural approach and concluded that students with higher levels of acculturation were more skeptical and ambivalent about their future, similar to discussions by Boutakidis, Guerra, and Soriano (chap. 3, this volume).

Clearly, there are several reasons why Latino youth join gangs, and a complete review of risk factors for joining gangs and specifically for joining Latino gangs is beyond the scope of this chapter. Among the more frequently mentioned reasons are protection/defense, something to do, economic gain, family problems, and peer pressure (Sanchez-Jankowski, 1991). These factors seem to operate across regions and even countries. For example, in a survey of youth street gangs in El Salvador, participants reported joining gangs for four main reasons: (a) the experience or "el vacil" (40%); (b) family problems (21%); (c) peer pressure (20%); and (d) protection/defense (12%). Most violent aggressions (63.2%) were directed against rival gangs. Gang members were at high risk for victimization, mainly by rival gangs and the police. In the previous year, more than 90% of members reported physical aggression;

60% had been injured by a knife or other nonfirearm, and 60% of males had been injured with firearms. Moreover, 48.8% of female gang members reported being raped (Santacruz & Concha-Eastman, 2001). Thus, for Latino youth, gangs are one of the most significant risk factors for violence perpetration and victimization. Accordingly, prevention and intervention efforts must address the gang problem.

PREVENTION AND INTERVENTION WITH LATINO YOUTH

Unfortunately, there have been few successful gang prevention and intervention programs for Latino youth. In contrast, most programs emphasize less serious violence and are often conducted in schools and with younger children (Thornton, Craft, Dahlberg, Lynch, & Baer, 2000). Because Latino youth and families tend to live in poor, urban areas, many prevention programs conducted in these communities have engaged Latino youth. In general, these programs have not been specifically tailored to Latino youth, but many have incorporated issues of ethnic/cultural awareness and pride, getting along with others, conflict resolution, and prosocial competencies.

Those programs that have adapted to Latino culture generally address what Wright and Zimmerman (chap. 9, this volume) refer to as *surface structure*. This refers to the external characteristics of a culture (e.g., language, food, appropriate messages) that increases familiarity of respondents with the activities. As such, parent communication, lessons, and assessments are translated into Spanish and may include reference to common situations encountered by Latino families. Cultural adaptation, however, does not necessarily address the "core cultural values" inherent in many Latino families discussed previously, or what Wright and Zimmerman consider *deep structure*. There is a need for preventive interventions that consider both surface structure and deep structure in a fashion sensitive to specific Latino cultural values that can have protective functions based on their emphasis on collective engagement and responsibility.

One example of an effort to address both surface structure and deep structure is The Students for Peace Project (Murray, Kelder, Parcel, Frankowski, & Orpinas, 1999) described by Wright and Zimmerman (chap. 9, this volume). In this study, a randomized controlled trial of a parent education program to prevent violence among middle school students was conducted. For Latino families, this was translated into Spanish and renamed Padres Trabajando por la Paz (Parents Working for Peace). Parents received bilingual newsletters designed to increase parental monitoring. Stories were developed from interviews with Latino families to reflect specific issues of most relevance. The intervention resulted in higher levels of parental monitoring as reported by both children and their parents.

Several other school-based violence prevention programs have also included large numbers of Latino children and families and have increased cultural sensitivity by having materials available in Spanish, using bilingual and often bicultural trainers, and trying to capture situations of particular relevance to Latinos. For instance, the Resolving Conflict Creatively Program, which has been evaluated in New York City with more than 8,000 children in 15 elementary schools, served a population that was almost 50% Latino. This program provided classroom lessons, teacher training, and peer mediation activities for students with a focus on teaching skills to facilitate prosocial problem solving, self-control, and positive engagement. In a recent evaluation, the program was found to increase emotion regulation and prosocial behavior, and to reduce the increase in aggression found in the control group for children who were in a high-dosage group. However, the effects were smaller on high-risk males (Aber, Brown, Chaundry, & Samples, 1996).

Similarly, a large-scale, school-based prevention program in the Chicago area (Metropolitan Area Child Study, 2002) served low-income, inner-city, and urban children, with approximately 40% of the children of Latino heritage (primarily from Mexico). Three levels of intervention were provided, including classroom lessons and teacher training on social–cognitive skills, a peer group intervention to enhance modeling and use of these skills, and a family intervention to teach parenting skills and develop a parent support group. The intervention was provided during the early or late elementary school years in schools that were either low or moderate in resources. Results indicated that younger students who received all components of the intervention in the moderate resource schools displayed less aggression than students in other intervention conditions and the control group. These differences maintained regardless of ethnicity; that is, they were constant for both White youth and ethnic minority youth (predominantly Latino and African American children).

Although there are many agencies and programs serving Latino youth across the United States, few of these programs have been systematically evaluated with large populations of Latinos. Furthermore, interethnic distinctions based on region, beliefs, identity, and so on, have rarely been addressed in assessment, intervention, or interpretation of effects. Programs that are culture-specific and try to build on the core cultural values and their possible role as protective factors are scarce. Although this approach has received considerable attention in the African American community, as discussed by French, Kim, and Pillado (chap. 2, this volume), fewer programs have been developed for Latino youth and families that address these deep structure issues and focus on cultural strengths.

CONCLUSION

Latinos are the largest minority group in the United States, with 37 million people residing in the continental United States and an additional four million living in Puerto Rico. The term *Latino* appeared in the census only in the beginning of the 21st century. Regarding race, a large proportion of Hispanics do not consider themselves Black or White. This preference seems to question the validity of the concept itself and points to the possibility of a difference in conceptualizing race and ethnicity. A significant proportion of Latinos (about 10%) who live in Puerto Rico are not usually included in the statistics published in the mainland. An even greater proportion of Latinos who lack official documentation are excluded from official statistics.

Latinos are younger and less educated than other ethnic groups in the United States and live in a variety of locations. The clearest indicators of youth violence in Latino males are homicide rates that are three times greater than for Whites. When nonfatal as well as fatal injuries are considered, however, rates for Hispanics are lower. Latino youth receive harsher sentences and are more likely to be arrested and assigned to restrictive placement.

In terms of primary prevention, school and household surveys place Hispanic youth at an intermediate level of risk for violent behavior. The rates of reported violent behaviors such as carrying weapons consistently show Hispanics with higher rates than Whites but lower than Black students. Puerto Ricans surveyed in the island rank below Hispanics in continental United States in such reports. It is of great concern that Hispanic youth report more crime in their neighborhood and more street fighting than their White peers.

An extensive review of official reports, surveys, and research studies related to Hispanics in general, and to the problem of violence in Latino youth, reveal that the information is scattered and remains understudied. For Puerto Ricans residing on the island, the problem is greater because they are frequently not included in the statistics. Detailed information about the Latino youth population and its subgroups is warranted, in view of their diverse historical, political, and socioeconomic backgrounds. Furthermore, there is a need to assess how these subgroups have adapted (or not) to American culture/values and how this relates to youth violence.

Additional studies are needed to study the risk and protective factors in this heterogeneous population. The sociodemographics of the Latino population indicate that many Hispanic youth reside in communities where multiple risk factors coexist, such as low socioeconomic status, educational barriers/disparities, high unemployment rates, and lower-income jobs. In addition, their community environments may provide greater access to firearms, drugs, and/or alcohol. These circumstances, in combination with other individual and family characteristics, may place Latino youth in certain U.S. communities and Puerto Rico at greater risk for violence and delinquent behavior.

There is a need for culturally competent initiatives for youth violence prevention in this population. Outcome studies have been limited by small Latino sample size and the availability of culturally sensitive instruments. Many preventive interventions in urban areas have been translated but not culturally adapted before implementation. Meanwhile, Latino youth continue to suffer injuries and chronic disabilities because of violence—at least four Latino youths die each day in the United States as victims of an assault. Future initiatives should focus on strengthening assets, including cultural values, of Latino youth, families, and communities, and developing resiliency in this population. Research should also carefully assess how these assets can be harnessed to reduce youth violence through strategic prevention and intervention.

REFERENCES

Aber, L., Brown, J. L., Chaundry, N., & Samples, F. (1996). The evaluation of the Resolving Conflict Creatively Program: An overview. *American Journal of Preventive Medicine, 12*, 82–90.

Adler, P., Hocevar, D., & Ovando, C. (1984). Familial correlates of gang membership: An exploratory study of Mexican–American youth. *Hispanic Journal of Behavioral Sciences, 6*, 65–76.

American College of Surgeons. (2004). *National Trauma Data Bank Report, 2004.* Chicago: Author.

Anderson, R. (2002). Deaths: Leading causes for 2000. *National Vital Statistics Report (NVSS), 50*, 16.

Anderson, R. N, & Smith, B. L. (2003). Deaths: Leading causes for 2001. *National Vital Statistics Report (NVSS), 52*, 1–86.

Aquilino, W. S. (1992). Telephone versus face-to-face interviewing for household drug use surveys. *International Journal of the Addictions, 27*, 71–91.

Belitz, J., & Valdez, D. (1994). Clinical issues in the treatment of Chicano male gang youth. *Hispanic Journal of Behavioral Sciences, 16*, 57–74.

Brener, N., Lowry, R., & Barrios, L. (2004). Violence-related behaviors among high school students—United States, 1991–2003. *Morbidity and Mortality Weekly Report, 53*, 651–655.

Bureau of Justice. (2002). *National Crime Victimization Survey. Criminal victimization in the United States, 2000 statistical tables.* Washington, DC: Office of Justice Programs.

Buriel, R. (1984). Integration with traditional Mexican–American culture and sociocultural adjustment. In J. L. Martinez Jr., & R. H. Mendoza (Eds.), *Chicano psychology* (2nd ed., pp. 95–130). New York: Academic Press.

Buvinic, M., Morrison, A., & Shifter, M. (1999). *Violence in Latin America and the Caribbean: A framework for action.* Washington, DC: InterAmerican Development Bank.

Carolina Population Center. (2002). *National Longitudinal Study of Adolescent Health, wave I.* University of North Carolina, Chapel Hill. Retrieved June 30, 2003, from http://statweb.unc.edu

Centers for Disease Control and Prevention. (2002). *Youth risk behavior surveillance system.* Retrieved July 12, 2003, from http://www.cdc.gov/nccdphp/dash/yrbs/index.htm

Centers for Disease Control and Prevention. (2004a). Surveillance for fatal and nonfatal injuries—United States, 2001. *CDC Surveillance Summaries, Morbidity and Mortality Weekly Report, 53,* 1–57.

Centers for Disease Control and Prevention. (2004b). Youth risk behavior surveillance—United States, 2003. *CDC Surveillance Summaries, 53* (SS02), 1–96.

Centers for Disease Control and Prevention. (2005). *Youth Violence: Fact Sheet.* Retrieved January 24, 2005, from http://www.cdc.gov/ncipc/factsheets/yvfacts.htm

Chavkin, N. F., & González, J. (2000). Mexican immigrant youth and resiliency: Research and promising programs. *ERIC Digest.* Charleston, WV: ERIC Clearinghouse on Rural Education and Small Schools.

Concha-Eastman, A., & Villaveces, A. (2001). *Guías para el diseño, implementación y evaluación de sistemas de vigilancia epidemiológica de violencia y lesiones.* Washington, DC: Panamerican Health Organization, World Health Organization.

Cook, P., & Ludwig, J. (1997). *Guns in America: National survey on private ownership and use of firearms. Research in brief.* Washington, DC: National Institute of Justice.

Dahlberg, L., & Potter, L. (2001). Youth violence: Developmental pathways and prevention challenges. *American Journal of Preventive Medicine, 20,* 3–14.

Federal Bureau of Investigation. (2004). *FBI Uniformed Crime Report.* Retrieved December 22, 2004, from http://www.fbi.gov

Federal Communications Commission. (2000). *FCC releases new telephone subscribership report.* Washington, DC: Author.

Gotsch, K., Annest, J., Mercy, J., & Ryan, G. (2001). *Surveillance for fatal and nonfatal firearm-related injuries: 1993–1998.* Office of Statistics and Programming, Division of Violence Prevention/Centers for Disease Control and Prevention.

Grieco, E., & Cassidy, R. (2001). *Overview of race and Hispanic origin, Census 2000 Brief.* Washington, DC: U.S. Census Bureau.

Hawkins, D., Laub, J., Lauritsen, J., & Cothern, L. (2000). *Race, ethnicity, and serious and violent juvenile offending*. Washington, DC: U.S. Department of Justice, Office of Justice Programs.

Johnston, L. D., Bachman, J. G., O'Malley, P. M., & Schulenberg, J. (2004). Monitoring the future: A continuing study of American youth (8th- and 10th-grade surveys), 2003 [computer file]. Conducted by University of Michigan, Survey Research Center. Ann Arbor, MI: Inter-university Consortium for Political and Social Research.

Klevens, J., & Roca, J. (1999). Nonviolent youth in a violent society: Resilience and vulnerability in the country of Colombia. *Violence and Victims, 14*, 311–322.

Males, M., & Macallair, D. (2000). *The color of justice: An analysis of juvenile adult court transfers in California*. San Francisco: Youth Law Center.

Marin, G., & Marin, B. V. (1991). *Research with Hispanic populations*. Newbury Park, CA: Sage.

Martin, P., & Midgley, E. (1994). Immigration to the United States: Journey to an uncertain destination. *Population Bulletin, 49*, 2–45.

Maternal and Child Health Bureau. (1999). *Youth violence prevention in Latino communities: A resource guide for MCH professionals*. Newton, MA: Education Development Center.

McAuliffe, W., Labrie, R., Woodworth, R., & Zhang, C. (2002). Estimates of potential bias in telephone substance abuse surveys due to exclusion of households without telephones. *Journal of Drug Issues, 32*, 1139–1154.

McLoyd, V. C. (1999). Changing demographics in the American population: Implications for research on minority children. In V. C. McLoyd & L. Steinberg (Eds.), *Studying minority adolescents* (pp. 3–28). Mahway, NJ: Erlbaum.

Metropolitan Area Child Study. (2002). A cognitive–ecological approach to preventing aggression in urban settings: Initial outcomes for high-risk children. *Journal of Consulting and Clinical Psychology, 70*, 179–194.

Miller, S. (2003). *Hispanics replace African as largest U.S. minority group*. Washington, DC: U.S. Department of State, International Information Programs.

Mirabal-Colón, B. (2003). Developing a center for Hispanic youth violence prevention. *Puerto Rico Health Sciences Journal, 22*, 89–91.

Murray, N. G., Kelder, S. H., Parcel, G. S., Frankowski, R., & Orpinas, P. (1999). Padres Trabajando por la Paz: A randomized trial of a parent education intervention to prevent violence among middle school children. *Health Education Research, 14*, 421–426.

National Alliance for Hispanic Health. (2001). *A primer for cultural proficiency: Towards quality services for Hispanics*. Washington, DC: Estrella Press, Health Resources Services Administration, & Office of Minority Health, Department of Health and Human Services.

National Youth Gang Center. (2002). The national youth gang survey trends from 1996 to 2000. *OJJDP Fact Sheet*. Washington, DC: United States Department of Justice.

Office of Applied Studies. (1998). *National household survey on drug abuse 1998.* Rockville, MD: U.S. Department of Health and Human Services, Substance Abuse and Mental Health Services Administration.

Office of Applied Studies. (1999). *National household survey on drug abuse 1999.* Rockville, MD: U.S. Department of Health and Human Services, Substance Abuse and Mental Health Services Administration.

Office of Applied Studies. (2000). *National household survey on drug abuse 2000.* Rockville, MD: U.S. Department of Health and Human Services, Substance Abuse and Mental Health Services Administration.

Office of Applied Studies. (2001). *National household survey on drug abuse 2001.* Rockville, MD: U.S. Department of Health and Human Services, Substance Abuse and Mental Health Services Administration.

Office of the Surgeon General. (2001). *Youth violence: A report of the surgeon general.* Washington, DC: Department of Health and Human Services, U.S. Public Health Service.

Pastore, A., & Maguire, P. (Eds.). (2002). *Sourcebook of criminal justice statistics 2002, Bureau of Justice Statistics.* Retrieved March 20, 2003, from http://www.Albany.edu/sourcebook

Poe-Yamagata, E., & Jones, M. (2000). *And justice for some.* San Francisco: Youth Law Center.

Puerto Rico Health Department. (2004). *Cause of death by age group and gender, 2002.* San Juan, Puerto Rico: Department of Public Health.

Puerto Rico Trauma Registry. (2005). *Preliminary data on 2004 admissions due to intentional injuries in youth.* San Juan, PR: Author.

Rennison, C. M. (2002). Bureau of Justice Statistics Special Report. *Hispanic victims of violent crime, 1993–2000.* Washington, DC: Bureau of Justice Statistics.

Reyes, J. (2003). *Estudio Epidemiológico sobre la prevalencia de violencia entre los adolescentes escolares en Puerto Rico, sus factores de riesgo y de protección: Bases empíricas para el desarrollo de estrategias de prevención.* Unpublished doctoral dissertation, Universidad de Puerto Rico, San Juan.

Rodríguez, M., & Morrobel, D. (2002). *Latino youth development: A vision of success in a period of empirical drought.* Retrieved February 16, 2005, from http://www.edmeasurement.net/aera/papers/rodriguez.pdf

Rosa, T. (2005, January 20). With the highest murder rate in the US, Puerto Rico needs immediate solutions. *Caribbean Business.*

Sanchez-Jankowski, M. (1991). *Islands in the street: Gangs and American urban society.* Berkeley: University of California Press.

Santacruz, G., & Concha-Eastman, A. (2001). *Barrio adentro: La solidaridad violenta de las pandillas.* San Salvador, El Salvador: Instituto Universitario de Opinión Pública/Organización Panamericana de la Salud.

Senger, J. M. (2004). *Lost opportunities: The reality of Latinos in the U.S. criminal justice system.* Washington, DC: National Council of La Raza.

Suarez-Orozco, C. E., & Suarez-Orozco, M. M. (1995). The cultural patterning of achievement motivation: A comparison of Mexican, Mexican immigrant, Mexican American and non-Latino White American students. In W. A. Cornelius & R. G. Rumbaut (Eds.), *California's immigrant children: Theory, research and implications for educational policy* (pp. 161–190). San Diego: University of California, San Diego, Center for U.S.–Mexican Studies.

Suarez-Orozco, M. M. (1989). *Central American refugees and U.S. high schools: A psychosocial study of motivation and achievement.* Stanford, CA: Stanford University Press.

Therrien, M., & Ramirez, R. (2000). *The Hispanic population in the United States: March 2000. Current Population Reports.* Washington, DC: U.S. Census Bureau.

Thornton, T. N., Craft, C. A., Dahlberg, L. L., Lynch, B. S., & Baer, K. (2000). *Best practices in youth violence prevention: A sourcebook for community action.* Atlanta, GA: Centers for Disease Control and Prevention.

U.S. Census Bureau. (2000a). *Puerto Rico. Profile of selected economic characteristics: 2000.* Washington, DC: U.S. Department of Commerce.

U.S. Census Bureau. (2000b). *Current population survey. Ethnic and Hispanic Statistics Branch, Population Division.* Washington, DC: U.S. Department of Commerce.

U.S. Department of Justice. (1999). *1999 National Report Series, Juvenile Justice Bulletin.* Washington, DC: Office of Justice Programs.

U.S. Department of Justice. (2005a). *Homicide trends in the U.S.: Age trends.* Washington, DC: Office of Justice Programs, Bureau of Justice Statistics. Retrieved January 24, 2005, from http://www.ojp.usdoj.gov/bjs/homicide/teens.htm

U.S. Department of Justice. (2005b). *Homicide trends in the U.S.: Long-term trends and patterns.* Washington, DC: Office of Justice Programs, Bureau of Justice Statistics. Retrieved January 24, 2005, http://www.ojp.usdoj.gov/bjs/homicide/hmrt.htm

Valdez, A. (1999). *A history of California's Hispanic gangs. National Alliance of Gang Investigators Associations.* Retrieved November 15, 2004, from www.nagia.org

Valdez, A. (2000). *Mara Salvatrucha. National Alliance of Gang Investigators Associations.* Retrieved November 15, 2004, from http://www.nagia.org

Vélez, C. N. (2003). An overview of reported youth violence in Puerto Rico. *Puerto Rico Health Sciences Journal, 22,* 61–67.

Vigil, J. D. (1988). Group processes and street identity: Adolescent Chicano gang members. *Ethos, 16,* 421–445.

World Health Organization. (2002). *World report on violence and health.* Geneva, Switzerland: Author.

5

YOUTH VIOLENCE PREVENTION AMONG ASIAN AMERICAN AND PACIFIC ISLANDER YOUTH

GREGORY YEE MARK, LINDA A. REVILLA, THOMAS TSUTSUMOTO, AND DAVID T. MAYEDA

The social and economic development of the United States has been enriched by the contributions of many Asian Americans and Pacific Islanders, both immigrant and indigenous alike. More than 150 years ago, Asian immigrants arriving from China, Japan, Korea, Okinawa, and the Philippines struggled to make ends meet on sugar plantations of Hawaii, gold mines, canneries, and agricultural fields of the West Coast, and cities across the country; they challenged exclusion and racial discrimination, and built strong and vibrant communities. Indigenous to the Hawaiian islands, Native Hawaiians have struggled to maintain their language and cultural traditions while their monarchy was forced to abdicate and their land was annexed to the United States. Recent immigrants from Micronesia, Samoa, Tonga, Southeast Asia, and elsewhere are also Asian Americans and Pacific

The authors would like to thank the following individuals for their support in writing this chapter: Vanessa Cunanan, Orlando Garcia-Santiago, Michael Goshorn, Linda Minamoto, Sophia Monroy, and Stephanie Okihara.

Islanders, or APIs, whose history and culture resonates along the margins and mainstreams of American life.

This chapter reviews a subject matter heavily neglected in the academic literature—youth violence issues and prevention strategies among Asian American and Pacific Island youth. Before delving into this topic, however, it is important to define the broad terms *Asian American* (or *Asian*) and *Pacific Islander*. Asian refers to those having origins in any of the original peoples of the Far East, Southeast Asia, or the Indian subcontinent including, for example, Cambodia, China, India, Japan, Korea, Malaysia, Pakistan, the Philippine Islands, Thailand, and Vietnam. Pacific Islander refers to those having origins in any of the original peoples of Hawaii, Guam, Samoa, Tonga, Fiji, Micronesia, or other Pacific Islands.

The Asian and Pacific Islander population is not a homogenous group; rather, it is includes many groups who differ in language, culture, socioeconomic status, educational attainment, family structure, immigration history, health status, geographical residence, and length of residence in the United States (U.S. Department of Commerce, 2003). Recognizing this diversity and the significant differences between Asian Americans and Pacific Islanders raises questions about the appropriateness of using terms such as Asian Pacific Islander or Asian Pacific American when speaking of Asian Americans and Pacific Islanders (Mayeda & Okamoto, 2002). Thus, in discussing the topic of youth violence among API, we endeavor to name specific ethnic groups as reported by the studies to attain a more accurate portrayal of how the different groups are faring.

GENERAL POPULATION TRENDS AND CHARACTERISTICS

American popular culture and academia historically have tagged Asian Americans and Pacific Islanders as "Orientals," "Asiatics," "exotics," and so forth (Takaki, 1987; Trask, 1999). Today, Asian Americans and Pacific Islanders are still located as "others" somewhere between "Black" and "White" (Yu, 2002). Research on API youth is particularly sparse. A recent review of the API juvenile delinquency literature found most studies focused on Chinese Americans, Vietnamese Americans, and an aggregate of Asian Americans (Le, 2002). Pacific Islanders—often located within the rubric of "Asian Americans"—have largely been misunderstood and overlooked. As an example, Native Hawaiians continue to struggle in overcoming more than 200 years of colonial oppression since the arrival of England's Captain Cook in 1778 (Trask, 1999). The range of problems that contemporary Native Hawaiians endure include homelessness, poverty, health concerns, discrimination, and disproportionate minority confinement, often related to the use of alcohol and substance use.

In 1965, the United States passed an immigration act that ended Chinese exclusion acts and abolished the national origins quota system established by the 1924 immigration law (Takaki, 1990) This immigration act eliminated the use of national origin, race, or ancestry as a basis for immigration to the United States and also sparked a new wave of immigration that continues to affect contemporary Asian Americans and Pacific Islanders. According to the U.S. Census Bureau, Asian Americans and Pacific Islanders now number approximately 12.5 million in the United States, about 4.4% of the population if APIs of more than one ethnic background are included (U.S. Census Bureau, 2000).

Shinagawa and Jang's (1998) article presenting disaggregated population statistics from the 1990s on Asian Americans and Pacific Islanders illustrates the diversity of the API community. In 1990, 68.2% of APIs were foreign-born, contrasting with only 6.2% of the general population. However, among API groups, the proportion of foreign-born varies as such: Laotians (93.9%), Cambodians (93.7%), Asian Indians (70.4%), Filipinos (64.7%), Samoans (35.5%), and Japanese (28.4%). In terms of statewide distribution, examples of the largest API groups by state are California: Filipinos; New York: Chinese; Hawaii: Japanese; Texas: Vietnamese; and New Jersey: Asian Indians. Shinagawa and Jang (1998) examined the data in more depth, finding cities and counties with the largest API groups. For example, these include Koreans (Los Angeles County and city); Laotians (Fresno County and city, CA); Cambodians (Los Angeles County, Long Beach city); Thais (Los Angeles County and city); and Tongans (Salt Lake County and city, UT). Looking at age distribution, in 1994, APIs had a median age of 32 years. Japanese Americans had a median age of 36 years, Cambodians had a median age of 19 years, and Hmongs had a median age of 13 years.

Educational attainment statistics also show disparities. Although bachelor's degrees were held by 38% of all Asian Americans, educational attainment varied between and within groups. For example, 58% percent of the Asian Indian population held at least a bachelor's degree, 11% of Pacific Islanders, and 6% or fewer of Tongans, Cambodians, Laotians, and Hmongs held the same degree. The lowest poverty rates among APIs were with Filipino (5%) and Japanese (3%) families, whereas the highest were among Hmong (62%) and Cambodian (42%) families. Among Pacific Islanders, Samoans (26%) and Tongans (23%) had the highest poverty rates. Hmong families are the largest in size, with an average of 6.6 members. Filipino, Vietnamese, Cambodian, Laotian, and Pacific Islander family sizes average more than 4.0 people, while Japanese average 3.1 people (Shinagawa & Jang, 1998).

Perhaps the most common fallacy cast on Asian American youth is their generalized characterization as "model minorities" who are passive, sacrificial, academically successful, and eventually able to attain secure employment. As this chapter outlines, however, Asian American and Pacific Island youth are diverse, while still sharing many of the same concerns with youth from other ethnic groups (Lee, 1996).

VIOLENCE AND ASIAN PACIFIC ISLANDER YOUTH

Analyzing youth violence among APIs is a new avenue for most researchers. In many crime data sets, Asian Americans and Pacific Islanders are not listed or are part of the "other" category. In sections to follow, offenses perpetuated by and crimes of hate against APIs are discussed. During the past two decades, API youth arrests increased drastically by 726% (Asian/ Pacific Islander Youth Violence Prevention Center, 2001), at a time when adult arrests for the general population were relatively stable. Offenses attributed to this increase include crimes against families and children, curfew violations, embezzlement, gambling, robbery, runaways, and sex offenses (Lee & Zhan, 1998).

In an important study that disaggregates juvenile delinquency and substance use rates among API youth, Nagasawa, Qian, and Wong (2001) found that Pacific Island and Filipino youth in California had significantly higher risk rates than youth from other API backgrounds (Asian Indians, Chinese, Japanese, Korean, and Southeast Asian). Furthermore, this study found that as assimilation into Western, individual culture increased, API youth were more prone to report using marijuana, consistent with findings regarding potentially negative effects of acculturation cited by Boutakidis, Guerra, and Soriano (chap. 3, this volume). With regard to API youth protective factors, the authors write, "youth who have social and cultural capital (strong ethnic family ties and traditions) are likely to resist adopting the normative behavior of either the teen-drug or delinquent culture" (p. 369). Similar studies on aggregated API youth have also found Western assimilation to increase delinquent behavior (Chen, Unger, Cruz, & Johnson, 1999).

Arrests and Crime

Hawaii and California were chosen as the focus of this discussion on API youth arrests and crime because these states have the highest proportions of Asian Americans and Pacific Islanders in their populations. These locations also provided more data on arrests and delinquency between API communities. For the following sections, arrests are analyzed for specific Asian Americans and Pacific Islanders nationally, based on the Federal Bureau of Investigation (FBI) Unified Crime Reports (FBI, 2001b), locally

TABLE 5.1
Arrests of Various Ethnic Groups in the United States, 18 Years of Age and Younger: 1995 to 1999

Ethnicity	1995	1996	1997	1998	1999
African American	27.9%	27.3%	26.5%	26%	25.1%
Asian or Pacific Islander	1.8%	1.8%	1.7%	1.6%	1.7%
White	69.2%	69.7%	70.6%	71.3%	71.9%
American Indian	1.2%	1.2%	1.3%	1.1%	1.3%

Note. Data from Federal Bureau of Investigation (2001a).

for one major Bay Area region—San Francisco County, and for the city and county of Honolulu, Hawaii.

Examining National Crime Data, the FBI Uniform Crime Reports provides national statistics on total arrests and types of crimes or offenses. With respect to race, the Uniform Crime Reports provides data on "Whites," "Blacks," "American Indian or Alaskan Natives," and "Asian or Pacific Islanders." (Data on specific Asian ethnic groups are not provided in the Unified Crime Reports.) Table 5.1 displays data on arrests for Asian Americans and Pacific Islanders. National Uniform Crime Data on trends for Asian American and Pacific Islander juvenile arrests are not broken further into more specific ethnic categories. Although the changes in arrest proportions were minimal over the 5-year span, there was a gradual decrease in arrest proportions among African Americans from 27.9 to 25.1% and among Asian or Pacific Islanders overall from 1.8 to 1.6%. In the same time frame, there was a gradual increase in arrest proportions among Whites from 69.2 to 71.9%. Furthermore, the figures tend to make Asians and Pacific Islanders appear as having low arrest rates in comparison to youth from other umbrella ethnic categories. In the following section examining arrest data on youth in San Francisco and Honolulu Counties, however, more specific categories are analyzed, and a different image emerges.

The Bay Area: San Francisco County

California is the state that numerically has the largest number of APIs (more than 3.6 million). San Francisco County makes up a portion of the northern California "Bay Area" with one of the highest concentrations of Asians and Pacific Islanders in the nation. Le and colleagues' (Le, Arifuku, Louis, & Krisberg, 2001a; Le, Arifuku, Louis, Krisberg, & Tang, 2001b) studies of this Bay Area county and studies in Honolulu demonstrated the similarities and differences among API juvenile crime patterns in varying locations. Table 5.2 shows juvenile population and arrest statistics for all races in San Francisco County. Table 5.3 shows juvenile population and arrest statistics for specific API groups. As Table 5.3 illustrates, Cambodian,

TABLE 5.2
San Francisco County: Juvenile by Ethnicity, Population, and Arrest (1999)

Ethnicity	Juvenile population		Arrests	
	Number	Percentage	Number	Percentage
American Indian	189	0.3%	37	1%
API	23,482	38%	907	19%
Black	8,921	15%	2394	49%
Hispanic	12,426	20%	775	16%
White	16,277	27%	651	13%
Other	—	—	103	2%
Total	58,825	100%	4867	100%

Note. Populations are estimates provided by California Department of Finance (2000). Estimates by age and race breakdown were not available from the U.S. Census at this time. Population estimates by API ethnic group have not been released for 2000; population estimates reflect 1990 U.S. Census figures. Data from Alameda County Juvenile Probation Department; U.S. Census Bureau (1990); California Department of Finance (2000); Le, Arifuku, Louis, and Krisberg (2001a).

TABLE 5.3
San Francisco County: Juveniles by API Ethnic Group, Population, and Arrest (1999)

API ethnic group	Juvenile population (1990)		Arrests	
	Number	Percentage	Number	Percentage
Asian Indian	269	1%	5	1%
Cambodian	272	1%	24	3%
Chinese	12,182	59%	393	43%
Filipino	4,483	22%	185	20%
Hawaiian	59	0.3%	0	—
Japanese	492	2%	8	1%
Korean	618	3%	15	2%
Laotian	147	0.7%	9	1%
Samoan	383	2%	115	13%
Vietnamese	1,644	8%	121	13%
Other Asian	325	2%	18	2%
Other Pacific Islander	34	0.2%	14	2%
Total	20,509	100%	907	100%

Note. Populations are estimates provided by California Department of Finance (2000). Estimates by age and race breakdown were not available from the U.S. Census at this time. Population estimates by API ethnic group have not been released for 2000; population estimates reflect 1990 U.S. Census figures. Data from San Francisco County Juvenile Probation Department; U.S. Census Bureau (1990); California Department of Finance (2000); Le, Arifuku, Louis, and Krisberg (2001a).

Laotian, Samoan, and Vietnamese youth are arrested at rates that clearly exceed their overall juvenile population.

Honolulu, Hawaii

Oahu is the most densely populated of the Hawaiian islands and comprises the city and county of Honolulu. Numerically, there is no clear

TABLE 5.4
City and County of Honolulu Population of Selected Ethnic Groups in 2000

Ethnicity	Number	Percentage
African American	20,619	2.3%
Asian Indian	1,191	1.3%
Chinese	53,332	6.0%
Filipino	124,072	14.1%
Hawaiian/Part Hawaiian[a]	153,117	17.4%
Japanese	161,224	18.4%
Korean	21,681	2.4%
Micronesian	9,621	1.1%
Samoan[a]	25,856	2.9%
Vietnamese	7,392	—
White	186,484	21.2%
Total[b]	876,156	100%

Note. [a]Native Hawaiians and Samoans alone or in any combination. Data from U.S. Census Bureau (2000).
[b]Includes ethnic groups not listed.

majority ethnic group in Honolulu, although collectively APIs constitute a majority of the population. Table 5.4 shows the residential distribution of some of the larger racial and ethnic groups in Honolulu.

Although Hawaii is often portrayed as a paradise free from social ills, crime rates are comparable with most major cities across the United States. A closer look at offenses as they occur in Honolulu County and the state as a whole among various ethnic groups reveals that youth from specific ethnic groups are more prone to be arrested.

Juvenile arrests are generally higher for Hawaiians (39%) and Samoans (6%) when compared with their cohorts (ages 10–17 years) in the general population. See Table 5.5. Hawaiian youth, for example, typically comprise about 50% of all juvenile arrests for alcohol-related disorderly conduct. Turning to arrests specifically for offenses involving interpersonal violence,

TABLE 5.5
Juvenile Arrests by Ethnicity in Honolulu County and the State of Hawaii: 2000

Ethnicity	Honolulu		State of Hawaii	
African American	454	5.0%	489	3.7%
Chinese	172	1.9%	189	1.4%
Filipino	1353	15.1%	2043	15.8%
Hawaiian	3477	38.8%	4846	37.5%
Korean	434	2.0%	221	1.7%
Samoan	149	6.0%	550	4.1%
Other	825	9.2%	1036	8.0%
Total	8,948		12,896	

between the years 1996 and 2003, Hawaiian youth (who represent about 30% of all 10- to 17-year-olds in Hawaii) accounted for 38.5% of all juvenile arrests for aggravated assault and for 43.1% of all juvenile robbery arrests. Showing extreme disproportionality in arrests for violent offenses, Samoan youth (who represent barely more than 2% of all 10- to 17-year-olds in Hawaii) made up 8.6% of all juvenile arrests for aggravated assault and 22.4% of all juvenile robbery arrests between 1996 and 2003 (State of Hawaii, Department of the Attorney General, 1997–2004).

Gangs

Much of the research on youth gangs in the United States has focused on ethnic minority communities. Still, there has been a dearth of scholarly research and publications concerning Asian American and Pacific Islander youth gangs. Historically, much of the literature covering Asian gangs in the United States has been sensationalized journalism that induces unnecessary public fear and exacerbates racial stereotypes (see, for example, English, 1995; Huston, 1995). More recent studies of API gang involvement suggest that many of the factors that predict gang involvement generally are similar to the experiences of other ethnic minority and immigrant youth. However, within API, just as within other ethnic groups, there appear to be further divisions within ethnic groups based on country of origin and immigration history that require an additional understanding of the unique features of this group.

For example, Hunt, Joe, and Waldorf (1997) interviewed 91 Vietnamese gang members, ages 14 to 38, in San Jose, California. According to this study, Vietnamese youth gang members frequently feel alienated from mainstream institutions in the United States. In the midst of a rapid acculturation process, youths often perceive gangs as a place of refuge. Du (1996) also argued that Vietnamese youth gang members feel unaccepted in school by peers and teachers. In addition, less-educated and acculturated Vietnamese parents have difficulty connecting with their children, who then begin to internalize individualistic and material Western values. Feeling estranged from parents and school, some Vietnamese youth turn to gangs for acceptance and self-esteem (see also Kent & Felkenes, 1998). Notably, these causal factors of gang membership are shared by other ethnic minority populations that have high immigrant populations, such as the Latino experience described by Mirabal-Colón and Vélez (chap. 4, this volume).

Vigil (2002) added that in some cases, the refugee experience has stood as a more unique global factor that can affect gang membership among Vietnamese adolescents and young adults, whose families fled to the United States to escape political persecution in Vietnam. Vigil noted that the refugee experience occurs with other Latino groups, also influencing gang membership in the United States. However, Vigil added that a distinctive aspect of some Vietnamese gangs includes the aggressive house robberies, termed "home invasions," in which Vietnamese gang members specifically target immigrant families within their own ethnic communities. Vietnamese immigrant families are targeted because of their distrust of American banks and police, stemming from their distrust of the government in their country of origin. In effect, gang members are more confident that Vietnamese immigrant families will keep large amounts of cash and jewelry in their homes and that they will be less apt to contact American authorities after being victimized. Hamamoto (1994) reminded us that media portrayals of Vietnamese youth focus far too much on this aspect of gang violence, despite the fact that the majority of Vietnamese youth do not join gangs and engage in violent activities.

Chin's 1990 book, *Chinese Subculture and Criminality*, focused on New York Chinatown gangs, examining Chinatowns, Chinese secret societies, the development of Chinese gangs nationally, Chinese gang patterns and characteristics, and social sources of Chinese gang delinquency. He studied the relation of adult Chinatown organizations and Chinese criminality, and why and how Chinese gangs formed, claiming that New York Chinatown Chinese gangs and the tongs have a symbiotic relationship that deeply intertwines both bodies. The tongs are secret societies that originally were formed to overthrow the Manchus who ruled China from 1644 to 1911. In the United States, they became in part social clubs, and since their inception (1860s), some were involved in gambling, prostitution, and other criminal activities.

According to Mark (1997), in the development of Chinatown gangs, many American-born Chinese (ABC) had negative ethnic identities—in other words, they were ashamed to be Chinese. These feelings brought them into direct conflict with Chinese immigrants ("fresh off the boat" or "FOB") primarily from Hong Kong. As a result of these conflicts, the immigrant youth were forced to band together for protection from their American-born cousins. These groups evolved into the early Chinatown gangs in the 1960s. This lack of a positive ethnic identity has played a role in the formation of other API gangs, such as Filipino gangs in Hawaii (Alegado, 1994; Revilla, 1996). The role of ethnic identity search and youth gang affiliation is important given the relative paucity of research on the role of ethnic identity and youth violence among API youth (for a more detailed discussion of ethnic identity and youth violence, see French, Kim, and Pillado, chap. 2, this volume).

Much of the API gang and youth violence literature (other than Chinese and Vietnamese) has been centered in the state of Hawaii.

According to qualitative research conducted by Joe and Chesney-Lind (1995), youth from varying ethnic and gender backgrounds cited different reasons for why they joined gangs. Joe and Chesney-Lind interviewed 48 self-identified gang members in Hawaii (35 boys with a mean age of 16.7 years, and 13 girls with a mean age of 15.3 years), the majority of whom were Filipino or Samoan. Interviewees from both genders claimed a perceived need for protection as one reason for joining a gang, although boys and girls declared needing protection from different types of conflict. Whereas boys from this study more frequently cited needing protection from male peers, girls were more inclined to report physical and/or sexual abuse histories, indicating a highly gendered backdrop to using gang affiliation as a means for protection. As Joe and Chesney-Lind wrote, "Many youth are drawn from families that are abusive, and particularly for girls, the gang provides the skills to fight back against the violence in their families" (p. 230). This gendered explanation to youth gang affiliation resonates with other research on girls and gangs among African American and White youth (Miller, 2001).

For boys, gangs reportedly serve multiple functions, ranging from the more typically discussed physical confrontations as an alternative means of establishing masculinity to the more socially based desire to "pick up girls" and be part of a social circle (Mayeda, Chesney-Lind, & Koo, 2001; Messerschmidt, 1993). "The displays of toughness and risk taking described by the boys in our study are a source for respect and status in an environment that is structurally unable to affirm their masculinity. Their acts of intimidation and fighting are rooted in the need for protection as well as the need to validate their manliness" (Joe & Chesney-Lind, 1995, p. 230).

VICTIMIZATION AND ASIAN AND PACIFIC ISLANDERS YOUTH

A recent study by the National Institute of Justice (Davis & Erez, 1998) addressed the issue of immigrant populations as crime victims. The national survey of police chiefs, prosecutors, and court administrators found that 67% of all officials agreed that recent immigrants report crime less frequently than other victims. They named Asians and Latinos as the groups most likely to underreport crimes. The officials thought that domestic violence was the crime least reported, as well as sexual assault and gang violence. Officials listed language and cultural barriers and unfamiliarity with the justice system as challenges to immigrant victims. Interestingly, those immigrants who reported crimes and appeared in court later described the experiences to be positive ones. In Philadelphia, Vietnamese, Cambodian, and

Korean victims interviewed as part of the study described the majority of victimization incidents involved perpetrators and victims from the same ethnic group. Most (about one third) of the crimes described were robberies and burglaries, whereas 8% described domestic violence.

Hate Crimes

In the 1990s, as the API population increased in size and visibility, incidents of anti-Asian violence and hate crimes also increased. The 1982 murder of Vincent Chin, the victim of White auto workers in Detroit, Michigan, who had assumed Chin was Japanese and blamed him for their lost jobs, remains the most infamous hate crime (Espiritu, 1992). Since the Chin murder, many other Asian Americans have been killed in acts of hate. In 1989, a White gunman opened fire at a school in Stockton, California, killing five Southeast Asian children and wounding 30 others. In 1999, Joseph Ileto, a Filipino American postal delivery person in Los Angeles, was murdered by a White man who had previously shot at people in a Jewish Community Center (Guillermo, 1999).

After the September 11, 2001, terrorists attacks on the United States, Asian Indians have increasingly been the victims of hate crimes. Although most of the hate crime victims have been adults, API children have also been victimized. According to the National Asian Pacific American Legal Consortium's (NAPALC) annual audit of violence against APIs, many students have been the targets of racial slurs and assaults in schools since 2001. The same report stated that hate crimes continue to be underreported and misreported because of inconsistent or faulty procedures on the part of the police and language and cultural barriers as well as fear of the police and the U.S. Immigration and Naturalization Service (INS) on the part of the victims. The report also noted that despite the Hate Crime Statistics Act of 1990, local law enforcement often do not collect adequate data on hate crimes (NAPALC, 2001).

In his comprehensive discussion on the increase in anti-Asian violence, Fong (2002) posited that the root causes for these anti-Asian sentiments and violent acts are both structural and individual in nature. At the same time, three easily identifiable factors are lighting rods that serve to exacerbate tensions between Asian Americans and other groups: (a) an increase in anti-immigrant sentiment; (b) economic competition between racial and ethnic groups; and (c) poor police–community relations. He noted that "It will take far more effort and political will than is currently being shown by local and national leaders to solve this important social problem. In the meantime, individual, small group and community pressure must be applied to make a difference" (p. 182).

Racism

As Uba (1994) noted, Asian Americans often face unique stressors not shared by their mainstream American counterparts—stressors that can lead to negative mental health consequences. As described throughout this volume, although ethnic minorities may have different histories and cultural norms, in many cases they all share the minority experience in the United States, which is often characterized by racism and oppression. In its most overt form, racism is linked to violence by hate crimes. Perhaps less obvious, however, is the link between racism and API youth violence. Uba stated, "Racism is a source of stress because it is a source of oppression" (p. 121). Oppression can lead to feelings of powerlessness. Feelings of powerlessness, coupled with anger and frustration can result in alienation and marginality and other negative responses.

In terms of more unique racialized stressors, Lee (1996) discussed the ways that more acculturated Asian American youth (in Lee's study, Korean Americans) often come into conflict with less acculturated Asian American youth (Cambodian, Chinese, and Vietnamese Americans), who in turn, begin to develop an ethnic identity rooted in resistance to Asian American assimilation. Lee noted that because Asian Americans are frequently typecast as meek and passive, resistant Asian American youth may sometimes respond to this stereotype in violent manners, thereby reclaiming a sense of authority and power.

Lee's study also pointed out that Asian American youth are frequently presented in opposition to African American youth, with Asian Americans racialized (often times inaccurately) as the "model minorities," who do well in school, follow conventional American norms, and do not get into trouble. Conversely, African American youth are cast (again frequently inaccurately) as high-risk youth, who should follow the example of the "good" Asian Americans. Pinderhughes's (1997) ethnographic study in New York City found similar results, in which African American and Asian American youths resented one another because of the opposing ways in which they were racialized by others. Notably, in Hawaii, Samoan adolescents expressed being stereotyped in the same ways as African Americans—being physically tough and good in high-contact/collision sports but academically unmotivated. Mayeda, Chesney-Lind, and Koo (2001) theorized that this racial stereotype promoting brawn over brains contributes to Samoan youths' high rates of arrests for offenses involving interpersonal violence because some Samoan youths realize society values them for their perceived physical prowess rather than their intellect.

Young and Takeuchi (1998) noted the scarcity of research on the psychological impact of racism on Asian Americans. They discussed three studies with Chinese and Japanese American samples that also show mixed results with regard to this topic. Nagata (1998, as cited in Young & Takeuchi, 1998) examined the intergenerational impact of racism. Her study of third-generation Japanese Americans whose parents were placed in internment camps during World War II reported that silence about the internment experience within the family is pervasive. Explanations for this silence range from cultural explanations, to shame, to symptoms of posttraumatic stress.

RISK AND RESILIENCY

The chapters throughout this volume stress that relations between many risk and resiliency factors and youth violence do not vary by ethnicity but vary in the likelihood they will occur within the distinct developmental ecologies experienced by ethnic minority youth. It is also important to note that many studies of youth violence within ethnic minority populations have focused on risk factors rather than protective or resiliency factors. Researchers examining violence etiology, prevention, and intervention programs need to highlight protective factors, or what is right in communities, instead of only focusing on what is wrong. As Guerra and Williams (chap. 1, this volume) point out, it is too easy to characterize ethnic minority youth as "disadvantaged," a label that can blind observers to the positive features of culture and communities that facilitate successful adaptation. This is important for all ethnic minority communities, including API youth.

Fortunately, there is a research tradition focused on resiliency that can be highlighted with API youth. In particular, Werner and Smith's (2001) hallmark study on risk and resilience covering youth on the Hawaiian island of Kauai, *Journeys From Childhood to Midlife: Risk, Resilience, and Recovery*, provided key insights into the adjustment of API youth. This longitudinal study is unique in that it chronicled the lives of 698 infants born on Kauai in the post–World War II era, beginning in 1955. Most of the participants in the study were Japanese, Filipino, Portuguese, Chinese, Hawaiian, and/or of northern European ethnicity. One of the shortcomings of the study is that the authors did not focus on ethnicity, culture, or gender as being significant risk or protective factors.

However, the study did find certain risk and protective factors to be particularly influential for these youth. In particular, risk factors, such as prenatal stress, unstable home environment, alcohol abuse and dependence, predicted negative outcomes for youth and adults. In contrast, the study also examined the positive forces that serve to protect youth from adverse conditions. They found that three factors were particularly important. These included (a) strong family support; (b) serving in the military; and (c) a strong informal support network through school, work, and/or church. The study suggested that if these particular protective factors were present, children could more easily transcend negative circumstances. It should be noted, however, that citing the military as a protective factor is especially problematic in Hawaii, given that the military has stood as a volatile institutional imposition on indigenous Hawaiian lands and has been considered more as a risk for Hawaiian communities in general (Trask, 1999).

Nagasawa, Qian, and Wong (2001) examined teenage drug and delinquent cultures. They argued that the variable rate of marijuana use and delinquency in API communities can be explained by the theory of segmented assimilation. This theory states that the process of assimilation has become segmented into several distinct forms of adaptation: (a) acculturation into the dominant society; (b) assimilation into the underclass; and (c) maintenance of ethnic culture and ties via social networks in the community. The major theoretical finding was that as API subgroups assimilated, drug use increased, as did overall delinquent behavior. For example, the less assimilated Chinese American youth cohort, as opposed to the Filipino, Korean, Southeast Asian, Asian Indian, and Pacific Islander youth cohorts, exhibited the lowest risk for drug use and delinquency of all the API subgroups. Again, this is consistent with the findings reported by Boutakidis, Guerra, and Soriano (chap. 3, this volume), who note the generally negative effects of adopting the norms and behaviors of the dominant, majority culture.

PREVENTION AND INTERVENTION WITH ASIAN AMERICAN AND PACIFIC ISLANDER YOUTH

On one level, many issues related to risk and protective factors for youth violence and associated prevention and intervention programs can be applied to all youth. Furthermore, as suggested throughout this volume, because of conditions of development for ethnic minority youth, these programs may be even more important for ethnic minority youth who are afforded fewer resources and opportunities than their nonminority counterparts. For example, at a national conference on family violence, work groups strategizing on assessment, interventions, media, prevention, and professional education emphasized the importance of "interdisciplinary collaboration, empowerment of victims, perpetrator accountability, violence prevention, and the strengthening of families and communities" (Witwer & Crawford, 1995, p. 17). Key to all strategies is community involvement, which can be applied to ethnic communities, particularly where families and communities are highly valued. For example, one recommendation—that communities create a family violence coordinating council to coordinate local efforts—should be extended. Although membership in such councils would be open to "all interested parties . . . encouraged to join" (Witwer & Crawford, 1995, p. 19), councils should go one step further and actively recruit community leaders, victims, educators, and others from affected ethnic groups to participate.

Still, it may be particularly important to address the specific cultural practices and historical circumstances of distinct API groups as part of prevention and intervention programming. This is in part, because of the high levels of diversity within the API population, with many unique histories and variations on the minority experience. Furthermore, as we have discussed, the stereotypic models of Asians as "model citizens" can further negate their stressors, struggles, and difficulties, requiring attention to these unique experiences within a general context of risk and resilience.

A recognition of this need came recently, when former California governor Gray Davis signed a bill encouraging 7th- through 12th-grade history teachers to include in the curriculum the Hmong and Iu Mien role in the Vietnam War. The bill was authored after a dozen Hmong teenagers committed suicide in the Fresno area between the years of 1998 and 2002. A local Hmong educator attributed the suicides to feelings of being lost in America; reportedly, a significantly high percentage of Hmong youths are unaware of their history and do not feel proud of their heritage (Maganini, 2003). As this example illustrates, the "deep structure" aspects of cultural sensitivity examined by Wright and Zimmerman (chap. 9, this volume) may be particularly acute for Asian and Pacific Islander youth. As Lee and Zhan (1988) pointed out, "It is important to understand the state of children and youths through their own perceptions of their world; we need to know how they view their own existence in this society, whether they experience stress, and what their perceptions are of the social supports within their social milieu" (p. 157).

CULTURALLY SPECIFIC APPROACHES TO PREVENTION

In recent years, there have been a number of prevention programs directed at API youth and communities. However, only a small percentage of these programs are actually violence prevention or intervention programs, and even a smaller fraction of these programs have been formally evaluated. Thus, at this point in time, it is difficult to present a list of successful "best practice" programs in Asian American or Pacific Islander communities. Similar to other programs for ethnic groups cited throughout this volume, API community responses to their youth problems often focus on educating youth about their history, traditional values, and cultural practices, in an attempt to strengthen the youths' sense of ethnic identity. Speaking about Filipino youth in Hawaii, Alegado (1994) commented, "Ethnic awareness, in the view of youth workers, can impart a richness lacking in the emotional lives of young people, as well as a sense of personal history: links across time, generation, and place generally unavailable to immigrant youngsters raised in anonymous, turbulent inner-city environments" (pp. 17–18).

Although the attributes of gang membership are frequently similar across various ethnic gangs, literature on API gangs suggests that culturally specific approaches to prevention also should be taken seriously. Le (2002) asserted that outreach to young Asian Americans who are inclined to join gangs needs to address "institutional and cultural disorganization in ethnic neighborhoods, and in the ability of ethnic social agencies to exercise control with the community" (p. 64).

As paradigms of intervention evolve, new programs emerge. In 1997, Hawaiian girls, who make up more than 60% of female population incarcerated at the Hawaii Youth Correctional Facility (HYCF), were extremely overrepresented compared with their general youth population proportion (Freitas, 2000). With an overrepresentation of Hawaiian and Pacific Island boys and girls in Hawaii's youth correctional facilities, more recent literature suggests that intervention programs need to emphasize and utilize models of intervention that account not only for culture but also gender-specific needs.

Along with conventional components such as anger management treatment for addiction and abuse, culturally based programs should focus on healing instead of punishment. Ho'omohala I Na Pua (Freitas, 2000) is a model program currently being implemented in modified form that offers a culture-based program designed to service at-risk Hawaiian girls (Mayeda & Okihara, 2003). This intervention incorporates Hawaiian values and concepts to combat traumatic experiences in a "deep culture theoretical framework." As a protective factor imbedded in the intervention, Hawaiian cultural values and activities such as mo'olelo (story telling) that showcase successful female characters, Hawaiian epistemology, spirituality, self-identification, and knowledge offer an alternative to punishment.

Hui Malama o ke Kai (HMK) is a grassroots youth violence prevention program that began in 1998 in Waimanalo, Hawaii. In partnership with the John A. Burns School of Medicine at the University of Hawaii at Manoa Native Hawaiian Center of Excellence and the Office of Minority Health (Family and Community Violence Prevention Initiative), the program seeks to improve community health through family and community violence prevention. The program currently serves approximately 40 at-risk 5th- and 6th-grade youths from the local community through year-round after-school and weekend activities aimed at strengthening family bonding, providing academic support, and increasing awareness and pride in Hawaiian culture and values.

Waimanalo's proximity to the ocean lends itself to great opportunities to incorporate skills such as a canoe paddling, surfing, sailing, and so on, into the program curriculum. In addition, traditional Hawaiian values such as respect for the *aina* (land) are fostered through activities such as stream restoration and working in a *lo'i* (taro patch). The curriculum integrates the teaching of traditional Hawaiian values such as *laulima* (cooperating, working together), *lokahi* and *malama* (care for and preservation of the land and ocean) with components addressing conflict management, problem-solving techniques, and other life skills training through hands-on, experiential learning. In addition to the exposure to Native Hawaiian cultural practices, the curriculum also includes activities that highlight the unique characteristics of other ethnic groups in Hawaii as well as activities that take the children to places across the state, opening their eyes to the possibilities and locales beyond Waimanalo. Hui Malama o ke Kai's goal is to help develop the physical, mental, emotional, and spiritual health of children, and by extension their entire families, thereby improving the quality of life not only for the youths and their families but the community of Waimanalo as a whole.

The Hui Malama o ke Kai Impact Survey was conducted in June 2002 (Takeshita & Takeshita, 2002). Its purpose was to measure the program's effect on the youth participants. Three surveys were conducted: (a) student impact survey, (b) parent impact survey, and (c) staff impact survey. The surveys were designed to assess youth changes in attitude and abilities in the categories of academic development, personal development, cultural and recreational enrichment, and career development. The survey results were clearly positive. Both students and parents believed that positive change occurred with the program participants. The greatest positive impact was the youth's pride in being Hawaiian, and holding a greater concern for the ocean and land. Student comments included: "It has changed my attitude about being Hawaiian by me being more proud." "The program helped me think good (sic) about myself" (p. 11).

CONCLUSION

Asian Americans and Pacific Islanders are predominantly young populations who are rapidly growing and whose place in American society is constantly evolving. Youth violence in API communities is a serious issue within these communities. Asian American and Pacific Islander youth violence is not one-dimensional. Racism, minority status, stereotyping, stressors related to acculturation, ethnic identity, intragroup conflicts, immigrant or refugee status, and a lack of structural opportunities are factors related to youth violence and victimization. Research must address these issues as well as their variance in different API groups in different communities. API youth violence research must also push the envelope further and look more closely at issues such as the impact of trauma from war in relationship to violence causation and the intensity of the violence.

The API communities must be educated as to the etiology of youth violence and work together with outside agencies to develop and implement programs and procedures to address youth violence issues. More prevention and intervention programs need to be developed to serve the diverse API communities, especially programs emphasizing resiliency, and ethnic and gender-specific factors that promote positive cultural identities. Community history has taught us that to truly make a difference, it is imperative that the impetus for community mobilization against youth violence must originate from the communities themselves. Only then can partnerships with other community-based organizations, social service agencies, research institutions, educational institutions, and government agencies become successful.

REFERENCES

Alegado, D. (1994, December). *Immigrant youths from the Philippines: Embedded identities in Hawaii's urban community contexts.* Paper presented at First World Congress on Indigenous Filipino Psychology and Culture.

Asian/Pacific Islander Youth Violence Prevention Center. (2001). *API currents.* Oakland, CA: National Council on Crime and Delinquency.

Chen, X., Unger, J. B., Cruz, T. B., & Johnson, C. A. (1999). Smoking patterns of Asian–American youth in California and their relationship with acculturation. *Journal of Adolescent Health, 23,* 321–328.

Chin, K. (1990). *Chinese subculture and criminality: Nontraditional crime groups in America.* New York: Greenwood Press.

Davis, R. C., & Erez, E. (1998, May). *Immigrant populations as victims: Toward a multicultural criminal justice system.* National Institute of Justice, Research in Brief Report.

Du, P. L. (1996). *The dream shattered: Vietnamese gangs in America.* Boston: Northeastern University Press.

English, T. J. (1995). *Born to kill: America's most notorious Vietnamese gang, and the changing face of organized crime.* New York: William Morrow.

Espiritu, Y. L. (1992). *Asian American panethnicity: Bridging institutions and identities.* Philadelphia: Temple University Press.

Federal Bureau of Investigation. (2001a). *Hate crime statistics, 2001.* Retrieved June 3, 2003, from http://www.fbi.gov/ucr/cius_00/hate00.pdf

Federal Bureau of Investigation. (2001b). *Crime in the United States 2000: Uniform crime reports.* Retrieved June 3, 2003, from http://www.fbi.gov/ucr/cius_00/00 crime212.pdf

Fong, T. (2002). *The contemporary Asian American experience: Beyond the model minority* (2nd ed.). Upper Saddle River, NJ: Prentice Hall.

Freitas, K. (2000). *Ho'omahala I Na Pua: A gender specific and culture-based program for Native Hawaiian girls.* Honolulu: University of Hawaii Center for Youth Research.

Guillermo, E. (1999, August 26). The trouble with hate crime laws. *Asian Week, 21*(1), A1.

Hamamoto, D. Y. (1994). *Monitored peril: Asian Americans and the politics of TV representation.* Minneapolis: University of Minnesota Press.

Hunt, G., Joe, K., & Waldorf, D. (1997). Culture and ethnic identity among Southeast Asian gang members. *Free Inquiry in Creative Sociology, 25,* 9–21.

Huston, P. (1995). *Tongs, gangs, and triads: Chinese crime groups in North America.* New York: Universe.com.

Joe, K. A., & Chesney-Lind, M. (1995). "Just Every Mother's Angel": An analysis of gender and ethnic variations in youth gang membership. *Gender and Society, 9,* 408–431.

Kent, D. R., & Felkenes, G. T. (1998). *Cultural explanations for Vietnamese youth gang involvement in street gangs.* Westminister, CA: Westminister Police Department, Office of Research and Planning.

Le, T. (2002). Delinquency among Asian/Pacific Islanders: Review of literature and research. *Justice Professional, 15,* 57–70.

Le, T., Arifuku, I., Louis, C., & Krisberg, M. (2001a). *Not invisible: Asian Pacific Islander juvenile arrests in San Francisco County.* Oakland, CA: National Council on Crime and Delinquency.

Le, T., Arifuku, I., Louis, C., Krisberg, M., & Tang, E. (2001b). *Not invisible: Asian Pacific Islander juvenile arrests in Alameda County.* Oakland, CA: National Council on Crime and Delinquency.

Lee, L. C., & Zhan, N. W. (1998). *Handbook of Asian American psychology.* Thousand Oaks, CA: Sage.

Lee, S. J. (1996). *Unraveling the "model minority" stereotype: Listening to Asian American youth.* New York: Teachers College Press.

Maganini, S. (2003, July 11). Hmong war heroism to join history texts. *Sacramento Bee,* pp. A3, A5.

Mark, G. Y. (1997). Oakland Chinatown's first youth gang: The Suey Sing boys. *Free Inquiry in Creative Sociology, 25,* 41–50.

Mayeda, D. T., Chesney-Lind, M., & Koo, J. (2001). "Talking Story" with Hawaii's youth: Confronting violent and sexualized perceptions of ethnicity and gender. *Youth and Society, 33,* 99–128.

Mayeda, D. T., & Okamoto, S. K. (2002). Challenging the "Asian Pacific American" rubric: Constructions of ethnic identity among Samoan youth in Hawaii. *Journal of Poverty, 6,* 43–62.

Mayeda, D. T., & Okihara, S. (2003). *Disproportionate minority confinement in Hawaii: A review of culturally effective youth programming* (Vol. II). Honolulu: State of Hawaii Office of Youth Services.

Messerschmidt, J. (1993). *Masculinities and crime: Critique and reconceptualization of theory.* Lanham, MD: Rowman & Littlefield.

Miller, J. (2001). *One of the guys: Girls, gangs, and gender.* New York: Oxford University Press.

Nagasawa, R., Qian, Z., & Wong, P. (2001). Theory of segmented assimilation and the adoption of marijuana use and delinquent behavior of Asian Pacific youth. *Sociological Quarterly, 42,* 351–372.

Nagata, D. K. (1998). Internment and intergenerational relations. In L. C. Lee & N. W. Zane (Eds.), *Handbook of Asian American psychology* (pp. 433–456). Thousand Oaks, CA: Sage.

National Asian Pacific American Legal Consortium. (2003). *Fact sheet: Local law enforcement enhancement act.* Retrieved July 14, 2003, from http://www.napalc.org/programs/antiviolence/resources/llea.pdf

Pinderhughes, H. (1997). *Race in the hood: Conflict and violence among urban youth.* Minneapolis: University of Minnesota Press.

Revilla, L. (1996). Filipino Americans: Issues for identity in Hawaii. In J. Okamura & R. Labrador (Eds.), *Pagdiriwang 1996: Legacy and vision of Hawai'i's Filipino Americans* (pp. 9–12). Honolulu: Center for Philippine Studies, University of Hawaii.

Shinagawa, L. H., & Jang, M. (1998). *Atlas of American diversity.* Walnut Creek, CA: Altamira.

State of Hawaii, Department of the Attorney General. (1997). *Crime in Hawaii: A review of Uniform Crime Reports.* Honolulu: Author.

State of Hawaii, Department of the Attorney General. (1998). *Crime in Hawaii: A review of Uniform Crime Reports.* Honolulu: Author.

State of Hawaii, Department of the Attorney General. (1999). *Crime in Hawaii: A review of Uniform Crime Reports.* Honolulu: Author.

State of Hawaii, Department of the Attorney General. (2000). *Crime in Hawaii: A review of Uniform Crime Reports.* Honolulu: Author.

State of Hawaii, Department of the Attorney General. (2001). *Crime in Hawaii: A review of Uniform Crime Reports.* Honolulu: Author.

State of Hawaii, Department of the Attorney General. (2002). *Crime in Hawaii: A review of Uniform Crime Reports.* Honolulu: Author.

State of Hawaii, Department of the Attorney General. (2003). *Crime in Hawaii: A review of Uniform Crime Reports.* Honolulu: Author.

State of Hawaii, Department of the Attorney General. (2004). *Crime in Hawaii: A review of Uniform Crime Reports.* Honolulu: Author.

Takaki, R. (1987). *From different shores: Perspectives on race and ethnicity in America.* New York: Oxford University Press.

Takaki, R. (1990). *Strangers from a different shore: A history of Asian Americans.* New York: Penguin.

Takeshita, C., & Takeshita, I. (2002). *Hui Malama o ke Kai: Impact survey results, June 2003.* Waimanalo, HI: Hui Malama o ke Kai.

Trask, H. (1999). *From a native daughter: Colonialism and sovereignty in Hawaii.* Honolulu: University of Hawaii Press.

Uba, L. (1994). *Asian Americans: Personality patterns, identity, and mental health.* New York: Guilford Press.

U.S. Census Bureau. (2000). *City and county of Honolulu population of ethnic groups in 2000.* Retrieved November 15, 2003, from http://www.census.gov/

U.S. Department of Commerce. (2003). *Current population reports: The Asian and Pacific Islander population in the United States.* Washington, DC: Author.

Vigil, J. D. (2002). *A rainbow of gangs: Street cultures in the mega-city.* Austin: University of Texas Press.

Werner, E. E., & Smith, R. S. (2001). *Journeys from childhood to midlife: Risk, resilience, and recovery.* Ithaca, NY: Cornell University Press.

Witwer, M. B., & Crawford, C. A. (1995). *A coordinated approach to reducing family violence: Conference highlights.* Washington, DC: U.S. Department of Justice.

Young, M., & Takeuchi, D. (1998). Racism. In L. C. Lee & N. W. Zane (Eds.), *Handbook of Asian American psychology* (pp. 401–432). Thousand Oaks, CA: Sage.

Yu, H. (2002). *Thinking Orientals: Migration contract, and exoticism in modern America.* New York: Oxford University Press.

6

UNDERSTANDING AMERICAN INDIAN YOUTH VIOLENCE AND PREVENTION

SAMANTHA HURST AND JACK LAIRD

This chapter explores issues of American Indian[1] youth violence related to circumstances and behaviors that have been shown to place Native adolescents at high risk for becoming victims or perpetrators of violence. These include historical patterns of oppression and poverty, intergenerational problems of discrimination, abuse of alcohol and other drugs, association with delinquent peers, and previous victimization. Most mainstream efforts have done little to identify effective interventions that demonstrate sensitivity to the social and cultural experience of American Indian adolescents. For violence prevention to work effectively in American Indian youth populations, service providers must recognize and understand the differences and strengths of American Indian people and consider how culture, family, and community play an important role in prevention and intervention initiatives for Native youth.

---

[1] Throughout this chapter the terms *American Indian*, *Native American*, *Native people*, and *Indian* are used interchangeably. When specific tribal groups are the focus of the content, they are named.

Many American Indian youth live under difficult conditions involving violence and victimization in their homes and communities. Considering that American Indians are among the youngest and fastest growing ethnic groups in the United States, the challenges from current population growth alone will compound the difficulty of resolving these issues (Gover, 1998; U.S. Department of Health and Human Services, 2001). General population statistics collected by the Indian Health Service (1999) report that 17% of Indian males and 16% of Indian females are under the age of 15 years compared with 11% for both sexes in the United States The U.S. birth rate for teenagers 15 to 19 years ranks American Indian teens third (67.8 per 1,000), compared with Hispanic (94.4 per 1,000) and Black (81.9 per 1,000) teenage mothers (National Center for Health Statistics, 2002).

Understanding issues in population growth and change are critical to resolving the existing combination of social, economic, and health problems that have contributed to a serious breakdown in the stability of today's American Indian family. Also complicating the overall management of youth violence prevention is the inadequate coordination of data available on Native youth violence and violent crimes reported by reservations and local and federal agencies (Wakeling, Jorgensen, Michaelson, & Begay, 2001). There is still much we do not know about the extent of youth violence in Indian country, but what data is available suggests a major reason for concern.

According to estimates reported by the U.S. Department of Justice, from 1992 to 1996, the violent crime rate for American Indian males of age 12 or older was more than double (153 per 1,000) that found among all males (60 per 1,000) of other ethnic groups. Among the different age groups, the violent crime rate for Native adolescents of ages 12 to 17 (171 per 1,000) was nearly 1.5 times the violent crime rate of Whites (118 per 1,000), Blacks (115 per 1,000), and Asians (60 per 1,000) in the same age cohort (Greenfeld & Smith, 1999). Data from the Federal Bureau of Investigation (FBI) and the U.S. Bureau of the Census for 1980 to 1999 present a substantial increase in simple assault rates for American Indian youth of ages 10 to 17 (185%) compared with Whites (160%), Blacks (133%), and Asians (39%; Snyder, 2001).

Although American Indian youth make up just 1% of the U.S. population of ages 10 to 17, they represent 2% to 3% of juveniles arrested for such offenses as liquor law violations and larceny–theft (Coalition for Juvenile Justice, 2000; Snyder & Sickmund, 1999). Arrest and conviction rate data for alcohol-related violations (1,341 per 100,000) were twice the national average (649 per 100,000), and total property violations (3,026 per 100,000) were slightly higher than the national youth average (2,783 per 100,000; Greenfeld & Smith, 1999; Snyder 2002).

Data compiled by the Indian Health Service from 1994 to 1996 report that Native youth are more likely to die from accidents, homicide, and suicide than other adolescents in the general population. Estimated rates of violent victimization reported by the U.S. Department of Justice from 1992 to 1996 are higher for American Indians in every age group than that of all races (Greenfeld & Smith, 1999). In particular, the average annual number of violent victimizations for American Indians of age 12 or older (124 per 1,000 people) was more than twice the rate for the nation (50 per 1,000 person) with slightly more than half (52%) of these crimes occurring among individuals from 12 to 24 years of age. Likewise, between 1993 to 1998, the rate of intimate partner violence was higher for American Indian females of age 12 or older (23.2 per 1,000) compared with rates for Blacks (11 per 1,000), Whites (8 per 1,000), and Asians (2 per 1,000; Rennison, 2001).

One of the most prevalent youth victimization crimes in Indian country takes the form of child abuse. As a consequence of the 1990 judicial hearings on hundreds of documented child sexual abuse cases at the Hopi, Navajo, and North Carolina Cherokee Indian reservations, Congress enacted the Indian Child Protection and Family Violence Prevention Act of 1990 (Pub. L. No. 101-360, tit. IV, § 411). From 1992 to 1995, American Indians and Asians were the only racial or ethnic groups to experience an increase in the rate of abuse and neglect of children under 15 years of age, as measured by incidents recorded by child protective service (CPS) agencies. On a per capita basis, the 1995 National Child Abuse and Neglect Data System indicate an estimated 1 substantiated report of an American Indian child victim of abuse or neglect for every 30 American Indian children of age 14 years or younger. Nationwide, the 1995 estimates translate into about 1 American Indian child victim known to CPS for every 58 children of any race, 66 White children, 30 Black children, 80 Hispanic children, and 209 Asian children (Greenfeld & Smith, 1999).

Researchers suggest that violent victimization is in fact a warning sign for future violent offending among juveniles. Violent victimization and violent offending share many of the same risk factors, including new or continuing alcohol or drug use, male gender, offending or victimizing incident within the last year, and depression (Shaffer & Ruback, 2002). Risky and aggressive behavior may be interpreted as a defense against experiencing painful affect, and delinquent behaviors can additionally serve as a catalyst for further dangerous activities that lead to arrest and detention, or even suicide (Borowsky, Resnick, Ireland, & Blum, 1999; Hurst & Lefler, 2003).

Not surprisingly, American Indian youth are overrepresented in the juvenile justice system, and juvenile recidivism is also high. The number of Native American youth in Federal Bureau of Prisons (BOP) custody has increased 50% since 1994 (Andrews, 1999). It is estimated that on any given day more than 70% of the approximately 270 youth in BOP are American Indians. Once entangled with law enforcement, young Native offenders are often detained in facilities that are located hundreds of miles from their rural reservations, therefore disconnecting youth from their family members and tribal contact. For adolescent offenders growing up in metropolitan areas, the juvenile justice system may seem equally as unsupportive by overlooking or misidentifying urban American Indian youth as "other" or of Hispanic ancestry.

Approximately 30% of Native adolescents make their home on one of the 619 federal or state reservations, the remainder live in large urban areas such as New York, Los Angeles, Phoenix, Anchorage, and Oklahoma City (Snipp, 2002). Considering that one third of U.S. states have no federally recognized American Indian tribes, a disproportionate number of arrests are taking place in states with significant American Indian communities, but national data may be masking the disparity (U.S. Census Bureau, 2002). Overrepresentation exists, in part, because crimes committed off the reservation are more likely to violate local and state laws, whereas crimes committed on tribal property are considered federal offenses (Andrews, 1999). As a consequence, the U.S. Constitution does not shield American Indian youth from double jeopardy. Data concerning American Indians living off the reservation are likely to be captured in general population data, if they are captured at all. According to estimates from the U.S. Census Bureau (2003), there are currently 1.4 million youth less than 18 years old who identify themselves as American Indian, whether of heterogeneous ancestry or tribal heritage alone.

Chronic exposure to violence is a common condition on the reservation that many American Indian adolescents regard as the social norm. Countless American Indian youth live in reservation communities where families continue to be affected by persistent historical problems resulting in long-term economic disadvantage and social distress, thus perpetuating feelings of isolation, alienation, and hostility. Data reported by Indian Health Service from the 1990 census indicate that 33.1% of 12- to 17-year-old Indians live below the poverty level in contrast to 16.3% for the all races and 11.0% for White populations (Indian Health Service, 1998).

Anecdotal accounts from a number of Indian families enrolled in one of the estimated 321 tribes involved in gaming operations suggest that growing revenue from tribal casino profits has had no substantial impact on decreasing levels of violence, addiction, and victimization on their reservations. These accounts are in sharp contrast to published evidence reported by the National Indian Gaming Association (2001). Additional analysis is most certainly warranted. As a consequence, unemployment, which may be high for both gaming and nongaming tribes, is also frequently associated with high levels of substance abuse and crime (U.S. Department of Interior, 1999).

FACTORS CONTRIBUTING TO YOUTH VIOLENCE
AND DELINQUENCY

The fact that American Indian youth and their families are exposed to a variety of risk factors associated with violence and violent behavior is not necessarily unique. Consistent with chapters in this section and throughout this volume, it is clear that ethnic minority group members share risk factors with all youth in general as well as with ethnic minority youth in particular. Furthermore, there are unique risk factors experienced by virtue of specific historical circumstances of different ethnic groups. For Native youth, the challenge of overcoming multiple problems has been greatly compounded by contemporary pressures of assimilation and lateral oppression, all of which have been influenced by historical trauma, substance abuse, depression, and gang involvement (Fisher, Storck, & Bacon, 1999; O'Nell & Mitchell, 1996).

Historical Trauma

The impact of historical events on present-day issues is deeply felt by most American Indians. Native people have been subject to social and legislative domination unlike any other ethnic or cultural group living in the United States. Since the early 1800s, government policies have attempted to extinguish Indian identity through a number of federal programs such as forced removal of entire communities, relocation to urban areas, and adoption by non-Indian families (Duran, Duran, & Brave Heart, 1998). The aftermath of these programs has left generations of Native American individuals in emotionally distraught and vulnerable life situations (Duran & Duran, 1995). Indeed, many American Indian families are still undergoing a massive recovery from government policies and programs designed to strip them of their traditional Native identity.

Perhaps one of the most emotionally devastating campaigns to assimilate American Indians, however, came from the attempted extinction of tribal religion, language, and culture through residential boarding school. For the span of nearly a century, thousands of American Indian children relinquished the innocence of their formative years to residential boarding schools. The federal Bureau of Indian Affairs began opening boarding schools in the 1870s, joining a parallel system of religious boarding schools for Indians run by Christian missionaries. Anecdotal accounts by former students and boarding school historians say the methods were often violent and deeply humiliating (Adams, 1995; Child, 1998; DeJong, 1993).

Spiritually, as well as emotionally, children were stripped of their culturally integrated beliefs and behaviors and forced to change their names, to wear uniforms, and to cut their long hair. Parents were often denied requests to visit their children and children were often not allowed to leave the boarding schools for up to 4 and 5 years, depending on the age of the child (Child, 1998). In many cases, Indian children were subjected to militaristic discipline, excessive physical labor, and harsh punishment for speaking their native language even though the majority could not speak English (DeJong, 1993). Students were instructed in domestic, manual, and industrial skills that were appropriate to Euro-American gender roles, which for many led to confusion, alienation, homesickness, and resentment (Adams, 1995).

At both government and mission schools, the goal was the same—obliterating all Indian culture through forced assimilation. One of the dominant characteristics found in the off-reservation boarding schools was a system of work and study referred to as the "outing system." Designed by retired Army officer Richard H. Pratt, the outing system was created to place Indian children in the homes of White families where they would learn the "virtues" of living in White America (DeJong, 1993). The outing system served as a model for many Indian boarding schools with the intent of placing schools as far away as possible from the tribes and families.

By 1931, nearly one third of Indian children were in boarding schools, a total of about 24,000 children. As Indian children became adults they were painfully unprepared to raise their own families within the values of a traditional American Indian context (Braveheart & DeBruyn, 1998). The effects from boarding school trauma have continued to affect American Indians for generations, resulting in a nexus of social problems such as depression, drinking, violence, and suicidality (Brave Heart, 1999a, 1999b; Brave Heart & DeBruyn, 1998).

Substance Abuse

The first stage of risk for substance abuse in Native Americans occurs in utero. A developing fetus is highly susceptible to the toxic effects of alcohol exposure. The presence of birth defects caused by maternal consumption of alcohol during pregnancy is known as fetal alcohol syndrome (FAS). In addition to deficits in general intellectual functioning, children with FAS often demonstrate difficulties with mental health and social interactions (Abel, 1998a). Secondary disabilities associated with FAS may include hyperactivity, disruptive behavior in school, and difficulties with alcohol and drug problems, which make them especially susceptible to involvement with the police and crime (Streissguth, 1996).

Studies in the 1980s revealed an FAS rate of 2.9 per 1,000 total births in American Indians (Chavez, Cordero, & Becerra, 1988). This rate is approximately 30 times the rate reported for Caucasian infants (Vanderwagen, 1990). More recently studies conducted with American Indians in high-risk communities have yielded FAS rates among the highest known in the world (May & Gossage, 2001). For some of the Plains and Plateau cultural tribes the average FAS rates were 9 per 1,000 births among children of ages 1 through 4 years. Tribes representing the southwestern United States ranged from 0.0 to 26.7 per 1,000 births for children from infancy to 14 years. Average rates measures between major cultural groups ranged from 1.4 and 2.0 to 9.8 per 1,000 births. Although the actual prevalence of FAS in Indian country may be difficult to establish, the maternal risk factors for substance abuse are quite clear.

To a great extent, FAS depends on the quantity, frequency, and timing of maternal drinking. The most commonly reported pattern of drinking among Native Americans is generally accepted as binge drinking (May, 1996; Robin, Chester, Rasmussen, Jaranson, & Goldman, 1997). Of significance here is a comparison of population studies across countries of the Western world, which suggest that the most severe and major symptoms of FAS result from mothers who consume substantially large quantities of alcohol in short time periods, as opposed to those who consume less but with a greater daily frequency (Abel, 1998b). Thus the prevalence of FAS and effects from secondary disabilities may still be substantially underestimated in association with other coexisting morbidities in American Indian children.

American Indian youth have consistently experimented with drugs and alcohol at significantly higher rates compared with all U.S. adolescents (Beauvais, 1992; MacDonald, 1989; Plunkett & Mitchell, 2000). A summary of annual averages based on findings collected from 1999 to 2001 by the Substance Abuse and Mental Health Services Administration indicate that 38.7% of American Indian adolescents, 12 to 17 years old, had reported heavy use of alcohol in the past month compared with White (26.4%), Latino (21.4%), African American (23.2%), and Asian American (15.3%) youth (National Household Survey on Drug Abuse Report, 2003). Among individuals of age 12 or older in 2002, the rate of substance abuse or dependence was highest among American Indians (14.1%; Substance Abuse and Mental Health Services Administration, 2003). The next highest rate was among people reporting two or more races (13.0%).

Native American youth report using alcohol and drugs at a younger age, continuing use after initial experimentation, and often developing more abusive or dependent stages of combined substance abuse (Beauvais, 2000). Percentages of individuals of age 12 or older reporting past year dependence on or abuse of any illicit drug or alcohol were also higher for American Indians (13.9%) than reported for all other "racial/ethnic groups" (7.3%; National Household Survey on Drug Abuse Report, 2003). American Indian adolescents also make up 2% of all juveniles arrested nationwide for public drunkenness and driving under the influence, as well as 3% of all juveniles arrested for liquor law violations (National Center for Juvenile Justice, 1999). Furthermore, it has been reported that American Indian males and females have had higher overall rates of alcohol-related death in most age categories than the total U.S. population (May, 1996).

Young American Indians living on the reservation also have higher rates of illicit drug use when compared with most other young people, particularly for marijuana, inhalants, and stimulants (Plunkett & Mitchell, 2000). Recent data from the National Household Survey on Drug Abuse 2002 reported among adolescents of ages 12 to 17, the rate of current illicit drug use was more than twice as high for Native youth (20.9%) as the national average (11.6%; Substance Abuse and Mental Health Services Administration, 2003).

Depression

There is little doubt that most Indian youth perceive trauma and stress to be a fairly common issue within their lives. American Indian adolescents are frequently traced to homes marked by intergenerational family violence, parental substance abuse, kinship and family disruption, poverty, and child abuse/neglect (Hurst & Lefler, 2003; Novins, Beals, Shore, & Manson, 1996). Generally speaking, it is often difficult to separate the underlying stress from the effect of stress itself, neither of which may even be decipherable to the Native adolescent. The research on risk factors associated with American Indian youth point to many of the same variables that place them at risk for depression, substance abuse, posttraumatic stress disorder (PTSD), and suicidal behavior (Beals et al., 1997; Borowsky et al., 1999; Cummins, Ireland, Resnick, & Blum, 1998; Gray, 1998).

The effect of traumatic events has been associated with an increased prevalence of behavioral disorders and substance abuse or dependence disorders (Bechtold, Manson, & Shore, 1994; Jones, Dauphinais, Sack, & Somervell, 1997; Pfefferbaum, Pfefferbaum, Strickland, & Brandt, 1999). For example, Manson and colleagues (1996) summarized findings from three studies exploring the prevalence of psychopathologies among American Indian adolescents (Health Survey of Indian Boarding School Students; Flower of Two Soils Reinterview, and Foundations of Teens). The studies, conducted between 1988 through 1992, involved interviews of 477 Native American youths between the ages of 13 and 20 years. All interviews took place on reservations or in tribal secondary schools. Among respondents from the Health Survey of Indian Boarding Schools Students, the three most common diagnoses were conduct disorder (18%), major depression (15%), and alcohol dependence (13%). Of particular concern was the fact that 25% of the students indicated that they had made a previous suicide attempt, which for many had taken place within the last 6 months. Adolescents participating in the Flower of Two Soils Reinterview also similarly presented with disruptive behavior disorders (22%), conduct disorder (9.5%), and substance use disorders (18.4%). Of these individuals, 20.2% qualified for a single diagnosis only, while the remainder were assigned multiple or comorbid diagnoses. In response to the Foundations of Teens study, 51% of Native students reported experiencing at least one traumatic event, with 37% reporting more than one, and 16% reporting four or more. Approximately half of the students experiencing a traumatic event met the criteria for eight or more of the PTSD symptoms (of 17 possible) on the self-report survey.

Not only do traumatizing events occur at an overwhelming rate in the lives of American Indian youth, but each generation is faced with the cumulative effects of unresolved intergenerational trauma, discrimination, alcoholism, and violent death, thus affecting the emotional strength of every new cohort of young Native males and females. As a result, suicide is often the overwhelming consequence of the failure to address and treat these family and community issues. For the past 15 years, suicide has been reported as the second leading cause of death for 15- to 24-year-old American Indian youth (Nissim-Sabat, 1999). General mortality statistics collected by the Indian Health Service from 1994 to 1996 indicate the three leading causes of death for 15- to 24-year-old Native youth were accidents, suicide, and homicide/legal intervention (Indian Health Service, 1999). The respective rates of accidents and suicides for Indian youth were two to three times the U.S. population rate for the same age group.

The high rate of suicide among American Indian youth has generated a number of studies attempting to identify modifiable risk factors and culturally appropriate interventions. General factors associated with suicide and related behaviors have involved association with friends or family members attempting or completing suicide, a history of physical or sexual abuse, being female, emotional problems, availability of firearms, and substance abuse (Borowsky et al., 1999; EchoHawk, 1997; Grossman, Milligan, & Deyon, 1991; Manson, Beals, Dick, & Duclos, 1989).

Novins, Beals, Roberts, and Manson (1999) explored differences in factors associated with suicidal ideation in 1,353 high school students representing three culturally distinct American Indian tribes. In the multivariate analysis, not one correlate of suicidal ideation was common among all three tribes; however, correlations were derived from within the social structure of each tribe related to cultural concepts of individual and gender roles and community support systems. Identified correlates of suicidal ideation in the Pueblo youth reported the recent loss of a close friend through suicide, perceived lack of social support, and depressed affect. Among youth of the Northern Plains tribe, suicidal ideation was associated with low self-esteem and higher levels of depressed affect. Finally, among adolescents from the Southwest, suicidal ideation was related to youth who experienced increased interpersonal stress and a destabilizing household structure. It is important to note that while substantial heterogeneity exists in factors associated with suicide ideation between the tribes, a small percentage of youth in each of these tribes may experience serious and recurrent thoughts about suicide. Results from a study by Middlebrook, LeMaster, Beals, Novins, and Manson (1998) have suggested that although completed suicide rates for Native youth are higher than in general populations, the suicide rates vary considerably between tribes.

Gang Involvement

American Indian youth gangs have become a focus of concern on many reservations during the past decade (Arrillaga, 2001; Hernandez, 2002; Khoury 1998). For troubled Native youth, particularly those already adrift as a consequence of dysfunctional families, establishing peer relationships with other distressed youth may be a motivating factor in finding a new sense of belonging to something. Most of these youth are also reportedly heavily involved in alcohol, drugs, crime, and violence, leading to serious problems in school and detachment from their community and traditional culture (Henderson, Kunitz, & Levy, 1999). Although gangs clearly are not indigenous to Native American communities, the poverty, alcoholism, domestic abuse, and sense of hopelessness on many Indian reservations have placed a burden on Native adolescents and a challenge on parents and families (Campbell, 2000; Clarke, 2002).

Over the years, research efforts to document American Indian youth gangs have evolved from a number of surveys. These studies include the FBI (Conway, 1999), the Bureau of Indian Affairs (Juneau, 1998), an academic master's thesis (Hailer, 1998), and a collaborative effort between the Office of Juvenile Justice and Delinquency Prevention (OJJDP) and the Judicial Branch of the Navajo Nation (OJJDP, 1995). Data from the FBI study was based on telephone interviews with tribal law enforcement officers from 40 reservations experiencing severe gang-related difficulties. Findings from the Bureau of Indian Affairs survey identified names of male and female gangs affiliated with specific reservations, along with a list of referring offenses and the degree to which tribes had taken necessary steps to enact antigang legislation and develop community-based prevention programs (Juneau, 1998). The Bureau of Indian Affairs survey was based on a mailed question- naire with results from 75 tribes confirming a nationwide distribution of Native youth gangs on reservations. Hailer's survey (1998) of Indian area law enforcement agencies examined the formation of gangs, the reported presence of gang activity and the characteristics of individual gangs recognized by tribal law enforcement officers. Thirty-four of the 67 respondents to Hailer's mailed questionnaire identified from 1 to 33 different gangs on separate reservations, with a majority of reservations listing 3 or 4 gangs.

In 1995, the first on-site study was conducted between the OJJDP and the Judicial Branch of the Navajo Nation (OJJDP, 1995). Funding for the project was in response to concerns coming directly from Navajo judges, law enforcement officials, social service agencies, and schools. Reservation staff hired to oversee the data collection interviewed 103 gang members, 192 "stakeholders" (agencies), and 25 off-reservation law enforcement officials. Conclusions from the surveys and interviews supported a number of previous research findings in that Navajo gang members were typically drawn from a highly troubled segment of youth who experienced academic problems and truancy, had virtually no parental guidance or support, no knowledge of their clan affiliation, and were likely to be nonspeakers of their native language.

In 2001, the National Youth Gang Center (NYGC) surveyed a total of 577 federally recognized tribal entities across the United States, initially targeting tribal leaders but later including law enforcement agencies that serve American Indian reservations and communities (Major & Egley, 2002). Overall, 52% responded to the survey, and 23% of those tribal communities reported experiencing a youth gang problem in 2000. Gang members were most often reported as male. Types of crimes they were involved in varied significantly, but often included vandalism and graffiti.

A self-report survey was conducted with 393 male and 465 female American Indian adolescents between 1989 to 1993 by Donnermeyer, Edwards, Chavez, and Beauvais (1996). This sample came from 7th- through 12th-grade Native youth attending school on reservations and in urban settings in Montana, New Mexico, Oklahoma, and South Dakota. Roughly 5% of the males and less than 1% of the females reported actual gang membership but the level of drug use and involvement in juvenile delinquency was higher for youths in gangs and those who associated with them compared with those adolescents who reportedly were not involved. Whereas other studies have associated risk factors for gang activity based on poverty, discrimination, and loss of cultural identity, the diffusion of gang culture from this adolescent survey was based on contact between Indian and non-Indian youth who had knowledge about gangs.

A comparable study by Whitbeck, Hoyt, Chen, and Stubben (2002) surveyed 212 adolescents from three Indian reservations in the upper Midwest. Results show that 30% of the youth reported being approached to join a gang by the time they were in 8th grade. The emerging profile among the 5th- to 8th-grade Native students who reported gang involvement described either a male or female that engaged in delinquent activity and/ or substance abuse and lived in a single-mother household where the mother had a history of antisocial behavior. In addition, that adolescent had most likely experienced multiple life transitions or losses in the past year and was doing poorly in academics. Interestingly in some cases, the more the adolescents were involved in traditional activities (e.g., "the more conspicuously American Indian"), the more likely that they would be involved in gangs and the more likely that they would experience discrimination. The authors interpret this finding to suggest that those youth who are more traditionally involved, not including spiritual practices, may view gangs as protective or at least as a source of identity through association with other American Indian adolescents (Whitbeck, Hoyt, McMorris, Chen, & Stubben, 2001). This interpretation of gang involvement as a means of coping with perceived discrimination is comparable with findings pertaining to gang membership and other ethnicities. Moreover, many of the factors used to explain Native American youth gang involvement meet nearly the same criteria used to explain gang membership among other ethnic groups (OJJDP, 2000).

PREVENTION AND INTERVENTION STRATEGIES

To address the increasing rates of juvenile violence and crime on Indians reservations, the U.S. Congress appropriated funding to establish the Tribal Youth Program (TYP) in 1999 (Pub. L. No. 106-113, 1999) under the administration of the OJJDP (Andrews, 1999). Several broad program areas were established by TYP to promote funding for the development and design of violence and delinquency prevention: (a) mental health and substance abuse prevention; (b) coordination of community infrastructures to control crime, violence, and drug abuse; (c) training and technical assistance for program implementation; and (d) research and evaluation (McKinney, 2003).

The basic strategy behind the TYP is to empower American Indian communities to determine the resolution of their social problems, using the spiritual and cultural aspect of their specific Native traditions. Transforming Native American communities in crisis requires that many of interventions involve the entire family. The buffering effects of protective factors such as family and social support are well recognized as one of the survival strengths of American Indian culture. Western cultural values that focus on individualism and individual choice are frequently at odds with Native values of consensus and extended family and are seen as obstacles in recovery when Native youth and their families are forced to work within a dominant culture framework.

Significant interventions that have been initiated in TYP prevention programs include the development of youth tribal courts that incorporate cultural traditions in dealing with young people (Tanana Chiefs Conference in Fairbanks, Alaska), and youth mentoring activities that include police officers and home detention systems reducing the need to place youth away from their families (Ysleta Del Sur Pueblo in El Paso, Texas). Other noteworthy activities developed through the TYP Mental Health Project involve behavioral and psychological assessments and therapies including talking circles, sand tray painting, and adventure-based programs (Confederated Tribes of Siletz Indians, Oregon), and an inpatient treatment center and residential treatment services for at-risk males of ages 13 to 18 (Osage Nation/Pawhuska, Oklahoma; McKinney, 2003).

General activities that may be incorporated in any number of tribal programs include teen pregnancy prevention, participation of community elders to mentor and promote positive behaviors among youth, teen parenting skills classes, and health education forums. These activities may also be presented in the context of ceremony and rituals and learning activities that involve participation in traditional forms of song and dance, gathering food, fishing, shepherding, storytelling and harvesting crops (Sanchez-Way & Johnson, 2000).

Another "best practice" prevention program that is also adaptable to different tribes and tribal groups is the Gathering of Native Americans (GONA), which focuses on community and family healing from historical and cultural trauma. The GONA curriculum was developed in 1992 to 1994 under contract to the Center for Substance Abuse Prevention (CSAP) by a team of American Indian trainers and curriculum developers from across the United States (Center for Substance Abuse Prevention, 1999). Based on values that are inherent to traditional tribal culture, the GONA training program is based on four stages of development—belonging, mastery, independence, and generosity. The underlying message to youth is that healthy personal development requires each child, adult, and community to evolve sequentially through stages of the cycle of life. If a stage is missed, the individual or community must go back and reprocess that stage in order to fully mature. Considering that so many American Indian families and communities have been traumatized by historical grief, poverty, substance abuse, and violence, the GONA model is a positive and cathartic experience in personal and community healing and the reclaiming of American Indian identity and pride.

CONCLUSION

It is imperative to consider that while the historical past may seem far enough away from the present day, the lives of many American Indian youth are still coming to terms with the history of their ancestors and the contemporary experience of life in this time. In the rapidly changing U.S. society, American Indians find themselves constantly and inevitably surrounded by non-Indian people and non-Indian culture. The fact that American Indians have held to a distinctive set of values, practices, and traditional beliefs, despite a history of cultural struggle and assimilation, suggests that the identity of American Indians is a deeply rooted connection that is central to their survival. It may also be that the heart of Native cultural differences stem from a vision that cannot and should not be obscured by dominant Western cultural paradigms.

Although successful youth violence prevention programs currently operate across Indian country, there are still too few programs existing to serve the needs of both reservation and urban American Indian populations. A number of tribes are undertaking educational and interventional approaches to youth violence prevention, but the programs themselves may not be inclusive enough to address the multiple and interacting problems associated with crime, violence, and substance abuse. It is also important to keep in mind that cultural diversity between tribal groups, as well as differences between reservation versus urban Indian residents, make it impossible to precisely describe "American Indian youth violence," as well as to prescribe a general violence prevention and intervention program that will apply for all Native youth. Thus, service providers and juvenile justice administrators must become partners with their respective American Indian communities to create unique and effective violence prevention programs that convey a responsiveness to individual tribal needs, reflecting the distinct cultural and ceremonial practices of each community. Prevention models must emphasize the resiliency and cultural strengths of American Indian families that are crucial to building a positive cultural identity for American Indian adolescents. Non-Indians often do not understand this important reconnection to traditional Indian values.

With regard to plans for the future direction of research and evaluation of American Indian youth violence and prevention programs, it is necessary to actively engage the collective voices of American Indian youth themselves, who are the focus of the research. Identifying the full range of violence problems is essential in deconstructing the relative importance youth attribute to violence and violent behaviors. The use of informal interviews, talking circles, and "violence episode narratives" can generate knowledge and discussion necessary to taking action that is appropriate for individual, family, and tribal needs. These types of qualitative methodologies can also provide important contextual information for use in more structural assessments of violence behaviors such as feelings of alienation, self-worth, and lack of familial socialization found in many distressed American Indian adolescents.

The best long-term solutions to challenges facing Native youth are through reversing the patterns of violence and victimization by jointly addressing high rates of alcohol and drug abuse, homicide, suicide, depression, and delinquency. Violence prevention strategies and educational programs must match the risks, traditional needs, and contemporary expectations of American Indian communities. Native authors Duran and Duran (1995) have advised that "the Native American community can help itself by legitimizing its own knowledge and thus allowing for healing to emerge from with the community" (p. 53).

REFERENCES

Abel, E. L. (1998a). *Fetal alcohol abuse syndrome*. New York: Plenum Press.

Abel, E. L. (1998b). Fetal alcohol syndrome: The American paradox. *Alcohol and Alcoholism, 33,* 195–201.

Adams, D. W. (1995). *Education for extinction: American Indians and the boarding school experience.* Lawrence: University Press of Kansas.

Andrews, C. (1999). *Tribal youth program.* Fact Sheet (FS 99108). Washington, DC: U.S. Department of Justice, Office of Justice Programs, Office of Juvenile Justice and Delinquency Prevention.

Arrillaga, P. (2001, April 15). Stuck between cultures: Indian youth struggle with violence, dependency, and depression. *Los Angeles Times,* p. B1.

Beals, J., Piasecki, J., Nelson, S., Jones, M., Keane, E., Dauphinais, P., et al. (1997). Psychiatric disorder among American Indian adolescents: Prevalence in northern plains youth. *Journal of the American Academy of Child and Adolescent Psychiatry, 36,* 1252–1259.

Beauvais, F. (1992). An integrated model for prevention and treatment of drug abuse among American Indian youth. *Journal of Addictive Diseases, 11,* 63–80.

Beauvais, F. (2000). Indian adolescence: Opportunity and challenge. In R. Montemayor, G. R. Adams, & T. P. Gullotta (Eds.), *Adolescent diversity in ethnic, economic, and cultural contexts* (pp. 110–140). Thousand Oaks, CA: Sage.

Bechtold, D. W., Manson, S. M., & Shore, J. H. (1994). Psychosocial consequences of stress among Native American adolescents. In R. Lieberman & J. Yaeger (Eds.), *Stress and psychiatry* (pp. 101–116). New York: Plenum Press.

Borowsky, I. W., Resnick, M. D., Ireland, M., & Blum, R. W. (1999). Suicide attempts among American Indian and Alaska Native youth. *Archives of Pediatric Adolescent Medicine, 153,* 573–580.

Brave Heart, M. Y. H. (1999a). Gender differences in the historical trauma response among the Lakota. *Journal of Health and Social Policy, 10,* 1–21.

Brave Heart, M. Y. H. (1999b). Oyate Ptayela: Rebuilding the Lakota nation through addressing historical trauma among Lakota parents. *Journal of Human Behavior in the Social Environment, 2*, 109–126.

Brave Heart, M. Y. H., & DeBruyn, L. M. (1998). The American Indian holocaust: Healing historical unresolved grief. *American Indian and Alaskan Native Mental Health Research, 8*, 56–78.

Campbell, B. N. (2000). Challenges facing American Indian youth: On the front lines with Senator Ben Nighthorse Campbell. *Juvenile Justice, 7*, 3–8.

Center for Substance Abuse Prevention and Indian Health Service. (1999). *The gathering of Native Americans (GONA)*. Rockville, MD: Author.

Chavez, G. F., Cordero, J. F., & Becerra, J. E. (1988). Leading major congenital malformations among minority groups in the United States, 1981–1986. *Morbidity and Mortality Weekly Report, 37*(SS-3), 17–24.

Child, B. J. (1998). *Boarding school seasons: American Indian families, 1900–1940.* Lincoln: University of Nebraska Press.

Clarke, A. S. (2002 January). Social and emotional distress among American Indian and Alaska Native students: Research findings. *Eric Digest EDO-RC-01-11.* Retrieved April 19, 2003, from http://www.indianeduresearch.net/edorc01-11.html

Coalition for Juvenile Justice. (2000). *Enlarging the healing circle: Ensuring justice for American Indian children.* Washington, DC: Office of Juvenile Justice and Delinquency Prevention.

Conway, M. K. (1999). *SIAU intelligence report: Gangs on Indian reservations.* Washington, DC: Federal Bureau of Investigation.

Cummins, J. R., Ireland, M., Resnick, M. D., & Blum, R. W. (1998). Correlates of physical and emotional health among Native American adolescents. *Journal of Adolescent Health, 24*, 38–44.

DeJong, D. H. (1993). *Promises of the past: A history of Indian education.* Golden, CO: North American Press.

Donnermeyer, J. F., Edwards, R. W., Chavez, E. L., & Beauvais, F. (1996). Involvement of American Indian youth in gangs. *Free Inquiry in Creative Sociology, 24*, 167–174.

Duran, B., Duran, E., & Brave Heart, M. Y. H. (1998). Native Americans and the trauma of history. In R. Thorton (Ed.), *Studying Native America* (pp. 60–76). Madison: University of Wisconsin Press.

Duran, E., & Duran, B. (1995). *Native American postcolonial psychology.* Albany: State University of New York.

EchoHawk, M. (1997). Suicide: The scourge of Native American people. *Suicide and Life Threatening Behavior, 27*, 60–67.

Fisher, P. A., Storck, M., & Bacon, J. G. (1999). In the eye of the beholder: Risk and protective factors in rural American Indian and Caucasian adolescents. *American Orthopsychiatric Association, 69*, 294–304.

Gover, K. (1998, October 20). Speech by Kevin Gover, assistant secretary—Indian Affairs, Department of the Interior, before the 55th Annual National Congress of American Indians, Myrtle Beach, SC.

Gray, N. (1998). Addressing trauma in substance abuse treatment with American Indian adolescents. *Journal of Substance Abuse Treatment, 15*, 393–399.

Greenfeld, L. A., & Smith, S. K. (1999). *American Indians and crime*. Washington, DC: U.S. Department of Justice, Bureau of Justice Statistics.

Grossman, D. C., Milligan, B. C., & Deyon, R. A. (1991). Risk factors for suicide attempts among Navajo adolescents. *American Journal of Public Health, 81*, 870–874.

Hailer, J. A. (1998). *A loss of traditions: The emergence of American Indian youth gangs*. Master's thesis, San Jose State University/Administration of Justice Department, San Jose, CA.

Henderson, E., Kunitz, S. J., & Levy, J. E. (1999). The origins of Navajo youth gangs. *American Indian Culture and Research Journal, 23*, 243–264.

Hernandez, A. (2002, December). Can education play a role in the prevention of youth gangs in Indian country? One tribe's approach. *ERIC Digest EDO-RC-12*. Retrieved April 4, 2003, from http://www.ael.org/eric/

Hurst, S., & Lefler, L. J. (2003). *American Indian adolescent co-morbid treatment issues*. Manuscript in preparation.

Indian Health Service. (1998). *1998–1999 Indian health focus—Youth*. Washington, DC: U.S. Office of Public Health, Office of Planning Support, Program Statistics Team, Department of Health and Human Services.

Indian Health Service. (1999). *1998–1999 trends in Indian health*. Washington, DC: U.S. Office of Planning, Evaluation, and Legislation, Department of Health and Human Services.

Jones, M. C, Dauphinais, P., Sack, W. H., & Somervell, P. D. (1997). Trauma-related symptomatology among American Indian adolescents. *Journal of Traumatic Stress, 102*, 163–173.

Juneau, S. K. (1998). *1998 Annual report: Gangs in Indian country*. Artesia, NM: U.S. Department of the Interior, Bureau of Indian Affairs, Indian Police Academy.

Khoury, K. (1998 July 9). Fighting back against Indian gangs. *Special to The Christian Science Monitor*. Retrieved April 19, 2003, from http://www. csmonitor.com/durable/1998/07/09/p4s1.html

MacDonald, D. I. (1989). *Drugs, drinking, and adolescents*. Chicago: Year Book Medical.

Major, A. K., & Egley, A., Jr. (2002). 2000 Survey of youth gangs in Indian country. *National Youth Gang Center Fact Sheet*. Retrieved April 19, 2003, from http://www.iir.com/nygc

Manson, S. M., Beals, J., Dick, R. W., & Duclos, C. (1989). Risk factors for suicide among Indian adolescents at a boarding school. *Public Health Reports, 104*, 609–614.

Manson, S. M., Beals, J., O'Nell, T., Piasecki, J., Becktold, J., Keane, E., et al. (1996). Wounded spirits, ailing hearts: PTSD and related disorders among American Indians. In A. J. Marsella, M. J. Friedman, E. T. Gerrity, & R. M. Scurfield (Eds.), *Ethnocultural aspects of posttraumatic stress disorder: Issues, research, and clinical applications* (pp. 255–284). Washington, DC: American Psychological Association.

May, P. A. (1996). Overview of alcohol abuse: Epidemiology for American Indian populations. In G. D. Sandifur (Ed.), *Changing numbers, changing needs: American Indian demography and public health* (pp. 235–261). Washington, DC: National Academy Press.

May, P. A., & Gossage, J. P. (2001). Estimating the prevalence of fetal alcohol syndrome: A summary. *Alcohol Research and Health, 25,* 159–167.

McKinney, K. (2003, May). OJJDP's tribal youth initiatives. *Juvenile Justice Bulletin.* Washington, DC: Office of Juvenile Justice and Delinquency Prevention.

Middlebrook, D. L., LeMaster, P. L., Beals, J., Novins, D. K., & Manson, S. M. (1998, October). *Suicide prevention in American Indian and Alaska Native communities: A critical review of programs.* Paper presented at a meeting of the National Suicide Prevention Conference, Reno, NV.

National Center for Health Statistics. (2002). Births: Final data for 2000. *National Vital Statistics Reports, 514–521.*

National Center for Juvenile Justice. (1999). *Juvenile offenders and victims: 1999 national report.* Washington, DC: U.S. Department of Justice, Office of Juvenile Justice and Delinquency Prevention.

National Household Survey on Drug Abuse Report. (2003). *Substance use among American Indians or Alaska Natives.* Rockville, MD: Substance Abuse and Mental Health Services Administration, Office of Applied Studies.

National Indian Gaming Association. (2001). The national evidence on the socioeconomic impacts of American Indian gaming. *Newsletter.* Retrieved September 12, 2003, from http://www.indiangaming.org/library/newsletters/newsletter 9-00.html

Nissim-Sabat, D. (1999). *Suicide: A crisis within the American Indian and Alaskan Native community.* Congressional testimony submitted to the Hearing on Native American Youth Activities and Initiatives before the Senate Committee on Indian Affairs.

Novins, D. K., Beals, J., Roberts, R. E., & Manson, S. M. (1999). Factors associated with suicide ideation among American Indian adolescents: Does culture matter? *Suicide and Life Threatening Behavior, 29,* 332–346.

Novins, D. K., Beals, J., Shore, J. H., & Manson, S. M. (1996). Substance abuse treatment of American Indian adolescents: Co-morbid symptomatology, gender differences, and treatment patterns. *Journal of American Academy of Child Adolescent Psychiatry, 35,* 1593–1601.

Office of Juvenile Justice and Delinquency Prevention. (1995). *Field-initiated gang research: Finding and knowing the gang Nayee in the Navajo nation.* Washington, DC: U.S. Department of Justice.

Office of Juvenile Justice and Delinquency Prevention. (2000). *1998 national gang survey*. Washington, DC: U.S. Department of Justice.

O'Nell, T. D., & Mitchell, C. M. (1996). Alcohol use among American Indian adolescents: The role of culture in pathological drinking. *Social Science and Medicine, 42*, 565–578.

Pfefferbaum, B., Pfefferbaum, R. L., Strickland, R. J., & Brandt, E. N., Jr. (1999). Juvenile delinquency in American Indian youths: Historical and cultural factors. *Journal of Oklahoma State Medical Association, 92*, 121–125.

Plunkett, M., & Mitchell, C. M. (2000). Substance use rates among American Indian adolescents: Regional comparisons with monitoring the future high school seniors. *Journal of Drug Issues, 30*, 575–591.

Rennison, C. (2001). *Violent victimization and race, 1993–98*. Special Report. Washington, DC: U.S. Department of Justice, Office of Justice Programs, Bureau of Justice Statistics.

Robin, R. W., Chester, B., Rasmussen, J. K., Jaranson, J. M., & Goldman, D. (1997). Relationship of binge drinking to alcohol dependence, other psychiatric disorders, and behavioral problems in an American Indian tribe. *Alcoholism: Clinical and Experimental Research, 22*, 518–523.

Sanchez-Way, R., & Johnson, S. (2000). Cultural practices in American Indian prevention programs. *Juvenile Justice, 7*, 20–30.

Shaffer, J. N., & Ruback, R. B. (2002, December). Violent victimization as a risk factor for violent offending among juveniles. *Juvenile Justice Bulletin*, n.p.

Snipp, C. M. (2002, April). *American Indian and Alaska Native children in the 2000 Census*. Baltimore: Annie E. Casey Foundation/Population Reference Bureau.

Snyder, H. N. (2001, December). Law enforcement and juvenile crime. *National Report Series Bulletin*. Washington, DC: Office of Juvenile Justice and Delinquency Prevention.

Snyder, H. N. (2002, November). Juvenile arrests 2000. *Juvenile Justice Bulletin*. Washington, DC: Office of Juvenile Justice and Delinquency Prevention.

Snyder, H. N., & Sickmund, M. (1999). *Juvenile offenders and victims: 1999 national report*. Washington, DC: Office of Juvenile Justice and Delinquency Prevention.

Streissguth, A. (1996, September). *The challenge of fetal alcohol syndrome: Overcoming secondary disabilities*. Paper presented at the International Fetal Alcohol Syndrome Conference, Seattle, WA.

Substance Abuse and Mental Health Services Administration. (2003). *Overview of findings from the 2002 national survey on drug use and health*. DHHS Publication No. SMA 03–3774, NSDUH Series H-21. Rockville, MD: Substance Abuse and Mental Health Services Administration, Office of Applied Studies.

U.S. Census Bureau. (2003). *American Indian and Alaska Native heritage month: November 2003*. Facts for Features, CB03-FF.16. October 20, 2003 [Quotes and Radio Sound Bites]. Washington, DC: Author.

U.S. Census Bureau. (2002). *The American Indian and Alaska Native population: 2000.* Census 2000 Brief. Washington, DC: U.S. Department of Commerce Economics and Statistics Administration.

U.S. Department of Health and Human Services. (2001). *Mental health: Culture, race, and ethnicity. A supplement to mental health: A report of the surgeon general.* Rockville, MD: U.S. Department of Health and Human Services, Public Health Service, Office of the Surgeon General.

U.S. Department of the Interior. (1999). *Indian labor force report.* Washington, DC: Bureau of Indian Affairs, Office of Tribal Services.

Vanderwagen, C. (1990, December 10). Statement by the acting associate director in the office of health programs, Indian health services before the Subcommittee on Social Security and Family Policy Committee on Finance, U.S. Senate.

Wakeling, S., Jorgensen, M., Michaelson, S., & Begay, M. (2001). *Policing on American Indian reservations: A report to the national institute of justice.* Washington, DC: National Institute of Justice, Office of Justice Programs, U.S. Department of Justice.

Whitbeck, L. B., Hoyt, D. R., Chen, X., & Stubben, J. D. (2002). Predictors of gang involvement among American Indian adolescents. *Journal of Gang Research, 10,* 11–26.

Whitbeck, L. B., Hoyt, D. R., McMorris, B. J., Chen, X., & Stubben, J. D. (2001). Perceived discrimination and early substance abuse among American Indian children. *Journal of Health and Social Behavior, 42,* 405–424.

7

PREVENTING YOUTH VIOLENCE AMONG AFRICAN AMERICAN YOUTH: THE SOCIOCULTURAL CONTEXT OF RISK AND PROTECTIVE FACTORS

EMILIE PHILLIPS SMITH AND LA MAR HASBROUCK

Youth violence is a problem that disproportionately affects African American youth, both in terms of victimization and perpetration, causing disparities in life expectancy. Given these disparities, a considerable amount of attention has focused on understanding further the etiology of youth violence based on risk factors that are shared with all youth or with other ethnic minority youth, as well as risk factors that reflect unique circumstances and characteristics of African American youth. In this chapter, we rely on the epidemiological triad to frame the role of risk for youth violence with a focus on factors that seem to be especially salient for African Americans. We also review violence prevention programs that have been implemented and evaluated with significant numbers of African American youth, and we discuss how the programs are linked to shared and unique risk factors. As we point out, there is still a need to understand better the sociocultural context of youth violence etiology and prevention for African Americans.

THE SCOPE OF THE PROBLEM

Youth violence involves behaviors ranging from physical fighting to more severe forms of physical assault that can result in serious injury or death. Any discussion of violence as it relates to African American youth must begin with a brief restating of the already familiar and dispiriting statistics showing the disproportionate burden on this population. The decade between 1983 and 1993 was marked by an epidemic of increasingly deadly violence that was associated with a large rise in use of firearms, involving primarily African American males (U.S. Department of Health and Human Services, 2001). Since 1994, however, there has been a decline in homicide for all racial groups. African American youth have followed a similar pattern. Although these recent downward trends are encouraging, rates of youth violence among African American youth remain at historically high levels and have not declined to pre-epidemic levels before the mid-1980s.

In 2000, violence (homicide and suicide) was the number one leading cause of death for African American youth and young adults that year (Centers for Disease Control and Prevention, 2005). Moreover, official statistics show that African Americans are victimized by and arrested for violence disproportionately. Differences in the rates of violence across racial and ethnic groups must be viewed in terms of the life circumstances of various groups. For example, in the year 2000, poverty among African Americans with children under 18 was 25.3%, down from 31.2% in 1990, yet nearly three times the 7.7% rate for non-Latino Whites (U.S. Census Bureau, n.d.-a). This means that at least one in every five African American children live in poverty.

Another way to measure the disparate impact of violence on African Americans is to consider the contribution of deadly violence on life expectancy. According to a recent study (Centers for Disease Control and Prevention, 2001), Whites lived 6.2 years longer than African Americans. Homicide accounted for 9.7% (0.6 years) of the difference in life expectancy, despite accounting for less than 1% of the total deaths for the U.S. population in 1998. For males, homicide accounted for 14.1% (0.9 years) of the 6.4 years difference in life expectancy. For females, the contribution of homicide to the 4.4-year life expectancy gap was less; 4.5% or 0.2 years. Homicide primarily affects people in their second and third decade of life, whereas death from heart disease and cancer—the number one and number two leading contributors to the life gap—primarily affects people in their fifth and sixth decades of life. Homicide results in more years of young lives lost. In addition, the mortality burden from homicide on African Americans is much greater than for Whites. Death rates from homicide have historically been six- to eight-fold greater for African Americans compared with Whites.

THE AFRICAN AMERICAN EXPERIENCE
IN THE UNITED STATES

This section provides a brief historical background and demographic portrait of African Americans in the United States. Africans came to the Americas through the slave trade as early as 1518 and to what is now the United States in the early 1600s. This slave trade began after a Golden Age in West Africa during which West African countries regularly traded salt, gold, and slaves with Northern Africa, Spain, and Italy (Davidson, 1998). Slaves in this society could buy, marry, or complete a period of limited servitude and some suggest that slavery in Northern and West Africa was less bound by color lines. Scholars debate exactly how many Africans were brought to America. Estimates suggest that during the course of about 250 years, 30 to 70 million Africans were transported with about one-third surviving the middle passage across the Atlantic Ocean to arrive in the United States. Others regularly threw themselves and their children into the ocean to avoid enslavement, and the slave traders regularly dumped the bodies of dead and infirm Africans into the ocean (Davidson, 1998).

Once in America, enslaved Africans were forbidden to maintain their names, native language, cultural practices, or celebrations, practically erasing any visible signs of culture and forcing their integration into the fabric of slave society (Haley, 1980). African American and abolitionist resistance to the institution of slavery grew, but increasingly rigid laws in the United States limited their freedom and the ways by which they could attain their freedom. A moral divide emerged in the country that culminated in the Civil War and the Emancipation Proclamation of 1863 freeing the enslaved Africans. The years following did not bring the "40 acres and a mule" promised to African Americans by the government. Indeed, laws were passed legalizing racial segregation (i.e., *Plessy v. Ferguson*, 1896). During the period of the early to mid-1900s, thousands of African American men were lynched in the South, brutally hung from trees, burned, and often castrated. Between 1882 and 1968, there were 4,743 individuals lynched in the United States; more than 70% of the victims were African Americans (Brundage, 1993). Race riots in the early 1900s resulted in the destruction of entire African American communities (e.g., Rosewood, Florida, and Tulsa, Oklahoma) triggered by racial animosity. As late as the 1950s, "Jim Crow" laws in the South designated movie theaters, restaurants, and even bathrooms and water fountains as "Colored" or "White only" (Meier & Rudwick, 1976). In the 20th century, it is a challenging task to document the amount of discrimination and lingering poverty caused by hundreds of years of slavery, oppression, and discrimination.

According to data from the U.S. Census Bureau (2005b), 34 million African Americans reside in the United States, making up nearly 14% of the population. African Americans are concentrated in the South and the nation's urban areas because of migration patterns toward industrialized work and employment. Although historically large gaps have existed in educational attainment, the African American high school completion rate of 80% now rivals the 86% completion rate of European Americans. However, similar to Americans overall, the marriage rate among African Americans has been decreasing, albeit more drastically, from 80% in 1960 to approximately 47% in 2005 (U.S. Census Bureau, n.d.-b). Single parents are more likely to be impoverished; the poverty rate for African Americans stands at 22% overall and at 32% for African American female-headed households (U.S. Census Bureau, n.d.-a).

RISK AND RESILIENCE AMONG AFRICAN AMERICAN YOUTH

A central premise of this volume is that the relation between risk and resiliency factors and youth violence in many cases does not vary by ethnicity; rather, ethnic minority youth experience developmental ecologies and environmental conditions that make it more likely these risk factors will occur. Furthermore, as has been pointed out, some additional risk factors are unique to ethnic groups or to the minority experience, such as the link between ethnic identity and youth violence. We now turn to a discussion of risk for youth violence among African American youth and illustrate how risk and resilience play out within this ethnic group. We anchor our discussion in the epidemiological triangle.

The epidemiological triangle or triad is the traditional model for examining acute disease conditions (e.g., infectious diseases); however, it has been used for noninfectious conditions as well (Haddon, 1968). The model has three components: an external agent, a susceptible host, and an environment that brings the host and agent together. We use this triad as a framework for our discussion of violence among African Americans. For our purposes, the concept of agent can be broadened to refer to weapons used to cause the violence-related injury (e.g., body parts, knives, blunt object), perhaps none more important than firearms. Host factors influence an individual's exposure, susceptibility, or response to a causative agent. For example, age, race, gender, emotional state, social skills, and early antisocial behaviors are some of the many host factors that affect a person's likelihood of exposure. Lastly, environmental factors are extrinsic factors that affect the agent and the opportunity for exposure. Some of the environmental factors for violence include factors such as peer affiliation, poor relations with parents, parent disciplinary practices, exposure to family violence, physical surroundings (e.g., housing, recreational facilities), and socioeconomic factors such as crowding and residing in a poor community with diminished economic opportunities (see Guerra & Williams, chap. 1, this volume).

Agent, host, and environmental factors interrelate in a variety of complex ways to produce violent behaviors and violence-related morbidity and mortality in the African American community. To better inform future directions in research and prevention strategies, we examine the contributions of all three factors, and their interactions. Finally, based on our analysis, we briefly describe approaches that build on existing best practices for effective prevention and control of violence among African American youth.

Agent Factors

In the case of violence, the agent factors that are most important are those associated with the method or mechanism of the violent act, namely the weapon. The concept of weapon can be broadly defined to include not only firearms, but also knifes, blunt objects, body parts (e.g., fist, foot), suffocation, and others. An examination of homicide rates during the epidemic and postepidemic period of youth violence (1983–2000) shows a steep rise and fall associated with increased firearm use. Both total and firearm-related homicide rates increased dramatically for individuals aged 10 to 19 years, peaking in 1993, and have declined since then. Likewise, the downward trend in homicide arrests beginning in 1993 was traced to declining firearm usage (U.S. Department of Health and Human Services, 2001). Virtually all of the increase in firearm-related homicides involved African American youths (Snyder & Sickmund, 1999). In 1983, African American youth were killed by someone using a firearm 69% of the time; 31% were killed by other weapons, such as a knife or body part. By 2000, the proportion of young African American homicide victims killed by a firearm had increased to 85%.

Clearly, firearms are critical agents for violence as youth have engaged in more fatal forms of violence. The easy availability of guns, changes in the types of guns manufactured—with cheaper, larger caliber guns flooding the market—and recruitment of youths into crack cocaine and other drug markets, where carrying guns became routine, have been postulated to explain the upsurge in firearms use among all youth (Blumstein & Wallman, 2000). These factors are particularly important for African American youth who are more likely to reside in poor neighborhoods beset with violence, drug abuse, and crime, making these youths more vulnerable to the danger of alternative economies (Johnson, Golub, & Dunlap, 2000).

Host Factors

African American youth are far more likely to experience violence at the hands of a peer or acquaintance than a stranger (Hammond & Yung, 1993). Although some view the amount of violence among youth acquaintances as evidence for the need of more constructive conflict resolution (Mercy & Rosenberg, 1998), others view interpersonal violence among these youth as reflecting society's lack of value for African American life, a form of self-hatred (Poussaint, 1985). The self-hatred hypothesis for violence has received little empirical attention; however, interest in the role of identity, and specifically ethnic identity in youth behavior, has grown in the past decades. On one hand, ethnic identity might result in more violence particularly when expressed among youth in oppositional peer groups that eschew successful integration into society. Another perspective of ethnic identity postulates that greater levels of self and group pride function in protective fashion, leading to greater self-efficacy and reduced involvement in violence and aggression. French, Kim, and Pillado (chap. 2, this volume) point out that ethnic identity may operate differently in different ethnic groups. As they discuss with data from the Adolescent Pathways Project, ethnic group esteem is related to reduced later delinquency for African American adolescents but not for Latino youth.

Other individual host factors that have been shown to increase violent behaviors among youth include antisocial attitudes and beliefs, a positive attitude toward violence, aggression in boys (and young men), involvement in serious nonviolent offenses, and substance use (U.S. Department of Health and Human Services, 2001). For African American youth who tend to report less substance abuse, the risk of substance use may lie more in the situations in which drug use and violence co-occur than in the effect of the substance on behavior. In the late 1980s, young adolescents were welcomed into the crack cocaine markets because they were less likely to consume the drug and received lighter sentences than adults if caught (Johnson et al., 2000). Cocaine and crack drug-trafficking provided access to alternate forms of income, firearms, and the belonging and protection of a gang or "crew" (Johnson et al., 2000).

The crack market was pivotal in increased access to and deaths because of firearms among adolescent gangs who wielded weapons to avert being caught by police, robbed, or harmed by competing gangs; innocent bystanders were often caught in the crossfire. The tough policing standards introduced to curb the crack market (versus the standards used for cocaine, the drug of the more affluent) resulted in long sentences for possessing even small amounts of crack and increased the proportion of African American males jailed from 25% to 33% between 1989 and 1994 (Blumstein, 2003; Johnson, et al., 2000). Drug-trafficking involved a mix of economic need of the youth, young age of the youth involved, nature of the crack drug producing impulsiveness and paranoia, and increased use of firearms in the crack market resulting in increased death and jailing of African American youth and in particular males.

There has been a clear link between exposure to media violence and aggression demonstrated by longitudinal studies spanning nearly two decades that show a persistent association between media violence consumed and aggression (Huessman, Moise, Podolski, & Eron, 2003). African Americans watch more television than any other racial group regardless of their socio-economic status (Comstock & Paik, 1991; Wilson, 1987). Although more likely to be consumers of television and other media, African Americans are often portrayed in limited, stereotypical, and often violent ways in the media (Murray & Mandara, 2002). At times, one wonders whether invisibility in the media would be better for youth development than consuming persistent stereotypical portrayals. Alternatively, young people are active partners in the video music industry, portraying images of African American masculinity and femininity that have been criticized for glamorizing violence and sexism. Television has a greater effect on the development of aggression when the aggressive behaviors learned by viewing media are not countered by a norm against such behavior. In recent years in the movie industry, portrayals of African Americans have expanded a bit. Some actors initially known for their roles as gun wielding "gang-bangers" are now portraying roles as fathers and businessmen (see Amber, 2005, discussing Ice Cube). It would be of interest to examine empirically the emerging variability of roles for African Americans and the opportunity to capitalize on the role of the media in positive youth development.

In summary, individual host factors that act to increase or buffer the likelihood of violence include being male, older age, hyperactivity and impulsiveness, social skills, and problem-solving abilities. Ethnic group es-teem, involvement in drug use or trafficking, and being exposed to various forms of violence through the media are factors that may be especially important to African American youth.

Environmental Factors

Environmental factors such as the family, peer, neighborhood, and larger society likely interact with individual host characteristics. Some of these various factors include parental disciplinary practices, being exposed to family violence, having delinquent peers, and being reared in violent neighborhoods with few opportunities for occupational advancement (Dishion, Patterson, Stoolmiller, & Skinner, 1991; Sampson & Laub, 1994; Vissing, Straus, Gelles, & Harrop, 1991; Wilson, 1987). Much more atten-tion has been given to the risk factors for violence and delinquency. In this section, environmental risk and protective processes that may be of particular salience for African American youth will be explored.

Family Factors

Research has found that there are descriptive characteristics of families, that is, single-parent status, and potentially socioeconomic status, that are related to youth involvement in violence and delinquency. Some of these variables are quite likely proxies for actual family processes. For example, single-parent status may be a marker for the level of parental monitoring and discipline available to young people, an important variable related to less involvement in violence and delinquency (Bank, Forgatch, Patterson, & Fetrow, 1993). Single parents carry the responsibility for the multiple needs of the family with one less adult to monitor children's activities and whereabouts. Monitoring among African American families is increased when extended families members (e.g., grandmother, aunt, etc.) are present in the household (Dornbusch et al., 1985). Another example is that of family socioeconomic status (SES). Across ethnicity, poorer, often female-headed, households are more likely to reside in lower-income–higher-crime neighborhoods, with fewer resources to monitor children and resulting in increased exposure to violence (Laub & Lauritsen, 1998). African American families are more likely to live in poor neighborhoods with severely concentrated disadvantage and increased deleterious effects (Wilson, 1987). Examining the actual family processes veiled by family descriptive characteristics is of value for developing effective prevention approaches.

Harsh, lax, or inconsistent discipline is often described as a risk factor for problem and aggressive behavior (Patterson, Reid, & Dishion, 1992). In families with inconsistent rules and guidelines, children do not have a clear sense of the behaviors that are expected, encouraged, and sanctioned in the household. Consistent disciplinary practices help young people to identify consequences and set limits for their behavior. Discrepant views exist as to what constitutes positive parenting practices and its effects within families of diverse ethnic backgrounds. Uninvolved parents and permissive parents have few if any behavioral standards and have children with poorer behavioral outcomes, regardless of the ethnicity of the family (Lamborn, Dornbusch, & Steinberg, 1996). Authoritarian parenting, in which parents have strict guidelines, rules and punishment, and with little discussion with children of the underlying reasons is found to result in reduced children's ability to make competent decisions. Authoritative parenting that includes both behavioral standards and communication seems to result in more optimal behavior and competence (Baumrind, 1972).

There is some dispute over findings showing that African American families tend to be less democratic with their children (Lamborn et al.,

1996). However, this reduced level of democracy and more parental decision making is related to positive child behavioral and academic outcomes among African American families. Some researchers concede that parents in challenging, racist, violent, and dangerous contexts may need swifter compliance and fewer debates from their young concerning the reasoning underlying parental demands on the child's behavior (Spencer & Dupree, 1996). Some African American parents in more violent neighborhoods with children who seem to fare well often do not allow their children to play outside as often, do not allow them to affiliate as much with other children in the neighborhood, and keep their children involved in structured recreational and enriching activities (Spencer & Dupree, 1996). This view of more parent-directed approaches acknowledges the role of potential social influences on families exerting more control in their children's lives.

Similarly, there is considerable debate arising in the field concerning African Americans and what has been defined as harsh punishment. Most often, the term *harsh discipline* refers to the use of corporal punishment, a policy already widely debated in the field. A significant amount of research, particularly among European Americas, has found harsh punishment to be related to increased violence (Deater-Deckard, Dodge, Bates, & Pettit, 1996). However, the research that has examined this dimension separately across ethnic groups has revealed that more African American families support corporal punishment among their disciplinary strategies but with no deleterious increase in violence and delinquency (Deater-Deckard et al., 1996). These findings do not include families who are clearly violent and abusive toward their children.

In some of the findings examining parenting across ethnicity, ethnicity is most often confounded with socioeconomic status (Murry, Smith, & Hill, 2001). Parents with lower levels of parental education and socioeconomic status report greater reliance on physical punishment as a method of child discipline (Pinderhughes, Dodge, Bates, Pettit, & Zelli, 2000). These family approaches seem, in part, to be a result of parental stress experienced by resource-poor families. Importantly, there is much to be learned about parenting in research where socioeconomic status and ethnic background are not confounded, including middle-class African Americans, so that one can decompose effects due to class and those potentially due to culture. Although middle-class African Americans still lack the amount of wealth possessed by European Americans, half of African American children grow up in middle-class families (Huston, McLoyd, & Garcia Coll, 1994). Furthermore, the vast majority of all African American youth, 80% to 90%, are not involved in violent crime (U.S. Department of Health and Human Services, 2001).

Our limited conceptualization and measurement of parenting may in part contribute to lack of understanding about African American parenting (Okazaki & Sue, 1995). The dimensions of parenting that have been identified as important have emanated from studies of mostly European American families. It is unknown as to whether there are other dimensions of parenting, particularly well-suited for diverse families. Furthermore, parents are frequently categorized along one dimension, for example, harsh parenting, without attention to other dimensions. Several investigators have emphasized the importance of investigating parental directiveness and the level of warmth in the family (Brody & Flor, 1998; McLoyd & Smith, 2002), a type of parenting Brody and Flor have branded "no-nonsense parenting." Research on parenting in diverse contexts is needed attending to multiple potentially beneficial dimensions and constellations of parenting.

Although some view African American parenting styles as emanating from the demands of a violent and racist context, still others propose that some aspects of African American families represent African cultural remnants (Sudarkasa, 1988). For example, the use of handles in the African American community even when preceding a first name (e.g., "Miss" Bettie or "Aunt" Dot) or, the participation of grandparents, augmented family, and friends in child-rearing exemplify the ways in which children are socialized to respect multiple adult authorities in their lives (Billinglsey, 1993). In West African society, and particularly among polygamous families, children were taught to respect multigenerational and multifamily adult authorities in their lives (Sudarkasa, 1988). This might have been adaptive to enslaved African children in the United States whose parents could be sold away from them suddenly without notice. The contemporary adaptation, "it takes a village to raise a child" reinvokes the practice of having multiple adults engaged in the discipline and training of children. The proviso, however, is that culture is dynamic and changing. Even as researchers are beginning to capture some of these sociocultural characteristics, they are changing in a society in which young people who are violent and armed feel less need to show deference to adult authority.

Peer and Gang Influences

During adolescence, the influence of peers relative to the family increases, although research has shown that the influence of negative peers is diminished in supportive families (Frauenglass, Routh, Pantin, & Mason, 1997). The strongest peer risk factors are weak ties to conventional peers, ties to antisocial or delinquent peers, belonging to a gang, and involvement in other criminal acts (Miller-Johnson et al., 2003). Gang membership is a more powerful predictor than having delinquent peers.

For African Americans, gang involvement dates back as far as the 1920s. These early gangs were loose associations consisting of family and neighborhood friends who were involved in limited criminal activities. It was not until the 1940s and 1950s that African American gangs became more organized, largely in response to resentment from the White community over growing migration of African Americans from the South and increasing movement into White neighborhoods (Alonso, 2005). Similar to the history of Latino gangs discussed by Mirabal-Colón and Vélez (chap. 4, this volume), much of the early growth for African American gangs began in southern California, particularly Los Angeles. Other African American gangs emerged in urban centers such as Chicago around this time period. Regardless of the city or community where they began, African American gangs shared with each other and with other ethnic minority gangs a sense of injustice, discrimination, and alienation from mainstream society.

The development of African American gangs into the 1960s and beyond was strongly influenced by the political circumstances for African Americans around civil rights and political activism. For example, in Los Angeles during the peak years of activism following the 1965 Watts riots, there were almost no active African American street gangs (Alonso, 2005). However, for various reasons, the influence of activist political groups declined in the 1970s. Furthermore, during this time period, there were many large plant closures and relocations in big cities including Los Angeles. Both of these factors coincided with the resurgence of African American gangs in cities throughout the United States. In Los Angeles, the Crips were the first large and organized gang on the scene with a distinct style of dress and orientation toward serious and violent criminal activity. Other African American gangs, most notably the Bloods, originated to protect themselves from the Crips. Eventually both the Crips and the Bloods divided into numerous smaller gangs. During the 1980s, they migrated to other cities in the United States and became much more heavily involved in narcotics trafficking. From the 1970s onward, much institutionalized gang activity was orchestrated from or connected to prisons.

Although gang violence is often sensationalized and linked with ethnic minority youth, only 5% to 6% of all youth are involved in gangs. Still, gangs account for the overwhelming amount of violence and serious offending (Huizinga, Weiher, Espiritu, & Esbensen, 2003). Thus, as has been pointed out in several chapters in this volume, it is important to consider the influence of gangs on African American and other ethnic minority youth when examining both causes and potential solutions to the problem of youth violence in a multicultural society.

School-Related Factors

The school experience for African Americans reflects disengagement and disadvantage, similar to what has been discussed by Hurst and Laird for American Indians (chap. 6, this volume). After their arrival to the United States in the 1600s and subsequently for more than 200 years,

African Americans were forbidden to learn to read, and someone teaching a Black child to read was subject to intense social and legal sanctions (Meier & Rudwick, 1976). Even in states traditionally considered progressive, such as New York, Pennsylvania, and Ohio, education was largely segregated for African American children. It was not until 1954 (*Brown v. Board of Education*) that segregation was declared illegal nationwide. The sobering statistic is that in the 21st century, African American children are still educated in predominantly segregated, frequently substandard conditions with more needs, fewer resources, and scarce attention (Kozol, 1992). These historical and contemporary experiences of discrimination are powerful for African American people.

In addition to the historical experience of marginalization and discrimination, research suggests that African American children may be particularly vulnerable to negative labels and low levels of support from teachers (Steele & Aronson, 1995). Perceived teacher support is a protective factor contributing to students' feeling competent and understood, especially when other areas of support are less available for the child (Bowen, Richman, Brewster, & Bowen, 1998).

Neighborhood and Community Influences

Many children grow and develop in urban settings where they are exposed to a myriad of stressful community influences including high levels of violence exposure, scarce resources, and economic disadvantage (Cantave & Harrison, 1999). As discussed by Guerra and Williams (chap. 1, this volume), neighborhood and community influences associated with disadvantage are more likely to occur for ethnic minority youth in the United States at this time. For African Americans, work on urban disadvantage has focused on structural changes in the inner city during the past several decades (National Institute of Justice, 1997). On the other hand, as Guerra and Williams also pointed out, communities have assets that can be mobilized to support healthy development.

YOUTH VIOLENCE PREVENTION AND AFRICAN AMERICANS

The epidemiological triangle is useful in identifying viable areas to be targeted by prevention programs for African Americans. These programs may be focused on agent, host, or environmental factors. Some previous programs have been targeted for youth growing up in disadvantaged urban and inner-city settings and often include large numbers of African Americans. Other programs focus on ethnic and cultural practices specifically tailored to African American history and values. Because several chapters in this volume have directly examined programs tailored to African American values and practices (in particular, see French, Kim, & Pillado, chap. 2, and Wright & Zimmerman, chap. 9), we focus primarily on violence prevention programs that have included large numbers of African American youth and/or have examined the relative effectiveness of a program for African Americans compared with other ethnic groups. We emphasize psycho-educational and therapeutic programs emphasizing both the host and the environment.

Approaches Designed to Strengthen Host Factors

In this section, we highlight examples of programs designed to build individual skills that have been implemented and evaluated with African Americans from early childhood through adolescence. Perhaps the most well-known example of early prevention is the High/Scope Perry Preschool program (Weikart & Schweinhart, 1997). This program was developed with attention to the needs of low-income African American preschool children. Student-directed learning activities, home visitation, and parent support were provided to enhance the cognitive and problem-solving skills of participating preschoolers. As discussed earlier, African American children and families have often felt disenfranchised from the U.S. educational system for multiple reasons (Comer, 1984; Smith, Boutte, Zigler, & Finn-Stevenson, 2004). This approach designed to support preschool children and their families was likely less stigmatizing given its universal approach and was attentive to the social welfare needs of poor families, freeing them to focus more on their child's cognitive development. The High/Scope Perry Preschool program has demonstrated cost-effective results well into adulthood resulting in higher levels of educational attainment and less delinquency (Weikart & Schweinhart, 1997).

As an example of a prevention program at the elementary school level, Aber, Brown, Chaudry, Jones, and Samples (1996) evaluated a universal, school-based conflict resolution curriculum, Resolving Conflict Creatively Program (RCCP), with children ranging from 1st to 6th grade in New York public schools. The study included substantial representation of African Americans (about 40% of the sample) and other ethnic minority youth. The focus of the study was to examine program effects alongside the process by which poverty and ethnicity interact with violence. The program was designed to enhance children's conflict resolution strategies. Among the program objectives were two that might be considered especially relevant to ethnic minority populations, namely encouraging children's respect for their own and other's culture, and teaching children to identify and stand against prejudice. Aber, Brown, and Jones (2003) found that when sufficient amount of program content was delivered by teachers, this resulted in reduced aggression, or in some cases at least reduced growth in aggression.

Farrell, Meyer, Sullivan, and Kung (2003) evaluated an individual skills program for sixth-grade children in predominantly urban African American communities. This program, Responding in Peaceful and Positive Ways, emphasizes social skills and problem-solving competencies. Considerable attention also focused on enhancing the cultural sensitivity for African American children by including respected African American men among the prevention specialists and attending to the role of culture in perceiving and interpreting cues related to violence and aggression. For instance, there is recognition that some language and behavioral cues that may be perceived as hostile by some may represent friendly peer bonding among African American youth (Meyer, Allison, Reese, & Gay, 2004). To date, effects of the program have been detected on disciplinary infractions but not on self-reported aggressive behavior.

In some cases, programs have been specifically tailored to African American youth. For example, Hammond and Yung (1991) developed an anger management program for use with African American adolescents. This program, Positive Adolescent Choices Training (PACT), was developed to include activities and videos with African Americans in scenarios relevant to their daily lives. Results from evaluation of PACT revealed higher skills gains among the participants compared with a nonrandomized control group (Hammond & Yung, 1991).

Hudley and colleagues (Hudley et al., 1998; Hudley & Graham, 1993) have examined programs designed to affect hostile attributions among African American and Latino elementary school boys, particularly those identified as highly aggressive. Programming was based on the fundamental assumption that aggressive children are more likely in ambiguous situations to "incorrectly attribute hostile attributions to a peer, to ignore social cues, and endorse retaliatory aggression" (Hudley et al., 1998, p. 272). The program included both aggressive and less aggressive males and was found to affect the attributions of aggressive boys and teacher ratings of aggressiveness (Hudley & Graham, 1993). Hudley and colleagues also discuss the limitations of attributional approaches across sociocultural contexts. The experience of a youthful participant is provided who was victimized by "gang bangers" who took his personal property. The youth stated that "if somebody does something to you, then you got to show them that they can't get away with it" (Hudley & Graham, 1993, p. 136). The scholars concluded that there remains much to learn about reducing violence and delinquency in ways that are sustainable with youth who live in dangerous settings where they have to exhibit both peace and strength to survive (Anderson, 1990).

Approaches Designed to Strengthen Environmental Factors

Prevention efforts to reduce aggression are likely more potent when multiple sources in a young person's life resound similar messages regarding violence and aggression. This section on environmental approaches provides an overview of prevention research designed to impact family, school, and community factors especially relevant to African American youth.

Family Programs

Family-based prevention and intervention programs designed to enhance parenting practices, monitoring, discipline, and academic performance have been the topic of considerable research (Farrington & Welsh, 1999; Sexton & Alexander, 2002). Some approaches have been tested specifically with African American families with children of various ages. For example, Olds and colleagues tested their pre- and postnatal nurse home-visiting program in Memphis, Tennessee, with a sample of African American mothers (Kitzman et al., 1997). In this study, parents receiving home visiting reported attitudes not supportive of child abuse and a more developmentally responsive home environment than mothers in the randomized control (Kitzman et al., 1997; Olds, 2002). However, long-term effects on adolescent violence have yet to be reported with this particular sample in Tennessee, although demonstrated in other studies (Olds et al., 1998).

Behaviorally based family intervention that also includes community advocacy has been found to be effective with adolescent juvenile offenders. The Adolescent Diversion program delivered 12 to 16 weeks of family behavioral contracting and community advocacy. Youth and their parents specified behavioral goals both for the youth and the parents, as well as contingencies to reward youth for attainment of these objectives. Advocacy for the youth and family often included connecting youth and families to important community resources (food banks, heating assistance, etc.), a feature that is critical for low-income families and minority families who disproportionately make up the poor. The model was developed and initially tested in a medium-sized town with predominantly White families; however, it has also been tested with African American juvenile offenders in a large metropolitan city. The program was designed to attend more to the social than the cultural context of families. In both samples, the program was found to significantly increase adolescent perceptions of positive features of family relationships and their identity, and to reduce officially reported delinquency (Davidson, Redner, Amdur, & Mitchell, 1990; Smith, Wolf, Cantillon, Thomas, & Davidson, 2004).

The Multi-Systemic Therapy (MST) model focuses on serious and repeated juvenile offenders and was designed based on an ecological and family systems model that views adolescent behavior as part of a family system. MST has been tested in both efficacy and effectiveness trials, and with study samples involving predominantly (81%) African American families in Charleston, South Carolina (Henggeler, Melton, Brondino, Scherer, & Hanley, 1997; Henggeler, Pickrel, & Brondino, 1999). The intervention is highly tailored to the needs and circumstances of the family and provides extensive advocacy to help the family with issues causing daily stress such as housing and interactions with the child's school and other human service systems. Again, this is likely an important feature for poor, ethnic minority families in general (including African Americans). Therapist adherence to the protocol was also examined, and with high treatment fidelity youth in the randomized MST experimental condition were found to exhibit 26 to 46% lower incarceration rates almost 2 years postintervention. The findings are significant in terms of the amount of reduction in delinquency, in incarceration, days out of the home, reducing overall juvenile justice costs for chronic offenders.

In the field of prevention science, there is consideration of whether cultural adaptation might result in more efficacious family-oriented programming (see Wright and Zimmerman, chap. 9, this volume, for a more detailed discussion of culturally specific approaches). The Strengthening Families Program has culturally adapted versions for African Americans, Latinos, and Asian Americans. The culturally adapted version implemented with rural African American families in Alabama and inner-city Detroit increased participation rates from 61% to 92% in Alabama and from 45% to 84% in Detroit when culturally relevant examples, graphics, and stories were included. Equivalent effects were demonstrated on youth and family outcomes relevant to substance abuse (Aktan, Kumpfer, & Turner, 1996). It seems important that prevention programming should be designed to demonstrate substantial efficacy and effectiveness with those most affected by the problem of youth violence.

In summary, family-based programs have demonstrated effects with African American families. Research on family intervention with pregnant mothers reveals that these models help interrupt abusive behavior often characteristic of young uneducated, highly stressed mothers unfamiliar with norms of child development. In these types of models and specifically nurse home-visiting, success has been demonstrated in engaging and benefiting African American families (Olds, 2002). However, it is clear that the program works via reducing more restrictive behavior among European American parents while it is not clear that the process of effects is similar for African American families, a question deserving empirical attention as to whether the same conceptual model fits both samples.

It is plausible that attention to the social situation of African American families is important. However, more research clearly is needed to disentangle the dynamics of effective family interventions that work for all families regardless of ethnicity versus programs that work particularly well for particular ethnic groups including African Americans. In some cases, programs have been found to work equally well for minority and majority youth and families, reducing the need to consider appropriate cultural adaptation (Wilson, Lipsey, & Soydan, 2003). Serious consideration should be given to whether the prevailing prevention prototypes in parenting actually make sense to and for these families given their social context and cultural values. Before change in cultural values are advocated, prevention scientists should ensure that parenting and family processes that characterize positive youth development are similar across ethnic groups and that change in parenting practices will produce the desired effects in the desired directions.

An important consideration derived from the more difficult life circumstances experienced by African America families is the extent to which life stress and the complexities of raising children under these conditions contributes to parenting difficulties and should be addressed in family interventions. For instance, as illustrated with MST, as families engage multiple systems such as child protective services and juvenile justice, their capacity for managing interactions in these systems is often taxed. As this suggests, it may be that these families are both most needy and most receptive to interventions (Davidson et al., 1990; Henggeler et al., 1997; Henggeler et al., 1999).

The question of whether family-based programs are in fact effective across diverse groups of families is rarely, if ever, analyzed in prevention science. In studies with families from multiple groups, the data is not always analyzed by ethnicity to examine if the program is equally effective for different ethnic groups. Often such small numbers of families of color are included that program effects by family ethnic background cannot be conducted. On the other hand, as discussed above, there have been some studies conducted with predominantly African American families that allow us to assess program outcomes.

The suggestion that program outcomes should be analyzed separately by ethnicity is not a suggestion we make unguardedly. What could be made of the results? If the program is found to be more effective for one group than another, does that mean that "nothing works" for the group less influenced by programming and that prevention efforts are useless? Would less effectiveness of the program for one group point to a need for revisions in the underlying theory or implementation of the program? It is apparent that these analyses by family ethnicity could raise additional research questions. However, given the already existing health disparities in youth violence, particularly for African Americans, it is important to identify approaches that are effective with those most at risk.

Environmental School Programs

Programs designed to affect the school environment are appealing because they can be integrated into the normal operations of the school and universally expose all students to prevention and health promotion. In doing so, it is important to remember that schools have the primary goal of educating children for academic attainment. Programs that limit the burden on school staff and advance the mission of the school are likely to be better received. School-based programs vary in terms of the theoretical rationale and focus of intervention. Some programs are designed to build strengths in the youth to help prevent violence and aggression. These programs have been discussed earlier in this chapter as host factors are their primary focus. Another approach attempts to impact and alter the structure of the school environment to foster improved behavior and achievement.

Just as parenting disciplinary practices are considered important in children's behavior, the teacher's disciplinary practices in the school setting also influence behavior. For example, a prevention program conducted with a largely African American student population in Baltimore, Maryland, reduced children's subsequent aggression (Ialongo, Werthamer, Brown, Kellam, & Wang, 1999; Kellam, Rebok, Ialongo, & Mayer, 1994). Specifically, highly aggressive children in intervention classrooms implementing effective management show reduced levels of aggressiveness compared with similar children in control classrooms.

Another school-level program, the Seattle Social Development Program, was designed to decrease violence, delinquency, substance abuse, and other problem behaviors by increasing bonding and attachment to school. The program supported teachers in using proactive behavioral strategies, and providing interactive teaching and cooperative learning experiences for children in Grades 2 through 6 (Hawkins et al., 1992). African American students have been included in the trials, making up approximately 25% of the sample. By the end of Grade 6, boys from low-income families in intervention classrooms had greater academic bonding and achievement, better teacher-rated behavior, and lower rates of violence and delinquency than boys in the randomized control classrooms (O'Donnell, Hawkins, Catalano, Abbott, & Day, 1995).

The Comer School Development Program has been developed as a process by which schools can examine the entire school environment (Comer, Haynes, Joyner, & Ben Avie, 1996). The SDP, designed particularly with children of color in mind, involves a process that (a) helps schools establish high standards of achievement, especially for poor and minority children; (b) enables teachers to understand and believe that their children can learn in spite of perceived challenges because of social and ethnic status;

(c) engages parents and teachers as partners in encouraging positive behavior and learning; and (d) empowers schools to reach out effectively to involve parents, teachers, staff, and community-based representatives in planning teams designing overall school improvement practices. Evaluation of the SDP has been conducted in "desperately poor" African American neighborhoods in Chicago (Cook, Murphy, & Hunt, 2000).

In analyses at both the school and individual level, program children were found to value achievement more, to view teachers as more concerned, and to evidence higher levels of achievement and better school behavior. SDP seems particularly well-suited for attending to the interaction of ethnicity and class and the educational barriers experienced by African American children described previously. Interestingly, similar results for the SDP were not found in suburban, more affluent, predominantly African American Prince George's County, Maryland. Apparently the program results in maximum effects in the communities in most need of improvement (Cook et al., 2000). Whole school models foster the formation of partnerships among parents, school staff, and community stakeholders, addressing issues of ethnicity, culture, and social class that would normally lead to reduced and/or strained relationships particularly for lower income families who typically are more disenfranchised from mainstream institutions.

The Comer School Development Model and the Schools of the 21st Century have been integrated in some sites to create a new model of home–school–community partnerships, with sites serving substantial numbers of African American families. The Schools of the 21st Century (21C Schools) is a model of making community resources more accessible to parents in the school year-round (Zigler, Finn-Stevenson, & Marsland, 1995). 21C Schools provide resources for before- and after-school care on sliding-fee scales, mental health support, and other community resources that reduce the stress of managing family life for parents, freeing them to be better parents and more involved in their child's schooling. With new federal policies, 21C school models are being implemented nationwide with findings forthcoming.

Multicomponent Programs

Multicomponent violence prevention programs (that focus on some combination of children, teachers, classrooms, families, and schools) have also been evaluated with substantial proportions of African Americans in the sample. For example, the Metropolitan Area Child Study (MACS) multicomponent violence prevention project used a design delivering various levels of intervention ranging from (a) treatment-as-usual control group; (b) universal classroom component that included a student skills development curriculum (Yes I Can) and a teacher-focused component providing support for classroom management and cultural competency; (c) classroom plus small peer group; and (d) the inclusion of all of the previous components plus a multiple-family group intervention. Schools were blocked by community and randomly assigned to condition (Huesmann et al., 1996).

The intervention design called for examining effects of this multicomponent program (evaluated at different levels) in a moderate resource urban area as compared with low-income, predominantly African American inner-city communities. Effects on violence prevention were noted only for the most comprehensive condition (individual, classroom, peer, and family), but only in the moderate resource urban area. Interestingly, in the overwhelmingly poor, urban, African American communities in Chicago, the multiple components including family intervention were found to result in more aggression from pretest to posttest in the intervention group than the controls for lower risk but not higher risk youth. The researchers concluded that family-based programs can "raise but not resolve" the complex issues of parenting strategies for youth residing in dangerous settings where parents do not want their children to be perpetrators, but neither do they want them to be victimized (Metropolitan Area Child Study Research Group, 2002).

The FastTrack Prevention trial is another multicomponent program including individual skills, peer intervention, and family involvement. This program was conducted in four sites around the country (North Carolina, Pennsylvania, Tennessee, and Washington), and included rural, suburban, and urban families of diverse ethnic and family structural backgrounds. The program was designed to enhance social skills, academic achievement, and positive-parenting strategies. Parents participated in multiple family groups and received home visits from staff hired from local communities to match the ethnic composition of the high-risk children. Various types of supports were given to families to help with child care, transportation, and connections to community resources that could be helpful in the lives of families. Children and families in FastTrack improved in both teacher- and parent-reported child behavior, social competence (better problem solving, reduced hostile attributions), increased positive parenting behavior (e.g., praise, encouragement), and reduced physical punishment (Conduct Problems Prevention Research Group, 1999, 2002). Of 76 possible interactions evaluated, one of the seven reaching statistical significance indicated greater effects in favor of the intervention on parenting behavior for European Americans, suggesting that the results were less demonstrative for African Americans. This is a result to be interpreted with caution given the number of possible interaction terms but again raises the possibility that more understanding is needed of the role of family processes and ethnicity in delivering prevention to African American families.

Community-Based Programs

Community-based programs are those conducted external to the family, peer, or school context and involve adults and youth in other areas of the young person's life. There have been fewer empirically validated community-based programs designed to affect violence and delinquency prevention. Some of the programs implemented in juvenile justice or youth services settings include boot camps, wilderness or marine programs designed to expose youth to new settings, roles, responsibilities, and discipline (Parent, 2003). Often, these types of programs concentrate on youth who are antisocial and/or delinquent, and frequently have disproportionate numbers of African American youth. Programs that include homogenous groups of antisocial youth can have deleterious, iatrogenic effects on problem behavior because these youth reinforce each other's antisocial values and behaviors (Dishion, McCord, & Poulin, 1999). To date, few if any positive benefits have been shown of boot camp and similar types of programs (Parent, 2003). Even if benefits could be accrued from participation in this type of programming, the issue becomes whether they are sustained once youth return to their family, peer, and community contexts that have likely not changed in the youth's absence.

The Big Brothers/Big Sisters of America (BBSA) is a blueprint program (Elliott, 1998) and a model for community-based youth development. In BBSA youth between the ages of 6 and 18 are carefully matched with a mentor who meets with the youth three times a month for 3 to 5 hours each time. Many of the participating youth are from disadvantaged, single-parent African American households. Youth participating in the mentoring program after 18 months are found to be less likely to initiate drug use, to be aggressive, and to have improved family relationships and school performance.

A model of community-based intervention that has demonstrated efficacy in one study but has not continued to demonstrate positive effects is the Quantum Opportunities Program (QOP; Lattimore, Mihalic, Grotpeter, & Taggart, 1998). The program based on opportunity theory is discussed here because it involves a popular approach in communities combining after-school and summer programming with career guidance, community service, mentoring, and tutoring across 4 years in high school and the opportunity to earn college scholarships on successful program completion. The participating students were mostly students of color, with 76% being African American. QOP has been found to have mixed effects with one study, demonstrating positive effects on high school graduation, college attendance, and arrests (Lattimore et al., 1998), and subsequent studies failing to replicate these results and even finding some deleterious effects (Sharon Mihalic & Delbert Elliott, personal communication, April 2005). This model is in need of additional rigorous effectiveness data, supporting the sustainability of effects, and substantiating this approach in multiple communities. This model is mentioned here because variations of this approach are popular and implemented in many communities.

CONCLUSION

The epidemiological triangle has provided a framework for examining the host, agent, and environmental factors influential in aggressive and violent behavior with particular attention to factors with saliency for African American youth. Prevention efforts designed to build skills among youth to consider their emotions, behavior, and ways to interact with others have been helpful with preschool and early elementary African American children. These approaches are more difficult with adolescents. For teenaged youth, there are other demands from peers in their community and the lure of other activities in the community that likely make these messages more complex to adopt for adolescents. Less attention in the prevention field has been given to the role of community and structural conditions and their interaction with the individual. How can one ignore the role of poverty, the lack of opportunity, and the availability of illegitimate goal attainment for youth in these communities that has likely led to increased high-powered weaponry and more violence (Blumstein & Wallman, 2000). Thus, many prevention approaches address individual host factors with African American youth while few address the community and structural circumstances of these youth, leaving a gaping hole in prevention science.

More much attention in prevention science has been given to building family relationships. Though some programs have demonstrated effectiveness particularly in early childhood and in adolescence with juvenile offenders, prevention trials have had a more challenging job. The typical approaches promulgated in prevention science may have a mixed reception among African American parents. One issue could be the difficulty of participation given the demanding circumstances of often single-parent households living in poverty (Orrell-Valente, Pinderhughes, Valente, Laird, & Conduct Problems Prevention Research Group, 1999). Another hindrance could also be that the parents are most receptive to hearing about parenting strategies at the early childhood developmental point. Another possibility is that there is a conflict in parenting values and goals between the programs and the families. More attention is needed to identify successful parenting approaches that are applicable to African American parents and children.

School can also be a buffer for children, particularly for those who can use as many positive sources of support as possible. Schools with staff who respect and welcome students and their families, who adopt proactive behavioral management with abundant encouragement and clear rewards and consequences and engaging instructional approaches result in positive outcomes for the children. Schoolwide approaches that promote nonaggressive behavior show promise for effectiveness and sustainability.

Future directions for prevention with African Americans include identifying important parenting practices and strategies to build positive families, more work to create peer communities, and community resources that support youth in nonviolent and constructive activities that can buffer them and assist families in promoting positive development and attainment among African American youth.

REFERENCES

Aber, J. L., Brown, J. L., Chaudry, N., Jones, S. M., & Samples, F. (1996). The evaluation of the Resolving Conflict Creatively Program: An overview. *American Journal of Preventive Medicine, 12*(Suppl.), 82–90.

Aber, J. L., Brown, J. L., & Jones, S. M. (2003). Developmental trajectories toward violence in middle childhood: Course, demographic differences, and response to school-based intervention. *Developmental Psychology, 39*, 324–348.

Aktan, G. B., Kumpfer, K. L., & Turner, C. W. (1996). Effectiveness of a family skills training program for substance use prevention with inner city African-American families. *Substance Use and Misuse, 31*, 157–175.

Alonso, A. A. (2005). *African–American street gangs in Los Angeles.* Retrieved April 2, 2005, from http://www.nagia.org

Amber, J. (2005, April 12). Men on fire: Ice Cube. *Essence, 35*, 131.

Anderson, E. (1990). *Street wise: Race, class, and change in an urban community.* Chicago: University of Chicago Press.

Bank, L., Forgatch, M. S., Patterson, G. R., & Fetrow, R. A. (1993). Parenting practices of single mothers: Mediators of negative contextual factors. *Journal of Marriage and the Family, 55*, 371–384.

Baumrind, D. (1972). An exploratory study of socialization effects of Black children: Some Black–White comparisons. *Child Development, 43*, 261–267.

Billingsley, A. (1993). *Climbing Jacob's ladder: The enduring legacy of African American families.* New York: Simon & Schuster.

Blumstein, A. (2003). The notorious 100:1 crack:powder disparity—The data tell us that it is time to restore the balance. *Federal Sentencing Reporter, 16*(1), 1–6.

Blumstein, A., & Wallman, J. (2000). *The crime drop in America*. Cambridge, England: Cambridge University Press.

Bowen, G. L., Richman, J. M., Brewster, A., & Bowen, N. (1998). Sense of school coherence, perceptions of danger at school, and teacher support among youth at risk of school failure. *Child and Adolescent Social Work Journal, 15*, 273–286.

Brody, G. H., & Flor, D. L. (1998). Maternal resources, parenting practices, and child competence in rural, single-parent African American families. *Child Development, 69*, 803–816.

Brundage, W. F. (1993). *Lynching in the new South, Georgia and Virginia, 1880–1930*. Urbana: University of Illinois Press.

Cantave, C., & Harrison, R. (1999). *Data bank fact sheet: Employment and unemployment*. Joint Center for Political and Economic Studies. Retrieved July 20, 2005, from http://www.jointcenter.org/DB/factsheet/employ.htm

Centers for Disease Control and Prevention. (2001). *Mortality and Morbidity Weekly Report, 50*, 780–783.

Centers for Disease Control and Prevention. (2005). *National Center for Injury Control and Prevention. Youth Violence Fact Sheet*. Retrieved April 11, 2005, from http://www.cdc.gov/ncipc/factsheets/yvfacts.htm

Comer, J. P. (1984). Home-school relationships as they affect the academic success of children. *Education and Urban Society, 16*, 323–337.

Comer, J. P., Haynes, N. M., Joyner, E. T., & Ben Avie, M. (1996). *Rallying the whole village: The Comer process for reforming education*. New York: Teachers College Press.

Comstock, G. A., & Paik, H. (1991). *Television and the American child*. New York: Academic Press.

Conduct Problems Prevention Research Group. (1999). Initial impact of the Fast Track prevention trial for conduct problems: I. The high-risk sample. *Journal of Consulting and Clinical Psychology, 60*, 783–792.

Conduct Problems Prevention Research Group. (2002). Evaluation of the first 3 years of the Fast Track prevention trial with children at high risk for adolescent conduct problems. *Journal of Abnormal Child Psychology, 30*, 19–35.

Cook, T. D., Murphy, R. G., & Hunt, H. D. (2000). Comer's School Development Program in Chicago: A theory-based evaluation. *American Educational Research Journal, 37*, 535–597.

Davidson, B. (1998). *West Africa before the colonial era: A history to 1850*. New York: Longman.

Davidson, W. S., Redner, R., Amdur, R. L., & Mitchell, C. M. (1990). *Alternative treatments for troubled youth: The case of diversion from the justice system*. New York: Plenum Press.

Deater-Deckard, K., Dodge, K. A., Bates, J. E., & Pettit, G. S. (1996). Physical discipline among African American and European American mothers: Links to children's externalizing behaviors. *Developmental Psychology, 32*, 1065–1072.

Dishion, T. J., McCord, J., & Poulin, F. (1999). When interventions harm: Peer groups and problem behavior. *American Psychologist, 54*, 755–764.

Dishion, T. J., Patterson, G. R., Stoolmiller, M., & Skinner, M. L. (1991). Family school, and behavioral antecedents to early adolescent involvement with anti-social peers. *Developmental Psychology, 2*, 172–180.

Dornbusch, S. M., Carlsmith, J. M., Bushwall, S. J., Ritter, P. L., Leiderman, H., Hastorf, A. H., et al. (1985). Single parents, extended households, and the control of adolescents. *Child Development, 56*, 326–341.

Elliott, D. (Ed.). (1998). *Blueprints for violence prevention.* Boulder, CO: Center for the Study and Prevention of Violence.

Farrell, A. D., Meyer, A. L., Sullivan, T. N., & Kung, E. M. (2003). Evaluation of the Responding in Peaceful and Positive ways (RIPP) seventh grade violence prevention curriculum. *Journal of Child and Family Studies, 12*, 101–120.

Farrington, D. P., & Welsh, B. C. (1999). Delinquency prevention using family-based interventions. *Children and Society, 13*, 287–303.

Frauenglass, S., Routh, D. K., Pantin, H. M., & Mason, C. A. (1997). Family support decreases influence of deviant peers on Hispanic adolescents' substance use. *Journal of Clinical Child Psychology, 26*, 15–23.

Haddon, W. (1968). The changing approach to the epidemiology, prevention, and amelioration of trauma: The transition to approaches etiologically rather than descriptively based. *American Journal of Public Health, 58*, 1431–1438.

Haley, A. (1980). *Roots: The saga of an American family.* New York: Dell.

Hammond, W. R., & Yung, B. R. (1991). Preventing violence in at-risk African–American youth. *Journal of Health Care for the Poor and Underserved, 2*, 359–373.

Hammond, W. R., & Yung, B. R. (1993). Psychology's role in the public health response to assaultive violence among young African-American men. *American Psychologist, 48*, 142–154.

Hawkins, J. D., Catalano, R. F., Morrison, D. E., O'Donnell, J., Abbott, R. D., & Day, L. E. (1992). The Seattle Social Development Project: Effects of the first four years on protective factors and problem behaviors. In J. McCord & R. Tremblay (Eds.), *The prevention of antisocial behavior in children* (pp. 139–161). New York: Guilford Press.

Henggeler, S. W., Melton, G. B., Brondino, M. J., Scherer, D. G., & Hanley, J. H. (1997). Multisystemic therapy with violent and chronic juvenile offenders and their families: The role of treatment fidelity in successful dissemination. *Journal of Consulting and Clinical Psychology, 65*, 821–833.

Henggeler, S. W., Pickrel, S. G., & Brondino, M. J. (1999). Multisystemic treatment of substance abusing and dependent delinquents: Outcomes, treatment fidelity, and transportability. *Mental Health Services Research, 1*, 171–184.

Hudley, C., Britsch, B., Wakefield, W. D., Smith, T., Demorat, M., & Cho, S. (1998). An attribution retraining program to reduce aggression in elementary school students. *Psychology in the Schools, 35*, 271–281.

Hudley, C., & Graham, S. (1993). An attributional intervention to reduce peer-directed aggression among African American boys. *Child Development, 64*, 124–138.

Huesmann, L. R., Maxwell, C. D., Eron, L., Dalhberg, L., Guerra, N. G., Tolan, P. H., et al. (1996). Evaluating a cognitive/ecological program for the prevention of aggression among urban children. *American Journal of Preventive* Medicine, *12*(Suppl.), 120–128.

Huesmann, L. R., Moise, T. J., Podolski, C. L., & Eron, L. D. (2003). Longitudinal relations between children's exposure to TV violence and their aggressive and violent behavior in young adulthood: 1977–1992. *Developmental Psychology, 39*, 201–221.

Huizinga, D., Weiher, A. W., Espiritu, R., & Esbensen, F. (2003). Delinquency and crime: Some highlights from the Denver Youth Survey. In T. Thornberry & M. Krohn (Eds.), *Taking stock of delinquency: An overview of findings from contemporary longitudinal studies* (pp. 47–91). New York: Kluwer.

Huston, A. C., McLoyd, V. C., & Garcia Coll, C. G. (1994). Children and poverty: Issues in contemporary research. *Child Development, 65*, 275–282.

Ialongo, N., Werthamer, L., Brown, H. B., Kellam, S., & Wang, S. B. (1999). The proximal impact of two first grade preventive interventions on the early risk behaviors for later substance abuse, depression, and antisocial behavior. *American Journal of Community Psychology, 27*, 599–642.

Kellam, S. G., Rebok, G. W., Ialongo, N., & Mayer, L. S. (1994). The course and malleablility of aggressive behavior from early first grade into middle school: Results of a developmental epidemiologically-based preventive trial. *Journal of Child Psychology and Psychiatry and Allied Disciplines, 35*, 259–281.

Kitzman, H., Olds, D. L., Henderson, C. R., Jr., Hanks, C., Cole, R., Tatelbaum, R., et al. (1997). Effect of prenatal and infancy home visitation by nurses on pregnancy outcomes, childhood injuries, and repeated childbearing: A randomized controlled trial. *Journal of the American Medical Association, 278*, 644–652.

Kozol, J. (1992). *Savage inequalities: Children in America's schools.* New York: Harper Perennial.

Johnson, B. D., Golub, A., & Dunlap, E. (2000). The rise and decline of hard drugs, drug markets, and violence in inner-city New York. In A. Blumstein & J. Wallman (Eds.), *The crime drop in America* (pp. 164–206). Cambridge, England: Cambridge University Press.

Lamborn, S. D., Dornbusch, S. M., & Steinberg, L. (1996). Ethnicity and community context as moderators of the relations between family decision making and adolescent adjustment. *Child Development, 67*, 283–301.

Lattimore, C. B., Mihalic, S. F., Grotpeter, J. K., & Taggart, R. (1998). The Quantum Opportunities Program: Book Four. In D. Elliott (Series Ed.), *Blueprints for violence prevention.* Boulder, CO: Center for the Study and Prevention of Violence.

Laub, J. H., & Lauritsen, J. L. (1998). The interdependence of school violence with neighborhood and family conditions. In D. S. Elliott, B. Hamburg, &

K. R. Williams (Eds.), *Violence in American schools* (pp. 127–155). New York: Cambridge University Press.

McLoyd, V. C., & Smith, J. (2002). Physical discipline and behavior problems in African American, European American and Hispanic children: Emotional support as a moderator. *Journal of Marriage and Family, 64,* 40–53.

Meier, A., & Rudwick, E. (1976). *From plantation to ghetto.* New York: Hill & Wang.

Mercy, J. A., & Rosenberg, M. L. (1998). Preventing firearm violence in and around schools. In D. E. Elliott, B. A. Hamburg, & K. R. Williams (Eds.), *Violence in American schools: A new perspective* (pp. 159–187). Cambridge, England: Cambridge University Press.

Metropolitan Area Child Study Research Group. (2002). A cognitive–ecological approach to preventing aggression in urban settings: Initial outcomes for high-risk children. *Journal of Consulting and Clinical Psychology, 70,* 179–194.

Meyer, A. L., Allison, K. W., Reese, L. E., & Gay, F. N. (2004). Choosing to be violence free in middle school: The student component of the GREAT schools and families universal program. *American Journal of Preventive Medicine, 26,* 20–28.

Miller-Johnson, M., Constanzo, P. R., Coie, J. D., Rose, M. R., Browne, D. C., & Johnson, C. (2003). Peer social structure and risk-taking behaviors among African American early adolescents. *Journal of Youth and Adolescence, 32,* 375–384.

Murray, C. B., & Mandara, J. (2002). Racial identity development in African American children: Cognitive and experiential antecedents. In H. P. McAdoo (Ed.), *Black children: Social, educational, and parental environments* (pp. 73–96). Thousand Oaks, CA: Sage.

Murry, V. M., Smith, E. P., & Hill, N. E. (Eds.). Race, ethnicity, and culture in studies of families in context. *Journal of Marriage and Family, 63,* 911–914.

National Institute of Justice. (1997). *Research in brief: A study of homicide in eight U.S. cities: An NIJ Intramural Research Project.* Washington, DC: U.S. Department of Justice, Office of Justice Programs.

O'Donnell, J., Hawkins, J. D., Catalano, R. F., Abbott, R. D., & Day, L. E. (1995). Preventing school failure, drug use, and delinquency among low-income children: Effects of a long-term prevention project in elementary schools. *American Journal of Orthopsychiatry, 65,* 87–100.

Okazaki, S., & Sue, S. (1995). Methodological issues in assessment research with ethnic minorities. *Psychological Assessment, 7,* 367–375.

Olds, D. L. (2002). Prenatal and infancy home visiting by nurses: From randomized trials to community replication. *Prevention Science, 3,* 153–172.

Olds, D., Henderson, C. R., Cole, R., Eckenrode, J., Kitzman, H., Luckey, D., et al. (1998). Long-term effects of nurse home visitation on children's criminal and antisocial behavior: 15-year follow-up of a randomized controlled trial. *Journal of the American Medical Association, 280,* 1238–1244.

Orrell-Valente, J. K., Pinderhughes, E. E., Valente, E., Laird, R. D., & Conduct Problems Prevention Research Group. (1999). If it's offered will they come? Influences on parents' participation in a community-based conduct problems prevention program. *American Journal of Community Psychology, 27,* 753–783.

Patterson, G. R., & Chamberlain, P. (1994). A functional analysis of resistance during parent training therapy. *Clinical Psychology: Science and Practice, 1,* 53–70.

Patterson, G. R., Reid, J. B., & Dishion, T. J. (1992). *Antisocial boys.* Eugene, OR: Castalia.

Pinderhughes, E. E., Dodge, K. A., Bates, J. E., Pettit, G. S., & Zelli, A. (2000). Discipline responses: Influences of parents' socioeconomic status, ethnicity, and beliefs about parenting, stress, and cognitive–emotional processes. *Journal of Family Psychology, 14,* 380–400.

Poussaint, A. (1985). Black-on-black homicide: A psychological–political perspective. *Victimology, 8,* 161–169.

Sampson, R., & Laub, J. H. (1994). Urban poverty and the family context of delinquency: A new look at the structure and process in a classic study. *Child Development, 65,* 523–539.

Sexton, T. L., & Alexander, J. F. (2002). Family-based empirically supported interventions. *Counseling Psychologist, 30,* 238–261.

Snyder, H. N., & Sickmund, M. (1999). *Juvenile offenders and victims: 1999 national report* (NCJ 178257). Washington, DC: U.S. Department of Justice, Office of Justice Programs, Office of Juvenile Justice and Delinquency Prevention. Retrieved July 20, 2005, from http://www.ncjrs.org/html/ojjdp/national report99/toc.html

Smith, E. P., Boutte, G. S., Zigler, E., & Finn-Stevenson, M. (2004). Opportunities for schools to promote resilience in children and youth. In K. I. Maton, C. J. Schellenbach, B. J. Leadbetter, & A. L. Solarz (Eds.), *Investing in children, youth, families, and communities: Strengths-based research and policy* (pp. 213–231). Washington, DC: American Psychological Association.

Smith, E. P., Wolf, A. M., Cantillon, D. M., Thomas, O., & Davidson, W. S. (2004). The Adolescent Diversion Project: 25 years of research on an ecological model of intervention. *Journal of Prevention and Intervention in the Community, 27,* 29–47.

Spencer, M., & Dupree, D. (1996). African American youths' ecocultural challenges and psychosocial opportunities: An alternative analysis of problem behavior outcomes. In D. Cicchetti & S. L. Toth (Eds.), *Adolescence: Opportunities and challenges* (pp. 259–282). Rochester, NY: University of Rochester Press.

Steele, C. M., & Aronson, J. (1995). Stereotype threat and the intellectual test performance of African Americans. *Journal of Personality and Social Psychology, 69,* 797–811.

Sudakasa, N. (1988). Interpreting the African heritage in Afro-American family organization. In H. P. McAdoo (Ed.), *Black families* (pp. 27–43). Newbury Park, CA: Sage.

U.S. Census Bureau. (n.d.-a). *Historical tables*. Retrieved April 4, 2005, from http://www.census.gov/hhes/income/histinc/histpovtb.html

U.S. Census Bureau. (n.d.-b). *Historical tables*. Retrieved April 11, 2005, from http://www.census.gov/population/www/socdemo/race/black.html

U. S. Department of Health and Human Services. (2001). *Youth violence: A report of the surgeon general*. Rockville, MD: Author.

Vissing, Y. M., Straus, M., Gelles, R. J., & Harrop, J. W. (1991). Verbal aggression by parents and psychosocial problems of children. *Child Abuse and Neglect, 15*, 223–238.

Weikart, D. P., & Schweinhart, L. J. (1997). High/Scope Perry Preschool Program. In G. W. Albee & T. P. Gullotta (Eds.), *Primary prevention works: Vol. 6. Issues in children's and families' lives* (pp. 146–166). Thousand Oaks, CA: Sage.

Wilson, S. J., Lipsey, M. W., & Soydan, H. (2003). Are mainstream programs for juvenile delinquency less effective with minority youth than majority youth? A meta-analysis of outcomes research. *Research on Social Work Practice, 13*, 3–26.

Wilson, W. J. (1987). *The truly disadvantaged: The inner city, the underclass, and public policy*. Chicago: University of Chicago Press.

Zigler, E. F., Finn-Stevenson, M., & Marlsand, K. W. (1995). Child day care in the schools: The school of the 21st century. *Child Welfare, 74*, 1301–1326.

8

YOUTH VIOLENCE PREVENTION AMONG WHITE YOUTH

ROBERT NASH PARKER AND LOUIS TUTHILL

A great deal of attention in the mass media and in academic research has been placed on the role of ethnicity in violence, particularly youth violence, in the United States. Almost exclusively, however, this focus has been directed toward minorities and youth of color as the ethnic and perhaps even cultural "source" of the ethnically linked violence of greatest concern to law enforcement, schools, government, families, communities, scholars, and the media. Given the hegemonic position of "Whites" in terms of economic and social power, the focus on "others" and related social categories such as "immigrants" and "non-Whites" is not surprising or unexpected. The impression that even an informed citizen might take away from all of the focus on ethnicities other than White and youth violence is that the linkage between ethnicity, culture, and violence is primarily a problem of youth of color.

Several persistent facts, however, continue to prove that the media and community attention is, in no small part, because of the dominance of Whites socially, economically, and politically, and the resulting ability to shift the frame of the discourse about ethnicity and youth violence away from Whites and toward others with less social and political power. Although ethnic minority youth may be disproportionately represented in arrest data, a preponderance of youth violence is still committed by White youth. Indeed, of those youth arrested for acts of violence in 1997 (the most recent data available) 53% were White, so that in terms of sheer numbers alone, it would be a mistake to ignore Whites in any consideration of ethnicity and youth violence (Snyder & Sickmund, 1999).

Of course, much of the violence committed by White youth shares a common etiology with violence committed by all youth. Otherwise stated, risk for violence is related to a number of genetic, biological, psychological, social, situational, and community factors independent of one's ethnicity or race. In some cases, White youth may be less at risk than youth of color because they simply are less likely to be exposed to social and situational constraints that foster violent behavior. As Guerra and Williams (chap. 1, this volume) point out, numerous studies of the effects of community disadvantage on violence rates have shown that disadvantage has largely the same pattern of effects in ethnic minority and White communities. In general, when levels of disadvantage are held constant, the effect of ethnicity on violence disappears. As these authors point out, however, ethnic minority youth in the United States simply are more likely to live under conditions of extreme and concentrated disadvantaged associated with higher rates of violence. Given their majority status in the United States, White violence overall (as opposed to rates per population) may largely reflect sheer numbers in the population.

Still, there is a unique subset of violence committed by White youth that can be considered ethnic in origin. That is, the reality of being "White" creates certain perceptions and beliefs that result in violent outcomes. For this reason, we draw a distinction between youth violence that is ethnic and that which is somewhat incidental to ethnicity, although the degree to which this is a distinction in fact versus an analytical distinction is subject to argument. Instead of trying to deal with this argument here, we focus on six types of youth violence that are prominent in research and in the public's eye and reflect violence among White youth that is related to their ethnicity: White supremacists, White survivalists, skinheads, hate crimes, White youth gangs, and school shooters.

In many cases, these types of violence are intimately connected with social "movements" led by adults, but youth are regularly involved as recruits and followers of these ideologies. Furthermore, although it is the case that several of these categories include more than youth who are involved in ethnic violence, these types of White ethnic groups provide ideologies and contexts for White ethnic youth violence in all six categories, in that they stem from a common genesis of hate and outrage at perceived injustices. Indeed, in 2003 there were more than 750 active hate groups operating across the United States (Southern Poverty Law Center, 2005a).

In addition, many accounts of White supremacists, skinheads, and survivalists, and to some extent, hate crimes, suggest that a religious thread runs through many of these movements and helps to justify the violence and other negative actions taken against people of color. In its extreme form, this so-called Christian Identity movement has strong links with the descendants of White groups from northern Europe and Great Britain, and this movement serves in some cases to reinforce the notion that violence against people of color is consistent with religious belief and practice. This is not to suggest that Christian Identity is a cause of White ethnic violence, but that in some cases, and among some groups of supremacists or survivalists, ideological justification for such acts can be found in the Christian Identity belief system (Kaplan, 2000).

THE RELATIVE ABSENCE OF RESEARCH
ON WHITE ETHNIC VIOLENCE

The astute reader of this volume will notice a qualitative and quantitative difference between this chapter and those focusing on Latino youth violence or African American youth violence. This chapter is quantitatively different in the sense that there are fewer studies cited, less detailed summaries of research, and a great deal less data displayed. Qualitatively, the discussion in this chapter is undertheorized and sparse, with few established patterns and facts to examine. Given that more violence is committed by White youth, and that White ethnic violence represents an extreme and often quite lethal type of violence, why is the literature so sparse and the data so incomplete?

The most obvious reason can be seen in the hegemonic position of Whites in the United States. Those in power generally do not engage in much self-examination, especially with regard to such deviant behavior as street crime. Hegemonic power can be maintained and even strengthened by having a convenient group of others to focus attention on, especially in the sense that any societal problems can be based on the other people, in this case, people of color. Conflict theory in sociology predicts this outcome as the working class loses its economic standing, the elites benefiting from that decline are beyond reach. The fact that one disadvantaged group targets another similarly disadvantaged group for blame and retribution also strengthens the power of the elites by dividing groups whose common structural position might be the basis for a united front against the elites, and by diverting attention of the media and citizens alike away from the structural cause of inequality and loss of status (see Reiman, 1994).

Furthermore, although the intent of recent government research initiatives involving the inclusion of traditionally understudied populations was clearly not to single out ethnic minorities as perpetrators of violence, in fact, these policies inadvertently help to support the idea that the source of the problem lies with youth of color. This is not to say that tremendous increases in knowledge have not come about from the forced inclusion of previously understudied populations; in fact, they have, and we know more about these groups and their role in violence because of their inclusion. However, it should not be missed that this positive trend in research has, in part, created somewhat of a vacuum on the other side of the color line in youth violence prevention research.

It is also important to note that historical evidence provides plenty of examples of White ethnic violence, from the Irish gangs of New York in the 19th century (and ironically, the recruitment of Irish immigrants into the ranks of the New York City Police Department in the same period) to the Italian and especially Sicilian "mafia" of the early to middle 20th century. A longer term view of the historical record suggests an even greater association between White ethnics and perceived to be out of control, irrational violence. The Romans built Hadrian's Wall in Northern Briton in the 2nd century A.D. to keep out the Picts, a violent race of "barbarians" who were later overrun by the Scottish ancestors of some of the politicians now decrying the out of control violence of youth of color in the United States in the 21st century (Simpson, 1991).

We now turn to a brief (and rather speculative) discussion that attempts to address the lack of theorizing about contemporary White ethnic youth violence by offering a framework within which the examples described here can be understood. We also examine the role White ethnic groups such as the Irish, Jews, and Italians have played in ethnic violence historically in the United States. The rest of this chapter will examine the nature, origins, and the ideological and cultural background of White ethnic violence in the six previously identified categories: White supremacists, survivalists, skinheads, hate crimes, White youth gangs, and school shooters. We conclude with a review of common themes underlying White ethnic violence, as well as implications for youth prevention programming.

A HEURISTIC FRAMEWORK OF WHITE ETHNIC YOUTH VIOLENCE

In an attempt to offer some guidance to future researchers interested in White ethnic youth violence, we offer a possible framework within which the types of violence and crime discussed here can be understood as they have played out in contemporary U.S. society. The evidence for this framework is incomplete and inconsistent, in part, because of limited research on White ethnic youth violence, but this discussion may serve as a point of departure for future endeavors.

One of the most discussed and persistent trends in the economic structure of the United States in the latter half of the 20th century has been the shift from an economy dominated by manufacturing to an economy dominated by information, to use one popular tag for the current economic emphasis. Others have described the transition as one leading to a service-dominated economy; and still others have described the process as the replacement of "red brick" industries with "high-tech" enterprises. What these descriptions have in common is that the fact that not all workers in the traditional economy have been successful at making the transition to the new economy. Wilson discussed how jobs left the inner cities and became beyond the reach of working-class African Americans and other inner-city residents of color (Wilson, 1996), However, in truth, it is more than the fact that these jobs left certain places; rather, the problem is that they simply disappeared, at least in the United States.

The jobs that replaced them were based on technical and informational skills that traditional working-class individuals often do not possess. Indeed, these are skills that often come from higher education, something that the traditional "blue-collar aristocrat" of the North and Midwest industrial belts, which so dominated the U.S. economy in the 1920s to the 1960s, generally eschewed and disdained (LeMasters, 1966). One the most telling symptoms of this change is that WalMart is now the largest employer in the United States (Hightower, 2002). WalMart's documented effects on local economies serve to hasten the decline of the working class by lowering average wages, driving competitors out of business, and creating minimum-wage, minimum-benefit jobs to replace the better-paying, and more likely to provide health benefits, jobs that were lost when alternative retailers are driven under. This process has also been accompanied by a parallel development in which other jobs have been continuously downgraded in terms of specialized skills and training required, so that now sophisticated machinery can be assembled by workers who only need to be trained to push a button, or turn a screw one quarter of a turn. This process has been described as the "deskilling" of jobs and workers (Abbott, 1993).

The important point is that working-class Whites in the United States have not prospered during these economic changes but have actually suffered a significant decline in economic status. Equally (if not more) important is the accompanying decline in cultural prestige associated with economic prosperity. The last four decades of the 20th century also were the time frame in which the culture of the country was increasingly recognizing nonmajority cultures as existing, at least. The increasing numbers of African Americans, Latinos, Asian Pacific Islanders, and other ethnic minorities on network television, in advertising, in the political and social discourses of equal rights, and in the realm of affirmative action have made issues of ethnicity and race front and center in American culture in a manner that was not the case in the earlier parts of the 20th century (Southern Poverty Law Center, 2005b).

Indeed, as a classic example of scapegoating, what is known about contemporary White ethnic youth violence suggests that it emerged in reaction to these shifts in status. Specifically, it appears to be motivated by a perception that (a) Whites have lost status and economic opportunity; (b) immigrants and people of color in general are to blame for this; and (c) federal, state, and local governments have not only stood by and allowed Whites to decline in fortune, but these government entities have actually hastened the process by policies such as affirmative action and minority rights. It makes little difference that the facts still show that Whites of all classes have higher incomes, lower unemployment, and better access to health care than African Americans and Latinos; it is the case that poorly educated and low-skilled White ethnics have suffered in the changing economy, and blaming others is not only convenient but provides a convenient target for such violence. For some people, it is possible that such insecurity can be converted into self-worth by relegating a person or group of people to lower status (Hoffer, 1989; Shafer & Navarro, 2003).

WHITE ETHNIC GROUPS AND IMMIGRANT VIOLENCE IN U.S. HISTORY

Most historical accounts of White ethnic violence discuss the Irish immigrants to the United States as the first and foremost example of a group who engaged in violence. It is noted that the Irish were major actors in the urban violence of the Jacksonian Age in America, from the 1830s until the beginning of the U.S. Civil War in 1860 (Feldberg, 1980). Irish immigrants played a major role in the 1863 draft riots during the war in New York City, both in terms of the rioters and the recently formed police force that finally suppressed the riot (Bernstein, 1990; Feldberg, 1980). Finally, the Irish, in the post–Civil War era, launched criminal/violent/ political machines in New York City, establishing the model later immigrant groups used in establishing criminal and violent organizations to gain political, social, and economic power. The first incarnation of the infamous Tammany Hall, which harnessed the violent tendencies of the Irish in the service of political corruption and power, collapsed in 1871, although its successors continue to Irish violence to dominate some aspects of city politics into the 1930s (Block, 1994), or at least through the turn of the 20th century (Bernstein, 1990; Kelly, Chin, & Shatzberg, 1994).

Why were the Irish so violent in early 19th-century America? One argument is that the Irish, both Protestant Anglo-Irish as well as the immigrant Catholic Irish, were products of a centuries-long violent and murderous oppression, beginning with the dreadful Cromwellian slaughter of Irish Catholics in the 17th century (Feldberg, 1980). The aftermath of Cromwell's so-called "invasion" of Ireland was the development of a long-term guerilla war waged by the Irish Catholics on their Anglo-Irish Protestant overlords, including "whiteboyism," in which Irish Catholic night riders carried out property destruction, robbery, and assassination to fight economic and political oppression (Feldberg, 1980). The Protestant Irish who emigrated to the United States had been used to organizing gangs and fire companies in the homeland for defense, and they brought similar tactics to their new home (Brown, 1991; Culberson, 1990; Feldberg, 1980). Thus, the Irish immigrants to the United States may have been predisposed to use violence as an acceptable political, social, and economic tool in their struggle to establish themselves in a new nation (Culberson, 1990).

Research on organized crime in U.S. history suggests that immigrant groups who followed the Irish became involved in organized crime and violence for similar reasons: poverty, discriminatory treatment by groups that arrived in the country before them, and the desire to gain economic, social, and political power (Bell, 1953; Kelly et al., 1994). Jewish immigrants and later Italian immigrants came to the United States and found limited legitimate opportunities; this does not mean that all immigrants were or are now involved in violence and crime. It should also be noted that especially before 1940, violence between Whites and African Americans mainly consisted of gangs of Whites invading African American neighborhoods and engaging in property destruction, looting, and murder of largely defenseless residents (Feldberg, 1980; Grimshaw, 1969).

Considering the involvement of later groups of White ethnic immigrants in violence and crime in the United States, it is clear that Italian immigrants played a major role in organized crime, especially before, during, and after Prohibition; exactly what role, and how organized this involvement was, is much less clear (Kelly et al., 1994). There is some evidence that eastern European Jewish immigrants also became involved in organized crime in New York City and perhaps elsewhere, and there is considerable evidence and scholarship now focusing on Russian immigrant involvement in violence and organized crime (Finkenauer, 1994). The history of the United States is full of examples, and continues to be so, of White ethnic groups being heavily engaged in violence.

TYPES OF WHITE ETHNIC VIOLENCE
IN CONTEMPORARY AMERICA

The basis of the various groups known as White supremacists is a misperception among some Whites that the hegemonic power of the White race is in decline or in fact has declined. Although such a view is difficult to sustain if one examines data on the relative social and economic power of Whites versus others in industrialized Western nations, the notion that the "darker" races have overthrown the hegemony of the White race, which is assumed by White supremacists to the natural dominant race, is the driving force behind most if not all White supremacists movements and ideologies (Arena & Arrigo, 2000). This perception may be driven by the fact that African Americans and Latinos have made some economic and social progress in the past 50 years. The literature cited by White supremacist groups speak of various manifestations of this "takeover," including such factors as White job loss to people of color, intermarriage between Whites and people of color thus creating "impure Hybrid" races, and supposed conspiracy among the United Nations, Jews, and "dark races" to enslave and dominate Whites. It should not be surprising to note the common themes among different White supremacist groups, as the Internet and computers have made communication and the spread of such ideas much easier during the past two decades.

The types of violence likely to result from this ideological base involve both antigovernment violence, as White supremacists are often convinced that the government, any government, is part of the mechanism whereby this conspiracy operates to force Whites into decline, as well as violence directed at ethnic and racial groups perceived to be the direct threat to White opportunities and success.

How does this ideology of White loss of power work effectively in the face of substantial evidence to the contrary? A major consideration is the class origins of the followers of such movements and their perception that blue-collar workers have suffered a decline in standard of living in the United States, in part, because of the influx of immigrants. Among the implications of globalization are increased stress on the working class of core nations, such that low-skill jobs have become a shrinking part of the economy of most postindustrial states. As the information economy continues to develop, fewer and fewer low-skill jobs in countries such as the United States are being sought by working-class Whites. Rather increasing numbers of immigrants seek these types of jobs, leaving Whites vulnerable to White supremacist ideology (Shafer & Navarro, 2003). In memory, most working-class occupations were denied to Blacks, Latinos, and other non-White ethnics, but legal barriers to discrimination have made for more competition for fewer positions in this part of the economy. Whites who find themselves disadvantaged in this sector of the economy might easily perceive that the White race has fallen from power. Indeed, an analysis of White supremacist and "patriot" organizational memberships confirms the impact of economic restructuring and the loss of family farm jobs as significant positive predictors of membership in such groups (Van Dyke & Soule, 2002).

The Ku Klux Klan

The Knights of the Ku Klux Klan (also called White Knights, Imperial Knights, Invisible Empire, etc.) is the oldest and best known of all the hate groups and White supremacist movements in U.S. history. Tracing its origins to the post–Civil War era, the Klan was seen as the protector of southern Whites from the twin depredations of federal Reconstruction and emergent Black political and social power, which were fostered by Reconstruction and the presence of northern troops until 1877 in most southern states (Lewis & Serbu, 1999). Once the White southern authorities reestablished their political, social, and economic power in the "Jim Crow" period after Reconstruction, the southern Klan seems to have faded to some extent, only to be reestablished in the 1920s in northern states such as Indiana and Ohio (McVeigh, 1999, 2001), and western locations such as Oregon (Horowitz, 1998) and California (Rhomberg, 1998). The Klan became a major issue at the national Democratic Party convention in 1924; a platform plank that would have specifically denounced the Klan was narrowly defeated, suggesting the strong influence the Klan had in national politics in that era (McVeigh, 2001).

Although the Klan traditionally engaged in violence and terrorism, such activities were not exclusively aimed at African Americans; the Klan has always maintained a strong anti-Catholic and anti-Jewish stance in rhetoric and action (Horowitz, 1998; McVeigh, 2001; Seltzer & Lopes, 1986). During the 1980s and 1990s, the Klan emerged into the limelight once again, drawing a great deal of media coverage for a mobilization drive in Wilkes-Barre, Pennsylvania, in the early 1980s and the unsuccessful campaign for governor of Louisiana by David Duke, a former self-styled Grand Wizard of the Klan, in 1991 (Keil, 1985; Kuzenski, Bullock, & Gaddie, 2002). A survey conducted in the mid-1980s in Tennessee showed that there was considerable support from a random digit-dial telephone survey sample for the Klan and its racist, anti-Catholic and anti-Jewish rhetoric (Seltzer & Lopes, 1986). At least two studies have suggested that recent Klan activities are likely to be more successful in places where competition from non-White ethnic and racial groups is more significant (Beck, 2000; Keil, 1985).

A related supremacist group that operates only in prisons is the Aryan Brotherhood. This group is a derivative of other supremacist groups outside of prison and of individual White prisoners convicted of hate crime against people of color. Many such individuals do not come to prison with an organized ideology of White supremacy, but to survive in the highly racialized settings that U.S. prisons have become (the Black Guerrilla Family or the Mexican Mafia serve the same functions for their ethnic male and female members), individuals have been drawn to the influence of prison-based White supremacist groups. The Aryan Brotherhood and other similar groups socialize and indoctrinate new recruits who become supremacists by the time they leave prison (see Levin & McDevitt, 1993).

Thus, from the fringes of the White American working class, White supremacist ideology has some appeal. However, it seems clear that an underlying perception of a decline in the status of the working class is driving this ideology, prompting such disadvantaged Whites to respond by attacking the "other," that is, people of color, who are vulnerable and equally powerless in society. Although youth do not dominate such violence per se, youth are involved in such movements through family connections and recruitment.

White Survivalists and the Expression of Antiethnic Violence

White survivalists and White supremacists share a great deal in terms of ideology. Whereas White supremacists believe that the power of the White race has declined and is threatened by "dark" races, and that by striking violently at these groups and at the government, Whites can reclaim their hegemonic position, survivalists argue that it is already too late for such action. Survivalist ideology typically argues that the fall of civilization, that is, "White civilization," has already occurred or, is so close to occurring that no possibility exists to prevent it through violence or political action (Berbrier, 1998). Survivalist thought suggests that the way to salvation is to withdraw from the corrupted society of today, create a self-sufficient local environment where the White race, culture, and way of life can be preserved uncontaminated by others, only to reemerge sometime in the future when the corrupted civilization has fallen of its own contradictions and inherent weaknesses (Mitchell, 2002).

This ideological approach makes it less likely that White survivalists will commit acts of violence. However, if such groups feel directly threatened, they are likely to lash out at the threat, whether it be from the government or an encroaching group of people of color perceived as a threat to the isolation of the group. For example, the siege at Ruby Ridge in 1992 by federal agents is a classic example of a survivalist group, generally based on a family or extended family, reacting violently to the intrusion of government agents. The 1993 siege of the Branch Davidian compound in Waco, Texas, is another example; this religious cult shared many antigovernment beliefs

of survivalist movements. Once again, although youth are not always involved in such violence, typically survivalist groups depend on youth to
supply much of the firepower when attacked. At Ruby Ridge, Randy Weaver's
14-year-old son, Samuel, was killed in the initial gun battle with federal
agents; and a large number of youth were involved in and died in the siege
of the Branch Davidian compound in Waco (Kaplan, 2000).

Skinheads

Skinheads is a term usually applied to an offshoot of the punk rock
music movement that developed in the 1970s in England and elsewhere as
a counterpoint to hippies and rock and roll in general. These "punk rockers,"
who perceived rock and roll as oriented to the middle class, were working-
class youths coming of age in a postindustrial Britain with little or no
economic opportunity (Kaplan, 2000). However, skinheads evolved in the
late 20th century to become similar to other urban and suburban youth
groups in the United States but with a racist aspect that involves Whites
against youth of color. This is somewhat ironic, because the original skinheads in London were multiracial and often specifically antiracist in ideology
(Kaplan, 2000; Smith, 2000). A significant branch of skinheads also developed in Norway in the 1980s (Fangen, 2000).

Although skinhead groups have proliferated in the United States in
recent years, there has been relatively little research on understanding and
preventing this type of activity. Still, some efforts have been made to
document types of skinhead groups, typical activities, and risk factors for
involvement. For example, the Federal Bureau of Investigation (FBI) recently completed a 7-year investigation of skinhead groups in Southern
California during the 1990s (Shafer & Navarro, 2003). According to their
findings, the skinhead groups they identified typically consisted of uneducated, young, White males between the ages of 13 and 24 who have little
prospects for long-term job and career success. In many cases, they lack
adequate parental supervision.

For youth who are disengaged and disenchanted with their lives, becoming a skinhead can provide an answer for their plight that conveniently
lays the blame elsewhere. Otherwise stated, the answer to the question of
"why can't I get ahead in life" is simple—because the rights to run this
country are being turned over to minorities. For those who have long
struggled to control their anger, the skinhead movement provides an organized form of expression for this anger and a type of "legitimacy" based on
group norms. Peer validation also bolsters their sense of self-worth, and at the
same time prevents introspection. Furthermore, joining a group empowers
individuals who feel otherwise ineffective—hate is the glue that binds them
together. Skinheads often see themselves as soldiers in a race war. To

sum up, White racial purity is the main item on the Skinhead agenda (Kleg, 1993).

Although hate is a common theme for all skinhead groups, they can be divided into two categories: criminally motivated and hate-motivated. According to the FBI report (FBI, 2003), criminally motivated skinhead groups focus on for-profit criminal activities. In other words, their primary motivation is economic gain, and crimes typically include drug sales and burglaries. Racially motivated hate crimes do occur, but they are somewhat incidental to their regular activities. These hate crimes are often designed to keep ethnic minorities out of their neighborhoods. In contrast, hate-motivated skinhead groups devote the majority of their time to hate crimes, although they may commit petty crimes to support daily needs. Hate-motivated skinhead groups often spend their time prowling the streets looking for ethnic minorities to attack. Indeed, interviews with members of each group reveal that criminally motivated skinheads identify themselves as criminals first and haters second. In contrast, hate-motivated skinheads feel that the world is against them and nothing will work for them. They regularly make reference to the fact that if they quit being a skinhead they would have "nothing."

Overall, most skinhead groups are not well-organized and lack the leadership found in many well-established street gangs. Despite this lack of organization, it is still common for them to establish a group identity through symbols, rituals, and mythologies, such as adopting the swastika, the Confederate flag, or other supremacist symbols. However, some skinhead groups are more organized. These groups frequently engage in active and well-planned recruitment through a variety of techniques. One former recruiter for skinheads tells of cunning recruitment strategies targeting children as young as 12 years old. "One strategy was to post hate flyers near schools and campuses. Minority students believed White students had posted them. When altercations occurred between White and minority students, the skinheads were always around to help the White students. This way the skinhead became the "savior, ingratiating himself with the White student" (Townsend, 2003, p. 1). The recruiter also describes the extensive network for recruiting youth that extends to music, magazines, comic books, and the Internet. Indeed, there are thousands of hate sites on the Internet, including several 24-hour Web radio sites that play hate music juxtaposed with old Nazi propaganda footage.

Hate Crimes

As discussed above, skinheads are composed of youth who are motivated, to at least some extent, by hatred of non-White groups. As such, much of their violent activity would be consider a form of hate crime. A hate crime, as defined by the FBI, is a criminal offense committed against a person or property that is motivated, in whole or in part, by the offender's bias against a race, religion, disability, ethnicity/national origin, or sexual orientation (Federal Bureau of Investigation [FBI], 2003). A number of organized hate groups exist in the United States at this time. However, as statistics reveal, most hate crimes are not actually committed by hate groups (FBI, 2003).

Hate or bias crime law is different from most criminal law in that it is based on the idea that the motivation of these crimes makes them especially harmful to the community and the victims (Jacobs & Potter, 1998). The passage of the federal Hate Crime Act of 1990 mandated that the Justice Department collect and publish annual statistics on hate or bias crimes. During the past decade, the FBI has reported about 8,000 hate crimes annually. However, participation in the Hate Crime Statistics report is voluntary, and several states do not participate fully, resulting in a likely underreporting. For this reason, data in regard to ethnicity of both offenders and victims must be viewed cautiously.

Considering all motivations for hate crimes in 2002, race and ethnicity accounted for about 63% of the incidents, with religion accounting for 19%, and sexual orientation about 17%. In terms of ethnicity of the perpetrator, in 2002, the latest year for which national data currently are available, crimes against people, the largest category of hate crimes reported, revealed an ethnic distribution of 62% Whites and 22% African Americans. In addition, hate crimes are much less violent overall then the other types we have discussed. Overall, crimes against people made up two thirds of the hate crimes reported, but of these, more than half consisted of intimidation, a type of crime that is more psychological than it is violent, in that it involves no physical contact between victim and offender (FBI, 2003).

Hate crimes have a long and inglorious place in U.S. history, and that history is dominated by both violence and an almost exclusive involvement of Whites as offenders of such violence and blacks and other people of color as victims. The most prominent example of this is the history of lynching, which in some places in the post–Reconstruction South became law de facto if not de jure (Culberson, 1990; Grimshaw, 1969). Even before the Civil War and during that conflict, lynching or the hanging of a victim by an illegal mob was a common method for Whites to express hate and bias against Blacks, Native Americans, and others (Feldberg, 1980; Jacobs & Potter, 1998). During the draft riots in New York City after the Emancipation Proclamation was issued by Lincoln in 1863, as many as 1,500 to 2,500 Blacks were murdered, many by lynching (Bernstein, 1990). Between 1889 and 1919, five southern states reported officially nearly 1,500 lynchings of

Blacks; this number does not include unreported lynchings (Jacobs & Potter, 1998). Hate crime toward other groups such as Native Americans and Catholics and later Jews was also relatively common both before and after the U.S. Civil War, and into the 20th century.

The degree to which these historical examples of hate crimes are congruent with the current view of hate crime is another issue. There is much evidence to suggest that many hate crimes both then and now are motivated by factors even beyond race and ethnicity. Anti-immigration has been a consistent theme, as has religious persecution, an interesting feature in a country supposedly founded on the principle of religious tolerance.

White Youth Gangs

As discussed previously, much of the youth violence, including organized youth violence, during the 19th century was carried out by White youth. Gangs were primarily Irish, Jewish, and Italian. However, from the 20th century to today, ethnic minorities are more likely than Whites to be involved in youth gangs. However, it is difficult to determine exactly how many White youth are involved with gangs. Estimates range from 5% to 25%, depending on the source of information and location (Howell, 1997). Communities with emerging gang problems, on average, report a larger proportion of White gang members than any other ethnic group (Howell, Egley, & Gleason, 2002).

Although police in smaller cities report emerging White ethnic gang problems, and some observers have reported contemporary White ethnic gangs (see Sanchez-Jankowski, 1991), detailed studies of gang joining and persistence continue to show that youth gangs are more attractive to youth of color and that such youth persist longer and are much more likely to become seriously involved (Farrington Gordon, Lahey, Loeber, & Stouthamer-Loeber, 1999). Klein (1997) presented convincing evidence that the majority of gangs and gang members in the major U.S. cities are African American or Latino.

School Shooters: An Almost Exclusive White, Male Club

Any listing of the major school shootings in the last few years shows a striking connection between ethnicity and the offenders of these horrific cases. More than 90% of these offenders are White, and more than 90% are male, giving this form of ethnic violence a distinctive profile (FBI, 2000). Why should this one type of violence be so exclusively linked to young White males?

Although these mass school shootings generate an enormous amount of media coverage, there are relative few of them in the United States. For example, between October 1997, when the Pearl, Mississippi, shooting occurred, and the May 2001, Santee, California, incident, there were four other major events—Paducah, Kentucky; Jonesboro, Arkansas; Springfield, Oregon, and the infamous Columbine incident in Littleton, Colorado. Despite the relatively small number of cases, some striking patterns have emerged. For example, the vast majority of the shooters were considered social outcasts by others and in most cases by the shooters themselves (Cornell, 1999). It has even been suggested that these shootings represent a "cultural war" between the outcasts of the junior and high school social scene and the dominant groups such as athletes, cheerleaders, and high achievers (Cook, 2000). Certainly some of these offenders were suicidal, while others were not, suggesting that the alienation felt by these outcast youth was not always self-destructive.

One study that examined school violence and compared Whites and African Americans found that for Whites, involvement in school violence was predicted by a sense that the conventional community in the school had rejected the respondent, yet among African Americans, this factor had no impact. In contrast, rejection by family was the best predictor for African Americans (D'Apolito & Wan-Tatah, 1998). This suggests that White youth may be more sensitive to the approval or rejection of the school social scene, thus making White youth more vulnerable and more likely to strike out externally if suicide is not a viable option.

Two additional factors—guns and media/entertainment—should also be mentioned in this context. A study of school shooters by the Centers for Disease Control and Prevention (CDC) found that most of the weapons used in the school shootings were obtained from relatives or friends (CDC, 2003). Some have argued that video games play a role in these school shootings; rushing into a building and trying to shoot everyone in the building, one expert pointed out, is reminiscent of the style of play in single player shooting-oriented video games (Cornell, 1999). In addition, mass media has some influence as well. It was said the Columbine shooters were inspired by an episode of the TV show, *Buffy the Vampire Slayer*, in which the school was rigged to explode to destroy an "evil" entity residing in the school; in their style of dress, the shooters in Colorado were obviously imitating the style of dress in a popular movie of that time, the *Matrix*. These factors are not the primary causes of these school shootings, but the easy access to guns and to games and movies that glorify such violence add to the likelihood that a young White male who is alienated and wishes to strike back at the dominant youth culture will find an extreme method for doing so.

CONCLUSION

Six types of White violence have been described in this chapter. It is clear from these descriptions that there are common threads in all six, although they vary in salience and degree. Typically, White ethnic violence involves the search for a scapegoat who can shoulder the blame for one's difficulties and problems. People of color or people who are marginalized because of particular circumstances become viable targets. These hate-motivated reactions are often facilitated by joining together with other like-minded individuals in an array of hate-focused affiliations.

The 1950s were a period of total White hegemony in the United States, during which people of color were all but invisible in the media and in public life. After the Civil Rights movement began, people of color served as scapegoats for all that was "wrong" with the nation among the fringes of the White population. This factor combined with the increasing marginalization of the least skilled and least educated members of the working class has created a potential for violent White reaction to people of color, as well as to other disenfranchised groups such as immigrants. Although these types of violence remain rare, White ethnic culture does contribute to the problem of violence in U.S. society and will continue to be a source of potential violence and victimization in the future.

What can be done to prevent or mitigate White ethnic youth violence? Clearly, some attention needs to be paid to address critical gaps in research and knowledge. What is needed in the case of White ethnic youth violence is basic empirical research in epidemiology, etiology, and greater theoretical development in both the areas of "Whiteness" or White ethnic culture and the youth violence that can spring from this dominant culture.

Prevention strategies must address the complex mixture of individual motivation and group processes. As discussed previously, when White ethnic violence is linked to membership in a particular group, the group becomes a source of legitimization, validation, anonymity, and diminished accountability. Group cohesion is solidified through a variety of rituals, symbols, and mythologies. Intervening to dismantle immature and disorganized groups should be easier than breaking down sophisticated groups or encouraging individuals to opt out of those groups. In the prior case, providing alternate options for positive engagement in schools, families, and the community via either school-sanctioned or court-mandated actions should prove useful. In the later case, where groups are more sophisticated or primarily criminally motivated, it is likely to require elaborate intervention strategies such as used more generally with criminal street gangs.

For example, a program based on Spergel's (1999) Comprehensive Model combined traditional gang worker individual intervention with a coordinated response form agencies such as police, probation, schools, and the business community to effectively and persistently intervene in targeted neighborhoods with severe gang problems. In a 5-year evaluation, this approach resulted in a significant decrease in youth gang and nongang violence in two targeted neighborhoods (Parker, 2002).

For White ethnic violence that is linked more to individual pathologies and problems than to group membership, different types of preventive interventions are warranted. In the case of school shooters, much effort has gone into enhancing efforts at early identification and threat assessment (FBI, 2000). Coordinated efforts to provide services for isolated and troubled youth in school settings may have a side-effect of reducing the likelihood that one of these White youth will become a school shooter. Additional efforts to enforce the existing laws and policies that are supposed to prevent access to high powered weapons among youth would also have a significant preventive impact on school shooters. Ultimately, more effective programs and interventions designed to prevent or control White ethnic violence can only be developed with additional research in schools, communities, courts, and juvenile detention facilities. An important but missing piece for understanding and preventing violence among White youth is to disentangle violence by White youth that results from the experience of Whiteness (as described in this chapter) from other developmental and community conditions that increase risk for violence among White youth but that are not linked to ethnic separatism based on Whiteness. As we have pointed out, although youth violence occurs disproportionately among ethnic minority youth of color, its significance as a problem perpetrated by White youth should not be overlooked.

REFERENCES

Abbott, A. A. (1993). The sociology of work and occupations. *Annual Review of Sociology, 19,* 187–209.

Arena, M. P., & Arrigo, B. A. (2000). White supremacist behavior: Toward an integrated social psychological model. *Deviant Behavior, 21,* 213–244.

Beck, E. M. (2000). Guess who's coming to town: White supremacy, ethnic competition, and social change. *Sociological Focus, 33,* 153–174.

Bell, D. (1953). Crime as an American way of life. *Antioch Review, 13,* 131–154.

Berbrier, M. (1998). Half the battle: Cultural resonance, framing processes, and ethnic affectations in contemporary White separatist rhetoric. *Social Problems, 45,* 431–450.

Bernstein, I. (1990). *The New York City draft riots: Their significance for American society and politics in the age of the Civil War.* New York: Oxford University Press.

Block, A. (1994). Organized crime: History and historiography. In R. J. Kelly, K. L. Chin, & R. Shatzberg (Eds.), *Handbook of organized crime in the United States* (pp. 39–67). Westport, CT: Greenwood Press.

Brown, R. M. (1991). *No duty to retreat: Violence and values in American history and society*. New York: Oxford University Press.

Centers for Disease Control and Prevention. (2003, March 7). *Morbidity and Mortality Weekly Report, 52*, 169–172.

Cook, D. T. (2000). Childhood is killing "our" children: Some thoughts on the Columbine High School shootings and the agentive child. *Childhood, 7*, 107–117.

Cornell, D. (1999). School shootings. Testimony before the U.S. House of Representatives Judiciary Committee, May 13, 1999.

Culberson, W. C. (1990). *Vigilantism: Political history of private power in America*. New York: Praeger.

D'Apolito, R., & Wan-Tatah, V. (1998). Social bonding and juvenile male violence: An empirical investigation. *Free Inquiry in Creative Sociology, 26*, 11–21.

Fangen, K. (2000). Skinheads (Norwegian). In J. Kaplan (Ed.), *The encyclopedia of White power: A sourcebook on the radical racist right* (pp. 281–283). Walnut Creek, CA: Altamira Press.

Farrington, D. P., Gordon, R. A., Lahey, B. B., Loeber, R., & Stouthamer-Loeber, M. (1999). Boys who join gangs: A prospective study of predictors of first gang entry. *Journal of Abnormal Child Psychology, 27*, 434–449.

Federal Bureau of Investigation. (2000). *The school shooter: A threat assessment perspective*. Washington, DC: National Institute of Justice.

Federal Bureau of Investigation. (2003). *Hate crime statistics 2002*. Uniform Crime Reports. Washington, DC: National Institute of Justice.

Feldberg, M. (1980). *The turbulent era: Riot and disorder in Jacksonian America*. New York: Oxford University Press.

Finkenauer, J. O. (1994). Russian organized crime in America. In R. J. Kelly, K. L. Chin, & R. Shatzberg (Eds.), *Handbook of organized crime in the United States* (pp. 245–265). Westport, CT: Greenwood Press.

Grimshaw, A. D. (Ed.). (1969). *Racial violence in the United States*. Chicago: Aldine.

Hightower, J. (2002, April 26). How WalMart is remaking our world. *Hightower Lowdown, 4*.

Hoffer, E. (1989). *The true believer: Thoughts on the nature of mass movements*. New York: Harper & Row.

Horowitz, D. A. (1998). The normality of extremism: The Ku Klux Klan revisited. *Society, 35*, 71–77.

Howell, J. C. (1997). Youth gangs. *OJJDP Fact Sheet*. Washington, DC: U.S. Government Printing Office.

Howell, J. C., Egley, A., & Gleason, D. K. (2002). Modern day youth gangs. *OJJDP Bulletin*. Washington, DC: U.S. Government Printing Office.

Jacobs, J., & Potter, R. (1998). *Hate crimes: Criminal law and identity politics*. New York: Oxford University Press.

Kaplan, J. (2000). *The encyclopedia of White power: A sourcebook on the radical racist right*. Walnut Creek, CA: Altamira Press.

Keil, T. J. (1985). Capital labor and the Klan: A case study. *Phylon, 46*, 341–352.

Kelly, R. J., Chin, K. L., & Shatzberg, R. (1994). Introduction. In R. J. Kelly, K. L. Chin, & R. Shatzberg (Eds.), *Handbook of organized crime in the United States* (pp. 1–16). Westport, CT: Greenwood Press.

Kleg, M. (1993). *Hate, prejudice, and racism*. Albany: State University of New York Press.

Klein, M. W. (1997). *The American street gang: Its nature, prevalence, and control*. New York: Oxford University Press.

Kuzenski, J. C., Bullock, C. S., III, & Gaddie, R. K. (Eds.). (2002). *David Duke and the politics of race in the South*. Nashville, TN: Vanderbilt University Press.

LeMasters, E. E. (1966). *Blue collar aristocrats: Lifestyles at a working class tavern*. Madison: University of Wisconsin Press.

Levin, J., & McDevitt, J. (1993). *Hate crimes, the rising tide of bigotry and bloodshed*. Boulder, CO: Westview Press.

Lewis, M., & Serbu, J. (1999). Kommemorating the Ku Klux Klan. *Sociological Quarterly, 40*, 139–158.

McVeigh, R. (1999). Structural incentives for conservative mobilization: Power devaluation and the rise of the Ku Klux Klan, 1915–1925. *Social Forces, 77*, 1461–1496.

McVeigh, R. (2001). Power devaluation, the Ku Klux Klan, and the Democratic convention of 1924. *Sociological Forum, 16*, 1–30.

Mitchell, R. G. (2002). *Dancing at Armageddon: Survivalism and chaos in modern times*. Chicago: University of Chicago Press.

Parker, R. N. (2002). *The evaluation of Project Bridge: 1994–1999*. Riverside: Report, Presley Center for Crime and Justice Studies, University of California.

Reiman, J. (1994). *The rich get richer and the poor get prison*. Englewood Cliffs, NJ: Prentice-Hall.

Rhomberg, C. (1998). White nativism and urban politics: The 1920s Ku Klux Klan in Oakland, CA. *Journal of American Ethnic History, 17*, 39–55.

Sanchez-Jankowski, M. (1991). *Islands in the street: Gangs and American urban society* Berkeley: University of California Press.

Seltzer, R., & Lopes, G. M. (1986). The Ku Klux Klan: Reasons for support or opposition among White residents. *Journal of Black Studies, 17*, 91–109.

Shafer, J. R., & Navarro, M. A. (2003, March). The seven-stage hate model: The psychopathology of hate groups. *FBI Law Enforcement Bulletin, 72*, 2–6.

Simpson, D. (1991). *Hadrian's Vale and Geordieland: The people, history, and folklore of River Tyne*. Durham, England: North Penmine.

Smith, E. (2000). Adult influence in youth subcultures: The case of Skinheads (Doctoral dissertation, University of Oregon, 2000). *Dissertation Abstracts International, 61*, 4953–4954.

Snyder, H., & Sickmund, M. (1999). *Juvenile offenders and victims: A national report.* Washington, DC: Center for Juvenile Justice, Office of Juvenile Justice and Delinquency Prevention.

Southern Poverty Law Center. (2005a). *Active U.S. hate groups in the U.S.* Retrieved March 30, 2005, from http://www.tolerance.org

Southern Poverty Law Center. (2005b). *Blood on the border.* Retrieved March 30, 2005, from http://www.tolerance.org

Spergel, I. I. (1999). *Youth gangs: Problems and response.* New York: Oxford University Press.

Townsend, A. (2003). *Ex-racist skinhead tells gripping story of hatred and redemption.* Retrieved November 1, 2003, from http://rickross.com/references/skinheads25html

Van Dyke, N., & Soule, S. A. (2002). Structural change and the mobilizing effect of threat: Explaining levels of patriot and militia organizing in the U.S. *Social Problems, 49*, 497–520.

Wilson, W. J. (1996). *When work disappears: The world of the new urban poor.* New York: Knopf.

III

DEVELOPING CULTURALLY COMPETENT YOUTH VIOLENCE PREVENTION PROGRAMS AND STRATEGIES

9

CULTURALLY SENSITIVE INTERVENTIONS TO PREVENT YOUTH VIOLENCE

JOAN C. WRIGHT AND MARC A. ZIMMERMAN

Some moralists suggest that there are no universal values that apply to everyone in all cultures. Instead, they argue, one way of doing things is as valid as any other, and acts are judged right or wrong only with reference to a particular cultural system. This is Protagoras's principle of relativism.

(Fearn, 2001, p. 10)

This chapter describes and discusses violence-prevention programs that adopt a strategy that includes some attention to cultural sensitivity. We begin by defining what we mean by cultural sensitivity and note both similarities and differences with other related constructs. We then discuss the general rationale for developing culturally sensitive prevention programs. Following this, we examine how cultural issues are addressed in the extant violence prevention efforts that consider culture. We conclude with a discussion of the limitations of these efforts, and provide suggestions for future directions to enhance our attention to culture in preventive interventions.

We focused our attention only on programs that addressed violent behavior (including aggressive behavior) or attitudes as an outcome. If a program included other outcomes in addition to violent behavior, it was still included. We chose, however, not to include programs focused more generally on problem behaviors, if specific reference to violence prevention was not included. We focused our attention in this way even though problem behaviors have many commonalities and similar antecedents, because violent behavior represents a unique type of problem behavior. Motivation for violent behavior may differ from other problem behaviors, the interpersonal nature of much violent behavior inevitably involves victimization, and violent behavior most often includes interpersonal involvement. Finally, because there is a dearth of controlled evaluations of violence-prevention programs that directly address cultural issues, some of the programs we included have not yet been rigorously evaluated.

Consistent with the definition of culture provided by Smith and Guerra (introduction, this volume), Braithwaite (1998) defined culture as a complex pattern of human behavior that includes perceptions, language, customs, values, belief systems, groups, and material traits of racial, ethnic, religious, or social groups. Given the potential implications of culture for health and behavior, researchers have suggested the need for and usefulness of culturally sensitive promotion and prevention programs (Braithwaite, 1998; Resnicow, Baranowski, Ahluwalia, & Braithwaite, 1999). Researchers, however, describe many strategies for addressing cultural issues and they use multiple terms to describe them.

The examination of the role of culture in learning, for example, has been occurring in educational research for decades (Hudley, 2001). The basic argument made by cultural discontinuity theorists is that teachers and students differ in their expectations of behavior and that their expectations are derived from experiences outside of the school environment in what sociolinguists call speech communities or speech networks (Taylor & Wang, 1997). Because there are individual experiences and variations in culture, these reflect differences in knowledge bases. This means that practitioners and participants may benefit from gaining an appreciation of various cultural experiences integrating relevant terms, values, norms, and historical context into culturally sensitive interventions (Taylor & Wang, 1997). Incorporating core cultural beliefs may help make interventions more sensitive to different ways of learning that may be more engaging for the individual.

Other traditional notions of cultural relevance, such as use of appropriate language and gender, are part of a culturally sensitive education program. Ladson-Billings (1994) defined culturally relevant instruction as a method of intervention that empowers individuals intellectually, socially, emotionally, and politically by using cultural referents to impart knowledge, skills, and attitudes. Cultural referents are indicative of attributes that describe culture, such as language, history, gender, cultural beliefs, and values. Finally, implicit in most culturally sensitive conceptualizations is the notion of a common ethnic background. Sale and colleagues (Sale, Sambrano, Springer, Turner, & Hermann, 1998) indicated that culturally focused programming includes activities that are designed to impart knowledge specifically related to cultural values, histories, or customs of groups of participants from a shared ethnic heritage.

Culture is infused into educational and health prevention programming in different ways. Nevertheless, few systematic efforts have been made to directly address issues of culture in the design, implementation, and evaluation of youth violence-prevention programs. This reflects a certain degree of unfamiliarity with cultural concepts. Conversely, practitioners and researchers do not have a clear set of guidelines about how best to integrate culture into these programs. A critical first step is to specify a broad framework that allows for incorporation of different cultural concepts. We believe that the concept of cultural sensitivity can provide guidance for these efforts.

WHAT IS CULTURAL SENSITIVITY?

The term cultural sensitivity has often been used interchangeably with terms such as *cultural relevance*, *cultural appropriateness*, and *culture based*. Resnicow and colleagues (Resnicow, Baranowski, Ahluwalia, & Braithwaite, 1999; Resnicow, Soler, Braithwaite, Ahluwalia, & Butler, 2000), however, distinguished between culturally based programs and culturally sensitive programs. Programs are culturally based if they combine culture, history, and core values as agents to encourage behavior change. Resnicow et al. (1999) suggested that culturally based interventions refer to those that include "messages that combine culture, history, and core values as a medium to motivate behavior change" (p. 11).

In contrast, Resnicow et al. (1999) defined cultural sensitivity as "the extent to which ethnic and cultural characteristics, experiences, norms, values, behavioral patterns and beliefs of a selected population as well as the relevant historical, environmental, and social forces are incorporated into the design, implementation, and evaluation of health promotion materials and programs" (p. 11). This framework provides a broader structure within which multiple factors can be integrated. Specifically, their conceptualization of cultural sensitivity includes both *surface structure* and *deep structure*. These two dimensions of cultural sensitivity draw on sociology and linguistics in which surface structure and deep structure have been used to describe dimensions of culture and language (Layton & Simpson, 1975; Liu, 1995; Mauner, Tanenhaus, & Carlson, 1995; Zuczkowski, 1994).

Surface structure includes the external characteristics of culture in an intervention for a selected population. Surface structure, for example, may involve using people, food, language, and music familiar to and preferred by the selected population. Surface structure refers to how well interventions fit within a specific culture and generally increases the receptivity, comprehension, or acceptance of messages (Resnicow et al., 1999; Simons-Morton, Donohew, & Crump, 1997). Surface structure also identifies what channels (e.g., media, African American facilitators) and settings (e.g., schools, community centers) are most appropriate for delivery of messages in culturally sensitive violence-prevention programs.

Deep structure reflects how cultural, social, psychological, environmental, and historical factors influence behavior differently across ethnic groups (Resnicow et al., 2000). It involves understanding how individuals in a particular subgroup perceive the cause, course, and treatment of an illness or risk behavior. Whereas surface structure increases the receptivity or feasibility of messages, deep structure refers to the salience or effect of multiple elements on behavior in the selected population. Mental health services, for example, often carry a stigma for Latino populations. Thus, simply calling someone a mental health worker rather than an outreach or support worker can have implications and reflects deep structure issues. Although most programs do not provide specific details as to how they incorporate surface structure and/or deep structure, these concepts provide a useful tool for assessing cultural sensitivity.

For example, Harris and colleagues (Harris et al., 2001) implemented a model composed of eight strategies to increase the cultural sensitivity of a smoking cessation clinical trial and developed a program that engaged African American young adults in activities to maximize the cultural sensitivity of the trial. The activities were conducted throughout three phases of the trial—project development, conducting the needs assessment, and pilot testing the trial. Although surface and deep structure components of the intervention were not discussed explicitly in the study, the article provides good examples of how surface and deep structure were operationalized in the program.

Examples of how surface structure was incorporated throughout each phase of the trial included recruiting African American counselors to conduct the counseling and developing a project logo depicting an African American, wearing African clothing, and using language familiar to participants. Examples of how deep structure was incorporated into the program included addressing ethical issues related to clinical research on African Americans and addressing participants' reluctance to seek treatment and take medication to quit smoking. Stigma of medical research on African Americans can invariably affect recruitment of participants and compliance in treatment. Therefore, addressing participant concerns in these ethical and treatment issues can be vital to the success of the program.

Culturally sensitive programs that involve deep structure integrate elements such as core cultural values (e.g., Afrocentric values) within programs. The basic assumption underlying surface and deep structure is that different ethnic groups have inter- and intracultural differences (differences within and among ethnic groups) and, therefore, are heterogeneous within a particular ethnic group (Resnicow et al., 1999). One of the crucial elements of culture for which heterogeneity might be assumed is ethnic identity. As discussed by French, Kim, and Pillado (chap. 2, this volume), during the past two decades, a number of conceptual models have been proposed to describe and explain ethnic (and racial) identity among African Americans and other ethnic minority groups. This suggests that consideration of cultural differences within ethnic groups may be necessary to achieve greater cultural sensitivity in programs regarding both surface structure and deep structure dimensions. Identifying ethnic groups as monolithic does not allow for within-group variation and may compromise the degree to which a culturally sensitive intervention can be achieved (Marks, Settles, Cooke, Morgan, & Sellers, 2004).

Another degree of complexity when thinking about making programs culturally sensitive involves the selection of specific cultures that must be incorporated into programming. In some cases, violence-prevention programs recruit youth from many different ethnic minority groups. This creates both conceptual and practical concerns. Should these programs develop specific programs for each group or subgroup of youth within a particular cohort? In addition to incorporating relevant themes and concerns around culture linked to ethnicity, it is also critical to consider the distinct features of youth culture that must be addressed. Indeed, the lack of meaningful economic and social opportunities for youth has been linked to the emergence and growing importance of a widely diffused youth culture. This culture is augmented by media advertising, economic factors that cater to youthful fads, and the growing buying power of the younger generation. Therefore, broadening definitions of culture to address youth culture might be helpful for the selected population.

Finally, interventions typically are considered culturally sensitive if they incorporate culture in how they are developed and the content of the activities (hence, surface and deep structure). Yet, interventions can also be culturally sensitive if they conceptualize culture as an asset to be enhanced as the prevention strategy itself. Similar to programs described by Hurst and Laird (chap. 6, this volume) for Native Americans, Zimmerman and colleagues (Zimmerman, Ramirez, Washienko, Walter, & Dyer, 1995) described an intervention that was designed to enhance Native American adolescents' identification with and pride in their native culture as a way to prevent alcohol and substance abuse (AOD). Thus, the *enculturation* (i.e., [re]discovering one's cultural heritage and traditions) process was the mechanism used to prevent AOD. Of course, this required the program to be culturally sensitive (how else could it help youth with enculturation), but it also differed in that the cultural context itself was the intervention and not merely a means to deliver a prevention message or set of skills. This is a form of deep structure, but rather than being a characteristic of an intervention that provides a means for delivering a message, the act of learning about one's culture is in fact the intervention. The Native American youth learned that alcohol put holes in their spirit and that tobacco ceremonies were the only appropriate use of that substance.

RATIONALE FOR CULTURALLY SENSITIVE VIOLENCE-PREVENTION PROGRAMS

Researchers and practitioners consistently note that violence prevention interventions need to be tailored to (a) the specific needs and strengths of the focus population and neighborhood; (b) the types, frequency, and severity of violence that exists within the population or neighborhood; and (c) the specific contexts and culture in which such violence occurs (American Psychological Association [APA] Commission on Violence and Youth, 1993; Corvo, 1997; Greene, 1998; National Center for Injury, Prevention, and Control, 1993; Tolan & Guerra, 1994). As emphasized throughout this volume, the rationale for focused and tailored violence-prevention programs across ethnic groups derives from differences in their rates of violence, differences in their prevalence of risk factors to engage in violence and assets that help them avoid violence, and differences in predictors of violence across ethnic groups.

As Guerra and Williams note (chap. 1, this volume), rates of violence, for example, are highest among ethnic minority youth living in poor, urban neighborhoods lacking resources. They note that ethnic minority children in the United States often grow up in disadvantaged ecological niches that are characterized by limited resources, concentrated poverty, and danger. Predictors of violence in these settings are not linked to race or ethnicity, but rather to the structural characteristics of these environments (Sampson, Morenoff, & Raudenbush, 2005). Although focusing on surface structure characteristics might be important in reaching children and families in these communities, it is also clearly important to address deep structure characteristics that contribute to this disadvantaged status.

Poverty, for example, has not been directly implicated in the etiology of violence. Rather, being poor under a specific set of historical and present circumstances can exert a unique influence on violence. We also must ask how the experience of racism contributes to individual development and can increase risk for violence. Similarly, what is the effect of marginalization from the mainstream economic forces in society on an individual's willingness to embrace a violent lifestyle? Clearly, deep structure refers to understanding the complexity of circumstance and how it can be addressed within a specific intervention.

Prevalence of assets among groups can relate to deep structure as well. The presence of assets that may help youth overcome or avoid the negative effects of violence, such as community involvement in the African American community, suggest that deep structure characteristics (e.g., making connections between poverty, community organization and disorganization, and violence) might be appropriate in interventions. Indeed, the chapters in section II of this volume that focus on violence prevention within distinct ethnic minority groups all emphasize the importance of building assets among ethnic minority youth, in part, to counteract negative labels and "risk" status often ascribed to minorities. In addition to prevalence of risk factors and assets, perceptions of risk might be different than actual risk of violence among youth (Stevenson, Herrero-Taylor, Cameron, & Davis, 2002). This suggests that addressing negative stereotypes among minority youth might be a vital deep structure component in violence prevention interventions as youth attempt to reject or appropriate these negative perceptions. These interventions can reflect how negative as well as positive images affect emotions and behaviors among youth.

Bringing together the experience of culture-specific art, drama, film, and other literary devices allows for the development of personal and culturally specific meaning within an intervention (Bourdieu, 1993). Yet, this approach alone only provides surface structure relevance to the intervention. While this may be vital to increase audience interest and enhance initial engagement in the program, it does not reflect a more nuanced understanding of culture. Interventions also need to incorporate the values, culture, and norms of the focus population so that learned behaviors can be more culturally familiar and more easily adapted (Spencer, 1990; Stack, 1974). Extended families, for example, are often vital in the lives of African American children (Spencer, 1990; Stack, 1974). As a consequence, violence-prevention programs that include a parenting component may be more relevant for African American youth if extended families are an integral part of the intervention content and implementation.

Robinson and Howard-Hamilton (1994) found that a social skills training curricula for African American youth that used Afrocentric content to promote positive social interactions provided participants with a greater understanding of their traditions, cultural contributions, and inventions. This, in turn, may help increase positive self images and attitudes toward others, reducing maladaptive social behaviors and promoting prosocial interactions. Gordon (1993) hypothesized that culturally sensitive instruction and content that focuses on cultural history enables children to critically view the messages of dominant society. African American youth, for example, can better construct how they have been negatively represented and perceived in mainstream society regarding violence and how this negative representation might influence attitudes toward violence and violent behaviors. Caldwell, Kohn-Wood, Schmeelk-Cone, Chavous, and Zimmerman (in press) found the negative effects of racial discrimination on violent behaviors were moderated by ethnic identity among urban, African American adolescents. Ward (1995) found that a strong and positive ethnic identity could help youth by building on a sense of belonging to a group whose very survival has been dependent on their ability to resist racism and oppression.

Reconnecting at-risk youth with cultural values that emphasize communal traditions enables youth to think more positively about self with regard to others (Ward, 1995). Robinson and Ward (1991) suggested that the traditional values emphasized by Afrocentric philosophy contribute to positive self-concept and prosocial functioning by helping African Americans avoid potential threats to healthy living such as drug use and addiction, failure in school, and community and interpersonal violence. However, as pointed out by French, Kim, and Pillado (chap. 2, this volume), most work on building ethnic pride has been conducted with African Americans; more research is needed within distinct ethnic minority groups to determine the dynamics of ethnic pride vis-à-vis youth violence and recommended intervention strategies.

CULTURALLY SENSITIVE YOUTH VIOLENCE PREVENTION PROGRAMS

As mentioned earlier, most of the violence prevention efforts that incorporate culture in some fashion have focused on African Americans and, to a lesser extent, Latino and Asian populations. Nevertheless, it is useful to note that although applications of culturally sensitive violence-prevention programs are limited to these ethnic groups, this discussion will provide foundation for developing a model on which future violence-prevention programs may be designed for other ethnic minority groups in particular and for ethnic minority youth in general. In addition, popular youth culture, more generally defined, may also be vital to consider regardless of ethnicity in order for violence prevention interventions to be successful.

The term *cultural sensitivity* does not frequently appear in the youth violence prevention literature. When it is used, it is with varied emphasis and meaning. It can be challenging to account for the deep structure complexities of culture when developing youth violence-prevention programming. One may have to consider various identities and contexts with which youth live. Ethnic identity, religious beliefs, developmental age, immigration status (e.g., citizen vs. noncitizen or first generation vs. second generation), socioeconomic status, political environment, and broader social norms are all possible aspects of culture that may affect how well a youth violence-prevention program will be received. The following examples illustrate how varying levels of surface and deep structure have been applied to violence-prevention programming that, at the very least, acknowledges culture. Table 9.1 summarizes each of the studies described.

Murray, Kelder, Parcel, Frankowski, and Orpinas (1999) evaluated a randomized-controlled trial of parent education to prevent violence among middle-school students. Called "Padres Trabajando por la Paz" (PTP; translated as Parents Working for Peace), the program is an extension of the Students for Peace (SFP) project. Ninety-four parents of middle-school students that participated in SFP participated in the intervention. Bilingual newsletters that relayed role model stories were developed to increase parental monitoring among Latino parents. The role model stories were created from interviews with Latino parents and were adapted into newsletter format.

Parents were randomly assigned to either an intervention or control group. Those parents in the intervention group received four parental monitoring newsletters over a 2-week interval during the school year. Evaluation data was collected through pretest and posttest interviews conducted in either English or Spanish. In addition, children of the parents completed pretest and posttest questionnaires at school. Results from the study indicated that parents that received the newsletters reported higher levels of parental monitoring than those parents who did not receive the newsletter. Children of parents that received the newsletter also reported higher levels of parental monitoring compared with the baseline group. Children of parents that did not receive the newsletter reported lower levels of parental monitoring at follow-up.

The PTP intervention incorporated surface structure aspects of culture into the intervention through the use of language and input from the participants, but deep structure elements were not evident. The design of this study, although including a surface structure-relevant component, could not determine if the culturally sensitive aspect of the newsletter was effective or if it was just the newsletter (regardless of its surface structure relevance) and attention to parents that was effective. Although attention to parents is consistent with Latino cultural values of the importance of family, this was not an explicit purpose of this aspect of the intervention. Future research that includes a condition where parents receive a nonculturally adaptive newsletter on parental monitoring to test the culturally sensitive effects of the newsletter would help tease these issues apart. This additional condition in the design would allow researchers to determine if sending a newsletter on parental monitoring would suffice or if there is an added effect of developing the newsletter with at least surface structure cultural relevance.

Another violence-prevention program, PROJECT 2000 (Holland, 1996), focused on school failure as a major risk factor for crime, violence, and other problem behaviors among African American youth. The primary objective of the program was to provide positive adult male role models, particularly African American men, in the daily school life of African

TABLE 9.1
Culturally Sensitive Interventions With Violence Prevention Components

Citation	Purpose	Sample	Cultural sensitivity	Outcome evaluation	Intervention
Alkon et al. (2001)	Safe Start—violence prevention only for child care teacher, directors, and parents.	N = 667; 27% African American; 25% Chinese; 15% White; 10% Latino, 14% Multiethnic	Surface and deep	None	Multicultural texts, role plays, cross-cultural counseling techniques
Banks, Hogue, and Timberlake (1996)	Adolescent Alternatives and Consequences Training Program (AACT)—violence prevention only for African American adolescents; uses social skills training curriculum along with Afrocentric value content.	N = 64 (33 females, 31 males); inner-city African American youth	Surface	2-group pretest/posttest design; group 1 (received culturally sensitive curriculum); group 2 (culturally sensitive curriculum plus Afrocentric value component)	Skills training (e.g., communication); use of instructional material using African American images, themes for role playing; conflict resolution
Caldwell, Wright, et al. (in press); Caldwell, Zimmerman, and Isichei (2001)	Flint Fathers and Sons Program—community-based program; aims to strengthen father–son relationships (focus on nonresident fathers) to prevent risk; addresses prevention of multiple-risk behaviors (e.g., violence, early sexual initiation); prevention of violent behavior and substance use among fathers and sons and early sexual initiation among sons	African American urban youth (8–12 years) and their nonresident fathers	Surface and deep	Pretest/posttest design with control group	Behavioral capacity/skill building (e.g., communication skills; self-efficacy to avoid violence); discuss issues related to social networks and social support (e.g., density, emotional closeness); foster positive racial identity and cultural pride/involvement in community (e.g., learning African values through teaching of history and culture, participation in cultural events)

Gabriel et al. (1996)	School-based violence prevention only; based on resiliency theory and relationship model.	$N = 326$; 7th, 8th, and 9th graders; African American; 51% males	Surface and deep	Longitudinal posttest only design (for 3 years) with comparison group	6 components: (classroom activities; exposure education; proactive education; mentoring; peer group; personal bonding); skill building; anger management; field trips focused on exposing kids to consequences of violence; students design their v.p. program
Gary and Lopez (1996)	The Smart Life—youth violence; AOD; sexual risk; school failure prevention-fostering independent and productive lifestyles.	African American rural youth (12–18 years) male and female	Surface and deep	None	Community-based; small group; commitment to growth contract; mentoring; impulse control; ethnic identity development
Greene, Smith, and Peters (1995)	"I Have A Future" (IHAF)—reduce incidence of early pregnancy, homicide, and violence, STD, and AOD.	African American adolescents (10–17 years) inner-city public housing	Surface and deep	Baseline data collected with two follow-up assessments (only baseline data reported)	Skills development (e.g., prosocial, conflict resolution) victim awareness; community development; personal responsibility; use of African spiritual principles
Marshall (1995)	Omega Boys Club—violence prevention; focus on youth involved in gangs; create awareness of social norms that foster violence (e.g., material values more important than family; use of derogatory language).	Ethnic minority youth and adults involved in gangs (11–18 years/ 35–40 years)	Surface and deep	None	Three-tiered program of change ■ discussion of social norms that influence violence ■ address emotional and identity aspects of being tied to gangs ■ enable gang members to leave by providing necessary life skills

(continued)

Note. AOD = alcohol and substance abuse; STD = sexually transmitted disease.

TABLE 9.1
(Continued)

Citation	Purpose	Sample	Cultural sensitivity	Outcome evaluation	Intervention
Murray, Kelder, Frankowski, and Orpinas (1999)	Padres Trabajando por la Paz (Parents Work for Peace)—violence prevention that aims to increase parental monitoring; parent education	$N = 38$ Latino parents of 8th-grade students	Surface	Outcome and process evaluation design; randomized trial with control group	Bilingual newsletters incorporating role model stories to address issues related to parental monitoring
O'Donnell et al. (1999)	Reach for Health Community Youth Service Program—community-based program; focus on violence prevention; alcohol and substance abuse (AOD); and sexual risk that can lead to HIV infection, STD, and unintended pregnancy; provides opportunities for urban middle school students to participate in community service	$N = 1061$ African American (7th and 8th grade); 68 classrooms; economically disadvantaged youth	Surface and deep	Baseline and 6-month follow-up data collected; control group did not receive community service component	Health education on drug use, violence, AIDS, sexual behavior; community service in nursing homes, clinics, day care centers; extensive input from parents and students to develop program
Okwumabua et al. (1999)	Community-based program aims to prevent violence by building self-esteem and providing social skills training	$N = 122$ African American male youth (3rd–6th grade) in public schools; West Tennessee	Surface	Pretest/posttest design; nonrandomized; no control group	Skills development (e.g., decision making; conflict resolution); cultural awareness through field trips, learning African American history

Ringwalt et al. (1996)	Supporting Adolescents with Guidance and Employment (SAGE)—African Rites of Passage violence prevention program; also addresses other risk behaviors	$N = 173$ African American male youth (12–16 years)	Surface	Process and outcome pretest/ posttest design (only baseline data reported); randomized control group	Rites of Passage component included male mentoring; increasing self-concept and cultural pride; education about risky behaviors; field trips; parent/ mentor meetings; graduation ceremony; Junior Achievement, summer job opportunities
Holland (1996)	PROJECT 2000—phase program (primary and secondary school) addresses early school failure as a major risk factor for crime.	$N = 53$ African American youth (1st grade)	Surface and deep	Posttest only design with control group; data collected in two phases—primary and secondary (no report on secondary data)	Skills development (e.g., listening); use of African American mentors to tutor, accompany on field trips
Wiist, Jackson, and Jackson (1996)	Community-based, longitudinal violence prevention peer leadership program; designed to influence leadership among African American and Latino students, diffuse skills that prevent violence to peers; strengthen social support and cultural pride	$N = 60$ student peer leaders in middle school (6th grade); African American and Latino youth	Surface and deep	Longitudinal randomized with control group	Skill building (e.g., problem solving); activities to encourage academic achievement; community engagement and leadership; educational field trips and recreational activities; parent education; community advocates address what the community perceived to be underlying causes of violence in their community

American boys. PROJECT 2000 was implemented in two phases (primary-school and secondary-school phase) to prevent early school failure and the development of negative attitudes toward academic achievement among inner-city African American youth, particularly males. The primary school phase included Grades 1 through 5, and the secondary school phase included Grades 6 through 12. More than 200 African American male volunteers from a historically Black college in Washington, DC, participated in the program through the 6th grade. They provided individual academic mentoring and tutoring for youth in the program.

In fall 1988, 53 first-grade students were selected from an elementary school in Washington, DC, and entered the first phase of the program. The second phase of the program began in fall 1993. Selection criteria were provided. Seventy-five students from a comparable elementary school participated as the control group. The control group received after-school tutoring and other extracurricular activities without the mentoring component of the curriculum. Volunteers for both conditions had little to no contact with the students outside of the school setting. Evaluation data was collected only at the end of the program. Results from the first phase revealed that PROJECT 2000 students had significantly higher grade point averages and standardized test scores than did the students in the control group. No current results have been reported on the secondary-school phase, but by the end of the second year of the project, significant improvements in grades were reported.

PROJECT 2000 incorporated surface structure aspects of culture into the intervention through the use of African American, male mentors. Volunteers from an all African American, male community organization staffed and sponsored the project. Young African American inner-city boys coming from predominantly female-headed households with few adult male role models provided the rationale for using African American mentors. Deep structure is emphasized in this program because it focuses on developing assets in the community. Local investments in community programs provided more resources to youth and a sense of respect and pride in their community. Deep structure is also evident in the program's objective to address unique risk factors for violence, such as school failure and lack of male role models in this group of youth.

Notably, culturally sensitive violence prevention interventions that include community components (e.g., involvement of community, engagement in particular community activities) enhance the possibility of containing deep structure because they must attend to the unique assets, values, history, and local experiences to be appropriately linked to the community. Carefully chosen community activities combined with information on how they are linked to risk behavior (either in terms of assets or risks) can help youth understand and internalize community values and norms that affect positive behavior and healthy development. Of course, a community component does not necessarily ensure cultural sensitivity unless local relevance and norms are considered. Mark, Revilla, Tsutsumoto, and Mayeda (chap. 5, this volume) provide an illustration of how community activities can be infused into violence prevention activities in general as well as within the Asian Pacific Islander community.

A limitation of the design of the PROJECT 2000 study is that tutoring and mentoring variables can be confounded. As in the PTP intervention, the design of this study could not determine if the culturally sensitive aspect of the program (e.g., mentoring with African American males) was effective, or if it was just the tutoring that made a difference. Future research that includes an analysis of the main effects of mentoring would be informative. It is also important to understand the role these variables play in violent behavior outcomes. Future research that examines the moderating effects of mentoring and academic achievement on violence outcomes would be helpful.

Wiist, Jackson, and Jackson (1996) evaluated a community- and school-based violence-prevention program that incorporated culture in its curriculum. This peer leadership program was designed to reduce violence among African American and Latino adolescents by training middle-school peer leaders and their parents to engage in and organize violence prevention activities in their school and community. The program was based on a social network model, which focuses on engaging individuals in a group to help modify their behavior. The authors used an experimental design where three predominantly African American and Latino matched pairs of middle schools in Texas were randomly assigned to either intervention or control conditions. The intervention was a 3-year education program that drew on community-based organizations to support middle-school peer leaders and parent education. Surface structure elements of the program were evident in that staff that were bicultural and bilingual were sought out to match the cultural and socioeconomic backgrounds of the program participants.

Sixty peer leaders at each of the six middle schools were identified from among 6th-grade students by using a questionnaire. All 6th-grade students were asked to identify the students in their grade whom they looked up to, admired, and wanted to be like. The students who received the largest number of nominations were chosen as peer leaders to participate in the program. The intervention peer leaders were taught how to strengthen social support, cultural pride, develop social skills for nonviolent problem solving, encourage career expectations, community service, and academic achievement, and how to organize their violence prevention activities. The intervention incorporated surface structure aspects of culture into the intervention through the use of bicultural and bilingual staff. Deep structure elements of cultural sensitivity include the use of curriculum that was designed to instill cultural pride (e.g., use of cultural ceremonies and traditions), and the involvement of families to enhance social networks. The students participated in the program once a week during the school year and four to five times during the summer over the 3-year period.

The parents of the peer leaders were invited to participate in a parent education program composed of lectures, discussions, and social activities. The parent portion of the program was conducted biweekly in English or Spanish as requested. Curricula for the parent education drew material from Effective Black Parenting (Alvy and Marigna's study as cited in Wiist, Jackson, & Jackson, 1996), Cara Y Corazon (Barrera's study as cited in Wiist, Jackson, & Jackson, 1996), and Padres Con Poder (Padres's study as cited in Wiist, Jackson, & Jackson, 1996) to match the cultural backgrounds of the African American and Latino parents. Within the curriculum, topics included communication, managing anger, conflict resolution, media violence, disciplinary techniques, cultural ceremonies, and crisis prevention tactics.

Another deep structure element of the program involved engaging individuals from the community to provide a social network and resources to address issues of violence in the community. At least 20 community members residing within the middle-school attendance zone were also approached to become Neighborhood Violence Prevention Advocates (NVPA). The community members were approached based on nominations as natural helpers, and their duty was to organize self-help groups, neighborhood associations, and coalition building among existing violence prevention organizations. Meetings were held in English or Spanish once a month.

Because Wiist et al. (1996) provided only preliminary baseline data, program effectiveness remains to be determined. Still, the considerations of culture are clear. Program staff was matched to the cultural backgrounds of the participants, bilingual efforts were made, cultural pride was emphasized, and the curriculum included cultural ceremonies. The program applied a medley of surface and deep structure cultural elements to youth violence prevention. A well-conducted evaluation would be beneficial to help determine whether or not the efforts were effective.

Gabriel, Haskins, Hopson, and Powell (1996) described the Self Enhancement Incorporated (SEI) program, a community- and school-based violence-prevention program run by a grassroots community service organization in Portland, Oregon. The program, guided by resiliency theory and a social relations model of interaction, focused on African American students in middle school and high school. The program incorporated classroom and community activities that addressed anger management skills and helped youth develop prosocial skills and attitudes. The SEI program also included activities to promote community involvement (such as recreational activities and job placement) and enhance support systems. Surface structure was evident in various ways (e.g., use of African American mentors). Deep structure was addressed via incorporation of African American cultural structures (e.g., media) and norms that shape attitudes and behaviors about violence (Gabriel et al., 1996).

Alkon, Tschann, Ruane, Wolff, and Hittner (2001) described the consideration of multiple cultures in the development of the Safe Start Project. This project provided a violence prevention education program for child-care staff and parents. The program was developed in response to the increase in neighborhood violence and the lack of violence prevention training for child-care teachers who work in these communities. The program was guided by an ecological model of prevention that emphasized the dynamic interaction of individual and environmental characteristics in determining behavior. The evaluation project was a 3-year randomized experimental study with a cross-sectional design conducted in 15 child-care centers.

The Safe Start Project was located in the ethnically diverse San Francisco Bay Area. It provided an educational training program designed for child-care teachers and parents. Objectives of the curriculum were to develop skills in self-awareness, cultural competency and sensitivity, violence intervention for young children, and counseling on violence prevention. Child-care teachers received nine credits at their local community college to develop the necessary skills. The curriculum for the child-care teachers was also adapted for parents. The classes provided violence prevention information for parents with diverse ethnic backgrounds and encouraged them to form social networks. More specific information about the violence prevention component of the program was not provided in the study.

The Safe Start program was developed as a result of a collaboration of professionals to make the program more culturally sensitive. An interdisciplinary diverse team of professionals from early childhood education, counseling, psychology, gay and lesbian studies, and African American, Asian American, Latino, Middle Eastern, and European American cultural groups designed the Safe Start Project curricula. The team of professional consultants contributed in each respective area of expertise. Surface structure cultural elements were evident in the intervention through the use of multicultural scenarios for role playing and multicultural textbooks. Therapists also developed a curriculum on cross-cultural counseling techniques. Deep structure was also evident through the involvement of parents in developing the intervention to promote parental support and the use of rituals to celebrate goals accomplished in the program.

Within the curriculum, child-care teachers and parents were encouraged to explore their family history and cultural backgrounds to gain understanding of different cultural child-care beliefs and practices. For the parent classes, translators were available for those that spoke Chinese or Spanish and written materials are available in English, Chinese, or Spanish. Much attention was also paid to hiring culturally diverse evaluation staff. Although surface and deep structure elements were incorporated into the program, it is not clear from the description of the training whether connections between culture and risk behaviors were emphasized. Unfortunately, to date, no outcome evaluation has been reported.

Marshall (1995) described another program in San Francisco, the Omega Boys Club, that focused on promoting life skills development among youth and adults from various ethnic backgrounds who were involved in gangs or gang activity. This program placed great emphasis on the deep structure elements of their program by helping youth understand the language used in gangs that put them at risk for violent activity. This program emphasized critical analysis of negative language (for instance, derogatory language against women), and provided positive language alternatives. Another distinctive element of deep structure in this program focused on addressing attitudes related to the fear of breaking free or discontinuing membership from the gang. The program helped youth develop the social and interpersonal skills that can enable them to leave a gang. This program is distinctive because its culturally sensitive characteristics are focused on gang and street culture, and not ethnic culture in particular.

The Flint Fathers and Sons Intervention (Caldwell et al., in press; Caldwell, Zimmerman, & Isichei, 2001) was designed to prevent violence, early sexual initiation, and alcohol, tobacco, and other drug use among African American males, of ages 8 to 12, through strengthening family relationships. Major emphasis was placed on strengthening relationships between fathers and sons in the program. The program is guided by multiple theories including social cognitive theory and the theory of reasoned action and behavior, as well as multiple conceptual models, including social support and ethnic identity, that address intentions and various risk and protective factors that may affect risk behaviors. The culturally based curriculum was developed with community partners. In each session the father–son pairs select their own theme (Caldwell et al., 2001). The curriculum includes 15 sessions that engage participants on multiple levels (individual, family, and community) with activities designed to (a) educate participants about the nature of various risk behavior; (b) impart skills (e.g., communication skills) among participants in order to prevent risk and promote family relationships; (c) involve participants in activities that engage them in community and school; and (d) influence cultural pride and ethnic identity through teaching cultural values and practices.

Both surface structure and deep structure elements are incorporated into each session. Surface structure elements, for example, involve the use of African American images throughout the risk-behavior presentations. More specifically, in the session where fathers and sons learn about how violence affects them and their community, participants are exposed to various images of African Americans and popular culture. The program uses African American facilitators recruited from the community and has conducted interventions in community organizations that provide services and resources to the African American community. Deep structure elements include the use of cultural values to help participants to understand the importance of cultural pride and respect in themselves, family, and community to prevent participants from engaging in activities that might harm themselves or others. The Flint Fathers and Sons Intervention is currently being evaluated and no results are available at this time.

Other programs similar to the Fathers and Sons Program with a primary focus on African American youth also focus on Afrocentric culture as a means to enhance self-esteem, cultural pride, and identity. Supporting Adolescents with Guidance and Employment (SAGE) is a multifaceted, community-based violence-prevention program in Durham, North Carolina (Ringwalt, Graham, Pashall, Flewelling, & Browne, 1996). Comparable to Fathers and Sons, this program engages participants' fathers; however, although fathers are encouraged to participate, it is not a requirement of the program. In the cases where fathers are not available, other adult males (not necessarily related to the child) participate to engage youth in an African Rites of Passage activity. This project uses both surface structure, through the involvement of African American mentors, and deep structure by incorporating a Rites of Passage activity. Yet, the connection of the Rites of Passage activity to violence prevention and risk is not explicitly made and may be less connected to the goals of the intervention than the Fathers and Sons project. These activities linked explicitly the creation of collective responsibility to encourage community involvement in their own business and mobilize the community to invest in its local resources. These are consistent with deep structure sensitivity because they are based on Afrocentric norms and values because of their communal characteristics.

Another similar effort, the Smart Life program, also focused on multiple risk outcomes (including sexual-risk behavior, violence behavior, and drug use) and applies social learning and identity development theories (Gary & Lopez, 1996). This program emphasized the development of independent and productive lifestyles among youth in north central Florida. The Smart Life program used African and African American culture to create an awareness and connection to other oppressed people throughout the world. Use of African American mentors and Afrocentric content illustrates how surface structure is incorporated into this intervention. Although this program had a particular focus on developing positive ethnic identity, it is unclear how these elements were used to create the deeper structure content of the intervention.

Unfortunately, outcome evaluations of many of these programs are limited. Greene, Smith, and Peters (1995) included two intervention and two matched control sites in the evaluation of their I Have a Future (IHAF) project. Two other violence-prevention programs (Banks, Hogue, & Timberlake, 1996; Okwumabua, Wong, Duryea, Okwumabua, & Howell, 1999) focused on Afrocentric values, promoting cultural awareness and self-esteem. They also included evaluation components in their program design, but the cultural sensitivity and linkages to violence prevention explicitly of these interventions were only clear for surface structure. Okwumabua and colleagues (Okwumabua et al., 1999) implemented a pretest/posttest design with no control group. They found that participants' relationship with their peers in the neighborhood and their ethnic identity improved from pretest to posttest, but without a comparison group these results are limited. Banks and colleagues (1996) tested two social skills training (SST) curricula using a two-group, pretest/posttest design where one group received SST curriculum with an Afrocentric component focused on African history and value systems while the other group received the SST curriculum without the Afrocentric component. They found that at posttest youth in the SST with Afroccentric components decreased trait anger and increased self-control as compared with those in the SST alone.

O'Donnell and colleagues (1998) evaluated the Reach for Health Community Youth Service program (CYS) effect on risky sexual behavior among seventh- and eighth-grade African American and Latino students in two northeastern urban middle schools. The Reach for Health CYS program was developed as a result of a collaborative effort between the Medgar Evans College of Nursing, Brooklyn School District 13, and community service agencies in east New York City, Brooklyn. The intervention was designed to provide opportunities for urban middle-school students to participate in organized service experiences that meet community needs. Although the program's primary focus was on risky sexual behavior, the Reach for Health classroom curriculum focused on three primary health risks faced by inner-city adolescents—drug use and alcohol use, violence, and risky sexual behaviors. Only risky sexual behavior outcomes were reported in this study. The CYS program involved community service in institutions and agencies to provide students with exposure to a variety of health settings and providers.

The study sites included two large public urban middle schools serving economically disadvantaged minority youth. The researchers used a quasi-experimental design where one school served as the intervention school (35 classrooms; $n = 477$) and the other served as the control school (38 classrooms; $n = 584$). The intervention school classrooms were randomly assigned to receive either the classroom curriculum or the curriculum enhanced by participation in the CYS program. The Reach for Health curriculum was delivered to all seventh and eighth graders at the intervention school. Students at the control school received only standard New York

City health education, most of which is implemented in eighth grade, with some lessons on drugs and HIV/AIDS in seventh grade. The CYS component required students to participate in three hours of community service per week at designated sites such as nursing homes, health clinics, and child day care centers. Students were expected to share their community service experiences in debriefing sessions with their health classes.

Evaluation results indicated that Reach for Health CYS participants reported significantly less recent sexual activity and exhibited less risk (as determined by the sexual activity index) than those in the control condition who only received the classroom curriculum. From the findings, the authors suggested that the intense community service portion of the program may have been primarily responsible for the intervention effects.

It is clear that deep structure elements were evident in the development of the intervention through the use of community collaboration to ensure that the curriculum addressed individual risk factors of the population (e.g., high-risk health profile, high-risk academic profile, and limited access to resources). A high-risk health profile was based on rates of violence-related injuries, HIV or sexually transmitted disease infection, teen pregnancy, and so forth. A high-risk academic profile was based on below-grade standardized test scores, low attendance, and low high school graduation rates. Deep structure was also evident in the intervention through student involvement in community service to increase community awareness and care for others.

CONCLUSION

Although some efforts have been made to make youth violence prevention more culturally sensitive, more efforts are needed. One reason such efforts are not more ubiquitous is that they are not easily developed and implemented. In this chapter, we focused particularly on the importance of both surface structure and deep structure in program design and implementation, and provided examples of how these can be addressed in programming. Still additional issues remain.

First, how culture is defined plays a vital role in the type of intervention developed. Additionally, the assumption that culture is monolithic may not be the case. Within-cultural differences are often as complex and disparate as those across cultures. Spanish language idioms and words, for example, differ across Spanish-speaking countries so even the surface structure for some interventions may not be appropriate. Consequently, implementation of culturally sensitive curriculum may be especially difficult when within-group cultural variation is pervasive. Unfortunately, the research literature does not include evaluation of programs that address within-group variation. Most programs that have diverse samples only compare behavioral outcomes across ethnic groups broadly and traditionally defined (e.g., African American, Latino, White, Asian Pacific Islander). As other chapters in this volume have noted, there is clearly a great deal of variation within ethnic groups based on factors such as native-born versus immigrant, country of origin, socioeconomic status, and community disadvantage that can differentially impact both the learning and prevention of violence.

It may be particularly useful to identify and study different content for surface and deep structural characteristics to reflect variation within ethnic groups. This would enable us to address the similarities in the local culture that make the groups interconnected, while simultaneously considering the differences that may distinguish members within a particular group. In order to develop a culturally sensitive program that considers these within-group differences, it is vital to include members of the focus audience so they can help the researcher and/or practitioner to understand the differences and similarities and develop strategies to measure and implement different approaches.

Second, most youth violence prevention interventions occur in multicultural contexts such as schools and community youth programs, and it is difficult if not impossible to develop an intervention that focuses on a single culture. A potential solution to this concern is to develop programs that address culture in general, while simultaneously allowing participants to provide meaning relevant to their own ethnicity or culture. This type of program could incorporate multicultural perspectives and would not be linked to the specific cultural practices of any group. This is consistent with the perspective of Hudley and Taylor (chap. 10, this volume) in their description of culturally effective programming.

Third, youth violence prevention must also consider popular youth culture. It may even be the case that youth culture is more important as the referent group than the youths' ethnic culture. Furthermore, in some cases youth culture and ethnic culture combine to create a set of values and beliefs that are linked to the mixture of these cultures. Thus, not only do researchers and practitioners need to consider multiple ethnicities to make their interventions culturally sensitive, but they probably need to attend to youth culture as well. The youth culture, however, may provide a common denominator for multicultural contexts and may be the central focus for making an intervention culturally sensitive.

Fourth, interventions must consider an ecological analysis and go beyond focusing only on individual change. Culture implies ecological factors that include family, school, and community context. Thus, interventions that are truly culturally sensitive must also incorporate elements that cut across attention to and development of an individual's cultural heritage to the settings and institutions in which the adolescent lives and experiences the very triggers for insensitivity, stereotyping, and frustration.

Fifth, practitioners must develop procedures for developing culturally sensitive interventions that are pertinent to the local context and acceptable to the focus audience. Several researchers have suggested ways to develop an insider's view of the issues, concerns, norms, values, and culture of a community (Caldwell et al., 2001; Kelly, 1988; Zimmerman, 2000). The general theme of these strategies is involving people from the audience for whom an intervention is intended, providing opportunities for them to have a genuine influence on program development and evaluation, and allocating time in the community to develop trust and social capital.

Although the development of culturally sensitive interventions to prevent youth violence poses several challenges, it also has several advantages. First, the programs may be more acceptable and relevant for youth. Efforts that indicate an understanding of, and sensitivity to, their world may motivate youth to take the program seriously, pay attention to its messages, and engage in efforts to change behavior. Culturally sensitive programs also enable researchers and practitioners to develop programs that are more closely connected to the youths' experience. This tailoring of the intervention will inevitably make the program more personal and consistent with youth culture. A culturally sensitive approach also helps the program be more responsive to the unique assets of marginalized groups. This may be especially important because adolescence is marked by the marginalization of youth. Attention to culture may also help address fundamental belief systems and behavioral norms. Cultural beliefs about risk and perceptions of risk may be partially determined by cultural norms and values. Consequently, understanding culture may also help researchers identify cultural beliefs and behaviors that promote or moderate behaviors such as violence. Cultural sensitivity may also enhance the focus of program on the identification and use of a strengths-based approach to prevention. Considered in this way, culture may help youth be resilient against the risks they face for violent behaviors.

In the final analysis, culturally sensitive interventions may be the best hope for developing sustained efforts that are both locally relevant and ecologically integrated. It will take more than teaching youth skills or changing their attitudes to address the problem of youth violence in America. Even as one considers culture as an asset for addressing youth violence, one is faced with the paradox of a culture of violence in the United States. The media, news, and everyday lives are filled with images of violence. Efforts to address the epidemic of youth violence requires attention to elements in individuals that connect them to other people they may not even know. Cultural connection can be that common thread because it provides a context in which to understand alternative behaviors, cooperation, and peaceful solutions. Yet, one is also faced with the daunting task of separating the messages and norms of competing cultures. Culturally sensitive interventions that focus on positive qualities of human interactions and help draw youth into a culture of pride, caring for others, and connections to others through a history that spans any one lifetime provide hope that one can create alternatives to violent behavior and begin to address youth violence in significant and enduring ways.

REFERENCES

Alkon, A., Tschann, J. M., Ruane, S. H., Wolff, M., & Hittner, A. (2001). A violence prevention and evaluation project with ethnically diverse populations. *American Journal of Preventive Medicine, 20*(1 Suppl.), 48–55.

American Psychological Association Commission on Violence and Youth. (1993). *Violence and youth: Psychology's response.* Washington, DC: Author.

Banks, R., Hogue, A., & Timberlake, T. (1996). An Afrocentric approach to group social skills training with inner-city African American adolescents. *Journal of Negro Education, 65,* 414–423.

Bourdieu, P. (1993). *The field of cultural reproduction.* New York: Columbia University Press.

Braithwaite, R. L. (1998). *Culturally-based health promotion: Practices and systems.* Technical Report #7 (DHHS Pub. No. 98-3238). Washington, DC: U.S. Department of Health and Human Services, Substance Abuse and Mental Health Services Administration.

Caldwell, C. H., Kohn-Wood, L. P., Schmeelk-Cone, K. H., Chavous, T. M., & Zimmerman, M. A. (in press). Racial discrimination and racial identity as risk or protective factors for violent behaviors in African-American young adults. *American Journal of Community Psychology.*

Caldwell, C. H., Wright, J. C., Zimmerman, M. A., Walsemann, K. M., Williams, D., & Isichei, P. A. C. (in press). Enhancing adolescent health behaviors through strengthening non-resident father–son relationships: A model for intervention with African–American families. *Health Education Research.*

Caldwell, C. H., Zimmerman, M. A., & Isichei, P. A. C. (2001). Forging collaborative partnerships to enhance family health: An assessment of strengths and challenges in conducting community-based research. *Journal of Public Health Management and Practice, 7,* 1–9.

Corvo, K. N. (1997). Community-based youth violence prevention: A framework for planners and funders. *Youth and Society, 28,* 291–316.

Fearn, N. (2001). *Protagoras and the pigs. Is man the measure of all things? Zeno and the tortoise.* London: Atlantic Books.

Gabriel, R. M., Haskins, M., Hopson, T., & Powell, K. E. (1996). Building relationships and resilience in the prevention of youth violence. *American Journal of Preventive Medicine, 12*(5), 48–55.

Gary, F., & Lopez, L. R. (1996). The smart life. *Journal of Primary Prevention*, *17*, 175–200.

Gordon, B. (1993). African–American cultural knowledge and liberatory education: Dilemmas, problems, and potentials in a postmodern American society. *Urban Education*, *27*, 448–470.

Greene, L. W., Smith, M. S., & Peters, S. R. (1995). "I have a future" comprehensive adolescent health promotion: Cultural considerations in program implementation and design. *Journal of Health Care for the Poor and Underserved*, *6*, 267–283.

Greene, M. B. (1998). Youth violence in the city: The role of educational interventions. *Health Education and Behavior*, *25*, 175–193.

Harris, K. J., Ahluwalia, J. S., Okuyemi, K. S., Woods, M. N., Backinger, C. L., & Resnicow, K. (2001). Addressing cultural sensitivity in a smoking cessation intervention: Development of the Kick It at Swope Project. *Journal of Community Psychology*, *29*, 447–458.

Holland, S. H. (1996). PROJECT 2000: An educational mentoring and academic support model for inner-city African American boys. *Journal of Negro Education*, *65*, 315–321.

Hudley, C. (2001). *The role of culture in prevention research*. American Psychological Association (APA). Retrieved February 1, 2003, from http://www.journals.apa.org/revention/volume4/pre0040005c.html

Kelly, J. G. (1988). A guide to conducting prevention research in the community: First Steps. *Prevention in Human Services*, *6*, 1–174.

Ladson-Billings, G. (1994). *Dream keepers: Successful teaching with African-American children*. San Francisco: Jossey-Bass.

Layton, P., & Simpson, A. J. (1975). Surface and deep structure in sentence comprehension. *Journal of Verbal Learning and Verbal Behavior*, *14*, 658–664.

Liu, D. (1995). Sociocultural transfer and its effect on second language speakers' communication. *International Journal of Intercultural Relations*, *19* (Special Issue), 253–265.

Marks, B., Settles, I. H., Cooke, D. Y., Morgan, L., & Sellers, R. M. (2004). African American racial identity: A review of contemporary models and measures. In R. L. Jones (Ed.), *Black psychology* (4th ed., pp. 383–404). Hampton, VA: Cobb & Henry.

Marshall, J. E. (1995). Street soldiers: Violence prevention over the airwaves, a phenomenon. *Journal of Health Care for the Poor and Underserved*, *6*, 246–253.

Mauner, G., Tanenhaus, M. K., & Carlson, G. N. (1995). A note on parallelism effects in processing deep and surface verb-phrase anaphora. *Language and Cognitive Processes*, *10*, 1–12.

Murray, N. G., Kelder, G. S., Frankowski, P. R., & Orpinas, P. (1999). Padres Trabajando por la Paz: A randomized trial of a parent education intervention to prevent violence among middle school children. *Health Education Research Theory and Practice*, *14*, 421–426.

National Center for Injury Prevention and Control. (1993). *The prevention of youth violence: A framework for community action.* Atlanta, GA: Centers for Disease Control and Prevention.

O'Donnell, L., Stueve, A., Doval, A. S., Duran, R., Haber, D., Atnafou, R., et al. (1999). The effectiveness of the Reach for Health community youth service learning program in reducing early and unprotected sex among urban middle-school students. *American Journal of Public Health, 89,* 176–181.

Okwumabua, J. O., Wong, S. P., Duryea, E. J., Okwumabua, T. M., & Howell, S. (1999). Building self-esteem through social skills training and cultural awareness: A community-based approach for preventing violence among African–American youth. *Journal of Primary Prevention, 2,* 61–74.

Resnicow, K., Baranowski, T., Ahluwalia, J. S., & Braithwaite, R. L. (1999). Cultural sensitivity in public health: Defined and demystified. *Ethnicity and Disease, 9,* 10–21.

Resnicow, K., Soler, R., Braithwaite, R. L. Ahluwalia, J. S., & Butler, J. (2000). Cultural sensitivity in substance use prevention. *Journal of Community Psychology, 28,* 271–290.

Ringwalt, C. L., Graham, L. A., Pashall, M. J., Flewelling, R., & Browne, D. C. (1996). Supporting adolescents with guidance and employment (SAGE). *American Journal of Preventive Medicine, 12,* 31–38.

Robinson, T. R., & Howard-Hamilton, M. (1994). An Afrocentric paradigm: Foundation for a healthy self-image and healthy interpersonal relationships. *Journal of Mental Health Counseling, 16,* 327–339.

Robinson, T. R., & Ward, J. (1991). A belief in self far greater than anyone's disbelief: Cultivating resistance among African–American adolescents. *Women and Therapy, 11,* 87–103.

Sale, E. W., Sambrano, S., Springer, J. F., Turner, C., & Hermann, J. (1998). *Toward a theory of prevention: Alternative correlates to adolescent substance use.* Paper presented at the annual meeting of the American Health Association, Chicago.

Sampson, R. J., Morenoff, J. D., & Raudenbush, S. (2005). Social anatomy of racial and ethnic disparities in violence. *American Journal of Public Health, 95,* 224–232.

Simons-Morton, B. G., Donohew, L., & Crump, A. D. (1997). Health communication in the prevention of alcohol, tobacco, and drug use. *Health Education and Behavior, 24,* 544–554.

Spencer, M. B. (1990). Parental values transmission: Implications for Black child development. In J. B. Cheatham (Ed.), *Interdisciplinary perspectives on Black families* (pp. 111–131). Atlanta, GA: Transaction.

Stack, C. (1974). *All our kin: Strategies for survival in a Black community.* New York: Harper & Row.

Stevenson, H. C., Herrero-Taylor, T., Cameron, R., & Davis, Y. (2002). "Mitigating Instigation": Cultural phenomenological influences of anger and fighting among "big-boned" and "baby-faced" African–American youth. *Journal of Youth and Adolescence, 31,* 473–485.

Taylor, R. D., & Wang, M. C. (Eds.). (1997). *Social and emotional adjustment and family relations in ethnic minority families.* Mahwah, NJ: Erlbaum.

Tolan, P., & Guerra, N. G. (1994). *What works in reducing adolescent violence: An empirical review of the field.* Boulder, CO: Center for the Study and Prevention of Violence.

Ward, J. V. (1995). Cultivating a morality of care in African–American adolescents: A culture-based model of violence prevention. *Harvard Educational Review, 65,* 175–188.

Wiist, W. H., Jackson, R. H., & Jackson, K. W. (1996). Peer and community leader education to prevent youth violence. *American Journal of Preventive Medicine, 12,* 56–64.

Zimmerman, M. A. (2000). Empowerment theory: Psychological, organizational and community levels of analysis. In J. Rappaport & E. Seidman (Eds.), *Handbook of community psychology* (pp. 43–63). New York: Plenum Press.

Zimmerman, M. A., Ramirez, J., Washienko, K. M., Walter, B., & Dyer, S. (1995). Enculturation hypothesis: Exploring direct and protective effects among Native American youth. In H. I. McCubbin, E. A. Thompson, & A. I. Thompson (Eds.), *Resiliency in ethnic minority families, volume I: Native and immigrant American families* (pp. 199–220). Madison: University of Wisconsin.

Zuczkowski, A. (1994). Language and experience: Deep structures as linguistic models for listening and intervening in psychotherapy. *Gestalt Theory, 16,* 3–20.

10

WHAT IS CULTURAL COMPETENCE AND HOW CAN IT BE INCORPORATED INTO PREVENTIVE INTERVENTIONS?

CYNTHIA HUDLEY AND APRIL TAYLOR

Youth violence in America continues to be a serious social problem with particularly damaging consequences for ethnic minority youth and communities. Differential rates of violence and victimization among youth of various ethnic groups, as described in previous chapters in this volume, offer a compelling reason to consider the role that culture might play in the prevention of youth violence. We explore that relation in this chapter and describe a conceptual model for the development of culturally competent violence prevention programming. We differentiate "cultural sensitivity" as discussed by Wright and Zimmerman (chap. 9, this volume), from "cultural competence." As mentioned in chapter 9, cultural sensitivity facilitates the tailoring of programs to one or more cultural groups, recognizing the unique customs, norms, and values within a specific culture. In contrast, our model is purposefully general in nature because we recognize that many programs must simultaneously serve youth of various backgrounds. We posit a series of principles that must be considered when developing prevention programming for any group, whether it includes members of one or multiple cultures. In this fashion, cultural competence involves the recognition of one's cultural beliefs and practices, an appreciation of other cultural systems, and the skills needed to work effectively across cultures (Sue, 1998).

The chapter is organized into five broad sections. First, we review and discuss the meaning of culture and its relevance for understanding and preventing youth violence. Next, we review current theorizing about the construct of cultural competence. Using theory as our foundation, we then turn to an examination of the significance of cultural competence for a number of areas in youth violence prevention programming. Following this, we provide examples of best practices in violence prevention that address important elements of cultural competence. Finally, we provide suggestions for programming for youth violence prevention that allow for incorporation of cultural competence.

CULTURE: WHAT AND WHY

Consistent with the systems view (e.g., Kitayama, 2002) and the definition provided by Smith and Guerra (introduction, this volume), we define culture as a set of variable, loosely organized systems of meanings that shape ways of living and are learned and shared by an identifiable group of people (Betancourt & López, 1993). These systems of meanings include beliefs, values, goals, and other foundations of social exchange. They organize group members' associated psychological processes and behaviors, including social norms, communication styles, and rituals, to adapt successfully within a particular ecocultural niche. An ecocultural niche represents the cultural and ecological contexts in which individuals live out their daily lives. This view of culture is particularly valuable for examining the relation between culture and youth violence prevention because it links culture in meaningful ways to cognitive and behavioral development and change.

Why, one might ask, should culture so defined have an influence on violence prevention programming? There is compelling evidence that theory and practice developed in one cultural context may not apply successfully in another context. These findings are not surprising once we understand culture as the system that organizes adaptation to a unique environment. For example, a substantial body of literature in human development has described how models of successful parenting behaviors originally developed in White middle-class cultural contexts may not adequately capture and define successful parenting in other ecocultural contexts (Baldwin, Baldwin, & Cole, 1990; Lamborn, Dornbusch, & Steinberg, 1996). Similarly, education research consistently finds that practices developed for one group are not equally successful with all groups in a diverse society, often resulting in a significant, culturally defined "achievement gap" (Garcia, 1993; McAllister & Irvine, 2000). Finally, research in the efficacy of mental health treatment practices has shown that a cultural match between client and service provider improves client participation and persistence (Sue, 1998).

In a similar vein, it therefore seems reasonable that models and methods for youth violence prevention will have a far greater chance for success if they are framed and presented in ways that are appropriate to participants' cultural systems (Roosa, Dumka, Gonzales, & Knight, 2002). Efforts to address the participants' ecocultural niche should increase the attractiveness and motivational impetus of prevention programs. The true measure of prevention programming is a capacity to bring about real change in particular communities. Youth and communities must actually believe that intervention programming will lead to lessened violence in their community if programs are to be successful and sustainable (Roosa et al., 2002).

Furthermore, cultures provide systems of meaning, thinking, and behaving that may successfully buffer youth in the face of multiple-risk factors for violence and victimization. For example, as French, Kim, and Pillado (chap. 2, this volume) point out, a positive ethnic identity can be a protective factor for aggression risk. Indeed, for some ethnic minority youth in the United States, this positive identity may counteract violent and racist messages that are so prevalent in the mainstream media (Hill, Soriano, Chen, & LaFramboise, 1994). Violence prevention efforts may be stronger if they build on participants' cultural strengths and may be hampered if they discount or marginalize these strengths.

Any analysis of culture and violence prevention must begin with the central role of violence in American culture and mythology. There are those who suggest that violence is integral to American history, thought, and behavior (e.g., Friedman, 1993; Malcolm X, 1965). The evidence for such a conclusion is compelling. Until recently, U.S. history represented violence against indigenous and enslaved populations as a pragmatic necessity and a moral right (Fegin, 1986; Friedberg, 2000). Popular culture often glorifies violence, and U.S. society rewards these violent images handsomely. At the same time, violent crime is substantially more pervasive in urban areas in the United States than in the major population centers of any other country in the industrialized world (McCord, 1997). Social critics, although swift to decry the role of the media in fostering a cultural belief that violence is normative, seem to have little to offer other than violent solutions (e.g., a return to corporal punishment, the death penalty for youth). Furthermore, the U.S. justice system uses institutional violence, such as confinement in adult institutions, most harshly against ethnic minority boys (Pope, Lovell, & Hsia, 2002).

It is against this backdrop that we examine the construct of cultural competence and its role in the development, implementation, and sustainability of effective programming to prevent violence by and against ethnic minority youth. These youth represent the fastest growing segment of the population (U.S. Census Bureau, 2002). Given the disproportionately high toll exacted by youth violence in ethnic minority schools and communities, these youth are also particularly likely to participate in some form of violence prevention programming before age 18. A consideration of the role of culture should be particularly useful for designing high-quality, effective preventive interventions that can be embraced and sustained by youth and their families and communities.

MODELS OF CULTURAL COMPETENCE

The construct of cultural competence has become an integral part of training and service delivery in a variety of helping professions, including health and human services, mental health, and education.

Health and Human Services

Within the past decade, the health services and mental health domains have generated a substantial literature around the construct of cultural competence (e.g., Pope-Davis & Coleman, 1997). Across these helping professions, practitioners view cultural competence as a necessary component for treating clients from diverse ethnic backgrounds. The prevalent theories of cultural competence include several themes. Self-understanding, viewed as the basis for cultural competence, provides an awareness of one's culturally grounded assumptions and expectations about human behavior (Sue, Arredondo, & McDavis, 1992). Beyond that, the culturally competent practitioner also recognizes and appreciates the worldview of other cultural groups and displays skills appropriate to work effectively across cultures (Sue, 1998).

The focus is on the competence of the professional practitioner to effectively serve an increasingly diverse client population. Cultural competence is attained through a therapist's developmental progression from unconscious incompetence to unconscious competence (Purnell, 2002). Recent reviews of the cultural competence literature have acknowledged the absence of the client's perspective (Pope-Davis, Liu, Toporek, & Brittan-Powell, 2001; Sodowsky, Taffe, Gutkin, & Wise, 1994). Nonetheless, this work has retained an emphasis on the practitioner's competence.

Cultural Competence and Education Research

Education research and practice have generated a rich and long-standing body of knowledge focused specifically on issues of culture (e.g., research in multicultural education). The education literature has introduced a variety of terms (*culturally appropriate, culturally congruent, culturally compatible, culturally responsive, culturally relevant*) to define particular models of cultural competence. Similar to other helping professions, all of these models posit self-knowledge, affirming attitudes toward the worldviews of other cultural groups, and the skills to successfully educate children from diverse backgrounds as foundational elements for culturally competent teachers (e.g., McAllister & Irvine, 2000).

This literature moves beyond a focus on the teacher, however, to incorporate specific instructional practices and desired student outcomes as equally necessary elements of cultural competence (Villegas & Lucas, 2002). Culturally relevant pedagogy makes up instructional practices that are responsive to and grounded in students' cultural patterns of learning and knowing and thus maximize academic learning for all students (Ladson-Billings, 1995). Cultural competence as defined from this perspective presumes that students are able to maintain the cultural knowledge and identity necessary to successfully navigate their ecocultural niche while succeeding academically (Ladson-Billings, 1994). Students' cultural competence, in turn, prepares them to become critical advocates for social justice by making visible the bias inherent in using a single cultural lens to understand a multicultural society such as that in the United States. (Villegas & Lucas, 2002).

CULTURAL COMPETENCE AND VIOLENCE PREVENTION

The comprehensive model of cultural competence represented in the multicultural education literature can serve a useful guide for the design of effective preventive interventions. Drawing on the literatures reviewed, our model of cultural competence for violence prevention programming comprises three elements (see Exhibit 10.1). Cultural competence refers to

1. The requisite self-knowledge, attitudes, and skills that allow youth-serving professionals to be effective with diverse populations of students. This usage is similar to the existing definition in the mental health field. We use the term *culturally effective* to refer to this specific subdomain of cultural competence.
2. Intervention methods and programming that are responsive to and respectful of youths' cultures and communities. Curricula present strategies for violence prevention (conflict resolution, peer mediation, mentoring, social and social–cognitive skill development) in ways that support participants' and families' cultural values and practices. Methods for assessment and

evaluation are similarly cognizant of the dynamics of participants' ecocultural niche. We use the term *culturally responsive*
to refer to this specific subdomain of cultural competence.
3. Participants' ability to successfully navigate their ecocultural
   niche. This includes cultural knowledge and cultural pride, a
   positive sense of self, bicultural competence, and the critical
   awareness to challenge inequality, hatred, and violence of all
   kinds. We use the term *culturally engaged* to refer to this specific
   subdomain of cultural competence.

There are a number of reasons why cultural competence as we define
it might be a particularly important element in youth violence prevention
programming. First and foremost, residents of communities that must contend with high rates of violent crime quite often are members of marginalized
ethnic groups (Bureau of Justice Statistics, 2003). Furthermore, ethnic minority communities, although still typically rigidly segregated by class, are
increasingly ethnically diverse (U.S. Census Bureau, 2001). Increased ethnic
diversity means that members of these communities regularly interact across
racial and ethnic lines in their daily lives. Therefore, cultural competence,
specifically cultural effectiveness and cultural engagement, are valuable competencies for all members (e.g., business owners, service providers, residents,
etc.) of those communities where rates of violence and victimization, as
well as social injustice, are the greatest.

In addition, schools and other agencies in communities with high rates
of violence and victimization usually provide some kind of programming to
address youth violence. As stated at the outset of this chapter, ethnic
minority youth tend to be overrepresented in the population of youth
participants in violence prevention programming, given the ethnic representation typically present in more economically disadvantaged communities.
We believe it only sensible, therefore, that programs should be responsive to
the unique cultural needs of children, their families, and their communities.

EXHIBIT 10.1
Cultural Competence Model

Tripartite Model of Cultural Competence for Violence Prevention Programming
- Culturally effective: Service providers' self-knowledge, attitudes, and skills equip
  them to function successfully.
- Culturally responsive: Curriculum materials and methods reflect participants' cultural
  strengths and support bicultural success.
- Culturally engaged: Participants successfully navigate their ecocultural niche. This
  includes cultural knowledge and cultural pride, a positive sense of self, bicultural
  competence, and the critical awareness to challenge inequality, hatred, and violence
  of all kinds.

Violence prevention programming at its best will be capable of promoting positive behaviors and skills appropriate for participants' specific ecocultural niche and will be delivered by those with a deep understanding and appreciation of that niche.

Our conclusions are grounded in the emergent thinking on positive psychology (Seligman & Csikszentmihalyi, 2000). For children, families, and communities to truly thrive, programs must concentrate explicitly on building positive skills and characteristics in addition to forestalling negative behaviors. In fact, we would add the development of cultural competence to previously identified competencies necessary for positive youth development in general (Catalano, Berglund, Ryan, Lonczak, & Hawkins, 2002). In the increasingly multicultural U.S. society, culturally competent violence prevention programming can facilitate interpersonal connections across cultural divides, increasing the potential for prosocial interaction while reducing the possibility of violent conflict.

Culturally Effective Service Providers

As previously defined, the culturally effective program leader is one with a particular constellation of knowledge, attitudes, and skills. Self-knowledge, the first component of cultural effectiveness, includes both an awareness of one's cultural worldview and the understanding that worldview is the product of previous life history and experience. Any one worldview is not universally shared; rather there are multiple worldviews mediated by a range of factors including social class, ethnicity, language, gender, and power relations. It is important to remember that ethnic match per se is not definitive of matching worldviews between participant and client.

Worldview may be particularly powerful in shaping one's judgments about and reactions to youth violence. Thus, cultural effectiveness is virtually unattainable for those who work in youth violence prevention in the absence of self-knowledge. Self-knowledge is a precursor to understanding how participants' cultural systems organize behavior, as it makes visible the distorting power of one's worldview. Evidence from counselor training research supports the link between self-knowledge and efficacy; awareness of one's cultural and personal biases has shown a positive relationship with multicultural counseling competence (Pope-Davis & Ottavi, 1994).

The attitude reflective of cultural effectiveness is one of affirmation. The culturally effective program provider sees the culture of each participant as a valid representation of ways of living, thinking, talking, and so on, that allows participants to respond to the particular demands of their dynamic ecocultural niches. The culture of the dominant group (i.e., middle-class Whites) is understood to enjoy high status because of institutionalized power inequality rather than an inherent superiority. Culturally effective providers realize that participants will need to become bicultural or multicultural to function successfully in the existing social hierarchy, a point to which we will return. However, providers recognize that participants benefit by maintaining their own culture; therefore providers see change as additive and transformative rather than the replacement of an inferior culture. Such an affirming attitude is particularly relevant in violence prevention work, as it protects both providers and participants from the toxic effects of stereotypes about particular groups of minority youth and violence.

Culturally effective skills may be specific to particular groups or more general competence in working in multicultural settings. Skills specific to a particular group are the product of explicit knowledge of that group, including the economic, social, and political pressures present in the group's unique ecocultural niche. Effective leaders understand and use culturally based interventions. They are able to translate general interventions into strategies that are appropriate for a given cultural group. Turning to general skills, effective group management in multicultural settings is critical. Culturally effective leaders are able to involve all participants in a manner that is comfortable. Participants will vary in their level of comfort with a variety of group processes (e.g., speaking in front of a group, interacting across gender boundaries, working independently). Leaders must know how to manage these varied needs, some of which will be culturally grounded, and create a constructive learning community.

In multiethnic communities, the potential for intergroup conflict in the context of violence prevention activities is a reality that must be managed sensitively. Leaders must create a safe environment for sharing and working together. Some argue that empathy in group leaders is a critical factor in creating safe spaces (Vacarr, 2001). Empathy, or the ability to understand another's feelings, is a particular blend of attitude and skill that may be central to a safe environment. However achieved, leaders must be facilitators of effective communication and interaction across cultural divides.

Culturally effective leaders are also committed to a safe and just future for all children and thus often function as advocates for participants and their communities. For example, many youth living in inner-city communities are exposed to multiple environmental risk factors (Osofsky, 1997). Youth violence is one possible consequence of these risk factors (such as early and constant exposure to violence). Culturally effective leaders understand how structural stressors present in the ecocultural niche increase vulnerability to violence, and they work to minimize or eliminate the effects of those stressors. Overall, leaders serve as coaches, models, and advocates for participants as leaders and participants together develop continuously and authentically toward cultural competence.

Culturally Responsive Materials and Methods

Culturally competent violence prevention programming should be designed to empower children within their unique cultural contexts. To illustrate this point, we consider a single possible component of violence prevention programming. Children who display problem behaviors in school may be rejected by their peers and therefore lack opportunities to build social skills. One appropriate part of a preventive intervention might therefore include social skills development. Culturally responsive social skills materials would honor the unique definition of socially skilled behavior that exists in the child's home culture, rather than imposing a universal (and most likely Eurocentric) standard of social skills. Cultures differ, for example, in their preferences for shaking hands, embracing, and defining appropriate physical proximity across gender and age divides. Social skills training should allow all children to develop skills appropriate for their culture.

Perhaps most important, in social skills training for violence prevention or any other component of a curriculum, students should have experiences that develop critical thinking and analysis skills. Critical analysis skills will help students identify the bias inherent in culturally defined worldviews in a manner similar to the awareness that is necessary for a culturally effective leader. Returning to our social skills example, students should learn to ask effective questions and pursue their analyses relative to differences and similarities in cultural rules for behavior. These activities teach students to understand and honor the basic humanity in everyone and reject interpersonal conflict based on behavioral preferences. A White man from the U.S. South, for example, might react aggressively to an overture toward physical contact from a man from a Mediterranean country. In many countries, an embrace is a typical greeting among men; this behavior is reserved for women in many regional cultures in the United States. Thus, culturally competent programming will include a mix of culture-specific and more general materials, methods, and experiences (Hudley, 2001).

More generally, culturally responsive methods and materials support students' development in a manner consistent with our discussion of culturally effective leaders. Recall that minority students must function successfully in their ecocultural niche as well as becoming skilled at navigating the dominant culture. Thus, violence prevention programs should help students identify those multiple and often competing demands present in their various ecocultural contexts. Culturally responsive violence prevention programming should make visible the existence of multiple cultural realms, the nature of the situation-specific demands that each context will exert, and the institutional bias that follows from the reality of cultural hegemony. We find proactive socialization to be an effective construct to capture this important quality in culturally responsive violence prevention programming. Proactive socialization is a deliberate effort to strengthen youth's cultural identification while developing personal skills and competence necessary for success in the mainstream culture (Hill et al., 1994; Spencer, 1984). The overarching goal of proactive socialization is to buffer youth against the powerful competing socialization messages toward violence present in the media, extant cultural stereotypes, and violent peer groups.

Previous research has demonstrated that an identity built on the strengths of the cultural group can moderate the display of youth violence (Hill et al., 1994). Specific methods for culturally responsive violence prevention programming might include inviting motivational speakers from various backgrounds drawn from the local community, conducting a cultural history of the local neighborhoods, engaging in political organizing to address issues of crime and victimization, conducting community service projects (clean-up, beautification) to enhance the local community, or cross-age mentoring in which youth are mentored by trained, caring members of the community and in turn mentor peers and younger students. In the process, youth develop leadership and organizational skills as well as a strong cultural identity; these are all important tools that will support their success in the mainstream culture, an important point to which we will return.

Methods for assessment and evaluation of violence prevention should be similarly cognizant of the dynamics of participants' ecocultural niche. When assessing ethnic minority youth, not all measures are appropriate. Assessment tools should be developed and validated with samples that are sufficiently diverse to ensure cultural appropriateness and measurement equivalence. Improper measures carry the risks of inaccurate matches between need and services, meaning that students may be improperly placed in services or may not receive needed services (Hudley et al., 2001). Improper placements can contribute to the labeling of entire social groups (e.g., "violent" African American teens; Pumariega, 2001). Furthermore, individual ethnic minority youth may develop negative self concepts if they identify with racist stereotypes of their own groups (Fisher et al., 2002). Conversely, the lack of needed services may lead to a host of maladaptive developmental outcomes (peer rejection, delinquency, mental disorder, etc.) that are documented consequences of childhood aggression and youth violence (Coie & Dodge, 1998).

CULTURALLY ENGAGED YOUTH

Cultural engagement is arguably the most important element in our model. Certainly, this component of cultural competence is difficult if not impossible to achieve in the absence of the other two components. Culturally effective leaders and culturally responsive programs provide the appropriate context. Although these elements are necessary, they are not sufficient. Our model makes clear that culturally competent youth violence prevention must attend specifically to youth outcomes. Recent research demonstrates that multiple stakeholders, including youth, place the development of positive competencies among the highest priorities of violence prevention programming (Lutenbacher, Cooper, & Faccia, 2002). We believe cultural engagement is an important competence that can militate against the development of youth violence (Grant & Haynes, 1995).

Culturally competent violence prevention programming will support participants' capacity to successfully navigate their ecocultural niches. As described earlier, urban neighborhoods, in particular, are home to residents of various ethnic groups, many if not all of whom experience systemic oppression from the institutions of the dominant culture (e.g., justice system, educational system, mental health system). Interactions across cultural divides can be a potent source of interpersonal aggression and violence in any community (Grant & Haynes, 1995). Thus, it follows that cultural engagement as defined by our model is a particularly valuable competence in an urban ecocultural niche as a positive force to counteract violence.

Recall that we define cultural engagement as cultural knowledge and pride, a positive identity, bicultural competence, as well as the skills to challenge inequality, hatred, and violence of all kinds. Cultural engagement is conceptually linked to ethnic identity, as the constructs of cultural knowledge and pride are components of many empirically validated models of ethnic identity (Phinney, 1990). Thus, culturally engaged participants will be grounded in a positive ethnic identity. By ethnic identity, we mean one's extent of identification with a distinguishable cultural and social group. Individuals with a strong ethnic identity have developed a knowledge of their cultural values (a process of exploration) and integrated a positive attitude toward the sociocultural group into their personal identities (arriving at commitment; French, Kim, & Pillado, chap. 2, this volume; Phinney, 1999). These elements of a positive ethnic identity map on to cultural knowledge and cultural pride, key elements of cultural engagement.

Knowledge of cultural values can be an important protective factor for youth violence. As highlighted in several of the chapters in this volume, interdependence, communalism, and spirituality are all salient values of the traditional cultures of many ethnic minorities in the United States that are explicitly in conflict with violence. Commitment to and pride in these traditional values can also protect against the debilitating effects of racism and stereotypes, known risk factors for the development of antisocial behavior (Utsey, Chae, Brown, & Kelly, 2000). Furthermore, cultural knowledge and pride have been investigated in the context of research on ethnic identity; these components of cultural engagement demonstrate a negative relationship with aggressive beliefs and behavior (McMahon & Watts, 2002).

From this base of an affirming ethnic identity, youth are better prepared to develop bicultural competence. Bicultural competence encompasses skills that allow participants to successfully access the mainstream opportunity structure without feeling they are compromising their identity or "selling out." LaFromboise, Coleman, and Gerton (1993) referred to this capacity to attain success in a dominant culture while maintaining a positive identity and connection within another culture as the "alternation model" of bicultural functioning. This kind of bicultural competence has shown a positive relationship with cognitive functioning, mental health, and self-esteem, all characteristics that militate against the display of violent, antisocial behavior (LaFromboise, Coleman, & Gerton, 1993). Boutakidis, Guerra, and Soriano (chap. 3, this volume) additionally highlight the importance of bicultural competence and its relation to adjustment and violence prevention.

A belief in the possibility of success in the mainstream culture can protect against the hopelessness that leads to antisocial behavior, affiliation with violent peer groups, and the violence that accompanies the illegal underground economy (Bolland, 2003). Our definition of cultural competence also incorporates a critical understanding of the role of culture in shaping one's beliefs, values, and behavior. Such understanding should lead participants to value cultural diversity, promote social interaction across cultural lines, and challenge acts of hatred and violence. The integration of efforts of this sort in mainstream White culture should also be important in the prevention of anti-ethnic violence committed by Whites that emerges from perceived lack of conventional opportunities, similar to what has been described by Parker and Tuthill (chap. 8, this volume).

Elements of cultural engagement are subject to developmental processes (e.g., identity development); thus the construct will take on age appropriate forms. We would expect cultural knowledge, attitudes, and bicultural competence to evolve as normative development progresses. For example, in childhood, participants may be developing an awareness of their ethnic and cultural heritage, as well as distinguishing their cultural heritage from those of other groups. Cultural engagement at this age will take the form of increasing cultural knowledge and positive attitudes toward participants' heritage as well as the heritage of groups other than their own. This form of cultural engagement should be effective in allaying or forestalling the development of negative attitudes toward other groups and developing participants' critical reasoning concerning fairness and social justice.

By early adolescence, children of color in particular have typically formed a stable ethnic identity (Phinney, 1999) and have an awareness of the broader society's attitudes toward their particular sociocultural group. They will also be ready to build on a foundation of cultural knowledge and critical-thinking skills. Cultural engagement for this age group should take the form of involvement in cooperative activities including community improvement projects, peer mediation, and volunteer opportunities to support justice and equality and reduce aggression among peers. As youth move through adolescence, cultural engagement should also include bicultural competence, a developmental process that will occur throughout adolescence and beyond. Youth at this stage and beyond should increasingly master the capacity to function successfully in the milieu of the dominant cultural group and overcome traditional risk factors for violence, such as poverty, unemployment, and lack of education. At the same time, youth should remain grounded in their home culture and thus buffered by a strong sense of positive identity. Building on experiences gained in school and community projects, cultural engagement will take the form of a progressively greater commitment to combat injustice, violence, and hatred of all kinds.

CULTURAL COMPETENCE IN PRACTICE

Up to this point, we have attempted to lay out a rationale for support of a three-component model of culturally competent youth violence prevention programming. This is a prescriptive model that represents the ideal for violence prevention rather than a description of the current state of practice. There is no dispute about the need for culturally competent prevention methods (National Center for Cultural Competence, 2002; Thornton, Craft, Dalberg, Lynch, & Baer, 2002). In reviewing available programs and strategies, we were not surprised to find that the multiple elements of this comprehensive model are not fully represented in any one violence prevention program strategy.

Although no single program has addressed all of these elements, several programs have addressed some of them. We now turn to a brief review of some of these promising elements. Clearly, a comprehensive review of prevention programming is beyond the scope of this chapter (see Coie & Dodge, 1998, for a review); this section briefly describes an array of examples that represent community-based and school-based programs as well as those grounded in a mental health tradition. We follow this with suggested guidelines for comprehensive, culturally competent youth violence prevention programming.

The BrainPower Program

The preventive intervention BrainPower Program, designed by the first author, began with a rigorously controlled experimental assessment of the theoretical linkages between social perceptions and aggressive behavior on which the curriculum is founded (Hudley & Graham, 1993). The initial study sample was restricted to African American elementary school-aged boys of low socioeconomic status (see also Smith & Hasbrouck, chap. 7, this volume). In subsequent research, the population of interest was expanded to also include low-income Latino boys (Hudley et al., 1998; Hudley & Friday, 1996). From its inception, the BrainPower curriculum materials were developed to be culturally responsive for a multicultural participant group. For example, open-ended stories are the vehicles through which participants discuss their experiences with peer aggression. A story about two friends meeting allows students to define the most likely meeting place within their ecocultural context (e.g., the park, the mall, the schoolyard). From there, the discussion centers on the specific issues, skills, and behaviors relevant to that group's niche.

The curriculum trains participants to social cues more effectively when they are interacting with peers. One of students' favorite activities involves observing their own social contexts (we refer to it as becoming an "intention detective") and reporting back the kinds of reactions that are typical of the people with whom they interact. Students learn simultaneously that not all people interact in the same way, there are many "good" ways to interact with others, and disadvantaging groups because of superficial styles of interaction is a bad idea that inhibits social cooperation. The benefits of this culturally responsive activity extend to age-appropriate cultural engagement in the form of critical thinking. Effects on behavior have been less apparent, although trends have been found that favor the intervention group. Additional modifications to expand this program beyond attribution retraining are currently underway.

The Quantum Opportunities Program

This community-based Quantum Opportunities Program addresses youth violence prevention by developing students' academic success as a vehicle to secure access to the mainstream opportunity structure (Lattimore, 1998). The goal of the program is to ensure that students graduate from high school and attend college with the requisite social and academic skills to thrive in a potentially difficult environment. The program provides academic assistance and basic skill instruction as well as cultural enrichment, personal development, and community service opportunities.

The Quantum Opportunities Program is focused on the development of cultural engagement. Students participate in cultural enrichment opportunities that allow them to explore their cultural and community histories; they also explore the cultural contributions and milieu of mainstream Euro-Americans. In addition, participants are exposed to role models of both genders from a variety of ethnic backgrounds. These opportunities directly facilitate the development of bicultural competence and the capacity to alternate appropriately between distinct cultural contexts. Students in the program also become culturally engaged through participation in community service projects including tutoring and counseling younger students. However, although initial evaluations of this program suggested positive effects on school-related factors and behavior, subsequent evaluations were less encouraging (for additional information about this program and related evaluations, see Smith & Hasbrouck, chap. 7, this volume).

Multisystemic Therapy

Multisystemic therapy (MST) is a general treatment strategy that assists parents in improving their youth's behavior problems and poor school performance (Henggeler, 1998; Henggeler, Cunningham, Pickrel, Schoenwald, & Brondino, 1996). MST's strengths have been in training culturally effective service providers to use culturally responsive treatment methods. MST typically comprises 50 hours of face-to-face therapist–family contact provided in the home, school, or a community location by counselors who are available 24 hours a day, 7 days a week over a period of 4 months (see also Smith & Hasbrouck, chap. 7, this volume).

During that time, the service provider's primary role is to identify barriers to effective parenting and build support networks for parents. Parent participants are full collaborators in developing treatment goals and plans. Together, parent and therapist focus on family strengths and consider how problems can be understood in light of participants' social–ecological context. This parent empowerment strategy affirms the cultural strengths of the participant and decreases the likelihood that treatment goals will be dictated by the worldview of the dominant culture. Proactively constructing informal support networks with extended family and community members also capitalizes on participants' cultural strengths.

Families and Schools Together

Similar to multisystemic therapy, Families and Schools Together (FAST) is a community intervention strategy that incorporates the vast array of relationships and settings affected by the youths' antisocial behavior (McDonald & Howard, 1998; McDonald & Sayger, 1998). FAST builds, sustains, and enhances relationships between youth and their families, peers, teachers, school staff, and other members of the community. FAST brings a group of families from the same community together for social activities and 2 years of monthly school–community meetings.

FAST highlights culturally effective leadership and culturally responsive methods. The program hires former program participants from the local community to serve as team leaders for each new cycle of the program in that community. Parent participants are considered the primary resource and prevention agent for their children, which naturally provides culturally responsive treatment. The social activities facilitate the development of support networks within the community that are developed and extended in monthly community–school meetings. FAST employs culturally responsive methods not only in its program design but in participant recruitment and retention. FAST team leaders meet program candidates in their homes at nontraditional hours including evenings and weekends and respectfully provide transportation, childcare, and meals to candidates. These strategies address barriers that might otherwise preclude program participation for stressed and low-income families.

CONSTRUCTING CULTURALLY COMPETENT PROGRAMS

Although elements of our model of culturally competent violence prevention programming are present in a number of programs, no single intervention that we identified has actively addressed all three components. However, the programs we have described are all consistent with the model and could easily be augmented to embody all of the components in actual practice. This seems a plausible supposition, given the substantial interrelatedness of the three components. For example, culturally effective leaders, as we have defined them, will actively work to develop bicultural competence in participants, an important element of cultural engagement. Such leaders will also either select or adapt program materials to make them culturally responsive. Similarly, culturally responsive materials will likely include the development of cultural effectiveness as a part of the normal training for program providers. As well, these materials will, by definition, provide activities designed to develop cultural engagement in participants. Culturally engaged participants, in turn, will be critical consumers of programs and services, making culturally effective leaders and culturally responsive materials a necessity to engage the sustained attention of this audience. In sum, programs that have already begun to incorporate an awareness and sensitivity to issues of culture are well on their way to becoming culturally competent preventive interventions.

Guidelines for Culturally Competent
Violence-Prevention Programming

Our discussion of cultural competence has obvious implications for program development. We have distilled the following general principles as a guide to the development of culturally competent violence prevention programming.

Develop Positive Competences in Youth

In line with the current interest in positive youth development, we agree that the distance between the absence of aggression or violence and the presence of competence to fully meet life's demands can be great indeed (Catalano et al., 2002). Violence prevention that promotes cultural engagement, a necessary competence in today's world, represents the best path to the reduction of antisocial behavior. Curricula, methods, and activities used in violence prevention should provide participants skills to thrive academically, culturally, and personally. Therefore, programming should be culturally informed and developmentally appropriate. As discussed previously, programs for primary grade students might emphasize the development of awareness of cultural and social knowledge, and programs for adolescents might focus specifically on cultural identity and pride. The sense of mastery that grows from competent functioning is a shield against hopelessness, which is an incubator of violence.

Prevention Efforts Should Embrace Multiple Settings

Positive functioning in the face of adversity requires that new skills are practiced and reinforced in multiple contexts. Risk factors for antisocial behavior emerge from multiple contexts beyond the individual (Catalano et al., 2002). Furthermore, youth who feel that they are valued by and connected to positive cultural and social groups such as family, church, and school are far less likely to engage in violent behavior (Hill et al., 1994). For all of these reasons, the strongest preventive intervention programs will be those that comprehensively engage the individual, family, school, peer group, and the broader community.

We acknowledge (from hard experience) the challenges inherent in engaging multiple stakeholders. Yet we remain firmly committed to broad-based program intervention. The key to comprehensive, sustainable intervention is respectful collaboration among stakeholders as equals from the start of program planning. Collaboration, early and often, to construct shared understandings and goals, is the path to successful comprehensive intervention that becomes an integral part of the community with effects that are felt over sustained periods of time.

Training for Program Providers Is Critical for Success

Finally, the success of any prevention program is highly dependant on the skills of program providers (Gottfredson & Gottfredson, 2002). This point is even more critical for the success of culturally competent violence prevention programming. Culturally effective program leaders, in particular, will be those who have been adequately trained not only in the specific program content but also in group process and cultural awareness. We deliberately are not arguing for an absolute match between the ethnicity of the leader and participants. That may not be possible, given the culturally diverse nature of most urban neighborhoods. Rather, we argue that all leaders, regardless of ethnicity, need appropriate training to develop the requisite self-knowledge, attitudes, and skills to function effectively within and across boundaries of race, ethnicity, language, class, and gender.

CONCLUSION

In closing, we would like to make explicit one final, important caveat concerning our model. Cultural competence is a developmental process that needs to be periodically revisited. Culture is a complex, evolving, living system that cannot be reified in a curriculum or training manual. Thus, those who work in youth violence prevention must engage in ongoing processes of program and self-evaluation to ensure the relevance of a particular program to the culture or cultures it is intended to serve.

REFERENCES

Baldwin, A., Baldwin, C., & Cole, R. (1990). Stress-resistant families and stress-resistant children. In J. Rolf (Ed.), *Risk and protective factors in the development of psychopathology* (pp. 257–280). New York: Cambridge University Press.

Betancourt, H., & López, S. R. (1993). The study of culture, ethnicity, and race in American psychology. *American Psychologist, 48*, 629–637.

Bolland, J. (2003). Hopelessness and risk behavior among adolescents living in high-poverty inner-city neighborhoods. *Journal of Adolescence, 26*, 145–158.

Bureau of Justice Statistics. (2003). *Violent crime victim characteristics.* Retrieved February 4, 2003, from http://www.ojp.usdoj.gov/bjs/cvict_v.html

Catalano, R., Berglund, M., Ryan, J., Lonczak, H., & Hawkins, J. (2002, June 24). Positive youth development in the United States: Research findings on evaluations of positive youth development programs. *Prevention and Treatment, 5*, Article 0015a. Retrieved January 30, 2003, from http://journals.apa.org/prevention/volume5/pre0050015a.html

Coie, J., & Dodge, K. (1998). Aggression and antisocial behavior. In W. Damon (Series Ed.) & N. Eisenberg (Vol. Ed.), *Handbook of child psychology: Vol. 3. Social, emotional, and personality development* (5th ed., pp. 779–862). New York: Wiley.

Fegin, J. (1986). Slavery unwilling to die: The background of Black oppression in the 1980s. *Journal of Black Studies, 17,* 173–200.

Fisher, C., Hoagwood, K., Boyce, C., Duster, T., Frank, D., Grisso, T., et al. (2002). Research ethics for mental health science involving ethnic minority children and youths. *American Psychologist, 57,* 1024–1040.

Friedberg, L. (2000). Dare to compare: Americanizing the Holocaust. *American Indian Quarterly, 24,* 353–380.

Friedman, L. (1993). *Crime and punishment in American history.* New York: Basic.

Garcia, E. (1993). Language, culture, and education. *Review of Research in Education, 19,* 51–98.

Gottfredson, D. C., & Gottfredson, G. (2002). Quality of school-based prevention programs. *Journal of Research in Crime and Delinquency, 39,* 3–35.

Grant, D., & Haynes, D. (1995). A developmental framework for cultural competence training for children. *Social Work in Education, 17,* 171–182.

Henggeler, S. (1998). Multisystemic therapy. In D. Elliot (Ed.), *Blueprints for violence prevention: Multisystemic therapy.* Denver, CO: C&M Press.

Henggeler, S., Cunningham, P., Pickrel, S., Schoenwald, S., & Brondino, M. (1996). Multisystemic therapy: An effective violence prevention approach for serious juvenile offenders. *Journal of Adolescence, 19,* 47–61.

Hill, H., Soriano, F., Chen, S., & LaFromboise, T. (1994). Sociocultural factors in the etiology and prevention of violence among ethnic minority youth. In L. Eron, J. Gentry, & R. Schlegel (Eds.), *Reason to hope: A psychosocial perspective on violence & youth* (pp. 59–97). Washington, DC: American Psychological Association.

Hudley, C. (2001, March). The role of culture in prevention research. *Prevention and Treatment* [online], *4.* Retrieved June 30, 2005, from http://journals.apa.org/prevention/volume4/pre0040005c.html

Hudley, C., Britsch, B., Wakefield, W., Smith, T., DeMorat, M., & Cho, S. (1998). An attribution retraining program to reduce aggression in elementary school students. *Psychology in the Schools, 35,* 271–282.

Hudley, C., & Friday, J. (1996). Attributional bias and reactive aggression. *American Journal of Preventive Medicine, 12*(Suppl. 1), 75–81.

Hudley, C., & Graham, S. (1993). An attributional intervention to reduce peer directed aggression among African American boys. *Child Development, 64,* 124–138.

Hudley, C., Wakefield, W., Britsch, B., Cho, S., Smith, T., & DeMorat, M. (2001). Multiple perceptions of children's aggression: Differences across neighborhood, age, gender, and perceiver. *Psychology in the Schools, 38,* 45–56.

Kitayama, S. (2002). Culture and basic psychological processes—Toward a system view of culture: Comment on Oserman et al. (2002). *Psychological Bulletin, 128,* 89–96.

Ladson-Billings, G. (1994). *The dreamkeepers: Successful teachers of African-American children.* San Francisco: Jossey-Bass.

Ladson-Billings, G. (1995). Toward a theory of culturally relevant pedagogy. *American Educational Research Journal, 32,* 465–491.

LaFromboise, T., Coleman, H., & Gerton, J. (1993). Psychological impact of biculturalism: Evidence and theory. *Psychological Bulletin, 114,* 395–412.

Lamborn, S., Dornbusch, S., & Steinberg, L. (1996). Ethnicity and community context as moderators of the relations between family decision making and adolescent adjustment. *Child Development, 67,* 283–301.

Lattimore, C. (1998). The quantum opportunities program. In D. Elliott (Ed.), *Blueprints for violence prevention: The quantum opportunities program.* Denver, CO: C&M Press.

Lutenbacher, M., Cooper, W., & Faccia, K. (2002). Planning youth violence prevention efforts: Decision-making across community sectors. *Journal of Adolescent Health, 30,* 346–354.

Malcolm X. (1965). *The autobiography of Malcolm X.* New York: Grove Press.

McAllister, G., & Irvine, J. (2000). Cultural competency and multicultural teacher education. *Review of Educational Research, 70,* 3–24.

McCord, J. (1997). Placing American violence in context. In J. McCord (Ed.), *Violence and childhood in the inner city* (pp. 78–115). Cambridge, England: Cambridge University Press.

McDonald, L., & Howard, D. (December, 1998). Families and schools together. *Office of Juvenile Justice and Delinquency Prevention Fact Sheet #88.* Washington, DC: U.S. Department of Justice.

McDonald, L., & Sayger, T. (1998). Impact of a family and school-based prevention program on protective factors for high risk youth. *Drugs and Society, 12,* 61–86.

McMahon, S., & Watts, R. (2002). Ethnic identity in urban African American youth: Exploring links with self worth, aggression, and other psychosocial variables. *Journal of Community Psychology, 30,* 411–431.

National Center for Cultural Competence. (2002). *Why is there a compelling need for cultural competence?* Retrieved February 5, 2003, from http://www.emplyee developmentsolutions.com/freearticles

Osofsky, J. (1997). *Children in a violent society.* New York: Guilford Press.

Phinney, J. (1990). Ethnic identity in adolescence and adults: A review of research. *Psychological Bulletin, 108,* 499–514.

Phinney, J. (1999). The structure of ethnic identity in young adolescents from diverse cultural groups. *Journal of Early Adolescence, 19,* 301–322.

Pope, C., Lovell, R., & Hsia, H. (2002). *Disproportionate minority confinement: A review of the research literature from 1989 through 2001. Juvenile Justice Bulletin.* Washington, DC: U.S. Department of Justice, Office of Juvenile Justice and Delinquency Prevention.

Pope-Davis, D., & Coleman, H. (1997). *Multicultural counseling competencies : Assessment, education and training, and supervision.* Thousand Oaks, CA: Sage.

Pope-Davis, D., Liu, W., Toporek, R., & Brittan-Powell, C. (2001). What's missing from multicultural competency research: Review, introspection, and recommendations. *Cultural Diversity and Ethnic Minority Psychology, 7*, 121–138.

Pope-Davis, D., & Ottavi, T. (1994). The relationship between racism and racial identity among White Americans. *Journal of Counseling and Development, 72*, 293–297.

Pumariega, A. (2001). Cultural competence in treatment interventions. In H. Vance & A. Pumariega (Eds.), *Clinical assessment of child and adolescent behavior* (pp. 494–512). New York: Wiley.

Purnell, L. (2002). The Purnell model for cultural competence. *Journal of Transcultural Nursing, 13*, 193–196.

Roosa, M., Dumka, L., Gonzales, N., & Knight, G. (2002, January 15). Cultural/ethnic issues and the prevention scientist in the 21st century. *Prevention and Treatment, 5*, Article 0005a. Retrieved January 30, 2003, from http://journals.apa.org/prevention/volume5/pre0050005a.html

Seligman, M., & Csikszentmihalyi, M. (2000). Positive psychology: An introduction. *American Psychologist, 55*, 5–14.

Sodowsky, G., Taffe, R., Gutkin, T., & Wise, S. (1994). Development and applications of the multicultural counseling inventory. *Journal of Counseling Psychology, 41*, 137–148.

Spencer, M. B. (1984). Black children's race awareness, racial attitudes, and self-concept: A reinterpretation. *Journal of Child Psychology and Psychiatry, 25*, 433–441.

Sue, D. W., Arredondo, P., & McDavis, R. (1992). Multicultural counseling competencies and standards: A call to the profession. *Journal of Multicultural Counseling and Development, 20*, 64–88.

Sue, S. (1998). In search of cultural competence in psychotherapy and counseling. *American Psychologist, 53*, 440–448.

Thornton, T., Craft, C., Dalberg, L., Lynch, B., & Baer, K. (2002). *Best practices of youth violence prevention: A sourcebook for community action.* Atlanta, GA: Centers for Disease Control and Prevention.

U.S. Census. (2001). *Profiles of general demographic characteristics.* Retrieved February 4, 2003, from http://www.census.gov/prod/cen2000/dp1/2kh06.pdf

U.S. Census. (2002). *Population by race and Hispanic or Latino origin for the United States: 1990 and 2000.* Retrieved January 21, 2003, from http://www.census.gov/population/cen2000/phc-t1/tab04.pdf

Utsey, S., Chae, M., Brown, C., & Kelly, D. (2002). Effect of ethnic group membership on ethnic identity, race-related stress and quality of life. *Cultural Diversity and Ethnic Minority Psychology, 8*, 366–377.

Vacarr, B. (2001). Moving beyond polite correctness: Mindfulness in the diverse classroom. *Harvard Educational Review, 71*, 285–295.

Villegas, A., & Lucas, T. (2002). *Educating culturally responsive teachers: A coherent approach.* Albany: State University of New York Press.

11

PREVENTING YOUTH VIOLENCE IN A MULTICULTURAL SOCIETY: FUTURE DIRECTIONS

NANCY G. GUERRA AND EMILIE PHILLIPS SMITH

Throughout this volume, we have emphasized the need to consider carefully the role of ethnicity and culture in the etiology and prevention of youth violence in the United States. As we have discussed, in many cases factors that increase or decrease risk for youth violence are shared across ethnic groups; however, the life circumstances of ethnic minority youth can increase the likelihood that risk factors will occur. In other cases, the minority experience (when shared by ethnic groups linked together by oppression and racism) may foster feelings of isolation, resentment, and anger that can contribute as well to violence. In still other cases, we must consider the unique life circumstances and historical experiences of individuals from particular ethnic groups as well as the important variations within these ethnic groups. These similarities and differences have clear implications for youth violence prevention in a multicultural society such as the United States. In summary, we address implications in six areas and their relevance to future research and practice: (a) ethnicity as a marker for culture, (b) ethnicity and disadvantage, (c) ethnicity and gangs, (d) levels of culture, (e) prevention in a multicultural setting, and (f) strength-based cultural competence.

ETHNICITY AS A MARKER FOR CULTURE

An understanding of the link between ethnicity, culture, and youth violence prevention first requires consensus on the meaning of ethnicity and culture and their relevance to development, behavior, and prevention. As discussed throughout this volume, ethnicity has been defined as group membership based on a perceived shared heritage typically derived from a sense of ancestry or geography. Culture represents a collection of social norms, roles, beliefs, and values that are learned and change over time. These belief systems and value orientations provide a way to understand the world and include guidelines for acceptable and appropriate behavior and "scripts" for routine social interactions. Thus, culture provides both a worldview and a way of living guided by multiple social forces in the environment.

To the extent that individuals from a common ethnic heritage view the world through a shared lens, ethnicity can serve as a marker for culture. Still, it can be a rather crude marker. In many cases, values, beliefs, and norms depend on a range of factors beyond ethnicity, including region (e.g., urban vs. suburban, north vs. south), generation, immigration status, country of origin, gender, and income (e.g., Nisbett & Cohen, 1996). As such, there is often a great deal of intraethnic variation, meaning that individuals from a common ethnic background do not necessarily stand together on attitudes, beliefs, and values relevant to specific behaviors or actions.

For instance, as Mark, Revilla, Tsutsumoto, and Mayeda (chap. 5, this volume) point out, Asian and Pacific Islanders, often referred to as an "ethnic" group, actually represent individuals from Asia or the Indian subcontinent (for example, Cambodia, China, India, Japan, Korea, Malaysia, Pakistan, the Philippine Islands, Thailand, and Vietnam) as well as the Pacific Islands (including Hawaii, Guam, Samoa, Tonga, Fiji, Micronesia, or other Pacific Islands). Although this ethnic tradition is often associated with "model minority" status, the minority experience actually is quite varied within this ethnic group. Similarly, as Mirabal-Colón and Vélez (chap. 4, this volume) illustrate, although Latinos have some shared cultural beliefs, such as *colectivismo* (collectivism), *familismo* (family-centered), *respeto* (respect), *simpatia* (pacifism), *personalismo* (person as a whole), and *religiosidad* (religiosity), they are a diverse group with many nonshared experiences related to country of origin, immigration status, generation status, income, and region of residence in the United States.

The "level of analysis" to be considered in understanding both the etiology of a behavior such as violence and appropriate interventions requires attention to issues of culture broadly defined as well as specific characteristics of the multiple "subcultures" that also define social interactions. As discussed throughout this volume, it is clear that each ethnic group shares commonalities with all other ethnic groups, commonalities with other ethnic minorities based on the minority experience in the United States, unique characteristics related to a specific historical and contemporary niche in society, and within-group variation. Hence, an important first step for future research and practice in youth violence prevention is to identify relevant subcultures and assess specific factors connected to etiology and prevention within these groups.

Hudley and Taylor (chap. 10, this volume) discuss the importance of understanding the cultural and ecological contexts in which people live out their daily lives, or their *ecocultural niche*. In some sense, the ecocultural niche may be the relevant level of analyses in understanding links between culture and behavior. However, a focus on subcultures related to within-group variation (or ecocultural niches) linking ethnicity with other markers of culture must be done with restraint, lest one identify an unlimited number of groups that vary by microlevel characteristics (e.g., third-generation, lower-class children, of Mexican descent, living in the southwestern United States, who speak Spanish). Still, a focus on culture broadly defined solely on the basis of ethnicity can mask relevant intraethnic variations and lead to overgeneralization of attitudes, values, and behaviors based on ethnic heritage. It can also lead to negative labeling of entire ethnic groups based on these overgeneralizations. This is also complicated by the fact that in a multicultural and diverse society, individuals increasingly come from mixed ethnic heritage and may identify with one or several ethnic groups.

The researchers' challenge becomes one of identifying characteristics of relevance to a specific behavior such as violence and including these characteristics in preventive efforts. For instance, although rates of youth violence arrests are higher among African Americans, this is largely because of the social and economic circumstances of many African Americans rather than any specific aspect of ethnic heritage. As discussed by Guerra and Williams (chap. 1, this volume) and Smith and Hasbrouck (chap. 7, this volume), elevated risk for violence is associated with living in economically isolated and disadvantaged communities, with few jobs, and concentrated poverty. These characteristics, not ethnicity, are most closely linked to violence. However, because of historical, social, and political forces, African Americans (and other ethnic minorities) are more likely to live in these communities in the United States at this time.

As this suggests, the appropriate level of analysis for understanding culture in relation to youth violence may not be ethnicity per se, but rather subgroups defined by ethnicity in combination with other relevant environmental factors. Furthermore, even within these subgroups, patterns of adaptation are not homogenous. For example, Anderson (1999) described the "code of the streets" that emerged in inner-city African American communities as an informal set of rules for social interactions, particularly among males, and often including prescriptions for revenge and retaliation. Yet, even in settings where the code of the streets is evident, violence is most often the exception and not the rule. Regardless of circumstances, most people live in relative harmony and do not use violence.

ETHNICITY AND DISADVANTAGE

As discussed earlier, ethnicity is often a proxy for a particular ecocultural niche in the United States marked by high levels of community disadvantage. The history of the United States has been a history of differential opportunities based, in part, on one's ethnic heritage. Indeed, disadvantage often weighs more heavily on individuals from certain ethnic groups or from certain countries. Individuals from the specific ethnic groups discussed in this volume have been particularly vulnerable to economic hardship. Latinos, certain Asian Pacific Islander groups, Native Americans, and African Americans have all experienced high levels of poverty when compared with Whites.

In some cases, this hardship is linked to the challenges of recent immigration. As discussed by Boutakidis, Guerra, and Soriano (chap. 3, this volume), new immigrants to the United States are less well off than those born in the United States. Although entry into the United States was often a ticket to improved economic status, in recent years, globalization and deindustrialization have placed constraints on the economy with fewer opportunities for upward mobility. Given that a large percentage of Asian and Latino families are recent immigrants, these ethnic groups are more likely to be poor and have fewer resources available.

In other cases, economic disadvantage is linked both to historical treatment of individuals from a particular ethnic group as well as changes in the economic structure of the United States during the latter part of the 20th century from a manufacturing economy to a service/information economy. This shift has been accompanied by an exodus of businesses and jobs to areas with low costs and a skilled workforce, often in other countries. As such, jobs have simply disappeared from many communities in the United States. The loss of jobs also resulted in a loss of related services and businesses and a general decline in the standard of living. As Guerra and Williams note (chap. 1, this volume) these transformations have created ecological niches for ethnic minorities that are scarred by multiple forms of disadvantage, inequality, and segregation of classes. In particular, African Americans living in large cities have experienced the most severe consequences.

However, as discussed by Parker and Tuthill (chap. 8, this volume), economic inequalities are not limited to ethnic minority youth and families. During the past few decades, many working-class Whites also have suffered a decline in economic status and an accompanying decline in "cultural prestige" associated with economic prosperity. Although Whites of all classes still have higher incomes, lower unemployment, and better access to health care than most ethnic minorities, it is still the case that many poorly educated and low-skilled White ethnics have suffered a decline in their standard of living. It is also the case that this perception of declining status as a result of the influx and favorable treatment of ethnic minorities has contributed to organizations of individuals that rally around their "Whiteness" as a cause to be promoted and defended at all costs, including violence.

Overall, economic disadvantage is associated with higher rates of violence. Comparing countries, homicide rates are significantly higher in countries with lower per capita incomes versus countries with higher per capita incomes (World Health Organization, 2002). Inequality also contributes to the violence, with higher inequality associated with higher rates of violence (Buvinic, Morrison, & Shifter, 1999). As the case of White ethnic violence suggests, it is not only absolute disadvantage but perceived disadvantage (or a decline in status) that contributes to violence, particularly hate crimes and other acts of violence targeted toward a particular group of individuals.

Structural differences in communities plagued by economic disadvantage have also been linked to higher rates of violence. These structural differences are more likely to be found in poor, urban neighborhoods where many ethnic minority children and families live. Thus, the link between ethnicity and violence is best understood as a link between ethnicity, disadvantage, and violence. Indeed, when disadvantage and related factors are held constant, differences in violence rates between ethnic groups tend to disappear (e.g., Sampson, Morenoff, & Raudenbush, 2005). This leads to the conclusion that it is structural differences among communities rather than ethnicity that produces heightened rates of violence.

Efforts to prevent or reduce levels of youth violence in disadvantaged settings must simultaneously attend to the impact of these structural differences through community-level interventions. For instance, in neighborhoods marked by high levels of crime and an *ecology of danger*, community policing and other locally based law enforcement approaches are needed. Similarly, concentrated disadvantage can be reduced via housing policies that create mixed-income communities rather than high-density, low-income housing developments. A responsive service delivery system hinges on viable and regular funding streams, connectedness to local resident needs, and knowledge of barriers to accessibility that may limit or enhance use of services.

Future prevention efforts must also address the effects of disadvantage and other structural factors on the children's development from birth through adolescence. In some cases, these factors can interfere with the accomplishment of developmental tasks (social, emotional, physical, or cognitive) and compromise healthy adjustment. In addition, disadvantage may create real or perceived "injustices" that can motivate individuals or groups of individuals to retaliate against other groups. In this fashion, ethnicity can serve as a symbol of group identity, and in-group/out-group differences can be identified based on ethnic ties. A word of caution about the positive and negative aspects of such group identity was discussed by French, Kim, and Pillado (chap. 2, this volume). Perhaps the clearest example of this in relation to youth violence is seen in the increasing significance of gangs in the etiology of youth violence and the role of ethnicity in determining gang affiliations.

ETHNICITY AND GANGS

As noted in several chapters in this volume, the prevalence of gangs and associated crime and violence is cause for concern. Gangs are found in all large cities and in most medium-sized cities. According to recent estimates, there are almost 25,000 known gangs in the United States. Gangs are largely formed around ethnic affiliations, with Latinos and African Americans accounting for the majority of gang members (National Youth Gang Center, 2002). In many cases, ethnic gangs have a long history in the United States. For instance, as discussed by Mirabal-Colón and Vélez (chap. 4, this volume) many youth involved in Latino gangs in the Southwest have parents and grandparents who were in the same gang. In other cases, gangs are a more recent and growing phenomenon and less is known about patterns of engagement. For example, as noted by Mark, Revilla, Tsutsumoto, and Mayeda (chap. 5, this volume), although prevalence estimates show a growing gang problem among Asian Pacific Islander youth, there are few scholarly studies and prevention efforts among this population.

Studies that have been conducted on gang involvement among ethnic minority youth point to a common set of risk factors. These include a sense of hopelessness, alienation, a need to belong, reaction against a negative ethnic identity, search for a positive identity, lack of family support and other family problems, peer pressure, as well as fun, recreation, protection, and economic gain. Although these factors seem to play out in some degree across ethnic groups, their relative salience is linked to the particular circumstances confronted by different generations of youth from different ethnic groups.

For example, as discussed by Mark, Revilla, Tsutsumoto, and Mayeda (chap. 5, this volume), Vietnamese youth caught up in a rapid acculturation process often feel alienated from mainstream institutions and turn to gangs as a place of refuge and support. Their less acculturated parents may also have difficulty understanding their children's needs in a new cultural context, contributing to increased family discord. In other instances, for example with Chinese youth, gang involvement may be linked more closely to the negative identities of American-born Chinese that brought them into direct conflict with recent immigrant youth and led to the formation of early Chinatown gangs in the 1960s. For Native American youth, as discussed by Hurst and Laird (chap. 6, this volume), gang involvement was more likely to provide a refuge from troubled families and a remedy for the sense of hopelessness that often characterized life on Indian reservations.

Clearly, gangs would not be so ubiquitous if they were not meeting at least some real needs of youth in certain settings. The appeal of gangs to ethnic minority youth suggests that these youth face the greatest difficulties in meeting basic developmental needs, such as affiliation, support, protection, identity, and a sense of future. These needs may vary slightly across ethnic groups in relation to historical conditions, but also reflect many common themes.

The challenge for prevention is to design and evaluate interventions that address these common underpinnings while simultaneously acknowledging the different histories of youth from distinct ethnic groups as well as differences in their current life circumstances. Otherwise put, interventions need to emerge from an understanding of the shared elements that contribute to gang involvement, but also be sensitive to how these play out differently in relation to the particular ecocultural niches of ethnic youth.

LEVELS OF CULTURE

Wright and Zimmerman (chap. 9, this volume) discuss the complexity of defining and operationalizing *cultural sensitivity*. They highlight an important distinction, based on the work of Resnicow and colleagues (Resnicow, Baranowki, Ahluwalia, & Braithwaite, 1999; Resnicow, Soler, Braithwaite, Ahluwalia, & Butler, 2000) between two levels of culture: *surface structure* versus *deep structure*. As they discuss, surface structure emphasizes the shared external characteristics of a culture such as food, language, and music. In contrast, deep structure reflects a more meaningful understanding of the experience of individuals within a culture and how this experience is colored by specific cultural, social, psychological, environmental, and historical influences. Surface structure increases the receptivity or feasibility of messages. Deep structure addresses the meaning attached to these messages and how they are delivered.

Although the distinction between levels of culture has not been used widely in the field of prevention, we believe that it holds much promise. As Hudley and Taylor (chap. 10, this volume) point out, effectiveness in multicultural settings requires both explicit knowledge of a groups' practices (i.e., surface structure) as well as an understanding and appreciation of the economic, social, and political pressures present in the group's unique ecocultural niche (i.e., deep structure). Although a shared ethnic heritage may facilitate greater awareness of specific practices, it does not necessarily translate to an understanding of deep structure issues, particularly for individuals who have not shared that experience. For instance, middle-class or upper-class African American teachers may actually have little understanding of the ecological niche of inner-city African American children, although they share a common ethnic heritage.

Much of what has been labeled cultural sensitivity or cultural competence, to date, has focused on surface-structure characteristics such as language (e.g., translating materials into Spanish or other languages), sharing ethnic food at family or community celebrations, or integrating holiday and other traditions into prevention programming. In many cases, hiring teachers, counselors, or caseworkers from the same ethnic background is used as a proxy for cultural sensitivity. Yet, as discussed above, cultural sensitivity also requires an understanding of the meaning of an individuals' experience in a specific ecocultural niche and how that shapes their worldviews.

This is not to say that prevention programs have neglected deep structure issues. Indeed, many of the chapters in this volume provide examples of efforts to address these issues. For example, Mark, Revilla, Tsutsumoto, and Mayeda (chap. 5, this volume) review several native Hawaiian culture-based programs, including Ho'omohala I Na Pua and Hui Malama o ke Kai. These programs place significant emphasis on incorporating Hawaiian values including spirituality, self-identification, cooperation, and care for and preservation of the land and ocean into broad social development and skill-building programs.

Similarly, Hurst and Laird (chap. 6, this volume) discuss the Tribal Youth Program, which was designed to engage Native American communities in the resolution of their unique social problems. This effort built on both the spiritual and cultural aspect of specific Native American traditions by fostering values such as consensus and family-support versus individualism and individual choice (traditionally Western values that may be obstacles to change for Native American youth). Many of the Rites of Passage programs for enhancing ethnic identity among African Americans also build on traditional cultural values and seek to build ethnic pride. However, there are very few well-designed evaluations of these programs vis-à-vis their impact on youth violence prevention. Hence, a challenge for future prevention efforts is to incorporate both surface structure and deep structure aspects of culture simultaneously in specific programs and to conduct systematic evaluations of these culturally sensitive efforts.

PREVENTION IN A MULTICULTURAL SETTING

In designing culturally sensitive prevention programs, one of the biggest challenges is how to attend to both surface structure and deep structure factors when programs are implemented in a multicultural setting. For instance, in ethnically segregated schools, programs can be designed that incorporate language, customs, and worldviews of a specific ethnic group. However, in schools with children from many different ethnic groups, it is difficult, if not impossible, to incorporate a meaningful understanding of these multiple cultural perspectives in preventive efforts designed to reach all children. As Wright and Zimmerman (chap. 9, this volume) discuss, in many cases violence prevention programs recruit and serve youth from many different ethnic groups. This presents a challenge in trying to integrate cultural dimensions into programming. For instance, should programs develop specific programs for each group or subgroup of youth within a particular setting, such as African Americans, Latino immigrants, Latino first generation students, and so on?

They suggest that interventions in multicultural settings can also become culturally sensitive by addressing issues of culture as part of the intervention. Culture becomes an asset to be enhanced, although the specific mechanisms for enhancement can still be rooted in an individual's unique cultural heritage. For instance, in a multicultural classroom, students could be encouraged to learn more about their native ethnic cultures, make presentations on accomplishments of individuals from their culture, and participate in activities designed to enhance and build pride in their culture. Learning about one's culture is not simply a means to deliver a message but the message itself. As Hudley and Taylor (chap. 10, this volume) also point out, it is important to incorporate an affirming attitude toward both one's culture as well as the culture of other groups.

At another level, not only is the United States composed of individuals from different ethnic and cultural backgrounds, but there are also other cultural imperatives that bear on youth violence. Some chapters in this volume have mentioned the impact of "youth culture" in the United States as well as the impact of the individualistic, achievement-oriented, and often violent "culture" of the United States in general. In many ways, violence has played a prominent role in American culture and history, whether against indigenous populations or through glorification of violence in media and popular culture. Even the justice system is predicated on violence as the ultimate punishment, in some cases extending the death penalty to youth. The penetration of violence in American society clearly presents challenges for prevention that must be addressed at the national level.

STRENGTH-BASED CULTURAL COMPETENCE

Against this backdrop of violence, a slightly different approach to cultural sensitivity emphasizes building on attitudes, beliefs, and values from different ethnic groups that foster harmony and cooperation and integrating these core values into mainstream programming. Rather than viewing ethnic minorities as disadvantaged groups needing help and services, prevention efforts can build on the strengths of each culture and develop strategies for enhancing and extending these strengths. Indeed, the findings discussed by Boutakidis, Guerra, and Soriano (chap. 3, this volume) showing that acculturation to the United States portends higher rates of youth violence for immigrant groups suggests that the U.S. culture itself may be fostering violence.

At a broad level, cultural classification systems have been used to distinguish cultures on key dimensions, such as individualism–collectivism. Individualistic cultures stress individual rights, autonomy, achievements, and independence. Collectivistic cultures emphasize group welfare, group harmony, and the importance of group needs. In the United States, higher violence rates have been attributed, in part, to an emphasis on individualism, as compared with collectivist cultures that tend to have lower crime and violence rates. Thus, principals of collectivist cultures are likely to be useful tools in broad-based violence prevention efforts that seek to infuse principles such as harmony and group welfare into systems, institutions, and programs.

However, branding the United States as an individualistic culture does little to acknowledge the existence and impact of multiple cultures and subcultures. As has been highlighted throughout this volume, many ethnic minority groups embrace values and goals that are more in line with collectivistic than individualistic cultures. Consider again the emphasis on *respeto* (respect), *simpatia* (harmony), and *personalismo* (importance of interpersonal relationships) in the Latino culture. Similarly, African American culture is based on a number of core values that should serve as protective mechanisms against youth violence, including *harmony, interrelatedness, communalism, mutuality, reciprocity,* and *spirituality*. Although Native American culture is quite complex because of the many different tribal entities and language differences, there are still a number of common world views antithetical to violence, including *harmony, noninterference, generosity,* and *noncompetition.* Among Asian Pacific Islanders, core values also emphasize *pacifism, harmony,* and *interconnectedness.*

CONCLUSION

Perhaps the most pressing challenge for future prevention programs is to reintegrate these cultural strengths into programs for ethnic youth, and to extend this programming beyond specific ethnic enclaves to benefit all youth. Cultural socialization and bicultural competence may help youth adjust to the multiple demands of their ethnic culture and mainstream culture, so that these cultural strengths do not preclude youth from navigating the larger social world. However, building these cultural strengths based on interconnectedness and harmony may, over time, also have a larger impact on preventing violence in mainstream U.S. culture as well.

REFERENCES

Anderson, E. (1999). *Streetwise: Race, class, and change in an urban community.* Chicago: University of Chicago Press.

Buvinic, M., Morrison, A., & Shifter, M. (1999). *Violence in Latin America and the Caribbean: A framework for action.* Washington, DC: InterAmerican Development Bank.

National Youth Gang Center. (2002). The national youth gang survey trends from 1996 to 2000. *OJJDP Fact Sheet.* Washington, DC: U.S. Department of Justice.

Nisbett, R., & Cohen, D. (1996). *Culture of honor: Psychology of violence in the South.* Boulder, CO: Westview Press.

Resnicow, K., Baranowski, T., Ahluwalia, J. S., & Braithwaite, R. L. (1999). Cultural sensitivity in public health: Defined and demystified. *Ethnicity and Disease, 9,* 10–21.

Resnicow, K., Soler, R., Braithwaite, R. L., Ahluwalia, J. S., & Butler, J. (2000). Cultural sensitivity in substance use prevention. *Journal of Community Psychology, 28,* 271–290.

Sampson, R. J., Morenoff, J. D., & Raudenbush, S. (2005). Social anatomy of racial and ethnic disparities in violence. *American Journal of Public Health, 95,* 224–232.

World Health Organization. (2002). *World report on violence and health.* Geneva, Switzerland: Author.

GLOSSARY

Because there is considerable controversy and overlap in the terms and definitions used in this book, the authors agreed on a common terminology as follows (listed alphabetically).

Acculturation: Acculturation refers to differences and changes in values and behaviors that individuals make as they gradually adopt the cultural values of the dominant society.

African American: The term *African American* is used to refer to people of African ancestry who by and large arrived in the United States via the transcontinental slave trade. Recently this term has been used along with and at times in place of the term, *Black*. African American encompasses the idea that the people are bound by perceived physiology as well as by shared experiences, values, and beliefs. Increasingly, other peoples of African ancestry are immigrating to the United States, including indigenous Africans and Afro-Caribbeans.

American Indian: American Indians are members of the aboriginal peoples living in North America when the Europeans arrived; the terms Native American, Native People, and Indian may also be used interchangeably, as well as specific Tribal names.

Asian and Pacific Islander: Asian and Pacific Islander is not a homogenous group; rather, it is composed of many groups who differ in language, culture, socioeconomic status, educational attainment, family structure, immigration history, health status, geographical residence, and length of residence in the United States. *Asian* refers to those having origins in any of the original peoples of the Far East, Southeast Asia, or the Indian subcontinent including, for example, Cambodia, China, India, Japan, Korea, Malaysia, Pakistan, the Philippine Islands, Thailand, and Vietnam. *Pacific Islander* refers to those having origins in any of the original peoples of Hawaii, Guam, Samoa, Tonga, Fiji, Micronesia, or other Pacific Islands.

Assimilation: Assimilation is a process by which a minority group assumes the norms of the dominant culture. This model emphasizes replacement of home culture with the host culture.

Culture: Culture represents a collection of social norms, roles, beliefs, and values that are learned and change over time. Group members may vary in their adoption of cultural values and practices. Cultural belief systems and value orientations are transmitted across generations and influence norms, practices, social institutions, and organizations. Thus, culture provides both a worldview and a way of living guided by multiple social forces in the environment.

Culture centered: Culture centered refers broadly to the need to view psychological processes and outcomes through a lens that acknowledges the importance of culturally learned patterns and how they can influence behavior. In other words, it involves the recognition that behaviors such as violence are shaped, at least in part, by one's cultural environment, be it one's indigenous culture or larger U.S. culture. Similarly, a culture-centered response requires that preventive and remedial responses are responsive to these culturally learned patterns.

Cultural competence: Cultural competence refers to the capacity to function effectively in a given cultural/ecological niche based on knowledge of relevant social norms, roles, beliefs, and values. It is often viewed as a continuum with different stages and indicators. It can also exist at multiple levels such as individual, professional, organizational, and societal.

Cultural identity: Although cultural identity is similar to ethnic identity, if is not constrained by one's perceived heritage and culture of origin. Rather, the term refers to one's self-definition based on membership in a distinct group defined by shared social norms, roles, beliefs, and values that are learned and change over time. For instance, someone born in the northern United States but raised in the south might embrace a southern identity.

Culturally based: This term refers to programs that combine culture, history, and cultural values as mechanisms for encouraging behavior change. For instance, a culture-based program working in collectivist cultures might build on this collectivist orientation in designing specific activities.

Culturally effective: A program or intervention is culturally effective if it is appropriately designed and communicated to produce a specific outcome for individuals who are members of a particular cultural group. In other words it contains the requisite self-knowledge, attitudes, and skills that allow professionals to be effective with diverse populations. The outcome is frequently measured in terms of compliance with a specific procedure and is most typically used in the medical field. This is another specific subdomain of cultural competence.

Culturally engaged: Participants are culturally engaged if they are able to successfully navigate their own culture and setting. This includes cultural knowledge and cultural pride, a positive sense of self, bicultural competence, and the critical awareness to challenge inequality, hatred, and violence of all kinds. This is also a specific subdomain of cultural competence.

Culturally focused programming: Culturally focused programming is specifically designed to enhance an individual's knowledge of cultural values, histories, and customs. For instance, programs designed to highlight the history of a particular ethnic group would be culturally focused.

Culturally relevant: Cultural relevance refers to the capacity to maximize the culturally defined strengths of the individual or group, enhance their critical consciousness and their ability to understand their niche. Culturally relevant programming is based on an awareness that unique features of different groups need to be considered.

Culturally responsive: This represents a specific subdomain of cultural competence. It refers to intervention methods and programming that are responsive to and respectful of participants' cultures and communities. Methods for assessment and evaluation also should be similarly cognizant of the dynamics of participants' cultures.

Culturally sensitive: Practices that are culturally sensitive recognize and appreciate individual differences based on ethnicity and culture. In other words, they strive to understand and incorporate the unique worldviews and cultural backgrounds of individuals they serve, with particular attention to relevant ethnic, linguistic, and cultural variations.

Culturally specific: A program that is culturally specific is tailored to the cultural norms and specific needs of a particular cultural group. This may be particularly important when providing services for groups of individuals whose world view and practices are quite distinct from the majority population, such as recent immigrant groups from dissimilar cultures.

Ethnic identity: Ethnic identify refers to one's self definition based on membership in a distinct group derived from a perceived shared heritage. In some cases, ethnic identity may be based on perceived racial grouping and would be called racial identity. Individuals may also have multiple ethnic identities that vary in salience across time and setting.

Ethnicity: Ethnicity is defined as group membership based on a perceived shared heritage typically derived from a sense of ancestry or geography. Individuals can choose to subscribe or not to that perceived heritage; that is, ethnicity is socially acquired and subject to change over time through the process of acculturation and assimilation. As members of ethnic groups interact with each other, ethnicity becomes a means by which culture is transmitted.

Latino: *Latino* and *Hispanic* are used interchangeably to refer to a broadly defined population that includes different ethnic groups who share a common language (Spanish) but represent distinct cultures, with influences from both Spain and Latin America. This usage is consistent with the U.S. Census Bureau category of *Hispanic/Latino*.[1]

Multiculturalism: Multiculturalism refers to competence and familiarity with more than two cultures. The nature of these multiple cultures can vary to include dimensions of race, ethnicity, language, gender, age, disability, religious orientation, and other cultural dimensions. Most frequently it refers to competence in more than two cultures that are defined along similar dimensions, such as White and African American cultures. When competence is limited to two cultures, the term *biculturalism* is used; competence in two languages is called *bilingualism*.

Race: Race is a social construction based on a collection of perceived shared phenotypical (and possibly genotypical) features. It is a broad category used to classify individuals, usually on the basis of externally visible characteristics. The term is often used to refer to group membership and collective identity that may carry a specific social meaning based on the individual's perception or the perception of others. As a construct, it provides no information about within-group variations important to understanding development. Race likely

---

[1] U.S. Census Bureau. (2000). *Census 2000. Public Use Microdata Sample (PUMS)*. Washington, DC: U.S. Department of Commerce Economics and Statistics Administration.

contributes more to understanding how others react to their own and others perceived group status given the wide range of intragroup variation. In this volume, we emphasize ethnicity vis-à-vis youth violence rather than race, although we acknowledge that much previous research and work cited has focused on race, particularly work with African Americans.

White: The term *White* can be used to refer to anyone who is not an individual of color. White is typically not considered an ethnic category because it does not refer to a particular shared heritage or ancestry. The term *Euro-American* is often used to refer to individuals whose ancestors came to the United States from Europe, and the term *non-Hispanic White* is often used to refer to members of the Caucasian race who do not consider themselves of Hispanic origin. In addition, some individuals profess a common bond by virtue of their "Whiteness" and define their social positions accordingly, usually in reaction to perceived advantages of specific minority groups.

AUTHOR INDEX

Numbers in italics refer to listings in reference sections.

SUBJECT INDEX

African American youth, *continued*
Multisystemic Therapy model, 183–184, 185
neighborhood violence, 173, 175, 176
Nigrescence model for, 54
and parenting styles, 176–178
PROJECT 2000, 229, 233, 234–235
and resiliency, 175
resistance culture and, 33
risk factors for violence, 8, 172–180
Rites of Passage activity, 239, 278–279
school-based violence prevention program, 186–187, 235–237
school experience, 179–180
and self-esteem, 239
and self-hatred, 174
sexual-risk behavior prevention program, 240–241
and smoking cessation program, 224
social skills training, 227
sociodemographics of, 170, 171–172
and substance abuse, 174
and urban disadvantage, 19–20
violence prevention programs, 180–190
violence rates, 4, 170
Aggression
and ethnic identity, 58–59
and neuropsychological problems, 29
and television, 175
and underachievement, 32
victimization and, 30–31
and violence, 6, 25, 27–28, 174
Alcohol abuse. *See also* Substance abuse
and American Indians, 150, 155–156
binge drinking, 155
fetal alcohol syndrome (FAS), 154–155
American Indians. *See also* American Indian youth
defined, 283
and ethnic identity, 53
and fetal alcohol syndrome (FAS), 154–155
and harmony, 92
historical experience, 153–154
sociodemographics of, 150
American Indian youth, 10. *See also* American Indians; Ethnicity;

Minorities; Prevention programs, youth violence
binge drinking, 155
boarding schools for, 153–154
and child abuse, 151
crime rates, 150–151
demographic characteristics of, 150
and depression, 156–158
and gaming operations, 152
gangs, 158–160, 277
juvenile justice system, 151–152
and reservations, 152, 156
risk factors for violence, 153–160
and substance abuse, 154–156, 157
victimization of, 149, 151, 152
violence prevention programs, 149, 160–161, 162
violence rates, 4
Arrests, of various ethnic groups in the United States, 131
Aryan Brotherhood, 207–208
Asian American and Pacific Islander youth, 10, 127–144. *See also* Asian Americans; Ethnicity; Minorities; Prevention programs, youth violence
versus African American youth, 138
arrest rates, 130–134
culturally specific approaches to prevention, 141–143
family support, 139
and gangs, 134–136, 276
hate crimes and, 137
and military, 139–140
racism and, 138–139
and resiliency, 139–140
risk factors for violence, 139–140
sociodemographics of, 5, 127–129, 272
and victimization, 136–139
violence prevention programs, 140–143
violence rates, 4
Asian Americans. *See also* Asian American and Pacific Islander youth
defined, 128, 283
educational attainment, 129
as immigrants, 77
Assimilation, 162, 283
and drug abuse, 130, 140
Autonomy, 56

Japanese Americans. *See also* Asian American and Pacific Islander youth
  and racism, 138–139
  World War II internment, 139
Judicial Branch of the Navajo Nation, 159
Juvenile justice system
  and American Indians, 151–152
  and Latinos, 110

Kauai, 139
Ku Klux Klan, 207–208

La Eme gangs, 7, 117
Laos, immigrants from, 77
Latino Americans. *See also* Latino youth
  and collectivistic culture, 83
  versus *Hispanic American*, 5, 104, 285
  versus *Mexican American*, 105
Latino youth, 9–10, 103–122. *See also* Ethnicity; Latino Americans; Minorities; Prevention programs, youth violence
  adult role models, 35
  and assimilation, 118
  family support, 114, 116–117
  gangs, 7, 116–119, 276
  homicide rates, 3
  and income levels, 106
  and juvenile justice system, 110
  neighborhood violence, 112, 121
  protective factors, 114–115
  racial identity model, 54–55
  risk factors for violence, 114–119
  school-based violence prevention program, 235–236
  sociodemographics of, 106–106, 121
  survey data on, 110–112
  and victimization, 112–113
  violence prevention programs, 119–120
  violence rates, 4, 106–112
Los Angeles, 118
  gangs, 178–179
Lynching, 171, 211

Mara Salvatrucha gang, 7, 117
Marginalization, 35, 36

Media
  influence on school shooters, 213
  portrayal of violence, 175
Mental health
  and acculturation, 80
Metropolitan Area Child Study, 187–188
Mexico. *See also* Latino Americans
  and immigrants to United States, 105
  and U.S. relations, 7, 117
Military
  and Asian American and Pacific Islander youth, 139–140
Minorities. *See also* African American youth; American Indian youth; Asian American and Pacific Islander youth; Culture; Development, ecology of; Ethnic identity; Ethnicity; Immigrants; Latino youth
  arrests of various ethnic groups in the United States, 131
  concentrated disadvantage, 23–24, 35
  and danger, 24–25
  and ecocultural niches, 18
  and neighborhood violence, 30–31
  and racism, 7
  resource scarcity, 17, 21–23
  risk factors for violence, 7–8
  and segregation, 17, 19–20, 23
  social transformations, 19–21
  and underachievement and lack of resources, 32
  and violence, 4
Monitoring the Future, 111
Moratorium, 49
Multiculturalism, 285
  violence prevention programs for, 257, 279–280
Multisystemic Therapy, 183–184, 185, 263

National Asian Pacific American Legal Consortium, 137
National Child Abuse and Neglect Data System, 151
National Crime Victimization Survey, 112–113
National Electronic Injury Surveillance System, 108

National Household Drug Use Survey, 110, 112
National Indian Gaming Association, 152
National Longitudinal Study of Adolescent Health, 112
National Trauma Data Bank (NTDB), 109
National Youth Gang Center, 117
  American Indian survey, 159
Native Americans. *See* American Indians
Neighborhood Violence Prevention Advocates, 236
New York City, 24
  Police Department, 202
  Reach for Health Community Youth Service, 240–241
Nigrescence model, 54

Office of Juvenile Justice Delinquency Prevention, 110
Omega Boys Club, 231, 238
"Outing" system, 154

Pacific Islanders. *See also* Asian American and Pacific Islander youth
  defined, 128
  educational attainment, 129
Padres Con Poder, 236
Parents. *See also* Adolescents; Children; Families
  and adolescent relationships, 88–89
  and childrearing, 6–7, 176
  parenting styles, 176–178
Parents Working for Peace, 119, 229, 232
Persistent fear response, 30
Philadelphia, 136–137
Positive Adolescent Choices Training, 182
Posttraumatic stress disorder (PTSD), 156
Poverty
  and concentrated disadvantage, 21, 23–24, 35
  and violence, 226
Prevention programs, youth violence, 68–69. *See also* Acculturation; Cultural competence; Culture;

Ethnic identity; Gangs; Interventions, culturally sensitive; Violence, youth
  and African American youth, 68, 180–190
  and American Indian youth, 149, 160–161, 162
  and Asian American and Pacific Islander youth, 140–143
  and biculturalism, 90–92
  and cultural competence, 253–258
  culturally sensitive, 227, 228–241
  culturally sensitive interventions, 230–233
  and Latino youth, 119–120
  in multicultural setting, 279–280
  and White ethnic youth, 214–215
Prison gangs, 7, 117
Project 2000, 229–230, 233
Puerto Rico, 106. *See also* Latino youth
  homicide rates, 108
  and youth violence surveys, 111
Puerto Rico Trauma Center, 109–110
Punk rockers, 209

Quantum Opportunities Program, 189–190, 262–263

Race, 285–286
Racism
  and Asian Americans and Pacific Islanders, 138–139
  and autonomy stage of identity development, 56
  and minorities, 7
Reach for Health Community Youth Service program, 232, 240–241
Religiosidad, 116
Resistance culture, 33
Resolving Conflict Creatively Program, 120, 181–182
Resource scarcity, 21–23
  effect on children, 32
Respeto, 116
Responding in Peaceful and Positive Ways, 182–183
Rites of Passage programs, 239, 278–279

Safe Start Project, 230, 237–238
Samoan Americans. *See also* Asian American and Pacific Islander youth
  poverty rates, 129
  stereotypes of, 138
San Francisco County, 131–132
  ethnic groups in, 132
  juvenile arrest rates in, 132
San Jose, California
  gangs, 134
Scapegoating, 204, 206–207, 274
Schools. *See* Education
School shooters, 212–213
Schools of the 21st Century, 187
Seattle Social Development Program, 186
Segregation, 17, 19–20, 23
Self Enhancement Incorporated (SEI) program, 231, 236–237
Self-esteem, 57, 58, 239
Self-hatred, 174
Self-knowledge, 255
Sexual-risk behavior
  prevention programs, 240
Simpatia, 92, 116
Skinheads, 209–210
Smart Life program, 231, 239
Smoking cessation program, 224
Social skills training, 240
Strengthening Families Program, 184
Stress, acculturative, 85–87
Students for Peace Project, 119
Substance abuse. *See also* Alcohol abuse; Drug abuse
  and acculturation, 80
  and African American youth, 174–175
  and American Indians, 154–156, 157, 225
  and National Household Drug Use Survey, 112
Suicide
  and American Indians, 151, 156–157
Supporting Adolescents With Guidance and Employment (SAGE) program, 233, 239
Surface structure, 11
  defined, 223–224, 277–278
  and Latino youth, 119
Survivalists, White, 208–209

Tammany Hall, 204–205
Television
  and aggression, 175
Texas, 235
Treaty of Guadalupe Hidalgo, 7, 117
Tribal Youth Program, 160–161, 278
  Mental Health Project, 161

Underachievement
  and aggression, 32
Unemployment
  and disadvantage, 119
  and violence, 34–35

Victimization
  and American Indian youth of, 149, 151, 152
  and Asian American and Pacific Islander youth, 136–139
  and children, 30
  and Latino youth, 112–113
  predictor of aggression and violence, 30–31, 151
Vietnamese Americans. *See also* Asian American and Pacific Islander youth
  teaching of Vietnamese history, 141
  youth gangs, 134–135, 277
Violence, youth, 3–5, 9. *See also* Gangs; Interventions, culturally sensitive; Prevention programs, youth violence; Victimization; Youth
  and acculturation, 80–81, 280
  and African American youth, 4, 169, 170
  and aggression, 6, 25, 174
  in American culture, 251
  and American Indian youth, 4, 150–151
  antiethnic, 208–209, 260
  among Asian Americans and Pacific Islanders, 4, 130–134
  and culture, 251
  and disadvantage, 18
  and ethnic identity, 6, 57–59
  homicide rates, 3, 107–108
  and immigration, 84, 204–205, 274
  among Latinos, 4, 106–112

ABOUT THE EDITORS

Nancy G. Guerra, EdD, is a professor of psychology at the University of California, Riverside. For the past 5 years, she has been the principal investigator for the Southern California Academic Center of Excellence on Youth Violence Prevention, funded by the Centers for Disease Control and Prevention. Before that, she was the principal investigator on a large-scale developmental and intervention study funded by the National Institute of Mental Health looking at individual, classroom, peer, and family influences on the aggressive behavior of inner-city and urban children. She has published numerous articles and chapters on risk factors for aggression and youth violence, the evaluation of prevention and intervention programs, the influence of ethnicity and culture on development and prevention, and international perspectives on youth violence prevention. She has worked with both the Inter-American Development Bank and the World Bank on youth development and violence prevention projects across Latin America and the Caribbean, and is currently working on projects in Colombia and El Salvador.

Emilie Phillips Smith, PhD, is an associate professor in human development and family studies at Pennsylvania State University. She has been involved in numerous local and national prevention studies designed to test the impact of universal, family, school, and community-based approaches on preventing youth violence and aggression. Before her arrival at Penn State, she served as a senior service fellow in the Division of Violence Prevention at the Centers for Disease Control and Prevention, where she served as the acting chief of the newly developed Prevention Development and Evaluation Branch and was honored for her role in developing the research agenda for the National Center for Injury Prevention and Control. She is a coinvestigator on a longitudinal, multicomponent prevention study in the southeastern

United States funded by the National Institute of Mental Health and the National Institute on Drug Abuse. She has published numerous articles and chapters on the role of family, school, and community factors in violence and aggression as well as on the role of ethnic identity and culture in child and family development.